The Secret

(of happiness)

Demosthenes Armeniades

Tinseltown
Press

ISBN 978-0-9843431-0-2

Printed in the United States of America by Tinseltown Press & Production LLC.

Author's Note

A portion of the proceeds from this book will be donated to help the homeless.

A Zoé, Constantin, et Isaure,
le vrai secret de mon bonheur.

Contents

1. Start Here

To: Dot
From: David
Subject: you know

Here it is. The whloe truth and nothing but, as they say.

PS: We'll be at Nemo's. Give me a call when you're done reading. Please.

(And don't bother correcting my typos :)

2. Me

THE TALL GUY is definitely looking straight at me. No doubt about it. I keep walking toward the parking lot. It's pitch black out here on this part of the campus. No one else around. Just me and him.

"Good evening, Mr. Finnegan," he says. "My name is Gupta Singh. May I have a brief word with you?"

I stop walking. *Who is this guy?* And how does he know my name? Judging from the fancy suit and tie, I doubt he's planning to jump me for my lunch money. Anyway, I respond:

"Pleased to meet you, Mr. Singh. How may I help you?" My syntax is craftily stilted to provide the needed rigor to my cocktail-impaired diction. I really shouldn't'a had that last shot.

Singh smiles ... movie guru-like, with a dash of film noir. And I'm standing there in the dark, wondering what he's going to say.

*   *   *

When we look back, we realize that certain moments change our lives forever. I didn't know it then, but after this precise instant my life would never be the same. If I'd known what was about to happen, would I have turned and run the other way?

But isn't that the catch? We never know it when it's happening.

I didn't run.

And here's what happened ...

3. Maximus

MAX SIMON stands in his office. It's about the size of a basketball court. Hundreds of thousands of books line the walls. The rest is a wild jumble of ethnic masks, sabers, shields, paintings, tapestries, statues, a magic wand won from an Antillean witch doctor in a poker game along with his lizard skin thong, and countless other trinkets he's gathered during his travels. The room would dwarf most men. But it fits Max just fine. Could be because he looks like he just stepped out from the pages of some sports fashion magazine ... tall, trim, finely chiseled features set around a large powerful nose with a mane of golden brown hair tumbling around his neck. But it's not that. Maybe it's his eyes. Intense eyes that seem to light up his face with their own glow.

He's staring out the window at the waves pounding against the shore of his private island. This is one of his favorite spots to think. And right now he's thinking about something that's bothering him. Niggling him like a mosquito just out of reach. Bzzzt. Bzzzt.

Over the years he's learned how to appraise a person's power like vintage wine. With a glance he can gauge where someone stands in that cosmic hierarchical structure. Of course the vast majority of humankind isn't worth swirling in the glass. But whenever he meets with some head of state, famous artist, baron of industry or other person of power or influence, he swirls, sniffs and tastes, like a connoisseur. He can tell instantly whether we're talking billions, or just millions. Whether it's an opinion-forming blockbuster or just a flash in the pan, a consolidated political powerbase or just a shaky run.

And of course Max can feel his own power. Immense power. He can do basically whatever he wants. At a whim he can meet with presidents or dictators. He can lunch with any celebrity. Jet around wherever he pleases on the planet. Buy anything he feels like. Do whatever he can dream up.

But with all this power, something else has developed. Something he hadn't planned on. Being able to do anything has taken something away. Insidiously. Without warning, that special spark vanished from his life. He's not quite sure when it happened. But somewhere along the way the challenge and novelty just evaporated. He'd done it all. Like those minerals replacing the organic tissue of a dinosaur to create a fossil, his enthusiasm somehow became replaced, cell-by-cell, with cynicism. The days began to feel like crosswords he'd already solved. Everything developed an aftertaste of déjà vu.

In short, that magic tingle disappeared.

He doesn't have a solution for this problem. And he doesn't like unresolved problems. It's a thorn in his side. Worst of all, it seems so trite. Feeling like a goddam walking cliché makes it even worse.

Then his mind skips away. Back to business. His refuge. Running the empire. He smiles in anticipation. Tomorrow he'll try out the new kid. Everything is already minutely planned, as always. No better way to test the mettle of a man than in actual battle. Sink or swim. Baptism by fire.

4. Dot

BY THE TIME DOROTHY PEABODY was a few hours old, everyone was already affectionately calling her "Dot." No one remembers where the nickname came from, or who thought of it, but it stuck.

Family legend holds that her great-great-grandparents arrived from England on a boat that sailed into New York Harbor, where they sold their worldly possessions to purchase a covered wagon and set out for a new life on the frontier, like a commercial plug for the American Dream. The Peabody Wagon continued obstinately westward until there was no more west to go. They'd arrived in the thriving Oregon frontier. Great-Great-Granddaddy Peabody looked out over the Pacific Ocean and decided they had found their new home.

Since their arrival in Oregon, it cannot be said that the Peabodies have prospered. But you could say they've settled into a sort of self-perpetuating socioeconomic stability. The male Peabodies enter various lumber-related professions beginning in their teens, work extremely hard their entire lives, and ultimately die with calloused hands, sore backs, and about as much financial liquidity as they possessed upon entering this world. And thus the Peabodies never vacation in Europe, never go to the opera, and rarely ever amass more than a few weeks' salary in life savings. But what the Peabodies clearly do possess is their staunch Puritan ideals. Over the generations, the Peabody Puritanism has manifested itself in many inter-denominational declinations, including the "UCC" (United Church of Christ), the "CCC" (Congregational Christian Church), and the "ERC" (Evangelical and Reformed Church) to name just a few. But whatever their various appellations, all the Peabody-elected houses of worship invariably have in common two things: deep Puritan values, and the best annual summer outdoor barbecue you could shake a stick at.

It was at one of these traditional summer congregational extravaganzas that Dot first set eyes on David. Always eager to earn an extra buck, David had signed on to work at the amusement booth concession. Given his non-Protestant lineage, he was quickly assigned to the dunking tank. He accepted the assignment, but only after negotiating (for the first time in local congregational history) to be paid on a commission basis at a hefty dime per dunk. He sat on a small seat suspended above a tank of water. The fun-seeking parishioners lined up for their chance to throw a baseball at a bull's eye mounted on a lever ultimately coupled to his precarious perch. Every few minutes, a contestant would successfully connect baseball to target, plunging David into the water amidst the jubilations of the crowd.

Transfixed, Dot watched him, sitting up there like a sodden little bird. Plummeting down—*splash*—over and over again. And each time he would crawl out, back up to his perch, with his right fist mysteriously clenched and raised in victory. She was enthralled to see how that waterlogged little creature with his T-shirt sticking to his bony chest could somehow transform those repeated dunkings into his own private little triumphs.

They were both thirteen years old. That mysteriously magical lightning bolt had struck. Her heart went out to him. Standing there at the church fair with her two feet planted firmly on the ground and her pigtails dangling in the wind, she resolved, right then and there, that he would be hers.

THE SECRET (*of happiness*)

There was something about David, Dot would often think to herself. She wasn't quite sure how, or why, but his face was flushed with a sort of radiant happiness. He always had that about him ... that inner glow. And Dot was happy whenever she was near him. One day, many years later, she asked him whether he'd always had that happy spark inside. He turned to her and said with that big smile of his that it all started when he met her. She always figured he'd just said that to be romantic. But sometimes, with a shudder of indescribable joy, she believed it was really true.

And so it is that thirteen years later, Dot is waiting for David's signature "rat-a-tat-tat" syncopated knock, exactly as planned ...

Why is he so late? He promised to leave the firm graduation cocktail on time. She's painstakingly planned every second of the tightly programmed evening. He shouldn't be late! After all, this is a big day for him—*for both of them*—and she wants it to be picture perfect.

5. Mr. Singh

I'M STILL STANDING here in the dark wondering, when Singh says:

"Mr. Finnegan, to be exact, it is my employer who would like to speak with you."

"Your Employer? About what?"

"He would like to make you a most interesting employment proposition."

"You're joking."

"No, I am very serious."

"But I've just signed up with—"

Singh is nodding knowingly. "Actually, today is Friday, and you wouldn't be signing until Monday. You can still change your mind. And that, Mr. Finnegan, is why I'm here. Out of all the graduating classes from every school on the planet, we've selected you."

Wow. I have to admit, this guy's very good. Highly effective flattery, appealing shamelessly to my over-inflated ego. And truth is, I haven't signed the papers yet. So I am *technically* still on the market. But that's just a formality. I'd decided to accept the job on Wall Street the very second it was offered. Who wouldn't? Who could turn down a job with such a great firm? But my mind's already double-tracking, streaking ahead catlike until I hear myself asking:

"What does your employer have in mind?"

Singh smiles and hands me a business card. No contact numbers. Just an embossed name. I read it out loud to avoid crimping the dialogue:

"Halcyon."

Singh does another one of his nods.

"Never heard of it," I say.

"Indeed. And as long as we're doing our job properly, you wouldn't."

I'm about to respond with something appropriately quippy and pith when my phone buzzes instead. "Would you excuse me a second?"

"Naturally."

I glance at the screen. Of course it's Dot, my girlfriend, texting me. *Where are you?? Everyone's waiting!* And of course she's right. I am late.

"I'm terribly sorry, Mr. Singh, but I really have to go."

"Yes, Mr. Finnegan. Your family is waiting to celebrate your graduation. But before you leave, please allow me to answer one question for you."

"I didn't ask a question."

"But you should nevertheless know the answer to it."

"OK ..."

"Why on earth would you ever want to give up working for a prominent Wall Street firm to come and work with my employer?"

"Good question."

"Well, Mr. Finnegan, for one thing, my employer would pay you at least five times as much."

As you can imagine, I'm totally shocked. But I try not to look like a complete spaz. "Did you say five?"

"Plus ample bonuses for success."

"Wow." Note to file: stop saying *wow*. It screams out hick.

"But Mr. Finnegan, that is not the real reason you would want to work with us."

"So what would the real reason be?"

"Because I'm offering you the life you always dreamed of. Beyond what you've dreamed. Opening doors where you never even imaged there were rooms. I invite you to take a tour of our facilities. The jet is waiting for us. We could meet tomorrow morning at the airport."

Doors? Rooms? What is this? Did he say tomorrow morning?

"Tomorrow morning? I can't! This is graduation weekend. My whole family is here. What could I tell them?"

"The truth, Mr. Finnegan. That you've just been offered a fabulous new job getting paid huge sums of money. I imagine they would be very happy for you."

Five times the salary! And they picked *me!* But what about Dot? She'll go apeshit at the thought of bailing on everyone. Christ! Singh's reading me like a teleprompter.

"Of course you could invite Dot to accompany you," he says, but his expression has shaded a tone darker, infusing his words with double entendre. "However, we've found in the past that it's usually more productive for a candidate to come out alone for the first visit. We *highly* recommend it."

I don't answer straight off. Part of me is seriously weirded out by the undeniably creepy fact that he knows my girlfriend's name, and even seems to have somehow anticipated her reaction, not to mention his suggestion that I go solo. And the whole mystical doors imagery thing. Should I just walk away and forget this guy? But part of me is already hooked. Curious to see where this is going. In any event, the guy's waiting for an answer ...

"I'll have to think about it."

"By all means. You can join me at the airport tomorrow morning at seven. I'll be at the private planes section waiting for you. Don't forget to bring your passport. Goodnight, Mr. Finnegan."

And then—just like that—he smiles, turns, and walks away. Totally Bogart. And I stand there watching him. Probably with my mouth elegantly gaping.

My passport? Of course. Halcyon is likely stashed quietly away in some offshore jurisdiction. I watch Singh walk towards the parking lot where a white-gloved chauffeur holds open the door to a Rolls Royce. Seriously! Incredibly suave. Singh steps in. The chauffeur shuts the door and they drive away. Awesome.

Five times the dough! That's a lot of cash. I'd make more in a week then I've made during my entire earthly existence. All those summers of toil ... waiting tables, delivering pizzas, scooping ice cream, tutoring the under-motivated and/or synaptically underequipped in every academic subject imaginable. Stocking warehouses, painting houses, mowing lawns, grooming poodles, selling encyclopedias, cleaning pools. All those mind-numbing backbreaking hours slogging away for peanuts. But that's all behind me now. Meet the new Mr. David Finnegan. The rich and powerful Mr. Finnegan. Oh crap, where the hell are my keys?

There, silently rusting in front of me, is the pitiful beat-up old wreck of a Volkswagen I've been constantly repairing. Somehow keeping it alive through my college years. I still can't find my keys. The body's so rusted there's actually a hole down by the clutch where the winter slush squeezes in like the spigot on a Slurpee Machine. Anyway, after all my beverages tonight I'm probably better off on foot. It's not a far walk and it'll give me time to call Nancy and check out this whole Singh thing.

So I whip out my cell, dial and start walking. My law school recruiting counselor. Where would I be without her? Come on, pick up Nance. I know you're there. I need you now. Can't wait till morning. Please pick up—

"Hello?"

"Hey, Nancy, it's David Finnegan."

"Finnegan? Why the hell are you pestering me so late at home?"

"I need your help."

"Of course, why else would you call?"

"Ouch."

"Never mind. What do you want? I put the film on pause, and I'll give you exactly one minute."

"Does a Mr. Singh from a company called Halcyon ring any bells?"

"Singh? Yeah, why?"

"He just met me on my way home from the cocktail party. You know him?"

"Know *of* him. He's sort of a myth around the recruiting gigs. Kinda our Keyser Söze. You actually met him?"

"Sure did. Just a few minutes ago. He offered me a job. Is he legit?"

"Yeah he's legit alright. Halcyon. They've been registered for ages with us, but they've never recruited anyone. Top class. Very small. Every year they pass our screening with flying colors. And rumor is they pay *lots* of money."

"Sounds like the same Singh. Should I go see them?"

"Of course. Wait a second, I'm pulling up Singh's file ... Halcyon, yes. Very nice. I'll send the file to you."

"Great."

"But don't blabber anything to your Wall Street mega-firm until you make a choice. They're so hyped up on themselves about being the best, they don't take well to new recruits losing the faith. Keep me posted, OK?"

"Sure, Nance."

"Knock 'em dead, wonder boy."

"Thanks."

"Yeah. Now leave me alone."

She hangs up. So do I. A few steps later my phone dings with the Email from Nancy. The recruiting office file on Halcyon. I click on it to see Singh's smiling face looking back at me ...

What to do? On the one hand, I could just forget about Singh and let everything keep moving along as planned. After all, everything's going fine right now. Dot's happy. Why rock the boat? But on the other hand, what if Halcyon is as wonderful as Singh says? What if Halcyon really is the perfect fit for me? And the money is huge. It would be stupid not to check it out. Right?

After all, I worked my butt off to get where I am. And I don't mean here at the corner of Mass Ave and Brattle. I mean law school and all. And Lord knows I'm not naturally clever. But I worked like a fiend. Like a fanatic. Yeah, sometimes it sucked, but I always felt for some reason that someday, somehow, it would pay off. Like that experiment where they put a piece of candy in front of toddlers and tell them they'll get more candy later if they resist the temptation to eat it now. Apparently most kids resist for a few seconds and then just reach for it and scarf it down. Well, I'd be the kid who didn't take the candy. Sitting there staring at it for hours because that's what the guys in the white lab coats said was the path to success. No pain, no gain. Drooling with desire, but working toward the promised reward at the end of the tunnel. I studied round the clock. When the other guys were partying and being popular, I had my nose in the books, not partying, and certainly not being popular. That's the trick. Really. Anyone can do it. You just have to work your ass off and avoid all extracurricular fun.

Hmm ... I think I may have lost the thread of where I was going with all this. Something or other crassly self-indulgent, no doubt. Oh well, I'll either remember later when I've regained the beneficial use of my neurons, or not. Anyway, I've reached my building. The hallowed crimson bricks and white woodwork trimming of HLS student housing. Up the stairs, two at a time. And now I'm standing here in front of my door with a goofy grin. Five times the salary! Plus bonuses! What a great night.

Dad always said I had a lucky star.

I knock.

6. Surprise!

IT WAS DECIDED that the event would be structured as a "surprise" party, despite the fact that everyone realizes I am, of course, fully aware of it. But that detail didn't seem to bother any of the party planners.

Everyone is already here. Mom and Dad flew in yesterday with Granny Finn. And this morning Uncles Liam and Billy arrived with wives and children galore. Ma and Pa Peabody rolled up at the wheel of their antediluvian Chevy SUV with Dot's younger brothers Jake and Todd seconds before commencement commenced. Pa Peabody is so proud of his flawless timing that he's already repeated the story of how they parked the car and entered the graduation ceremony "jyest when the music started" several times to anyone who'll listen.

It is thus into an apparently empty and suspiciously quiet living room that I now step as Dot holds the door open for me with an expectant smile stretching out to her ears. I sweep her into my arms, reinforcing everyone's willful suspension of disbelief. A roomful of Peabodies and Finnegans jump out of their hiding spots yelling: "Surprise!" as cameras flash to memorialize my look of utter and complete astonishment.

I make the rounds, hugging and kissing everyone. Welcoming them to my "humble East Coast abode." Catching up on recent happenings, birthdays, graduations, prom dates, boy crushes, girl exploits, noteworthy automobile acquisitions, etc. Teasing the teenagers, tickling the younger ones.

I save Dad for last, and grab him in a bear hug. It always sends me back in time when I feel the uneven pressure from Dad's one-armed hug.

"So, son, you really did it."

"Yeah, I guess so."

"I always knew you would."

"I know, Dad. That's what kept me going."

Then we do our thing. That long silent stare of ours deep into each other's eyes. I don't know how that started, but somehow over the years it's become our way. Our connection. Our way of communicating. I wouldn't trade a single one of those moments for anything in the world.

Over at the other end of the room I overhear Dot telling Granny Finn how much I like my new firm. And how we're so excited to be actually *moving* to New York City. I look at her with a smiling wink as she shouts into Granny Finn's left (and better) ear:

"Yeah, we've always dreamed of living in New York. I mean, New York City. It's incredible. The Big Apple."

"The what?"

"The Big Apple."

"No thanks, honey."

Louder: "New York."

"Where?"

Even louder: "New York."

"What about it, dear?"

"It's incredible."

"Come again?"

"Incredible."

"Oh yes."

Liam and Billy appear at my side, snapping my smiling eyes away from Dot. Of course they're holding a beer outstretched for me.

"I don't know guys, I'm already pretty toasted from my cocktail party tonight."

But Liam and Billy don't take no for an answer when it comes to beer. "Come on, man, you gotta toast with us," they chorus. And so of course I do. And soon we're laughing and clowning around like always. And somehow I must have had another couple of beers. You know how that goes.

Anyway, Dot is refilling the punch when she hears the sound of the spoon in my hand being pinged against a glass in that traditionally festive way of getting everyone to shut up and listen to a speech. She's never heard a Peabody speak in public, unless of course you count the jeers and tirades shouted around a mechanical bull or a parking lot brawl. On the other hand, we Finnegans do apparently possess that legendary Irish gift of gab. It therefore doesn't surprise her to see that it's a Finnegan tapping on the glass. And that the Finnegan is me.

The hoots and hollers provoked by the tapping take a while to die down. For although the Peabodies are not prone to public speaking, they do excel in most all other forms of non-verbal outbursts. Nevertheless, the last of the two-fingered whistles, rodeo hoots and catcalls finally fade, and I take the floor.

But as I open my mouth to speak, I notice that the floor is wobbling. I'm trying to focus to get a better view, but my eyelids are doing this independent fluttering thing, which doesn't help a damn bit. That's when I get an excellent idea: if I sway a little, I can compensate for the wobbly floor. There, that's better ...

"Everrawon, I have an announcemement to make," I announce.

I smile as my opening line (for some reason) inspires another wave of happy hollers and whistles, which is only silenced after I ping on the glass again. But then, all of a sudden, I'm having this really bad feeling about what I'm about to say. I'm thinking like it might be wiser just to go to the bathroom and barf. But unfortunately, tact and finesse have never figured amongst the recognized side effects of large quantities of alcohol. And sadly, this occasion provides no exception to the general rule. So instead of just sitting down and shutting up, I carry onward.

"I want to thank all of you for coming all the way out here."

—Hoots and hollers.

"I never could have made it this far without all your love and support, and so this is really your day, as much as it is mine."

—Appreciative heartfelt applause.

"And now I have something to announce, and I'm afraid I'm not sure exactly how to say it."

I can tell from everyone's grins what they're thinking about the fact that I'm swaying like an Oregon Pine in the wind, but if they realized it was all a carefully-studied strategy to alleviate the wobbly floor, they'd be wipin' off those grins. Anyhow, what was I saying? Oh yeah, now for the delicate part.

"The good news is that I've been offered a new job for lots of money, and, uh, the bad news is, that I ... uh ... have to leave tomorrow morning to go and visit them. So, um ... I won't be able to be with you over the weekend."

As might be expected from such an unexpected announcement, the reaction is not exactly homogenous. Of course everyone's disappointed that the weekend has been disrupted. But after all, this is great news, right? I'm in the fast lane now. Big business and all that stuff. Somewhere in the background Granny Finn keeps asking: "What'd he say? What'd he say?" And gradually, everyone manages to move towards me with warm congratulations for the awesome news of the totally awesome job.

Dot, however, is not among the congratulating throng. Where is she? I'm searching the room to see her reaction. Ah, there she is, refilling the pretzels and tending to the punch, or whatever that pink liquid stuff is. All smiles. I knew it! She's taking the whole gotta-leave-tomorrow thing perfectly in stride. She's really got the greatest attitude in the world. Which is just another reason why I adore her so much. She understands. She completely gets how things are starting to move so fast that you really have to go with the flow. Yeah, Dot is a real sport, one in a billion, my soul mate, the best of the best.

*   *   *

It's not until the wee hours of the morning that the party draws to a well-wishing close. It requires an intricate coordination of taxis (thank God for Dot's organizational skills!) to ferry the numerous Finnegans back to the Holiday Inn. Uncles Liam and Billy make repeated trips up and down the stairs to the waiting cabs with sleeping offspring in their arms.

Then, under Dot's directions, the parsimonious Peabodies bed down in the living room, sleeping bags hastily installed amidst a potpourri of crushed Cheetos, corn chips, pretzels, onion dip drippings, misguided celery sticks, and various other party remnants, all grinding their way between the cracks of the ancient hardwood floors and deep into the tightly packed polyester filament spirals of the well-worn carpets.

I fall backwards onto the bed crammed into the corner of our small bedroom. I'm exhausted. Floating somewhere between semi-sentient consciousness and totally hammered blackout.

"Wow, Dot. Great party. Thanks," I say, with slurred words, a dry throat and closed eyes, lying there on the bed on my back.

But in the moment of silence that follows, I don't need to open my eyes to know that all is not well in the state of Denmark. I can feel the charge in the air, like before one of those ferocious thunderstorms. I can feel her standing at the foot of the bed, staring at me. And as the alcohol-high gears down to a feel-like-shit reentry, I fumble around for the right thing to say, searching for the appropriate words in my cerebral haze. I can't seem to come up with anything even remotely close, so I settle painfully short for, "Please, Dot, it's not a big deal."

No spark could have ignited the powder keg with greater effect. She can't believe her ears. She's stunned. A public announcement calling into question New York and everything else which was already *planned* and actually already *decided on!* Not to mention running off like this with the whole family here visiting. She's furious. No, furious isn't the word. Way beyond furious, whatever that would be called. She's been wearing an actor's show-must-go-on smile all night since the "announcement" and now the explosion has attained that nuclear critical mass.

"Not a big deal?" she stammers with rage. "How is it *not* a big deal?" She's standing with her arms folded defiantly across her chest. Speaking through clenched teeth in a hushed but outraged tone intended to be low enough not to wake the sleeping Peabodies on the other side of the door. "Our families come across the country for you, and now we're just going to disappear? Like that? What's wrong with you? You're so incredibly selfish! You only think about yourself! I suppose it never occurred to you that we should just go in a few days when they leave!"

I squint, as if that could help me sift through her words, attempting to formulate some sort of coherent response. And as I listen to what she just said on internal playback, I realize that things are far worse than I'd originally imagined. Dot said *"we."* Like the other weekend firm outings, she was just *assuming* she was invited. Very very not good.

I absolutely have to say something significant now. That much is clear. Something cleverly soothing and understanding. But those sections of my brain seem to have clocked out for the night ...

"Dot, honey, I'm really sorry, but if I don't go tomorrow, I won't be able to make a decision before Monday—and that would screw everything up because I'm supposed to sign my contract on Monday ..." I realize my words are trailing off indistinctly. Partly because I'm presently struggling with this whole notion of formulating basic thoughts and stringing them into syllables, but also because I'm already cringing from what I know is about to come.

I sit up. Bad move. I was far better off lying down with eyes closed. Too late. She's got me in her sights.

"Don't you realize how selfish you're being? I mean, first of all, everyone has come all the way out here spending all that money just to be with us! And couldn't you have at least *talked* to me before making a public announcement? How could you just get up and announce something like that as though I didn't even exist? Without thinking of anyone else but your selfish, egotistical self-centered self? Don't you even care what I think?"

"Of course I—"

"I'm not finished."

"Sorry."

"Where was I?"

"Egotistical self-centered—"

"Exactly! It's already all been decided! We've already made all the plans. If you want to be with me you have to include me in the decisions. You can't just go and change everything at the last second without telling me! We've already decided! We've even picked out our apartment with a view of Central Park. They even bought a car for us. You remember how much you like that car, with the beige leather interior. You shouldn't be going to some other interview for some other job. We want to go to New York. We're already committed."

And that's where I hear some sort of mental click, right through the folded lobes of my soggy brain. As I hear her say that word *"committed"* I suddenly start to feel like I'm suffocating. Like I should be breathing into a paper bag or something. Or like I have been breathing into a paper bag and now all the oxygen is gone.

BUT WAIT! This isn't supposed to happen! This is like the exact opposite of what's supposed to happen. How did this get all screwed up? I've been working hard my whole life to get right exactly where I am now. This is the moment where I'm supposed to feel like I've made it. Like I've arrived at my destination. Like everything is in sync. Right? After all, that's what I was feeling at the firm's cocktail party tonight: *in sync*. It felt so good laughing and telling jokes with my future colleagues. In sync. Reveling in the great success of our mighty Wall Street firm and our personal excellence as the pillars of finance and all that horseshit. In sync! A great job on Wall Street with an awesome salary. An apartment already picked out and a brand new luxury car. I was feeling so good before Singh came out of nowhere like a stray bullet. I've never even questioned the goal. The goal was just always sort of assumed. And here I am. Standing right *at* the goal. Right next to the damn thing. In arm's reach for the first time. So why does it suddenly seem so important to get up and run off on Singh's jet?

"Well?" asks Dot.

Evidently just sitting there with a blank look is not a satisfactory answer to Dot's question. What is the question anyway? Never mind. Now's another spot ripe for something sensitive and constructive. I search, but seem caught in one of those loops where the hard drive just spins with that disappointing churning sound, coming up with nothing.

Silence reigns.

Dot glares.

And maybe she's right, after all. She usually is. Maybe this whole Singh thing is some self-destructive impulse that needs to be repulsed. Purged like a virus before it can contaminate an otherwise perfectly running program.

But I can't flush Singh out of my mind. As if he were holding out his hand, with a red pill and a blue pill in his open palm. Explaining in Morpheus' intense gravelly voice: *You take the blue pill the story ends. You wake up in your bed and believe whatever you want to believe. You take the red pill, you stay in Wonderland and I show you how deep the rabbit-hole goes.*

"Dot, I'm going out there today for the interview."

"You don't care at all about what *I* want!" she snaps.

Why is this happening? So tired. Oh so tired. Anything in exchange for a few minutes of sleep. My kingdom for a horse. No doubt about it, there's a monster hangover settling in. And the gravity's getting worse. Stronger and stronger. Impossible to resist. Dropping back on bed, eyes closed, rubbing temples.

"I do care about what you want, it's just that—"

How dare he flop on the bed with that put-upon sigh!

"No you don't care. All you seem to care about now is your big-shot career." She glares. Tears welling. Her inner voice screaming how unfair it is. Everything already planned! Now all spoiled, of course. The walking tour of colonial Boston with the whole family. The picnic dinner on Beacon Hill that coincides so incredibly perfectly with the free summer-concert-in-the-park program. All the planning! Enough paper plates, napkins, drinking cups, even the oversized ice chest already bought and ready. Not to mention the curtains in New York already ordered. Of course taken separately, detail by detail, it all seems stupid and mundane. But the details add up. Don't they? Someone has to care about it, or the whole thing just falls apart. Right? ... The truth of the matter is that Dot has reached that terrible point where she's liable to say things she doesn't really mean.

"Maybe you should just go ahead and decide whatever you want *without* consulting me. In fact, why don't we just take a *break* and you can decide whatever you want all by yourself. Period." As she utters these words, she wishes she could take them back. Just put them right back into her mouth! If only my eyes were open, I would surely see it in hers.

But my eyes are closed. Lying on my back, where I hear all of it through the thick molasses mush my brain seems now to be suspended in. Sure, our arguments have raised the specter of *the break* before, but it never really seemed serious. And of course it's not serious now either. And I'm ready to agree to anything just to be able to sleep. If only for a few moments. Still lying on my back, eyes still closed, borderline comatose, I mumble:

"Well, maybe you're right. Maybe we should take a break."

... I should have just shut the hell up! Why-oh-why couldn't I have just kept my mouth shut? As you might figure, Dot goes really wild now.

"How dare you actually *say* out loud that we should take a break? After all this time together you feel you can just spit me out like some old chewing gum you've already sucked all the flavor out of? After all these years I followed you around! Through thick and thin!"

She takes two steps forward and slaps me on the face as I lie on my back on the bed with my eyes closed. Then she runs into the bathroom, slams the door and locks it from the inside.

I sit up, rubbing my cheek. *Wow.* That's the first time Dot ever hit me. She must really be pissed. I should try to make up with her before it gets worse. But I notice the dawn beginning to seep in through the windows. I glance at my watch. It's late. If I'm going to meet Singh at the airport I have to go now. And as for Dot, don't worry, it'll all get patched up later. It always does.

I hesitate a moment, then stand up, throw together my overnight bag ... fresh pair of socks, underwear, toothbrush, etc., work my way into a fresh suit, a white starched shirt, and wrap a random tie around my neck.

Holding my bag, ready to leave, I step up to the bathroom door and knock. "Dot, honey. I gotta go." I wait a few seconds for her to answer, even though I know she won't. And of course she doesn't.

So I walk out of our bedroom, around the sleeping Peabodies, and out the front door.

Outside it's drizzling. Cold and predawn grey. But that fits my mood just fine. I let the door slam behind me, scowling.

Damn! My car is still on campus. Well ... the best place to try for a cab this early will be up by the all-night convenience store. I'm turning up my collar and bracing myself for the drizzly walk when I stop dead in my tracks. I can't believe it! Standing at the curb is a Rolls Royce with a chauffeur holding the door open for me!

... I guess I won't be needing that taxi after all.

My first reaction is to run inside to show Dot so we could have a good laugh. Normally she'd get a big kick out of something whacky like this, and she'd tease me and probably call me "Sir David" or something like that with an appalling Monty Python imitation. But given the present circumstances, I figure the timing's a bit off ... I'm not exactly in the mood for another smack on the face.

So I walk towards the Rolls. The chauffeur is dressed better than me, exuding the extreme confidence and stately deference of someone used to driving James Bond or a prime minister around.

"Good morning Mr. Finnegan," he says with an impeccable English accent.

I say hello and step inside.

For a brief second I glance over at my front door. I can already picture myself walking back through that door tomorrow when I come back home, probably with a huge bouquet of flowers for Dot, and maybe some perfume too, for good measure.

Then the strangest thing happens. I get this bizarre Twilight Zone feeling that I might never see that door again, as if Rod Serling were broadcasting live between my ears. I blink hard to chase away the weirdness. No ... that's totally ridiculous, I say to myself as the Rolls pulls away from the curb.

7. The Rainbow

THE BOARDING of private planes occurs in a discreet corner of the international airport that can only be reached after negotiating past a rigorously held security checkpoint. In other words, you don't get here by accident. You're either meant to be here, or you're not. Of course I'm wondering what the hell I'm doing here.

I see Mr. Singh through the glass doors of the entrance. Bond's chauffeur is opening the door for me while some guy in a spiffy uniform takes my bag from the trunk.

Singh steps outside to greet me. "Ready?" he asks.

"All ready."

"Good." He smiles and leads the way.

As we walk through the lobby, I get the sensation I'm entering a different world. Right through the proverbial looking glass. What I don't actually know yet is that I'm right. It is a *completely* different world, this world of *private jet money*. This isn't the upwardly mobile affluent world enjoyed by prosperous lawyers, businessmen, doctors, etc. That kind of money is pocket change where I've just entered. This place is exponentially grander. Light years away. Seeming to exist in its own dimension, functioning according to its own laws and principles diametrically opposed to everything else in that parallel world where the overwhelming majority of the population of the planet is born, lives and dies. In this universe of private jet money, where I've just placed an Armstrongian foot, there are no lines, no waiting, no logistic frustrations or hassles. No concern for how much day-to-day items cost. Money itself is an abstraction. Something multiplied or divided in bank accounts with vast amounts of digits, but never actually touched or handled. All the physical aspects are executed by those members of the *other* world who are here to serve. To facilitate the material variables of daily life: *the staff*.

I marvel as a smartly uniformed employee helps me with my bag and actually guides it through the security check, wishing me a pleasant day like he really means it. What a contrast to the surly rent-a-guards in the normal airport treating you like the subversive enemy! Devising countless ways to make you wait, beltless, shoeless, sweating in those interminable lines with countless others, late for planes ready to take off without you. Well, none of that here. The gracious, smiling, clean-cut staff pour their very souls into making sure that everything about your time spent with them is just grand.

Another set of magazine-perfect employees appear, this time holding umbrellas, clearly endowed with the mission of protecting our evidently exceedingly important persons from the unpleasantness of the drizzle. I feel a bit silly letting this well-built, well-meaning, well-smiling employee march next to me with an umbrella. But Singh-boy is doing it, so far be it from me to break stride.

And then I see *it*. The soundtrack plays crescendo in my brain. There it is, on the tarmac right in front of me, that talisman of power: the *private jet,* gleaming like a great sleek aluminum bird of prey.

I'd be lying if I said I don't feel a special sort of shiver as I climb up the stairs. Of course I realize it's a totally hedonistic *wow-look-at-me-now* type shiver that I should be feeling self-conscious about ... but come on, give me a break. Anyway, I feel like I'm climbing into some movie star world that I'd only just read about or seen in films before. And yes, it feels totally awesome.

Whether through carefully calculated design in order to avoid answering my questions, or force of habit, or merely because he's tired, Singh falls asleep immediately after takeoff.

I bask in the bliss of being in a private plane, and secretly wish that everyone in the world who knows me could see me now. Then I wander over to use the incredibly cool toilet, chat with the beautiful stewardess, drink a glass of freshly squeezed juice, sample the caviar and a host of other expensive delicacies, plop back down into the outrageously comfortable leather seat, and—exhausted by my sleepless night—decide that it would be wonderful take a nap like ol' Singh over there. I close my eyes and lean all the way back, perfectly horizontal. A moment later the stewardess has tucked me in with a soft fluffy blanket. I'm just about to slip off to sleep when a stabbing thought knocks me completely awake with a gut-wrenching lurch. Eyes wide open:

Dot!

Damn! No way I'm going to be able to doze off now. Why did she get so mad? I hate it when we fight like this. It makes me feel miserable. And of course there's no way I can sleep now. I've been through this a million times. After a fight with Dot I can't get to sleep until we make up. No matter how tired I am it's always the same. I just toss and turn till we're back in tune. So there's no use even trying. No ... use ... even ... trying ...

*   *   *

I wake up and look out the window as we drop below the clouds.

My eyes go wide in amazement. An Island! It's the most incredible thing I've ever seen. Unbelievably beautiful. Like that pristine tropical island paradise on the screensaver. The one in your mind's eye, with the perfectly powdery sand, crystal clear water, exotic trees, and creamy foam cresting over turquoise waves.

"It's gorgeous."

Mr. Singh smiles and points to a spectacular building perched on a cliff, constructed out of the island's natural rock to blend in perfectly, its entire ocean-facing side in glass. "That's the Hub, where we work," he says. He points to another large building ringed with tennis courts, an Olympic-sized swimming pool, and various athletic fields. "That's the gym, and the rest of those bungalows are where we live."

"Wow," I say, forgetting again to zap that from my vocabulary. The jet banks towards a small airport with a collection of other planes parked on the tarmac. Mind-boggling. Here I am, *David Finnegan*, landing on a private island because they want *me!*

I sit back in my plush leather throne, taking it all in, high on life, high on myself, high on the adventure of it all. From the back stem of some cerebral outcropping, a tune starts playing in my head. My inner voice starts humming the words, "Somewhere over the rainbow, bla bla bla ..." I laugh at myself, "Skies are blue, and the dreams that you dare dream, really do come true ..."

And, as the wheels of the jet touch down like a feather, with Judy Garland's voice singing sweetly in my head, I have to admit, I ain't in Kansas anymore.

8. Welcome To The Island

THE JET rolls to a stop. I follow Mr. Singh towards the exit. The stewardess stands at attention with choreographed grace. The pilot and co-pilot wave cheerily from the cockpit.

I climb down the gangway after Mr. Singh and out into the blinding tropical sun. Of course I forgot my sunglasses. Not exactly standard equipment back in Cambridge. I blink back the sun like a hick tourist arriving at a discount package-tour seaside destination.

Singh is talking with this amazingly stunning young woman dressed in a sober business suit. "David, this is Gwen," says Singh. "She's your Personal Assistant. She's here 24/7 to make sure you have everything you need."

Did I hear that correctly? *My* PA? Christ! How blatantly, yet effectively manipulative. I manage not to gawk in disbelief or drool on my tie or something equally endearing. She holds out an exquisite hand, which I of course shake.

"Hello David, welcome to the Island."

"Thank you, Gwen. I'm very pleased to be here."

As I release her hand I realize mine is all sweaty. Brilliant first impression. Grossing her out with a sticky palm.

"Gwen will help you get settled in," says Singh. "Then we can meet at the Hub, if that would be convenient for you?"

"Sure," I say.

I notice two futuristic-looking buggies waiting for us. Somewhere in their distant lineage must have been golf carts, but designers with penchants for sci-fi and unlimited budgets had clearly given them marvel-comic-makeovers so they now look capable of roving over the moon or ocean floor. The drivers, dressed in blindingly white uniforms, load Mr. Singh's luggage into one buggy and mine into the other.

Gwen climbs into the front seat next to the driver, and I get in the rear, feeling like I'm on some sort of shuttle borrowed from the Enterprise. Don't beam me up, Scotty, I like it here. We zip down the path and soon stop in front of what everyone has been referring to as a "bungalow." But let me tell you, as far as I'm concerned, it's a mansion. Gwen opens the door and I follow her in.

Inside is completely unreal. A sort of high-tech bungalow/loft. What you'd get if you locked Philippe Starck and Steve Jobs inside and told them to design the perfect lofty paradise without any concern for cost or for going too over-the-top.

A jovial looking woman dressed in white has just finished setting out a pair of awesome Ray-Bans (the kind I could never afford) on the coffee table, according (I presume) to Gwen's astute instructions during the buggy ride in. "Hello Miss Gwen," she says. She smiles at us both and disappears.

Gwen hands me a small screen that looks like a future generation iPhone. "Here's your Island Com. Just touch the screen and you can talk to anyone you want—on or off the Island."

"Would you like to see the view?" she asks.

"Sure." I glance around, puzzled to notice that there doesn't seem to be any windows at all. Gwen speaks into the air: "Reeves, could you please open the shades a bit." No sooner said than the far wall becomes translucent, revealing the breathtaking coastline. The entire wall is glass, now somewhat tinted against the sun. Spectacular blue ocean as far as the eye can see. "Reeves, a bit less sun if you would," whispers Gwen. Instantly the glass shades a tiny fraction, now perfectly adjusted for our eyes.

"My apologies," says an incredibly authentic sounding voice of the perfect English butler.

While maintaining my professional exterior, I'm totally losing it on the inside. Really, the butler thing is too much. "Just like a movie," I comment, then suddenly get the bright idea to add, "You wouldn't be some sort of bladerunner, would you?" And then (I kid you not) she actually turns to me and says: "Would that be Rachel, or Pris?" Can you believe that? She says it deadpan, without cracking a grin. Complete mastery. "It's all been downloaded. If you don't have any questions, I'll be back to pick you up in five minutes."

I nod. Totally blown away.

"And by the way, there's no dress code here. On the Island you can wear anything you feel comfortable in."

I glance down at my business suit. "How about this?"

She tactfully says *no* with her eyes. "Mr. Singh is probably the only person who wears a tie on the Island."

"OK, got it. Thanks Gwen."

She walks out the front door, leaving me to consider what to wear. On Wall Street there's never any question: suit, starched shirt and tie, like everyone else. Simple. But now after Gwen's advice, I'm not quite sure. Going too casual would be a mistake, since this is, after all, a job interview. But being the only dweeb with a tie would be equally lame. OK. Keep the suit, lose the tie and open the collar. Good enough.

9. Marcie

DR. MARCIE ROGERS stands at the podium of a large lecture hall filled with renowned scientists, select VIPs and journalists. She looks out at the standing-room-only crowd. Their admiring faces show how much they respect her scholarly work. She clears her throat, takes a sip of water, and continues her lecture in an impeccably academic tone of voice:

"And why do some people have such shitty lives and others have such fabulous ones? Why is one guy born dirt poor with a low IQ and a butt ugly face, and another one born handsome, clever and rich? Why does one poor schmuck get run over by a truck while another becomes the happy and fulfilled father of a loving family? Why such unfairness? Why such injustice? I'll tell you why." She pauses for emphasis ... Just look at their enthused faces, drinking at the fount.

"The answer is *luck*. Luck dictates whether we have happy lives or wretched ones. But what exactly is *luck?* The answer to that question has eluded us throughout the centuries. Until now. For I am pleased to announce today that my fully-documented research conclusively proves that luck is transmitted *sexually*." A wave of awe washes over the room.

"That's right. Sexually. Just like brown eyes, blond hair or an angular chin, there is a gene for luck, and it's found right here on this chromosome." Dr. Rogers pushes a button and a diagram of the genome in question appears on the wall screen. The audience buzzes with the excitement of such revolutionary scientific work, taking notes and exchanging comments in admiring scholarly tones.

"The ramifications of such a discovery are readily apparent. If luck is transmitted genetically, then unlucky parents will tend to pair up, driven together by their bad luck, thus breeding unlucky children and perpetuating their unluckiness. Instinctively, I imagine every one of you already realizes the truth of what I have scientifically proven. Think about your life. Think about those around you. Haven't you always wondered why certain people just seem to be blessed with good fortune, and others cursed? Well now you know why. Now you know why the rich, famous and beautiful breed rich beautiful offspring, and the poor, ugly, impoverished, criminal elements of our society perpetuate themselves."

Understanding spreads like a tidal wave across the auditorium. You could eat the eurekas with a spoon.

"And of course, since the fortunate winners of the genetic lottery don't procreate with losers, humanity is slowly but surely breeding itself into two distinct races: one with luck on its side, and one cursed with misfortune—"

Suddenly, the sound of a male voice interrupts her lecture. Her eyes darken at the impertinence of this voice that seems to be talking to her in an insistent and angered tone. How rude!

But the voice won't let up. Won't let her go. It snaps her out of her imaginary scientific lecture and back to reality, where she is in fact sitting in a plastic molded chair firmly planted in front of the large desk of her boss, the Senior Assistant Staff Manager for Wal-Mart Store #349. Marcie has been working at Wal-Mart for almost a year now, and this is already the second time she's been summoned to the Assistant Manager's office.

The voice drones on. "Do you even care about your job, Miss Rogers? Because if you don't care, you should quit right now. Do you want to quit your job, Miss Rogers? Is that what you want? Because I should really fire you. That's what I should do." The Assistant

Manager waits for an answer. Head cocked. "Well, do you have an explanation for your behavior?"

She fully reenters reality and looks straight at the pockmarked face of her boss staring at her like she's some sort of deranged halfwit. She summons her full reserve of sincerity and shunts it urgently to her face. With heartfelt eyes she looks earnestly at him and says:

"Well, Sir, I guess I'm just unlucky."

Unlucky? Did she say *unlucky?* What in hell does she mean by that? She was daydreaming at the register—staring into space, ignoring the customers trying to check out! What the hell does that have to do with *luck?* He's the unlucky one. Having to deal with smartass incompetent bitches like this. Then it dawns on him. She's making fun of him. She's mocking him. They're all the same! With their haughty eyes and contemptuous hips. Wonder how contemptuous you'd be with your smart ass fired out of a job? He seethes. But quickly reminds himself to keep his cool. To manage the situation. Managing is "key." K-E-Y. Exactly like he learned at those Wal-Mart Assistant Managers' training sessions. He clears his throat. His voice has that I'm-controlling-my-temper condescending timbre to it, adding a pleasant sheen to his clearly evident superiority.

"OK, Miss Rogers, would you explain to me how being *unlucky,* as you say, has anything to do with the incident today? And if it's not too much trouble, I'd like you also to explain to me why such unacceptable behavior should not result in the termination of your employment." He notes with pride that what he just said sounds very much like something you would hear on TV, or in some really good movie with a solid plot, thoughtful dialogue and truly likeable characters.

Meanwhile, Marcie's sweat glands writhe secretingly. She feels a frantic jab in her stomach as her self-preservation instinct kicks into full gear. Scrambling for an emergency plan. *Unlucky?* How the fuck could she have said that? Like paying the rent is a friggin joke. A fucking comedy act. Now something cleverly feline is needed. Designed to land on feet. Wait! No, on second thought clever repartee is *so* not the way to go with this chump. Feminine survival wiles much better. Complete submission is the ticket. Big time.

She brushes a strand of hair to the side. "Please, Sir," she says, looking up with those beautiful, pleading, sexy eyes. "I don't want to quit this job. I love my job. I need this job, and I promise I'll be more careful in the future." Unlike Dr. Rogers' academic diction, Marcie speaks with a slow southern lisp, producing a singularly sensual singsong resonance to her voice. She smiles wide, traces a big "X" over her ample bosom and adds:

"Cross my heart."

Marcie's sudden reasonableness completely disarms the Assistant Manager. She is smiling at him. Lips parted. Suddenly sincere. Understanding. Compliant. Obedient. Repentant. He feels a tingle in his loins and a flash of testosteronic vertigo. Those eyes, those lips. She's seen the light. She sees him for what he really is. Her lips ... still parted. She's seen through his skin-deep shortcomings straight into his true self, his debonair, masculine, true self. For a split second his thoughts run wildly like a pinball machine giving away a free game. This could happen! Is happening! She's gorgeous. They could go right now into the back room. *Right now!* But the moment of ecstatic fantasmic deliria lasts only until he looks into her eyes. There, in those eyes, he sees it immediately. He's totally off the mark. She would never want him! Ugh. The humiliation. That same old familiar humiliation. He quickly looks down at his desk, his pockmarked cheeks burning red. Screw her! They *are* all the same.

He starts shaking his head back and forth solemnly, with the gravity of an HBO drama, like he truly has no other choice but to sever her employment.

Hmm ... wonders Marcie. Why's he moving his head like that? That can't be good. Asshole.

The unexpected clanging of the phone makes her jump. He answers. Mumbles something into the receiver. Hangs up. Turns towards her and says: "Miss Rogers, I'll just be a minute."

"OK, sure." She nods with an exaggerated smile intended to exude maximum employee good attitude.

The plastic molded chair is now sticking sweatily to her back and butt. She watches the Assistant Manager stand up and start walking towards the door. He purposefully avoids looking at her as he leaves his office.

When he disappears behind the door, she lets her head collapse into her palms, covering her eyes, hoping desperately to pull out of the nosedive. Prayer time. *Please don't let me get fired. I'll do anything. Please.*

He closes the door behind him. Now he's in his favorite spot. He likes to think of it as his own personal Mission Control. It's nothing more than an oversized closet, but it's lined with a dozen security monitors linked up to the surveillance Cams throughout the store. He loves this place. From here he can observe this whole universe under his command. And he loves that little trick of pushing the button he had installed on his phone so that it rings a few seconds later creating the perfect pretext for him to leave someone alone in his office. That idea of his was a real stroke of genius.

He sits down in the big swivel chair and scans the monitors. Everything looks in order. But wait ... What's that? He looks closer and taps into a keyboard to zoom in on one of the Cams in the toy section. It's a man standing with his daughter. The little girl glances to make sure her father isn't watching, then reaches over to the display shelf, grabs a toy, and slips it into her pocket. *Aha!* It happens constantly throughout the day. Statistically there's an item stolen from his store—*right under his nose*—every hour. He zooms in closer. The quality of these new monitors is really excellent. He can actually see their expressions. Too bad there's no sound. He could alert security now and rub their stupid noses in the fact that he saw this while they were obviously asleep at the switch, but he decides to wait another moment. He watches as the man looks down to face his daughter, as if he'd caught her in the act as well.

*   *   *

"Zoey, what are you doing?"

"Nothing, Daddy."

"I saw that. What did you just put in your pocket?"

The little girl's eyes go wide. He saw her! She pulls out a small package from her pocket and looks guiltily up at her dad.

"What's that?" he asks.

"A Tamaguchi."

The man looks closer. It's a small plastic electronic device with an LCD screen showing some sort of a little pet-like creature.

"What's a Tamagoopy?" he asks.

"Tamaguchi."

"Whatever. What is it?"

"It's like alive. And if I care for it real good by giving it pretend water and food and stuff whenever it beeps, it will always stay alive. No matter what."

The man winces on the inside. If Skylark were here she'd know how to deal with this. He looks at the price. It's expensive. It's more than what he's already budgeted to pay the electric bill. He just can't afford it right now.

"OK ... but why was it in your pocket?"

She studies her shoes without saying anything.

"You know it's really bad to steal, don't you?"

She nods, but then looks up at him and asks, "Why? Why is it bad?"

The man thinks for a moment. "Well, it's bad because stealing is always bad. If everybody stole things, well ... we couldn't trust anybody. That's why we have rules like this. And you can't go against the rules, or the whole system falls apart. Do you understand that?"

The little girl nods, unsure.

"And besides, there are policemen everywhere in the store who are watching us, and if they see you stealing something it will be very very bad."

That she understands. She nods again. Then glances up where the sky would be if they weren't inside, and quickly back to her dad. "Do you think Momma saw me?"

"Maybe. I don't know. But I know I did. Now put it back."

Reluctantly, the little girl takes a last look at the toy she wanted and puts it back on the shelf.

The man smiles gently. "But don't worry, Sweetie, I'll buy you a Tamathingee."

The girl's face lights up. "Reeaaally?" she squeals with delight.

"Yeah. I can't do it right now, but real soon I'll come back and buy it for you, OK?"

"Sure. I can wait."

She grabs his hand with a huge smile and they continue to walk down the aisle.

*   *   *

Back at Mission Control, the Assistant Manager watches on the monitor as the man and his daughter walk away. So he won't have to alert security after all. Fine. He glances down at his watch. In another minute he'll go back in and deal with *her*.

10. Project F

MR. SINGH OPENS THE DOOR, ushers me into this enormous office, and withdraws without a sound. The place is gigantic. A cross between a museum and some sort of mad scientist's secret hideout.

And here he is, Max Simon, the man behind it all. He's dressed in a tennis outfit, covered in sweat, like he's just finished a set at Wimbledon ... Not exactly what I'd expected. He walks over to me with a big smile and an outstretched hand.

We shake.

"So I take it Mr. Singh didn't succeed in scaring you away."

"Not yet."

"Good. Now let's meet the team."

He pushes a button and this secret door-like thing opens into another vast room gorged with screens and keyboards. Inside are half a dozen late-twenty-something kids dressed like they're at the college campus cafeteria. They totally ignore us, continuing to sip their coffees and energy drinks as they tap on keyboards and stare into screens. Good thing Gwen tipped me off on the dress code or I'd feel even more uncomfortable than I already do.

Max calls out: "OK everyone, gather round, I'd like you to meet David." They look over at us and Max runs through the intros.

"This is Stacy. She's our information coordinator." She's tall, blond and tough-looking. The military fatigues she wears are right at home. Like Starbuck's twin sister from Battlestar Galactica. She nods army-like at me, which I try to return without looking like Radar or Beetle Bailey.

"Flo is our markets man, if he doesn't know about it, then it's not on a market and won't be any time soon." Flo looks like a nice guy. Chubby sort of roly-poly with an untamed afro and a welcoming smile. The kind of guy you'd go and sit down next to in a lunchroom if you didn't know anybody.

"This is Vlad, our hacker and techno-buff." Looks like they glued him together with the parts left over from Flo. The complete opposite. Cadaverous white, tall and lanky with a digital look to his eyes. Rather skip lunch than sit next to him.

"This is Goran, political liaison and research. Over there is our financial analyst, the number crunching Babz, and you'll meet Virgil later."

Introductions accomplished, Max turns to me with a devilish grin and says: "Now, how 'bout some *coke?*"

Yeah, I heard right: "*coke.*" Of course everyone in the room is staring at me, waiting to see how I'll react. Even I feel like I'm staring at me 'cause I don't have the foggiest idea what to say. I try to read Max's expression, but he's wearing a poker face. Clearly something witty is called for, but as so often in these types of key spotlight situations, I'm drawing a blank. Snap standup off-the-cuff comedy is definitely not my strong suit.

"Would you be referring to the beverage?" I ask, admittedly anemic.

"No," says Max, "I would not be referring to the beverage."

And then I get it. A beat behind, perhaps, but I get it.

"Well, then perhaps you'd be referring to the solid carbonaceous derivative from the destructive distillation of low-ash low-sulfur bituminous coal?"

Appreciative smiles and chuckles ripple through the floor.

Max grins approvingly. "Stacy, can you bring up a prep file on coke, and I don't mean the white stuff."

"Next time ask for something I couldn't do in my sleep," she says with a big smile and an attitude to go with. Seconds later every one of the dozens of screens in the room is filled with background data concerning industrial petroleum coke. Historical pricing, cross-indexed with every other commodity. Logistic analyses, tables for any transportation grid, everything imaginably relevant at your fingertips.

"So I guess now you understand why you're here," says Max.

"Not really."

Max smiles, obviously enjoying the theatrics. "Well, David, welcome to our little world. We call it the *Opportunity Hub*. From here we scan the planet, and when we find an opportunity we work our magic. There's so much out there! The possibilities are endless. The world is our oyster bed, so to speak, and I think you've discovered a very interesting pearl. Do you follow me?"

"Are you talking about the paper I wrote?"

"Yes I am."

"But it's nothing really. Just some research I did at school. Just school stuff. My prof didn't even take it seriously."

"He didn't?" Max smiles in mock surprise. "Well, unlike your *prof*, I found the paper very interesting. Especially the part where you criticize the prevalent market structure and postulate that current regulatory deficiencies could be exploited to manipulate cross-linked pricing by exponential factorization."

I smile. He read my paper.

"In fact, shortly after discovering your work, I started a little project. I call it Project F."

"F for factorization?" I ask.

"No. F for Finnegan."

"Wow."

"Indeed. And today we're going to bring Project F to life. Would you like to start us off by telling the gang about your idea in a nutshell?"

I'm not thrilled about being put on the spot like this. Especially in a room full of whiz kids waiting to hear me talk about something ridiculously called "Project Finnegan." But then again, I'm excited about sharing my idea with them.

"Well," I begin, "the concept is very simple. It's really just applying exponential matrix propagation to an unbalanced inter-related system in order to redistribute realization. Since the system is inherently linked, the idea is to start a chain reaction that spreads exponentially, the same way a virus or a dominant genetic mutation would spread through a population. The first transaction is the catalyst for two more transactions, each one causing two more, and so forth. Very rapidly the entire system becomes modified, and of course an investor who knows it's going to happen could make a lot of money."

As the words leave my mouth I'm patting myself on the back. OK, so I'm not great at the comedy bites, but I totally rock when it comes to nerd stuff. Wait. Strike that. I can't believe I actually just reveled in being a geeky nerd. How lame can you get?

"Fascinating," says Max.

"Yeah, well, it's just a hypothetical. I don't think anyone paid any attention to it."

"I paid considerable attention to it. And I still wonder, to this very moment, if your hypothesis is correct," responds Max.

"Well, even if the hypothesis were valid, and existing market imperfections could allow the price to be manipulated, that doesn't mean an independent investor could actually control such manipulation."

"But assuming it were possible, would it be legal?"

"Sure, it would be legal as long as it wasn't done through monopolistic market structures or collusion. But, from a financial perspective it would be risky."

"How risky?"

"Very."

"But interesting," pursues Max.

"I'll say." I'm now getting completely caught up in the game. If this is leading where it seems to be, then this guy is a complete nutcase, but he's also very cool.

"Would you like to try?" asks Max.

"That's impossible. We would need an enormous market stake."

"How enormous?"

"At least twenty-five million."

"Dollars?"

I nod. "With proper leveraging. But that would be crazy."

"You've run simulations on it though, haven't you?"

"Yeah, but the margin of error was huge. The variables are too complex for real-time modeling to be accurate."

"But you were able to pull it off on the models, weren't you?"

"Well ... sometimes."

"Would you like to try for real?"

My mouth is dry. Of course I'd like to try. It'd be great fun. But this is real money. Shitloads of real money. Standing there with Max egging me on, we're like two kids trying to get up the nerve to fly a kite in a thunderstorm with a key tied to the end of a string in a jar.

Max doesn't bother waiting for my answer.

"Stacy, load twenty-five into a trading shell," he says.

Her fingers fly over a keyboard, and on the main screen "US$ 25,000,000" is credited to a numbered account.

"Well, David, here's your chance."

"What if I lose it?" I'm wishing my words didn't come out so crackly.

"Then I'll have lost twenty-five million dollars *and,*" says Max loud enough for all to hear, "everyone in this room will take a hefty pay cut since of course their financial remuneration depends entirely on the profits generated out here on the floor." He nods his head in acknowledgment of some groans. "Yes, yes, here on the floor we rise and fall together. All for one and one for all."

Meanwhile, I'm getting serious cold feet, and deciding I'd just as soon call it a day. I guess I don't really have the guts to play Casino Royale with twenty-five million real dollars. So I glance at my watch, make a quick calculation, and conclude (thankfully) that I'm off the hook. The timing's wrong. It's too tight. The markets will begin overlapping convergence in two hours. There's no way I can gather all the data to make the calculations in time. I would have had to start setting it all up last night to be ready now.

So I shake my head and say: "I don't have enough time to get the data."

But Max ups the amps on his smile. "Good news. You don't need more time. You've got Stacy. She can give you anything you want before you finish your sentence." Stacy nods matter-of-factly that it's true. "Go ahead David," he urges, "give it a whirl. Nothing ventured, nothing gained."

Mom always said never give in to peer pressure. Pretty obvious what she'd be saying now.

Max is waving me into a chair. I don't know what's wrong with me, but I don't listen to Mom. Instead, I sit down. And I'm already regretting it big time as Commando Stacy sidles up to me and starts adjusting monitors and tapping on multiple keyboards.

"So, what you need, Captain?"

From the tone of her voice I can tell she means Crunch more than Kirk. But I smile anyway and say, "How about smelting output quantities, crossed with open steel orders, and future shipping rosters?" Stacy works the keyboard. And whatever she might lack in social grace, I immediately see she makes up for with results. Almost instantly, the info is on my screen.

"Wow. It takes me hours to compile this stuff."

"That's one of our edges," comments Max. "What others take hours to do, we take seconds."

OK, so I have a team of geniuses at my service. But it's me sitting in the hot seat. And at the risk of belaboring the metaphor, despite the perfect climate control, I'm already sweating like a pig. Stacy is barking commands to the team. The place looks like adopt-a-geek day at NASA.

Of course I'm scared shitless, but then I do what I always do in these types of situations. Somehow (thank God!) my inner calm Jedi Master takes over. It happens every time I have an important exam or get in some stressful situation. I get this Zen sorta concentration thing going and start thinking in fast motion. The Zen-me assumes command: "I'll need ten, no—eleven shells for the incoming funds."

The next two hours are grueling as the team feeds me the information I need to calculate and program the algorithms. Finally, my fingers flash over the keyboard for a few more seconds and suddenly stop. The room is silent.

"OK, I set the algorithms. All we have to do now is transfer the funds. But as soon as we do that, the money will be in play. We can't get it back. We'll have to wait for the cycle to run its course."

"How long?"

I glance at my watch, "Two hours from now."

"And then we'll know?"

"We'll know alright. If I've screwed up the money will be gone."

Max responds with a supportive "go team" smile and I scan the room. The team in question seems far more skeptical than enthusiastic.

"OK, let's do it," says Max.

Stacy looks at me, but I just shrug towards Max.

"As soon as David is ready," says Max.

Stacy looks back to me. Right at me with her eyes. Piercing eyes.

If one were foraging around for an appropriate adjective to describe the moment, one might opt for terrified. I'm on the spot. Totally. If I back down now I'd look like a complete gutless loser. Scratch that, I'd *be* a gutless loser. Man enough to write about it in a paper, sure. Yet spineless like a jellyfish when it comes to actually playing ball. Not an appealing option. But my motivation is not just the aversion to being de-masked as a total wimp. Seriously, my natural cowardice can trump any amount of peer pressure. After all, was it not I who actually climbed up to the ten meter diving platform, stood there for more than an hour trying to summon the balls to jump off, teeth and nuts clacking in the cold Oregon wind? And then actually *climbed back down* the ladder amongst the jeers of about everyone I knew in the entire universe rather than jump? Yup, that would be me. So I can definitely pocket self-esteem when it comes to being a coward for good valid reasons. I mean, ever think about what it would feel like to bank out of control into a belly flop from ten meters up?

No, this coke thing isn't about peer pressure. Like Max, it's about the adventure. The challenge. We're both drawn to it. Despite the risk, we both want to know. Like the astronomer searching for that star just beyond the visible spectrum, the test pilot yearning to break another speed barrier, the etymologist searching for that fabled undiscovered bug. *We want to know.* We want to know if something like this can really work in real life. It's the dare. The defiant mountain peak. The intellectual adrenalin rush. That's what kept me awake during those countless all-nighters when I was writing the paper, discovering my idea and developing the algorithms. That's what disappointed me so much when none of the faculty paid any attention to it. That's what still keeps me awake sometimes at night when I think back to my theory, wondering if it would really work. That's why Max picked me for his Island. That's why I'm here right now. That's why I'm just about to nod and bring Project F to life.

And so I nod.

Stacy pushes "enter" on the master control board, and the $25,000,000 disappears from the onscreen account. In its place pops up a column of "input" accounts where the profits or losses from the complex series of transactions will be transferred as each of the leveraged positions is unwound.

The entire room turns to watch the huge screen showing the input accounts on one side and a host of market variables on various bar charts and graphs on the other. For a few moments nothing happens as the positions are registered across the exchanges. That's perfectly normal. Within seconds the starting zero balances of the input accounts begin climbing, some edging already up. I watch the numbers multiply, having trouble believing it's for real. We're actually making millions of dollars. Real dollars. Just like that. Based on my idea! My silly idea that no one back at school took any interest in! I breathe a sigh of relief. Feeling already like a superstar. Despite myself, I know a self-congratulatory grin has crept into the subtext of my smile.

Then, suddenly, one after another, the accounts reverse themselves, dipping sharply negative. It feels like someone just kicked me in the gonads with a pair of football cleats. Needless to say the self-satisfied gloat has been sucked right off my face.

"Is this supposed to happen, Captain?" asks Stacy with a generous lilt of sarcasm.

"No."

I glance over at Max. His smile is gone too ... replaced by the poker face.

The floor kicks into high gear like a warship going into battle. Stacy organizes her troops as I frantically stare at the screen trying not to look as panicked and clueless as I feel. Why did I do this? Why did I ever get myself into this? I am such an ass!

I hear Stacy's whispered voice in my ear. "Vampire Vlad here is probably the best hacker on the planet, and given the deep shit it looks like you just dove into, you'd better pick his brains quick before it's too late."

Thankful for the advice I turn to Vlad. "Here, look. These are the algorithms I programmed. Here are the open orders, here are the leverage points and these are the reiterating parameters." Vlad absorbs it all in a flash. "Any ideas?" I ask.

A collective gasp rises from the floor. I look up at the big screen where the negative account balances have just spiked again. Shit! We're now down the $25,000,000 plus another $10,000,000 in open positions. I've already lost thirty-five million dollars in the past few minutes. My Zen Jedi-Masterness has totally skipped town. Leaving me alone with my Oregonian hick self. This is a fucking nightmare. And it's all my fault for ignoring my Mom and listening to the nutcase billionaire. What the hell's the matter with me?

Concentrate, damn it! Bitch and moan later.

"Would it help to see real time cross-market reactions since the play?" asks Vlad.

"You can do that?"

"If it'd help I can try."

"Hell yeah, it would help."

"Babz, Goran, get your butts over here," calls out Vlad. Stacy clears a station for them, and they start working their magic. Within minutes they've up-streamed the data, breaking it into bite-sized chunks and distributing it to the floor for analysis. As the analyzed data starts flowing back to me, I scramble for an answer—something to stem the hemorrhaging tide. Of course I'd seen problems like this when I was writing that stupid paper and running the models on my Mac. But I never really focused on it. After all, it wasn't real money back then. In a way I guess that's the difference between school and real life. No wonder profs are like they are.

OK, back to Jedi mode. Stacy, Vlad, Babz, Goran and the rest of the team are pumping an enormous amount of information into my screen. But now I know what I'm looking for and I'm back on Zen frequency turbo-charged overdrive. I slug down a double espresso and slog through the data.

"Faster," I say, and the numbers go blitzing over my screen like the Matrix.

"Slow down or you'll miss it," warns Stacy.

"Faster," I say.

I'm not trying to be macho, it's just that if I don't find what I'm looking for real quick it's going to be over and I'm going to have to face up to whatever they do to supposed superstars who blow forty million dollars their first day on the job.

The Matrix keeps flashing across my screen, but I can't find what I'm looking for. Neo, where the hell are you? White Rabbit? I glance up at the big screen to see that the losses are now over fifty million. That's it. I've blown it. Time to pull the plug and take the hit.

And then, thank God, or Allah, the Force or whoever else is out there smiling down on me at this precise moment ... I see it. "That's it!" I cry out. And there it is, right in front of me: *the cause.*

But now we have to move fast. Real fast.

"We hit a set of clustered options. They must be set up as self-triggering short sells. It's throwing everything off." My fingers fly over the keyboard. "Hurry. We need to reconfigure the algorithms factoring in the open positions." But before I even finish my sentence, the team's all over it.

"Problem is, we don't know what they look like."

Vlad's at my side, his fingers banging away at the keyboard. "Hang on, I'm working through the open orders."

"You can do that?"

"If it's digital, I can do it."

We're scrambling. I feel like I'm balancing Yoda and trying to levitate the spaceship out of the swamp at the same time. Then a few seconds later Goran calls out: "Got it!" A row of numbers flashes onto my screen. Halleluiah! We reprogram the order chains, and even as we type, the negative numbers in the accounts start moving upwards. You can feel the sighs of relief in the room. The numbers keep shooting skyward. Within thirty minutes we've climbed out of a negative position and the cash starts flowing into the accounts. Pouring in by the millions.

A bell rings. The markets are closed, and we're up thirty million!

A victory cheer roars through the room. Champagne corks pop like firecrackers.

*   *   *

"Congratulations, David. You put on a pretty good show out there today."

Max and I are now back in his palatial office. Just the two of us. I'm sitting next to a collection of shrunken heads mounted on the wall inches away from my own head. Max puts a glass of sparkling water down on a tray held by some sort of domestic robot reminiscent of R2-D2.

"Actually, I think you should take the production credit. I just walked on. You'd already set the stage."

Max laughs. "In any event, you made me thirty million dollars today. Thanks."

"Well, you took a big risk. Thanks for believing in me."

"I do believe in you, David. And I believe we can do great things together. So what would you like as a success bonus for this morning's work?"

"Success bonus?"

"Yes. Let me explain how the system works. Here on the Island we all have different talents and expertise. When one of us develops a proposal he or she submits it to the group and we either go ahead with it or put it on hold. It could be a hostile takeover of an oil field in Siberia or an LBO in Nebraska. Anything goes. Each member gets a share of the profits, and the one who developed the proposal and leads the deal gets a success bonus. Payment on the team is entirely by performance."

"But I was told I'd have a salary at least five times what my other firm wants to pay me."

Max bursts into laughter. Then, in between laughs, he says:

"Who told you that?"

"Mr. Singh."

This causes Max to laugh even more. But I'm not laughing at all. *Bait and switch* is what I'm thinking. The oldest trick in the book. Promise big numbers, then switch the offer to an entirely success-based formula. With the ratios fixed in favor of the house, of course.

"Mr. Singh, Mr. Singh ... I'm afraid I must apologize on his behalf. Mr. Singh would not be the most reliable source on this issue. You see, Mr. Singh, bless his soul, is far too conservative a man in these instances. He told you five times because he did not want to appear over-presumptuous, given the objectively undeniable reality that such figures are not in fact *guaranteed*." Max holds my stare. He can tell I'm annoyed, but it seems to amuse him. And as he looks into my eyes his complete confidence and sincerity wash away my skepticism.

"Salaries are for the staff, David. Or for the humdrum lawyers on Wall Street to whom we give our grunt work on the transactions. Truth is, if you made only five times what the other guys were offering you on Wall Street, then your performance here would be substandard, and if you were substandard, then you wouldn't have lasted here more than a month. You would have been handed a generous severance check and catapulted off-Island." His eyes twinkle amicably. "Personally, my bet is that you'll be making far more than what Mr. Singh indicated. After all, everyone you met this morning makes much more than that. Let's put it this way: what you'd make here is so much more than what you'd make at that job on Wall Street, it's beyond comparison. We're not in the same ballpark. We're not even in the same solar system."

I nod. Reassured. Tingling with excitement.

"So, David, are you ready to join us on the Island?"

Of course I'm ready, and I'm just about to say so when I think about Dot.

"Hesitating?"

I gulp.

"Perhaps I can assist you in your analysis. I'd like to offer you one million dollars for your work this morning."

"What? A million dollars?" My gulp turns to gawk. Max smiles. He's enjoying the moment profoundly. It's the joy of a successful pirate divvying the booty with his motley crew. Of Robin sharing with his Merry Men. The joy of amply rewarding someone who just made you richer. It's a joy that Max Simon visibly thrives on. The more he pays out, the more he makes. You can tell he loves the math on that.

I look at Max smiling at me. Then I notice a small painting of some sort of island cannibal tribal king hanging on the wall just above Max's shoulder. The caption explains that the cannibal king has just captured a young explorer, and has presented the unfortunate prisoner with a dilemma. The explorer has one question he can ask the king. If the king answers "yes" the explorer will be eaten for dinner. If the king answers "no" the young man will be fed to the sharks. But if the king must lie to answer the question, the explorer will take his place as king.

Max holds out his hand.

"Well, David, shall we shake on it?"

Max is waiting for my answer. I can't stall. This is the moment. One of those critical moments in life where you stand at a crossroads. There is no pause button. You either act or you let the moment flash past. Irretrievable.

"If the answer is *yes*, will I be fed to the sharks?"

Max smiles and shakes my hand.

And so, my beloved reader, what do you think? ... Did the cannibal king have to lie?

11. Conundrum Or QED?

BACK AT MY BUNGALOW I plop on the sofa and close my eyes for a sec. Reality check. Gotta stop and take stock. Breathe in deep. OK, today I almost lost fifty million real dollars, then actually ended up making thirty million for some billionaire weirdo who just offered me a million to come work on this private island that I couldn't even pinpoint on a map where I'll continue to make zillions and live in a dream pad with a computerized butler named Reeves and a PA who's so hot that—well never mind that.

And I guess that about sums up the day. In sum, this rocks. This totally completely rocks.

Gwen's voice comes over the invisible sound system as if she's sitting right here on the couch with me. "Hello David. I've prepared an *action item* list that you might want to consider."

I smile at the absolute perfectness of it all, looking out over the balmy blue ocean at my wild bungalow mansion ... "Sure, Gwen, that would be very helpful. Go ahead."

"First a draft letter to the Wall Street firm you were considering, explaining that you won't be joining them. I downloaded it to your screen."

Wow, they're fast! I'm already about to send a letter to my firm *turning down* their fabulous offer. The one I dreamed about all through school. Christ. The point of no return. If I blow them off now, they'll never take me back. But why do I care? I'm here! Think how surprised the guys at the firm will be!

I'm excited beyond anything I can remember. And of course I want to share it. I want to share it with my best friend in the universe. Truth is, ever since seeing the Island, I can't wait to tell Dot about it. I know she's going to love it here. It's perfect. She's going to be so psyched!

"Gwen, let's finish up a bit later. I have to make some calls."

"Of course." Gwen hangs up.

I reach for my phone and dial.

Dot answers, "Hello."

"Hey Dot babe!" My voice bubbles with excitement.

"Hello David." Her voice is sub-zero freezing. I guess she's still pissed off. But that'll change in a second when she hears the news.

"You're never going to believe it, Dot."

"What?"

"This is the greatest thing that's ever happened to us!"

"What is?"

"This place. It's just great. The job. Everything. It's fantastic here!"

"Where are you? Where's here?"

"Well, in fact it's an island."

"A what?"

"An island. And the guy who runs the business owns the whole island. It's beautiful. And the business concept is brilliant. We all live in bungalows. And work together as a team sharing profits. It's really wonderful. You're going to love it!"

"What do you mean: *I'm going to love it?*"

Cat now out of bag. Perhaps not the smoothest way to have broken the news. No time, however, for reformulating strategy. Must forge ahead. "Everyone lives in these amazing bungalows, and works in this huge office built right into the cliff over the ocean."

"David, what do you mean? You haven't already *accepted* the job, have you?"

I fumble for something to say. My razor wit might as well be a soggy Q-tip up against Dot.

"Without even *talking* to me about it?"

"Dot, honey, I wanted to talk to you, but there really wasn't any time."

"I can't believe it! You can't just decide where I'm going to live. Like I'm some dog or goldfish or pet turtle."

"Dot, please. The guy offered me a huge bonus and stuck out his hand to shake. I couldn't say '*no.*' What could I do? Just let his hand hang there and explain I have to ask my girlfriend's *permission* first?"

Of course I regret the words the second they leave my mouth. Dot's reaction is instantaneous. "That's a terrible thing to say!" she blurts. "How dare you try to make me feel like some shrew forcing you to ask for permission! We've been together since grade school! You can't just decide that we're going to live on some deserted island without even *asking* me! Like you don't even care what I think!"

"Of course I care what you think."

But something inside Dot has just burst. It's almost as if I can feel the explosion. Like some huge hot air balloon. Like a zeppelin or blimp or something. I can hear the tears rolling down her cheeks. But what can I do? How can I fix this?

"Dot, honey, I know you're going to love it—"

"That's not the point, David. If you're so eager to be making decisions without me, then maybe you should just keep on without me. Don't you realize you've just proven once and for all that you don't care about me? That I can't trust you? I told you this morning that if you want to be with me you have to include me in your decisions. So what do you do? You fly off to some island and you decide to live out there without even asking me what I think! So just stay on your stupid break, and stay on your dumb island!"

Click and then the dial tone.

I sit there staring at the phone. Pushing redial over and over. Calling back dozens of times. But she's not answering.

I can't believe what just happened. What's going on? How can such a small thing turn into such a big deal? I don't get it. I really don't get it. I mean I can understand her being peeved and all. I'm not a complete idiot. And I realize she was looking forward to New York, and the apartment on Central Park and the car and all that stuff. But things can't always go exactly as you plan. Right? And when things go better than you plan, well you just have to seize the moment, don't you? Deep down I know I'm right. But I also know Dot must be feeling just as righteous. I guess we're both right. That's the problem. Maybe we're just not right for each other. Oh my God. Is that what this is about? Is that what's going on? After all, think about it. Dot was so dead set on Wall Street that if I'd listened to her then I wouldn't even be on the Island now. I would have never come out here. And since being on the Island is obviously the best thing that's ever happened to me, then she's obviously wrong on that one.

Q.E.D.

So what should I do?

And that's when the doorbell rings.

12. Virgil

WHEN I OPEN THE DOOR there's a guy about my age standing there in jeans and a faded T-shirt proclaiming the excellence of the lobster gumbo of some illegible island dive.

"Hi David. I'm Virgil, your Guardian Angel."

"Guardian Angel?"

"Yeah, it's sort of a thing Max does to help a new guy get settled on the Island."

"Sounds good to me. Come on in."

"Yowza."

He steps in, pulls off his sunglasses and slumps into the sofa like he's lounging at home. "So bro', my only purpose in life for the next forty-eight hours is to make sure both of us have so much fun we're ready to work 'round the clock making gainful use of our brilliance starting Monday morning."

"Wow. What you have in mind?"

"Depends on you, buddy."

"I dunno, I'm kinda new here, what do you suggest?"

"Well, we could go night diving off the reef. There's always these monster manta rays out there which are really cool, and not dangerous if you don't harass them."

I let my aversion to aquatic adventures seep through the cracks of my polite smile.

"OK, so it's a pass on the mantas. How about we go night para-planing over the jungle, or take the submarine out for a spin."

"You guys got a submarine?"

Virgil mimics a cool nod, like James Bond (when it was Sean of course) and says with a charmingly poor brogue attempt, "Yes we have a submarine."

"OK. But at the risk of sounding like a total wiener, do you have a way to spend the evening that I haven't seen on the X-treme sports channel?"

Virgil sits up straighter in the couch as if to attribute the appropriate level of deference to the moment. "Yes, as a matter of fact, I have something that you've never seen on that channel. I myself have, shall we say, a certain predilection towards the type of fieldtrip I'm now about to propose. Nevertheless, I feel morally obliged to offer well-adjusted, healthy, meritorious, model-citizen-type entertainment options for you to choose from before giving you the *alternative* option."

"*Alternative* option?"

"In one word: *awesome*. In two words: *totally awesome*."

"Can you be a tad more specific?"

Virgil rolls his eyes, already reveling in the festivities to come. "First, we grab one of the planes, in say about ten minutes. And we fly to any number of incredible island party paradises. We check into the best hotel, go down to the casino, lose some money, and don't go back to our penthouse suite until we're accompanied by the most beautiful babes you've ever dared imagine, even in your most elaborate fantasies."

"Wow." And I know I'm trying to redact the *wows* out of my new worldly self, but this one really seems called for. Why? Well, for starters I'm about as much a swinging playboy as Mr. Bean or SpongeBob. So you can imagine the effect Virgil's proposition has on me. Or maybe you can't. On the one hand, of course it sounds amazing (if you're a guy). But on the other hand, I feel totally out of my element. Yet I can't deny the temptation. Let's face it, I've been a

nerd all my life. Terminally geek-like. Remember, I'm the guy in the
school lunchroom who sat at the far end with all the other losers
debating stuff about Frodo, Aragorn, Luke Skywalker and Klingons.
Shunned by the *in* crowd like we were lepers, or worse. And here's a
chance to step out of a whole life of geekdom and really be cool for
once.

And at the risk of appearing shamelessly self-serving, let's
nevertheless be clear on one point: even if I do go along with the
adventure, it'd be just a vicarious thing concerning the whole girl
angle. I'm not for one second tempted to cheat on Dot. I'd just be
tagging along for the ride. No harm in that. But then again, you don't
have to be Merlin to realize the impending evening would be fraught
with monogamistic peril. Cheech or Chong could figure that one out.
And at this point I could still easily pull out and go for the mantas or
the sub ...

And that's when Virgil slices through the Gordian knot by
jumping to his feet and walking out the door, yelling over his
shoulder: "Meet you at the airstrip in ten minutes! Yowza, yowza,
yowza!"

*   *   *

A few minutes later I'm zooming along in one of the space buggies.
Virgil's already there when I arrive, already chatting with the pilot
and stewardess. As I follow him up the gangway, he turns and says,
"Abandon all hope, ye who enter here."

Dante's Inferno of course. Then I get it. "I'll be damned, you're
Virgil."

"My parents had no idea."

Still chuckling, I climb aboard and see that this isn't the same jet I
arrived in earlier that day. Two big couches stretch out along the

fuselage like a living room. Virgil slumps into one and kicks off his shoes.

"This is the leisure version. Grab a couch."

I sit on the other sofa and notice an impressive hulk of a man sitting up with the pilot in a sober black suit with a completely bald head and the face of a marine field sergeant.

"Who's that?"

"That's Sal. He accompanies us on these little adventures, just in case."

"Just in case what?"

"I don't know. I've never had a *case*. But it's part of the program, and I'm personally thrilled to have him around. The man's a genius at facilitating fun. No matter what paradise island or third world urban shithole you drop him into, he's got local contacts up and running within minutes. Anything you want, that man can get. And if he says you don't need it, then he's probably right and you should slow down and reconsider. I'm not shitting you. This man is worth his weight in gold. And he's not light."

I glance over at him again. It feels weird to have a bodyguard.

"Anyway, he doesn't talk to us, and we don't talk to him, unless we need him, and then he's there for us. Until then, just forget about him. You probably won't even notice him."

"You mean he'll be following us around?"

"Yeah, but not like those creepy bodyguards the Russians drag around with them in six packs. Sal is discretion personified."

I'm thinking to myself that maybe Sal is also here to keep tabs on *us*. Or is that just paranoia? I decide to keep the thought to myself for now.

The stewardess hands us each a champagne glass. As a strictly objective and non-promiscuous journalistic comment, I might add that the stewardess is incredibly gorgeous. Anyway, we toast. The plane takes off with that inimitable private jet hum. As I watch the lights of my new home twinkle and disappear through the window, I can't help thinking about how much my life has changed since I first set eyes on the Island, *this morning*. And then, inevitably, my thoughts drift back to Dot.

I wonder what she's doing right at this moment. Probably already in bed, still pissed off as hell. I wish she weren't so mad, so we could just patch this whole thing up. Anyway, it'll work itself out. It always does. She won't stay mad for long. By Monday I'm sure I'll be able to convince her to move out to the Island with me. Wait until she sees the bungalow. She's going to love it!

Virgil's voice snaps me out of my thoughts. "OK, now I need to brief you on some of the basics."

"The basics?"

"Yeah. When we're out on these roving escapades, we fly incognito. Never any reference to our professional lives."

I adopt my serious business tone. It's still my first day on the job after all. "Sure, that's obvious."

"Yeah. But I don't mean the obvious *not discussing confidential legal matters* or *corporate strategy* and all the other usual business stuff you'd have working at some law firm or company. On the Island we have a special rule that's 100% airtight. No communication whatsoever about anything that links you to the Island or anything we do out there. It's Max's most important commandment. The Island is a *secret*."

"Understood."

"Well, it sounds straightforward, but in practice it's a bit tricky at first. For example, you can't just dodge the subject when people ask you shit like where you live or what you do, and you certainly don't want to contradict yourself by forgetting where you told someone you live. So the best way not to blow your cover is to make up a persona.

You know, the normal chitchat stuff: where you grew up, where you went to school, where you work, etc. Apparently this is what real spies do."

I smile, going along with it. "OK, Virgil, so where do you work?"

"I'm a freelance artist. Based out of New York, but spend my time traveling around the world catering to rich clients."

"What's your name?"

"What do you mean what's my name, bonehead? My name's Virgil."

I laugh.

"No, seriously, the guy who designs our security measures said we should keep our first names, and just change the last ones. This way, there's more of a chance that neophyte non-spy nerds like us won't totally screw it up. For the last names you go with some childhood friend that you won't forget after you've had a few drinks. After all, this isn't the Bourne Identity. We're not hiding out from the CIA or the Mossad. We're just putting together a protective persona so that our new casual acquaintances don't get too curious. A story about an island stocked with golden whiz kids would fetch a pretty good price with the gossip magz. And I guarantee you: Max would *not* like that. So listen to your Guardian Angel and make believe you're someone else for the weekend. Go wild. Be whoever you always wanted to be!"

"OK. I get it, but isn't it all a bit paranoid? Ever think it's just a facade to make us feel like secret agents fulfilling adolescent fantasies thereby enriching our productivity according to some highly paid management efficiency consultant?" I chuckle in good fun, but choke on it when I see that Virgil's dead serious.

"If somebody knew a position we were going to take on the market Monday morning, they could make multiple millions by noon. And you know how much it costs to have a guy kidnapped and tortured for information?"

"No idea."

"Well it's peanuts compared to the millions the information would be worth."

I gulp.

"Yeah. I don't like the cost/benefit numbers on that either. So, what's your persona?"

"I don't know yet. Give me a second."

One second later. "So, who are you?"

"I'm still working on it."

*   *   *

As we walk down the gangway to the tarmac, I realize there's a flaming red Ferrari convertible waiting a few steps away. Can you believe it? A liveried attendant hands Virgil the keys and he tosses them over to me.

"Wanna drive?" he asks.

"Hell yeah!"

We wave to the plane crew and close the doors of the car.

A Ferrari. A real Ferrari. The closest I've ever been to being behind the wheel of a Ferrari was borrowing Dad's Honda Accord. The sour grapes or Doubting Thomases might be thinking that it's just like being in any other car. But they'd be wrong. It's not. It's amazing. I start the engine. It purrs like Mufasa lounging in the sun on Pride Rock. I hit the gas and the G-force presses us back into our cordovan leather thrones. I feel like I'm at the helm of the Millennium Falcon.

"OK, turn off here," directs Virgil.

We roar out of the airport with the thrust of countless wild horses at the tip of my toe. In my rearview I see Sal tagging along in one of those black jeep-like Mercedes.

It still seems a bit strange to be tailed by a bodyguard, but a second later the thought's gone. *Here I am!* The invigorating smell of the ocean filling my lungs. Top down. Engine roaring. The road exotically skirting the rocky cliff. The stars in fairytale position with the ocean glowing all silvery in the moonlight. Virgil lets out a wild cry of pure joy, sitting up on the back of his seat, head out the top of the car, arms spread out like wings, howling to the moon. I join in, our howls mixing together like a pair of crazy werewolves.

Virgil climbs back in. "Yowza ... OK, slow down, when we come around this bend you'll see one of the all-time great scenic viewpoints of the world." And he's right. The car purrs around the curve and suddenly the whole bay is spread out in front of us. Like the night establishing shot for that perfect island paradise, with no FX needed. A crescent-shaped coconut tree-ringed beach of powdery white sand hugs the moonlit bay. But there's nothing barren or Gilligan-like here. Behind the ideal beach is a picture-perfect colonial style town complete with a grandiose hotel and casino that look like they're straight out of a Bond set, or vice versa.

I drive up in the Ferrari. The parking valets admire the suicide doors gliding open with that ultra cool sound.

I follow Virgil into the lobby where a bellhop is already waiting to show us to our rooms. And of course we don't have to mess with the hoi polloi hassle of checking in. Sal has organized everything in advance.

We follow the bellhop into an amazing suite with a breathtaking ocean view. Off from the salon are two bedrooms fit for royalty. Virgil tips the bellhop handsomely, who then proceeds to shut the door ceremoniously, stepping backwards like a Renaissance majordomo.

My room is the most luxurious place I've ever been. I feel like I'm in Versailles. At least from what I can glean from films and the

Internet, 'cause of course I've never set foot in Versailles. But screw Versailles, when I open my closet I'm totally blown away. Hanging there just for me are two tuxedos and a rack of white shirts!

"Time's a wastin'," calls out Virgil.

I put on the tux and admire myself in the flawlessly lit mirror of my gold-gilded bathroom. Given the fact I was bussing tables at my school prom, this is the first time I've ever worn one. And yes I do look great. Believe it or not, I really do.

Back in the salon, Virgil's already in his tux, holding out a glass of champagne. We clink.

"To the beginning of an epic evening," he says, handing me a money clip full of hundred dollar bills. "Spend as you wish. Everything we do this weekend is on the house. *Everything.*"

I slip the bills into my pocket and can't help laughing. Who would have thought when I was walking down that rainy Cambridge street this morning that I'd be *here* now? Life is truly amazing!

"Let's do it," say I.

"Wise words, Kemosabe."

We down the bubbly, and head downstairs to the casino. And what a casino! Lifted straight from Ian Fleming. The women are dressed in gorgeous evening gowns. The men are all in tuxedos. I notice that tuxedoes make anyone look good. Even ugly old men somehow look handsome and distinguished in a tux.

I wander around, soaking it all in while Virgil loses some money at the Texas Hold'em table. Eventually I notice two beautiful young women standing very close to Virgil, looking extraordinarily friendly. He shoots me a wink, sidles closer and suggests a drink out on the terrace. I nod, collect my chips and toss one to the croupier, exactly as Bond would do. Then I follow Virgil out to the enormous terrace overlooking the sea.

"David, this is Sveta, and this is Louba. Ladies, this is David."

We all shake hands, pleased to meet each other, etc., order a bottle of champagne and sit down at a table perfectly placed to bathe in the ocean view and the luscious sea breeze. It turns out that Sveta and Louba are best friends from Latvia, traveling around the islands seeing the sights. They're hands down the most beautiful girls I've ever seen. Period. They look like they've just stepped off the red carpet at Cannes. I watch as they laugh and fawn over Virgil.

"So what's it like being an artist?" Sveta (or is it Louba?) asks Virgil, with her ruby lips parted and her eyes sparkling in the moonlight.

Virgil seamlessly narrates amusing yarns about the joys and foibles of his fictionally artistic life. Not even a polygraph expert from the gulag could have spotted his smooth subterfuge.

"Yowza, it's tough, you know. When I was kid I just thought it would be all about the *art*. But it's not. And you know why? *Clients.* Oh my God." He hangs his head in mock penance. "It's the clients that kill me." He mimics a socialite complaining nasal voice: "But I thought it would be more *red*." The girls burst into appreciative laughter. Louba, whom I've now positively identified as the one in the sapphire blue sequined dress, is hanging on Virgil's every word and sympathizing artistically with her big blue beautiful eyes and her outstanding pair of lungs. I sip the sweet bubbly champagne. How incredibly good it all tastes!

Adroitly seizing a conversation breather, Sveta turns to me. "So what about you?" she asks, that charming accent gracing her perfect English.

I swallow a gulp of champagne for inspiration, suddenly intensely conscious of my complete and utter inadequacy next to these goddesses of perfection. Furthermore, because I've been with Dot ever since grade school, I've had exactly *zero* practice at the fine art of flirting, and consequently don't have the first clue.

"Uuhh ... I'm a ... musician," I mumble.

"Ooohh," say the girls. The exuberance in their voices is astounding. It's a first time experience for me to hear that sort of enthusiasm coming from actual real live human females.

"Have I heard your stuff on the radio? Do you have recordings of your work?" they chime.

I notice Virgil wincing, surely wondering how I'm gonna field this one.

"Sing something you've written. Yeah, please!" they beg.

Damn ... What I have I got myself into? What to do now? Hum something, I guess. But what? I let the champagne answer by itself. "Well, have you heard this?" I start humming the first tune that flits into my head, flying blind on autopilot. Sadly waylaid by the bubbly, however, I can't quite remember how the tune ends. Then it dawns on me that I've just hummed a pop tune that recently spent time on the top ten charts, and thus a very injudicious choice for someone trying to keep a low profile. But too late now. No choice but to go with it. And as I hum the refrain the girls' faces go ecstatic. Virgil shakes his head with ominous foreboding.

"My God, you play with that famous band?" exclaims Sveta.

Virgil looks at me with the face of someone reconciling himself with the realization that his new sidekick may be of dimmer wattage than previously anticipated. But I'm on a roll and take the question in stride, chuckling confidently.

"No, I'm not a stage man, I just write the songs and assign my rights to whoever wants to buy them."

The two girls look at me with unfettered admiration, like I'm a rock star, or ... "Like it's even cooler. Like he writes stuff for famous rock stars like songs and stuff," one girl is later overheard saying furtively to some jealous girlfriend into her cell phone.

Their admiration for me is like divine ambrosia. Virgil's whole persona thing is great. Much better than being myself. Pure bliss. And of course now I can't stop talking about my music career and my ultra cool fictional life. Sveta and Louba can't get enough of my evidently prodigious (and heretofore completely unsuspected) personal charm.

Eventually the girls walk off to "powder their noses" together. Virgil looks at me with playfully accusative eyes.

"Mind telling me what the hell that was?"

"What?"

"What? The whole genius songwriter thing."

"Great, huh? Did you see how they were looking at me?"

"Yes I saw it. You do realize you just blew my itinerant artist gig straight to hell."

"Yeah, sorry. It does sound a bit lame after me. Maybe I should hire you as my manager."

"In your dreams, pal."

"OK. Suit yourself. By the way, I've sorta been wondering ..."

"What?"

"Do all the guys on the Island lead a debauched and morally depraved social calendar?"

"No. Strangely enough we're in the vast minority. The others on the Island are the genuine authentic overachieving nerds. We were the overachieving nerds who secretly desired to be the cool jocks with the chicks but weren't."

"So what did the others do for their first weekend of leisure?"

"Depends. Everything is, of course, studied minutely and customized. Flo was taken to a secluded monastery for a special meditation reserved for only the most pious. Vlad went diving off the barrier reef with great white sharks. Babz spent the weekend in the chateau where Voltaire wrote his masterpieces. Others go on bird-watching safaris. You know, whatever makes them happy."

I can't help bursting out laughing.

"What?"

"Actually, I don't know whether I should be laughing or crying."

Virgil raises his eyebrows inquisitively.

"One guy watches birds, another prays all night, and I'm out with you spending shitloads of money carousing with loose women."

Virgil smirks. "Even after your crude reference to the enchanting evening we are currently spending in the company of ravishing young ladies, I must confess that I'd choose such a night against a safari, scuba dive or prayer meet any day of the week. You would too. Otherwise they wouldn't have assigned me as your Guardian Angel. And they don't make mistakes very often."

There's something infuriating about having been so accurately pegged by whoever is doing the psyche analyses. Something violating and foreboding, not to mention scary. And maybe I would have preferred the bird watching ... yeah right, who am I kidding?

The girls return. Virgil stands up and suggests taking the party upstairs. The girls immediately voice their approval and start following Virgil toward the elevators. No one seems interested on sounding me out on the question.

So I just sit there, watching them walk away. Despite my prodigious powers of self-deception, I nevertheless do realize that following Virgil and the girls upstairs to our suite would lead a good distance down that cheatingful path I'm not ready to tread.

And just then, I kid you not, Sveta, with some kind of crazy feminine sixth sense, chooses that very instant to look back at me cinematographically in slow motion, with her hair swooshing, and her eyes beckoning. Actually beckoning! One of the most beautiful sexiest girls on the planet. And *she* wants *me!*

Of course my more lucid self, somewhere deep down, beneath the bubbles, realizes that Sveta's infatuation just might be influenced by the fact that I've totally boldfaced lied to her about being some talented hip songwriter hobnobbing with the stars, and the subordinate, yet non-negligible corollary fact that I'm bunking in the Royal Suite and driving a flaming red Ferrari (oh so tasteful and discreet-like). But if such lucid self-cognizant realization does in fact take place, it's subconsciously buried deep enough to avoid polluting the crystalline beauty of the moment.

So what do I do? Do I run after her? No I do not. I actually pry my eyes away from her. Yes I do. I pull out my cell phone like it's some protective talismanic amulet, and dial Dot's number. I listen to the ringing. It rings and rings. I'm hanging on each millisecond. Hoping with each beat that the ring will be cut off by Dot's voice. But no. They continue their full cruel course and stop on their own. She doesn't answer.

What if she had? What if she'd picked up the phone? What if she'd answered? What if she'd thought it over and was ready to come join me on the Island?

Alas, we'll never know because she doesn't.

Then, somewhere along my neural pathways I must have given the command to stand up, because I do stand. But it must have occurred down the spinal cord around those reflex loops that function without consulting anything north of the shoulders. Like jerking your knee when the doctor hits you with the little rubber mallet. And once in motion, the autopilot just takes over. Come on, you know how that works.

As I walk toward the suite, I'm well aware of the fact that some part of me is experiencing serious misgivings. But somehow those sporadic flurries never coalesce into the coordinated expression that could even stand a second against the hormonal tidal wave crashing through my body, flowing up the cerebellum and washing through every fiber of my anatomy with overpowering force.

But then, as Virgil opens the door, I suddenly shake myself out of it. Like a cartoon character snapping out of hypnosis, I sternly remind myself that *I am no fool!*

If there's one lesson I gleaned from the gossip mill at law school, it's that a lawyer's libido is beyond doubt his most potent instrument of self-destruction, far beyond even the dangers posed by the profession's prevalent penchant towards unbridled financial greed. I've heard countless stories of successful lawyers who shamelessly self-immolated, destroying their happy home life over some hot secretary or cocktail hook-up. Of course I would never let something so absurdly asinine happen to me. I've struggled every waking hour of my life to rise up to where I am now, *at the very top!* And I, David Finnegan, am not the type of stupid jerk to detonate it all over some girl. I shall rise above the cesspool of my primeval instincts. And most of all, I am still very much in love with Dot—*break or no break.* With a self-saving interior laugh, I note for the record that anyone should be free to admire nature, like appreciating one of those skeletal beauties walking down the fashion runways. Certainly no harm in that.

In summation: I will party with them for a while and then gentlemanly retire to my bed alone. Honor intact. With a little force of character I'll come out of this whole thing squeaky clean ...

... *Won't I?*

13. Oops!

IT DOESN'T TAKE LONG FOR THE PARTY to start raging like some rock star after-the-concert uncut handy-cam sequence. It turns out that Louba has two Brazilian girlfriends who are "just, like hanging out, and could they, like, come over?"

"Well sure, the more the merrier," affirms Virgil. The bottles of champagne keep popping from a seemingly limitless supply.

Louba's Brazilian friends arrive. They turn up the music. They dance outside under the stars on the balcony overlooking the moonlit bay.

At one point, Sveta cries out: "Davey, look! There's a piano."

Sure enough, the Royal Suite has a grand piano in the corner. "Oh play us something!" says one of the Brazilian girls. Virgil winces, fearing an imminent persona implosion, but I just smile obligingly and walk over to the ivories. I pull out my new Ray-Bans, put them on, sit down, grin sightlessly into space, shoot the keys, and proceed to perform an absolutely flawless Ray Charles impersonation. Everyone claps and dances along. Virgil is thoroughly impressed.

Let me explain. I am clearly not a party animal. This Ray Charles bit is my party gig. My flash in the pan. All those years of belaboring the piano and memorizing arpeggios and scales become absolved in these brief moments of musically-contrived theatrically-canned exhibition. Scarcely a Finnegan family reunion could occur without Uncle Liam's and Uncle Billy's broods clamoring for "Ray Charles." It's my little thing I perfected in front of the mirror during countless adolescent hours. And I'm enjoying the payoff to the hilt right now.

In fact, with the girls dancing and singing around me in my tux in this incredible island palace suite, I'm thinking this is probably one of the coolest moments in my life. Like I'm living out some wild fantasy ...

And that's when I hear my cell phone: *RiiiiNG*.

I stop playing.

It's on the table over by the window where Louba is still gyrating to the music in her head. "Louba" I call out, "could you toss me my phone?" She smiles, a bit lopsided, picks up the phone, and tosses.

In one of those critical quirks of fate, it turns out that an inebriated Louba makes for a very poor tosser. The phone plunks down on the floor right between the legs of one of the short-skirted Brazilian girlfriends, presently very outstretched on the carpet. Apparently yearning to demonstrate she's not so drunk as to not even be able to deliver a phone properly, Louba slumps to the floor and reaches out for it. Quite the comedians, the Brazilian girl cries out and monologues as Louba's foraging digits wander over her thighs, inspiring peals of laughter from everyone, all in good fun.

Somehow, someone must have pressed the green *answer* button in the process.

Meanwhile, from her end of the line, sitting alone in our little Cambridge kitchen, Dot hears a very animated female voice say: "Hey Davey, here you go." Then a thud, then the voice laughing and saying: "Sorry Davey, I guess I'm so drunk I don't know what I'm doing." Then another thud, followed by a feminine screech and the voice asking playfully, *sexily*: "Why is your hand in my crotch?"

Once extricated from Brazilia's skirt, Louba smiles, zigzags across the room, and hands me the phone.

As I take the phone, I hope with all my soul that the reason it's no longer ringing is because the caller hung up. However, with a sudden sinking feeling in my gut, I see from the screen that the caller is *Dot*, and that she's very much still on the line. A bolt of panic zaps through me like lightning.

"Hi, Dot," I say, trying to sound as natural as possible. I stand up and walk into my room, shutting the door against the party brouhaha. I can plainly hear Dot's voice—electronic and far away, but nevertheless recognizably hysterical.

"David? Is that you? What's going on? Who was that woman?"

I take a deep breath with a face one might wear to a firing squad. "Hi, Dot," I say again.

"What's going on??"

"Nothing," I say as calmly and innocently as possible.

"*Nothing?* Who was that woman?" Her voice trembling and teary.

"Dot, really, it's nothing. I promise you, it's nothing."

Silence. I can imagine Dot's face. The tears beginning to form in the corner of her eyes. I desperately want to say something. But at this crucial instant I somehow can't summon the strength, or nerve, or decency, or indecency, or whatever lacking quality it would take to succeed in calming Dot down and making it all go away. As if none of it had ever happened ... shaken into oblivion like some wayward inadvertent misconceived doodle on the cosmic Etch-A-Sketch.

In fact, at this precise moment, numbed by champagne, consumed by guilt and self-loathing, I just can't find the words. Any words.

What am I doing here? I of course should have jumped on the jet straight back to Cambridge tonight instead of coming out here. Of course I *should have*. That's obvious now. I should never have left Dot alone like this. What was I thinking? Her teary voice is like acid pouring into my heart.

And on the other end of the line, Dot hears my silence as scathing guilt. Clear as a bell.

"You low-life cheating bastard."

"What do you mean?" I croak lamely. Oh my God ... this is spinning out of control!

"No, Dot, you have the wrong—"

"You cheating bastard!"

"Please, Dot, it's not—"

But she's heard enough. She's never felt so humiliated and betrayed and violated in her life. She makes a split-second decision and declares: "I'm going back to Portland. I'll pack your things and send them to your parents." Her voice is steely cold. "And don't bother coming after me. I don't ever want to see you again."

"Wait, Dot!"

Too late. She's hung up.

I slump down on the bed and try calling back. Dozens of times. But she's not answering.

It's been a very long day since I stepped on the jet with Mr. Singh eons ago, some light years away, on that drizzly Cambridge morning.

Still dressed in my tux pants and shirt (now open at the collar) I lie back on the bed.

So tired and weak ...

... Slipping off into a champagne-embalmed sleep.

14. Sex, Lies, And Saber Tooths

BACK ON THE JET SUNDAY AFTERNOON, headed home to the Island, Virgil is in the best of spirits.

"Awesome weekend," he says. "Four to one is perfect. The universe of positional permutations is mind-boggling. I still feel boggled. Makes you wonder why doctoral theses and other scholarly works aren't devoted to such things. Beats the hell out of Proust's ponderous proficiency with punctuation. But no one asks me, do they? Oh well, their loss." He glances at his watch. "Hey, you know. We'll be getting back before sunset. We could go straight to the beach and catch some waves before turning in. What do you say?"

Virgil is looking at me and evidently concluding that the Beach Boys invite has fallen on deaf ears. He's thinking to himself that I look like shit. Probably because I do. I've been staring out the window at the clouds streaming by, feeling like shit, so it's no wonder.

"Yowza dude, buck up! What more could anyone want? The blue marble is offering up its very best and we should be happy to partake. Harvesting the wonderful moments in the spring and vigor of our youth. Carpe diem and all that malarkey."

He pauses for a sip of champagne, then renews his motivational attack from a different angle. "You know, my mom thinks I'm wasting my life. When we indulge in our rare heart-to-hearts she says my life is meaningless, vacuous, empty, hedonistic, shallow, egotistical, and lots of other psycho-babbly words which are supposed to incite me to settle down and breed. But you know, all that stuff rolls off me like water off a duck. Why? Because she's totally wrong. I wouldn't change anything. As far as I can see, life just couldn't be any better."

I give Virgil a feeble smile, and can tell he's gearing up for some sort of commando guardian angel life-saving mission.

"Did I ever tell you why I don't have a steady girlfriend?"

I'm surprised by the unsolicited and unorthodox opening. But that doesn't faze Virgil. I shake my head.

"Well, it's because I refuse to go against the basic laws of nature. That, perhaps, is the secret of my perpetual cheeriness. And I wouldn't attempt to violate this basic law of nature any more than I'd try to outsmart gravity."

"What are you talking about?"

"Darwin, bro'. Natural selection."

"Say what?"

Virgil nods obligingly, as if he perfectly expects the neophyte to require further explication. "The fittest will survive and reproduce, thus preserving the traits most advantageous to survival of the species."

"I don't follow."

"Well, the butterflies with normal colored wings get eaten by hungry predators. But those with wings that look like leaves or flowers and shit can blend into their surroundings and thus survive to have baby butterflies with the same camouflaged wings."

"That would be caterpillars."

"Yeah, whatever. But the fact is, during those millions of years when human beings were living in caves, the best way for the species to survive and reproduce was to have the females pregnant all the time. And the best way to keep them pregnant was to have the men running around fornicating with boisterous evolutionarily-motivated diligence. Thus '*we men*' were conditioned over millions of years to try to copulate continuously with as many different females as humanly possible. We have no fucking choice in the matter. It's hardwired into us. Of course a few centuries of civilized decorum have tried to eradicate such behavior. But if you give into that, you're denying millions of years of genetic evolutionary selection in favor of a mere few hundred years of social conditioning. And that, in my humble opinion, can't be healthy."

Virgil takes a sip of champagne and continues.

"Of course for those with the double X chromosome, it's the opposite. Girls are evolutionarily programmed to be monogamous."

"Why's that, Professor?"

"Elementary. With all the men procreating as much as they can with as many different girls as possible—well, the cave chicks don't have any trouble getting knocked up. But then they *really* need a man to protect them from the wilds and shit." Virgil indulges a pregnant pause, then continues. "So the girls whose children will survive will be those who stick with one man because that man will protect her and her kids. I mean let's face it, if you saw your girlfriend being attacked by a saber-toothed tiger, would you jump in there to save her with your fucking wooden club if you'd just found out she'd been sleeping with the guy in the next cave?"

Virgil nods along with his narrative. Surfing on the philosophic rip tide. "Ordinary pedestrian love is clearly overrated. And even true love is most often a very bad way to go. Think about it. How did it turn out for Romeo and Juliet?"

"Movie deal?"

"True, but posthumously. Before that Romeo poisons himself by mistake, thinking Juliet is dead, and then she stabs herself out of grief."

"Point taken."

"Bet your ass. Not a good way to spend the afternoon. And what about Tristan and Iseult?"

I shrug my shoulders.

"Tristan waits for Iseult to return on a ship with a white sail if she's alive and a black sail if she's not. Some sailor screws up the color combo and raises the black sail. Tristan sees it and dies of grief when in fact Iseult was already stepping on shore with her dainty little princess foot. And when she sees him dead she stabs herself."

"The point being ..."

"These are not role models you want to emulate."

"What about *Princess Bride*?"

"Aha. *As you wish.* OK. There you got me. If you find the true love of Westley and Buttercup, then you should go for it."

I smile. But it's not a real smile. It's just a show smile for Virgil. On the inside I still feel terrible. A deep, horrible sadness. Since waking up this morning I've called Dot over and over. No answer. I e-mailed and texted her countless apologies, explaining how despite what it must have sounded like on the phone, *nothing* happened.

But no use. She's not taking my calls ... I guess that whole thing with the Brazilian girls must have sounded pretty awful.

15. Doterminism

EVER SINCE she broke up with David, she would often catch herself wondering about what really happened. She wondered if it had all somehow been inevitable. Whether their relationship had been doomed to fail. And if so, since when? From the start? She'd always secretly believed that they were *destined* to be together. But now that they've split up, does this mean they were *destined* to be apart? Or does destiny have nothing to do with it? Maybe the whole thing had been controllable, and she'd simply lost control somewhere along the way. Was there something she should have done differently to have kept it all on course? To keep it all as planned? According to the program?

At times she wonders if she did the right thing. After all, she could have just given up and gone to that stupid Island of his. But isn't that the point? Why should she give up? Hasn't she been doing that too much over the years? Following him around like a puppy dog. If he was going to be making decisions that completely derailed their lives without even consulting her, then isn't it better to call it off now? Before it gets worse? Before it gets so off-course that it's a total and complete disaster. But isn't that what it is anyways?

Damn! Wouldn't you know it? All this stuff about "destiny" and these strings of hypotheticals are just like those conversations with David back in college. How he loved to ramble on with his pseudo-philosophical monologues about determinism and free will and other such stuff. Dinner would be a bottle of inexpensive wine served ceremoniously up with some Chinese take-out or some of his "famous" pasta (the only thing he cooked). She remembers how on those special nights—so many of them!—She would set a beautiful candlelight table, even if they were just having leftovers or pizza. And they would talk and talk and talk, and then roll and tumble into bed together ... always. Those were good times. She smiles at the memories.

Back then David could go on for hours about whether they're bound by destiny, or whether they have the free will to determine what happens in their lives. If the universe is bound by the laws of cause and effect, and if we're made up of molecules, all governed by those same unyielding physical laws, then isn't everything being simply played out according to some already programmed chain of events?

She can't even begin to remember what any of the outcomes of those pop-existential debates might have been. All she knows is that back then, whatever they said always lead to the irrefutable conclusion that they were meant to be together. Where along the way had that all changed? How did the premises get switched around without her knowing it?

Oh David, how did we get it all wrong? After all this time together? Her thoughts drift back to him as a kid. Always so determined! Just like the little boy she fell in love with at the dunking booth when they were thirteen.

And there she goes, doing one of those things he hates. Mixing her metaphors. No, not the metaphor thing, this is another one of those things. When she jumps from one topic to the next with no logical link, just because a word sounds similar. Like determinism to determination. How that sort of stuff used to get his goat! She smiles. Oh David ...

Anyway, once he had a goal set, he would do anything to achieve it. She remembers the day during their sophomore year in college when he decided he'd go to law school. It all seemed so speculative and fanciful back then, like they were playing house or something. But from that day on, his approach to school and grades became completely different. If he wanted to rise out of this crappy state university and get a real piece of the American pie, he would say, he had to get into a top law school. And to get in, he needed to get straight A's and ace the LSAT exam. She remembers listening to him methodically lay out his plan. And of course with David, it wasn't *just* a plan. It wasn't just words. If he said it, he would do it. From that moment school became a science with him. Every waking hour was spent studying. If he had to go without sleep for days on end, so be it. Night after night she would nod off to sleep, only to wake up in the morning to find him still sitting at the kitchen table in his boxer shorts buried in his books before a test.

His determination was like that thing in those ancient Greek tragedies he loved so much. Hurbis, or whatever it's called. Like those Greek heroes who would have some character trait that was a source of their power, but also the seed of their downfall. Just like David. Now he's got his head set on something. On winning this dumb game of his he's playing of always trying to be the best. It's the same old David. Though now it doesn't mean staying up all night studying for an exam, it means going out to work on that stupid island with those other over-achievers making lots of money playing masters of the universe and completely forgetting about the people who love him.

She lets her mind wander over what his hurbistic determination would do to him. Would it destroy him, like in the Greek dramas? Or would it be more subtle, like that style he liked, "postmodernism" or whatever. A sort of postmodern hurbis where it doesn't actually destroy you physically, but rather indirectly, by destroying your love. She catches herself thinking that she vindictively prefers the version where it actually *destroys* him. But suddenly visions of David getting into a car wreck or some other disaster flash before her eyes and she immediately corrects herself, realizing that truthfully, if she has any say in the matter, she could never really want anything bad to happen to him at all. She even wants him to be happy without her, though in a sort of miserable, celibate way, preferably.

It was different before he got that idea about law school. Before then he was just crazy about music. His parents of course didn't have the money for lessons, but that didn't stop David. He took an extra paper route to pay for a piano teacher, and stayed after school to practice on the old rickety piano in the auditorium used for the school plays and the Christmas concerts.

She would stay with him, dutifully, every day while he practiced so that afterwards they could walk home from school together. He would play his lessons over and over again, keeping at it endlessly until he got every note perfectly right. And she would sit through it all, doing her homework, or just staring off into space and listening to him plunk out those wretched scales ... Do re mi fa so la ti do, do re mi fa so *wrong note* do do re ... do re mi fa so la ti do ... over and over and over.

But like everything else David did, the music paid off. He would rant on and on about how he had no musical talent, but that it didn't matter, what counted was the work you put into it. Talent was just a shortcut. What mattered was the time and devotion. The passion. In any event, at some point in time the scales and exercises started turning into tunes, and the tunes started sounding nice.

In high school he met Mr. Kowalski, the band instructor with those wobbly watery eyes, a harelip and matching tufts of grey fur spilling out from his ears and nose. It was something like love at first hearing between them. By then David had discovered jazz. He lived, breathed and slept jazz. It seemed at the time that's all he could think about. Red Garland, Ahmad Jamal, Wynton Kelly, Oscar Peterson, Bud Powell, Don Pullen, Horace Silver, Bill Evans, Dave Brubeck, Keith Jarrett, John Taylor, Joe Albany. He was crazy about them. And Kowalski found in David a fellow jazz junkie. Every day after class they would jam together. And even Dot, who had no ear at all, realized they sounded good, and started to love the music.

In college, he would sometimes play the piano to let off the pressure of studying till his brain turned to mush. That was when she loved his playing the most. When it was just for them during those late night sessions when he would really go wild—only the two of them in the world listening together in their little apartment. He would take a tune, usually one chosen by her. Some old pop tune, or a classical air, or even a snippet from a TV commercial or sitcom. He would start by first playing it in a standard type piano bar style. But then he would play it again, this time deconstructing it a layer, shifting the rhythm or the key ever so slightly. And he'd play it again, each time getting further and further away from the original melody. They would marvel at how far he could get from the tune, but still attached to it, still within the framework of the original notes, breaking out in joyous laughter as he would twist a classical melody or some commercial jingle into a wild blues riff.

Then somehow the music, those same tunes, those same notes, all got changed over time. Over the past few years, the law school years, those same tunes he would play started annoying her. Of course by then he wasn't playing much at all, but when he did play, it would grate on her nerves. The first time playing the tune, when he played it straight—well that was fine. But then, when he started improvising, strangely it annoyed her. As he would get further and further form the original melody, a little voice inside her started screaming: "Get back to the tune! To the tune I know. That I can hum or whistle. Whose notes I can predict." But of course he would keep moving further out. Sometimes she felt as though he was doing it just to spite her. Taunting her.

One time, a few years back, while she was clearing off the kitchen table, he was improvising on one of her favorite tunes, "Over the Rainbow." He started off playing it just beautifully. Better than you would hear on the radio. His tune was perfect. Then he started improvising. The beat picked up, the notes became jazzy and complex. Of course she realized it was probably technically impressive, but what if she wanted to hear the tune? She actually stopped him and told him how she felt. He looked like she'd slapped him in the face. He was so surprised. "I thought you liked my playing," he said. He looked so sad. "I do like your playing," she answered, "but you get so far away from the tune, it makes me—I know this sounds stupid—"

"No, go ahead."

"Well, it makes me angry." David's eyes almost popped out of their sockets.

"Angry?"

Dot nodded, suddenly feeling completely ridiculous and selfish and unsophisticated. And that's when David did the sweetest thing. His whole face lit up like he'd just received some brilliant illumination—instead of having just been nagged at by his silly unappreciative girlfriend. He kissed her and said "You're so right, I was playing without resolving the tunes, because I'd already resolved them in my head, and was starting to move on to the next one. But on the outside I just left them without any resolution." He looked so grave and serious and said, "Thank you, I'll fix that." And then he went off and played a great tune. "Summertime." And he played it beautifully. His improvisation, as always, took the tune out to orbit. But then, rather than stopping like he usually did, he played the tune straight again, with little bits and pieces of his improvisation still hanging on, like a blues note here and a jazz riff there. But there it was, the original tune, played beautifully. That was great.

And then, at some point, she must have just stopped listening, and just heard it all as background noise. If only she'd realized it back then. At that very second she stopped caring about his music, maybe that was the first blade of indifference creeping in like crab grass on a lawn, or like a cancer. If she'd known, maybe she could have weeded it out. Kept on listening and loving the music, and maybe stop the cancer, like having a breast amputated, or taking an antidote or something—anything to stop what was to come. How little by little every day it became more important that he not leave his dirty socks in the corridor than it was to listen to his music.

Of course, practically speaking, there was no good reason he couldn't play the piano and still put the socks in the dirty clothes bin. Dammit! Going off the point again. What was the point anyway? Oh yes, how was it that they had come so far together and now ended up so far apart? How was it that the little David at the dunking tank she loved so much for so long could end up turning into someone who could decide to go off and live on an island without caring what she thought about it? And what did she think about it? Nothing really. That's the point. No one asked her! As if she doesn't even exist! He just decided!

Then suddenly she wonders whether these two aspects might be irreducibly linked. Joined at the spiritual hip. Like a yin and a yang, or a proton and an electron, with one securely anchored at the center, and the other simply spinning around like a planet in orbit, though going so incredibly fast it looks like a solid shell. That maybe one can't be without the other without causing some sort of nuclear catastrophe. And if that were true, then maybe he really didn't have a choice. Maybe that determined over-achieving little thirteen-year-old David getting dumped in the dunking tank with whom she'd fallen in love could only exist within that same David who was so absorbed in himself that he would decide to live on an island without even asking her.

Damn. She wipes away a tear. Can't do this. Can't think thoughts like this and start crying. Mind's made up. Gotta stick to the program. Taking care of yourself now. Can't keep letting someone else disrupt all the plans. You have to be able to plan things out and stick to it. Otherwise you just go crazy. Like some wind vane blowing around and around and around without any real direction. Can't keep on living like some obedient puppy dog, always happy just to follow along. That's why it's so important not to talk or read his messages or even think about *him*.

Just like it said in that article in that magazine. After a breakup it's best if you don't have any contact, it said. Can't get derailed again. It's a question of self-preservation. Of survival.

She hasn't spoken with him ever since that terrible call with that terrible woman's voice with that foreign accent on his cell phone.

And she's deleted all his messages and e-mails without reading them. She has to pull her life together.

Oh Lord, *when can I just forget?*

16. Island Life

MR. SINGH WAS PERFECTLY RIGHT that evening back in Cambridge. It's not about the money. It's about the adventure. Every day on the Island is an exciting challenge. It's great.

Of course the money is great too, but strangely sort of irrelevant here. On the Island you can't even spend it. Everything is provided for. If you want something, you just tell your PA. And whatever it is, no matter how extravagant, or expensive, or difficult to find—it just appears with lightning speed—no questions asked. Money is simply no longer an issue. It just dropped out of the daily equation. Sort of like what Marx must have been thinking about before his thing got so screwed up.

There's just one piece missing. And that, of course, is Dot. I've called her a zillion times. Texted, voice-mailed, e-mailed, even telegrammed her. I wish she'd just answer me. Anything would be better than this silence. I'd even prefer her to be telling me what a selfish shithead I am. At least then we'd be talking. But I get it. She knows the silent treatment is the best way to punish me. So yeah, I get it, but I still can't help thinking about her every day. I just wish she'd agree to come out here and live on the Island. I'm sure she'd love it.

*   *   *

I wake up at five every morning. Exercise for twenty minutes, shave, shower, and sit down to eat the breakfast already set out for me on the terrace, overlooking the sun rising out across the ocean. Sometimes Virgil or one of the others wanders over for breakfast with me. By six o'clock I'm on the trading floor for a team meeting to discuss the day's strategy.

Each day is so jam packed with adrenalin-pumping excitement that it passes with the blink of an eye.

We often work around the clock. Pulling all-nighters. But let's face it. We love it. When we're into a project we'll do anything to reach the objectives. That's what got us this far.

And sometimes, at the completion of a project, when we can take a breather, we all get together in the dining room for a delicious meal, or head off to the beach for a swim or surf or volleyball game, followed by a picnic with tables stuck in the sand and an amazing array of tropical fruits and grilled seafood fresh out of the water.

Max and his wife Katya seldom join us for meals. But every once and while they stop by for a cameo appearance. Katya is from some isolated region in Siberia. The story goes that Max discovered her one day while backpacking through the mountain villages. He was sitting in a café when he felt something in his pocket. He reached down and grabbed Katya's hand just before it disappeared with his wallet. She was eighteen years old. One look into those defiant green eyes glaring at him through the dirt smudges on her face was all it took. Two years later, with Max's benevolent sponsoring, she was strutting down runways as a top model. And then they were married. A true-life fairytale.

When they drop by to visit with the team they laugh and joke with everyone. The perfect couple. Max sure got it right.

And now I'm a part of this world ...

... This perfect little Island world.

17. Misanthropy

MAX STANDS AT THE HELM OF HIS SAILING YACHT as it slices powerfully through the waves. He feels in complete control of his vessel, and yet terribly out of control of his life. As if his insides were somehow shifting—the amino acids being surreptitiously switched around like little colored Christmas lights on his DNA strands.

He's deep in thought. Thinking about how when he quarrels with Katya she almost always ends up calling him a misanthropist ...

She says it with that Slavic gargle to her voice, making it sound horrendously more vile than in English: "meezantghr*roa*peest." The guttural resonance alone would rank it somewhere between pedophile and serial killer. The ignominy. The sting. When she first brandished the accusation he naturally bridled in wounded self-defense. But she immediately retorted: "Well, do you even *have* any real friends?" "Of course I do," he countered in rapier-swift riposte. "Yeah? Who?" And the crazy thing is that she had him there. Completely disarmed.

He didn't know how to answer. Sure, technically he had loads of friends. Reams of them. Wealth attracts people like flies. But a real *friend?* Sadly, she was right. For some reason, over the past decade he'd been cutting off communication with anyone who could have jockeyed for position to be his friend. Why? It certainly wasn't intentionally planned. It was not his conscious ambition to become a social pariah. Like all those sorts of things, it happens gradually, growing invisibly in the dark like a stalactite. Drop by drop of drying solidifying sediment until lo and behold you're confronted with the rocky spike hanging in the cave of your subconscious that scares away even the most arduous socially amicable spelunker.

Katya says that all the people who used to be their friends (unspoken: *in the old days when we were happy*) now consider him to be "haughty." What she really means is that they all think he's an arrogant prick. But they've confused arrogance with boredom and indifference. He's bored to tears of the same incessant conversations over and over again.

He feels like he's trapped inside one of those toys toddlers play with. The one where you pull the string and an arrow spins around to land on the picture of some farm animal. "Hello, I'm a cow, moooo."

Socially correctly mixing during the cocktails, you move on to merge with another identical conversational cluster. You smile and shake hands. You pull the string again: "Hello, I'm a rooster, cock a doodle doo." "Hello I'm a farmer, subsidize my crops." Over and over. Identical conversations. Sure, the common nouns and proper nouns are different. But everything else is the same. Try as he might, he just doesn't care whether they prefer Bentleys or Rolls Royces, how hard it is to find a good chauffeur these days, or how bad the service has become in Ibiza.

For a while he continued to go through the motions. Determined to be a faithful, supportive marital unit. He continued pulling the string. "Hello, I'm a duck, quack quack." Laughing at their unfunny jokes, rolling along obligingly with the repetitive conversations. But it was all an act. And then the act itself started breaking down. The recording wore itself out.

It wasn't intentional, but at some point in time when he would dutifully pull the string the arrow would just fly on past the duck and the rooster and the pig to land on a newcomer to the menagerie ... a photo of himself, looking older and meaner and more reclusive than the pixels of his mind's eye ... "Hello, I'm a meezantghr*roa*peest and I don't give a fuck about what you're saying." And the disease, if you could call it that, just kept growing worse and worse. He bought the Island, staffed it with whiz kids, and soon had no conversations with anyone but *Islanders*. Which meant basically that he only talked with his employees.

And thus devolution into homo misanthropiens is consummated.

Why? It wasn't like this at the beginning. What went wrong?

What is the origin of this ... *affliction?*

Who knows? It did happen around the time he realized Katya didn't really love him. That he was in fact just a way out of poverty for her. Can't blame her of course. Growing up the way she did, there was only one rule: survival. No room for sentiments. But who says there's any link?

In fact, it probably already started happening long before. Probably started back with the money.

Money. It changes everything. Even if you don't want it to. Even if you promise yourself it won't. Of course the vast majority of wealth's byproducts are overwhelmingly positive and addictively enjoyable. You work for yourself, enjoy physical luxury, nifty toys, excellent health care, creature comforts, yada yada yada.

But there is a major detriment that is widely neglected. One crucial aspect of human life becomes unalterably compromised in the process: *trust.* When you're wealthy you never know if a person is interested because of you or because of your money. And since we all know how human beings will stoop to anything for money, the world suddenly becomes a very hostile place. People risk their lives and shoot others robbing convenience stores for a few hundred dollars. Imagine what they're capable of for millions? You can only protect yourself by trusting no one. And so gradually you don't trust a soul. And isn't love based on trust?

They didn't have children. He wanted to. Desperately. But what's the point without love? He would ask himself the question over and over again. It doesn't make sense without it. In fact somehow, somewhere along the line, it all stopped making any sense. The joy of it all just faded away, like some happy old snapshot left out in the sun until it turned into an unrecognizably diffused smudge. Like he'd contacted some sort of invisible foul disease cutting him off from the world. As if he's broken. As if some part of him just doesn't work any more. As if there's some proportional yin and yang mechanism taking over. Too much, and the balance warps. The extreme over-abundance of one thing takes something else away.

But of course that's just karmic babble. About as true as all the rest of those self-assuaging spiritual fantasies for the masses. But then again, too much CO_2, then not enough ozone, and there go the ice floes and coastal cities. But in the meantime, here he is, just going through the motions. A lone polar bear floating randomly lost on a mini ice floe.

What a sickening waste! How selfishly horrendous to have squandered all this good fortune!

And he'd do anything get it back. Anything to get back that feeling ...

But he's not groping to excuse his putative misanthropy. Not searching to excavate his psychological back-story in search of some cathartic purge. And he's not trying to shift the blame either. It's just a fact.

And of course no one in the world would have an ounce of pity. Why should they? Save your pity for the underprivileged, the poor, the starving, the sick. Right? No reason to lament some rich old schmuck who somehow screwed it up despite the odds all stacked in his favor.

But in the end the scorecard isn't based on net worth, is it? And if happiness is a gauge of anything, then he's somehow falling pitifully short of the mark.

Mea culpa.

18. Speeding In The Faust Lane

ONE MORNING Max calls me at my desk in the Hub and asks me if I feel like going sailing with him. I look around at my colleagues, wondering how guilty I'd feel if I bailed out on them. But I've never been sailing ... I decide I can deal with the guilt.

"Sure, when?" I ask.

"Now."

"Uh ... I'm in the middle of a project. Can I finish up and join you a bit later?"

"The wind's perfect now, David. Wind doesn't wait."

Twenty minutes later I'm climbing aboard the most amazing yacht you could ever imagine. Within seconds the lines are cast off and we're heading out to sea.

Max is behind the wheel in shorts and bare feet, his golden mane blowing in the wind. The crew scrambles under his directions. I watch, mesmerized, as the sails unfold like giant wings. The yacht surges with the wind. Lord knows I'm no great fan of extreme sports, but this is fantastic. We've all seen this sort of stuff in films, and it always looks kind of neat, but take it from me, what you've seen on a screen doesn't hold a candle to the real thing. Standing on deck as the boat bounds through the waves in those explosions of spray is truly amazing.

I feel a nearly irrepressible urge to run up to the front of the boat like Leo and yell "I'm king of the world!" You'll be relieved to know that I restrain myself.

The wind is blowing hard. Max revels. His eyes flash with the fun of it all. He calls over to me, yelling to be heard over the wind. "There's a full moon tonight and a great breeze. I was thinking about going for a sail around the next island and getting back here sometime tomorrow morning. You feel like coming along?"

The question is rhetorical of course.

The sun treats us to a dazzling display of orangey crimson heavenly perfection before swelling up into a fiery red ball and disappearing below the horizon. Max tells the captain that we'll take the first watch and that he and the crew should all get some rest. With the crew and captain below, we have the deck to ourselves. Max is at the wheel. I'm standing next to him.

"Have you ever sailed one of these before?"

I roll my eyes. "What do you think?"

Max laughs. "Well, it's never too late to start."

"I really don't know anything about—"

But Max has already released the wheel and stepped back, nudging me forward. This is clearly the sort of moment where the young Padawan can't refuse the challenge.

I grasp the helm and just stand there, wondering what I'm supposed to do now. And as nothing nautically disastrous happens, I muster my confidence and turn the wheel ever so slightly to the left. The movement is immediately felt on the ship and by the computer, whose screen tells me to correct back a degree. Max chuckles.

"It's generally a good idea to follow Guido the autopilot. He's very good at this. But you can do what you want up to a point. Experiment with the wind. Don't worry, the computer politely tells you when you're doing something less than optimal, and if you start doing something dangerous Guido takes over before you cause any damage."

I'm grinning. "Excellent." I can grasp the wheel with the poise of an adventurous mariner while nevertheless remaining under complete and comfortable oversight of the ship's computer. This is my kind of extreme adventure.

The yacht is nearly two hundred feet long with a mast that stretches up to the sky like a sequoia. With a dozen permanent crewmembers aboard, it's a miniature universe of pure luxury. But more than that, it's a racing machine.

"It seems really fast."

"Fast enough to beat Cutty Sark's record when we won last year's open Atlantic Challenge."

"Wow."

"There was a huge storm and we were the only ones crazy enough to sail right through it rather than going around."

"You must have been so happy when you won!"

I look over to see Max staring at me. A weird sort of stare. Like he forgot where he parked his next thought and is convinced for some reason that I can help him find it.

"Would you consider yourself to be a happy person?" he asks.

Of course Max's question makes absolutely no sense to me. I grin like I figure it must be the setup for some joke. But he looks back at me completely serious. Creepy serious. Clearly expecting an answer.

My God, what's happening to this conversation? Mayday Mayday. But Max is waiting ... For what? How do you answer something like that?

"Yeah, sure, I guess."

"I don't mean *content* or *glad*. I mean true, profound *happiness*."

Now I'm really not liking the way this conversation is going. First of all, as a general rule, I don't like these types of touchy-feely subjects. In fact, I avoid them like the plague. Even with Dot. And yet here I am, somehow caught up in this Hallmark moment from hell with ... *my boss!* I scramble for an emergency exit, wracking my brain for some way of deflecting it all into a joke. But then I see his eyes. Looking intensely at me.

"I'm sorry. Is this conversation getting too weird?" he asks.

"Kinda."

He smiles. "Well, despite the weirdness, you haven't answered my question."

Christ, the man's not a quitter. Oh well, roll with the flow. You gotta humor the guy who pays your bills, right? Anyway, doesn't look like there's much choice in the matter ...

Happiness? To tell you the gospel truth, I've never really thought about it. People have often told me I always seem happy. Of course if you consider how I've been feeling since this problem with Dot started, then miserable is the word, not happy. But the whole Dot thing is just a temporary glitch. We'll be back together soon enough. Anyway, that's not what Max is talking about. He's talking about the big picture. He's talking about that feeling deep inside.

"Yeah, I guess I'm generally happy."

Max continues to stare at me for a few beats as if trying to verify the truth of what he just heard with some internal sixth sense. Then he looks up at the stars, out to sea, breathes in deeply, and seems to concentrate on the beauty of the ocean. Whew ... that's a relief. The storm of touchy-feely bantering seems to have blown over.

But no such luck. Now Max is looking at me again. We've simply passed through the eye. Like those Perfect Storm guys before they decide to stay out and fish just a little longer.

"Tell me about it. Tell me about one of your moments of true happiness," he pursues.

Ugh. This will teach me to try my hand at water sports. And what's with this happiness bullshit? Some sort of psyche test he's running on me? Analyzing my answers with some expert consultant somewhere listening to us? OK, I guess I'm getting paranoid. But this sort of thing rattles me. I hate those gushy emotional TV shows where the guests come on and talk about their problems. It's just not my thing. Goddam nautical billionaire.

And as these recalcitrant thoughts swirl through the eddies of my mind, something in Max's penetrating gaze suddenly reaches out and grabs me. Holds me like we're in some strange dialectical tango, then spins me around. It's his sincerity that does it. Max is *sincerely* searching. Maybe it's just some sort of middle-age crisis pseudo-philosophical self-justifying search. But it's sincere. The insight scrambles my cynicism like tear gas at an anti-war rally.

"Well ..." I begin, without having the slightest idea where I'm going with the rest of the sentence. Hmm ... honestly, hundreds of happy moments come to mind. Everyday moments of simple happiness. And yet how can you explain the joy of just waking up in bed next to Dot, or the smell of your mom's pancakes? No. Max is looking for something else. Then the words just start pouring out by themselves, without checking in with the grey matter. I feel myself being swept up in my own narrative, carried along by the current. Oh well, here goes ...

"When I was twelve years old, my Dad worked at the lumber yard, like just about everyone in town. It was dangerous work, for minimum wage. But there wasn't anything else. Anyway, one day I had this little league baseball game I was playing in, and Dad promised me he'd be there. I remember standing out there in right field, punching my fist into my glove like I'd seen them do on TV. Squinting at the bleachers to see if my Dad had gotten there yet. Every single inning out there in the field, I waited for him to show up. But he never did. I was furious at him for not making it to the game as I got on my bike and started riding back home.

"When I got home I heard the bad news. There'd been an accident. Dad had gotten his arm mangled and his head bashed by one of those death trap machines at work. He was in a coma and they didn't know when he would wake up, if ever. So I got on my bike and pedaled like crazy to get to the hospital. When I got there they'd finished operating, but Dad was still in a coma. It was getting late, so Mom and everyone else wanted me to come back home with them, but I wouldn't listen. They tried to force me, but I wouldn't budge. Finally they let me stay with him for the night.

"I kept thinking the accident was all my fault for making him hurry to try to get to my game. It was horrible to see him lying on the bed, white as the sheets, with all those tubes stuck in him. My family had never been very religious, so I wasn't exactly sure how to go about praying. I struck all sorts of bargains with any brand of supreme being that might have been listening. If I could just get my Dad back! I promised to become a model citizen, to stop cursing, to start helping more around the house—anything I could think of. Eventually, I must have cried myself to sleep, my head resting on his chest. And then, sometime around dawn, I felt a hand on my back, holding me. I opened my eyes. My Dad was awake! Hugging me with his one good arm! It was the greatest feeling ever. Everything seemed to have fallen magically back into place. Nothing else mattered. The person I loved most in the whole world was back."

I stop talking. Suddenly terribly self-conscious. I can't believe I just gushed that whole story out like that. I've never done anything like this before. I'm just not the personal outpouring type. Christ! Next time I'll keep my trap shut.

We don't speak ... Just the sound of the wind and the waves. Then Max turns towards me:

"You've given me an idea, David."

"I have?"

"Yes. Ever since I met you, I thought you just might be instrumental in one of my projects. A particularly personal project. And now I have this idea. The idea seems so outrageous and preposterous that I'm thinking maybe it's a good one. You see, I learned long ago that the ideas which seem the most insanely off-the-wall at first, are often the real winners. After all, what do I have to lose?"

All through his speech I'm starting to think I'm working for a certifiable lunatic. "I'm afraid I really didn't understand much of what you just said."

"No of course not. Let me make myself more clear. I've decided to give a substantial sum of money to the person who can cause me to feel the type of happiness you just described."

I stare at Max for a moment, trying to figure out what's going on. He's looking at me deadpan serious, so I start chuckling as if this were part of some unfunny billionaire joke, hoping to coax out the punchline that's sure to come. But no. There is no punchline. Just Max standing there looking at me with his hair blowing in the wind.

So I stop the chuckling. "Are you serious?"

"Deadly."

I can't for the life of me imagine where all this is going, and I guess I'm still hoping it's all some sort of comical setup. In any event, the next line is obvious ...

"What do you mean by a *substantial* amount?"

"Well, it has to be enough to motivate someone who's already highly paid. Enough for him to drop everything and devote himself to the project as if his life depended on it. So I'd say ... well, something around, let's say ... ten million dollars."

What? Did I hear that correctly? He wants to give ten million dollars to someone who will make him happy? Now how insane is that? The man's a loony tune. Or maybe this is just part of the psych exam. Or some sort of candid camera punked thing he's pulling on me.

"You're joking, right?"

But he's looking at me with the most serious expression you could possibly imagine. He shakes his head slowly. He's not joking.

"Well, don't say it too loud, or they'll be lines of people wanting to try."

"No risk of that, it's only meant for your ears. And I stand behind what I say."

"But what do you mean? Happy every day? Happy for a week? Happy until you die?"

Max laughs out loud. "Happy until I die? No. I mean something much easier. Just the feeling you described. The feeling of true happiness. Even if it only lasts a brief moment."

"But how could one moment of happiness possibly be worth ten million dollars to you?"

"Because I have a theory. I think I've lost something. There's something missing. Something I've lost along the way. I don't know how or why it happened. But it did. And I've tried everything. I've consulted all the best shrinks in the world. They couldn't do anything for me. They just wasted a lot of my time, ended up telling me I was depressed, and gave me more pills. I've tried every chemical known to man, and then some. But the shrinks don't get it. They don't understand. You *get it*. And that's very rare. Now you just have to *get it* for me."

"And how could we know ... uh, I mean, verify?"

"I'm a man of my word, David. Don't worry about that. If you succeed, you'll have your money. Moreover, if you *do* succeed, I'll consider that I'm the one who made the better part of the bargain."

I shake my head, slowly, incredulously. This is all far too weird. Twilight Zone wrapped in Lewis Carroll and Willy Wonka with a Monty Python/Hunter Thompson turbo-charge. Just goes to show you that fact beats fiction any day of the week. Right off the starting block.

Max continues. "After all," he says, "it's no different than the deal we already have in place. Working on the Island you make a phenomenal amount of money because you make *me* a phenomenal amount of money. This is the same thing. The moment of true happiness you describe is worth much more than money to me. If I can ever feel it again, then I'll know there's hope. That it's not over for me."

I nod. Beginning to realize ... this is not a gag. It's bizarre. Outrageous maybe, but it's not a gag.

"You'll have one year from today to accomplish your task. I'll have a contract drawn up." He smiles. "I'm going to hit the hay. When you feel like turning in, give the captain a buzz. He'll take over."

I grip the wheel.

"And one more thing. This agreement between us must remain completely confidential. Just our little *secret*."

"Sure. OK. Just our secret."

Max disappears below deck.

My thoughts race—*Is this really happening?* Or will I wake up tomorrow and learn it was all a joke. Just a test to see how gullible the hick from Oregon really is. We'll all get a great laugh out of it tomorrow, right? Ten million dollars. Yeah, right! Dream on pal! I actually laugh out loud. Might as well, there's not a soul to hear me. I stand at the wheel, feeling the immense power of the yacht as it plunges through the waves.

My thoughts wander. The ship flies along through the blackness. It's dreamlike. I don't even feel the time passing. And then, at some point, the light seems to change texture. A rosy hint of dawn appears far away on the horizon.

A deep voice from behind makes me jump.

"Beautiful, isn't it?"

It's the captain with his thick Australian accent.

"Yes," I say.

"Yup, you can watch the sun rise over the ocean a million times, and every time it surprises you with how damn beautiful it is."

I nod, hand him the wheel, and go down to my cabin to sleep.

*   *   *

When I wake up, I see that an envelope has been delivered under my door. I scoop it up, plop myself into the plush leather chair cleverly designed to be comfortable regardless of the heel of the boat, and start reading. As I read my heart speeds up. By the end of the first paragraph it's beating like a drum. I can't believe what's happening ... can this be real?

The contract is eminently straightforward. It provides for me to have one year in which to cause Mr. Maximus Simon to feel the emotion of "true happiness." During the year I'll have no other assigned duties, in order to be able to devote myself fully to my task, and will have access to an appropriate expense account. If I fail, I forfeit all the money already slotted for me in my Island account for the work I've done thus far ... *Wait!* That's more than a million dollars. Every penny I have in the world. I hesitate for a moment over this provision. Of course I don't like it, but I see the logic. I'd be buying into a much more lucrative arrangement. Max is just trying to provide maximum motivation. Impeccable business acumen. Nothing ventured, nothing gained. After all, when I succeed I'll be getting ... *ten million dollars!*

A fountain pen lies suggestively next to the contract. As if in slow motion, I uncap the pen and sign. The words "ten million dollars" keep rattling in my head. I push the small white button seamlessly inlaid in the mahogany desk. Moments later there's a soft knock at the door.

"Come in."

"You rang, sir," says a gorgeous young woman dressed in the ship's uniform.

I hold up the signed document and am about to give my instructions when she says, "I'll take this to Mr. Simon right away."

"Thank you," I answer. And she's gone.

So it's done. Signed and delivered. I sit back in the chair, feeling the boat leaping forward through the waves. Ten million dollars! Beyond my wildest dreams. What are the odds of something like this? A lumber-mill brat from Oregon! But now this is actually happening. Coming true. I think for a second about the Chinese emperor who dreamed he was a butterfly and then always wondered whether he was just a butterfly dreaming he's an emperor.

But no ... this is real. I'm grasping my destiny. Finally. After all those years studying like a crazy fanatic. I'm finally becoming something exponentially beyond the suburban insignificance of that drab grey poor dumpy neighborhood I grew up in. Soaring now. Soaring to the heavens!

Ten million dollars! With that kind of money I can spend the rest of my life doing anything I want. Because of course I'm going to pull this off. I mean, armed with an unlimited expense account, getting Max to feel happy is going to be a slam-dunk ... It's as if the money's already in my pocket. Already mine. I'll be completely free. Completely independent.

And just as always, in these moments of happiness, my thoughts reach out to Dot. In a flash of seeming clarity, it dawns on me that maybe this thing with Dot is all turning out OK. I'll nab the money and then sweep her off her feet so we can live happily ever after. Yes! Everything is going to turn out just fine for me and Dot!

Of course by now I've figured out that Dot's not going to let me back into her life as long as I have anything to do with the Island. I'll have to make a clean break with all this and start over with her. A fresh start. A new foundation that we'll build together. So I can't do it now. I need to get the ten million first. And then we'll get back together. Back on track.

I need to tell her! I start writing her an e-mail, then notice the stationery decoratively set out in the mahogany shelves. So nineteenth century-ish. Awesomely romantic. I take out a sheet and write:

Dear Dot. I love you. I can't tell you the reasons right now, but we can't be together just yet. At first I didn't understand why you weren't answering my e-mails or calls or text messages. But now I realize you just need some time to cool off. To forgive me for deciding to stay on the Island. I understand. I think about you every day. Every minute of every day. I'm wrapped up in this huge project right now. It's for us. But in less than a year we'll be together again. And we'll be free to live out the rest of our lives together. Promise.

I♥UD

19. Like A Phoenix

GOING BACK TO PORTLAND was like some dreadful psychological torture for Dot. Like she'd lost everything and was forced to start over. This time older, without anything to show for it. Alone, and completely disillusioned. She remembers how it used to be when she was in high school. How many endless, beautiful hours she spent with David making plans. Bold plans. Together they could *and would* do anything! Nothing was impossible. They were going to get the hell out of Portland: *together*.

She spent the first few weeks back at her parents' house shut up in her room. Mostly sleeping. Ma and Pa Peabody would just shake their heads in despair. They didn't know what to do to make her feel better. She usually kept the shades down. Sometimes she would open them and sit on a chair watching the raindrops streak down the windowpane. Each drop slowly moving downwards until it joined with another drop. And then, suddenly, as if fueled by the strength of their joyful union, racing downwards together, mingling in perfect harmony to rejoin the Earth. Then she'd pull the shades down again and go back to sleep.

When David's letter from the yacht was delivered to her by Special Courier, she stared at it for hours in her room with the door shut. But she knew she wasn't going to read it. She'd already made up her mind. Whatever he had to say in that letter could only make things worse. Could only derail her plans once again. Only make the pain hurt even more. So she kept on staring at it without opening it. Then she picked up a match.

It was surprising how fast it went once it got started. The flames seemed to shoot up all of a sudden in a spontaneous burst. She watched as the fire devoured David's words, obliterating them—unread—forever. It burned her fingers as the ashes fell to the floor. But she held on. Something about the pain felt strangely soothing. Like it was sucking out some of the pain on the inside.

*   *   *

The days slip drizzly past. Finally, Ma Peabody can stand it no longer. She marches into her daughter's room and refuses to leave until Dot agrees to go with her to the grocery store.

Greg Maloney was the guy who sat next to Dot in many of her classes in high school. She'd always ignored him, just as she'd ignored every other boy in the universe after David.

Dot's failure to notice Greg was a deep source of pain for him. At first he persevered, maneuvering each time to get seated as close to her as possible in class. But he was no match for David, and soon abandoned hope. Still, he never forgot Dot. He recently weathered a miserable (but thankfully childless) divorce, and is now teaching history at his alma mater.

And so, when Greg enters the Price Chopper grocery store this afternoon, he's dumbstruck to see her. Not dumbstruck in a figurative sense, but actually literally struck speechless. There *she* stands right in front of him, right next to the cantaloupes.

After all these years, there she is! And he can't find a word to say. He just stands there staring at her. Paralyzed.

Ma Peabody has finished choosing a bunch of bananas and is heading back toward Dot and the shopping cart when she sees them. She instantly ducks behind the citrus fruit stalls, well out of view.

"You're Greg Maloney, aren't you?" says Dot with an easy smile when she sees him standing there staring at her.

Thankfully, this seems to break the spell, and Greg miraculously recovers the gift of speech. "Dot, I can't believe it's you."

The complete sincerity and enthusiasm that gushes out with Greg's words startles and amazes Dot. It seems to wake her up from a long sleepwalk. She blinks and sees Greg for the first time.

"Well, it's me," she says. But something in her voice makes it sound like she's acknowledging a defeat.

"Are you just back for a quick visit? Or ..." He holds his breath in anticipation.

"I guess I'm back for a while, at least for now." The note of defeat still hangs in her voice.

But from the looks of Greg's face, you'd think he'd just won the lottery. And as Dot realizes he's hitting on her big time, she has a split-second reflexive reaction to pull away—the reflex she'd acquired by always being with David since time began.

And then she realizes that the reflex has become outdated. Completely out of context. David isn't here. And he's not coming back.

She looks at Greg, bubbling over with joy at seeing her. Come to think of it, she's flattered, and pleased. And being a guy, Greg picks up on this immediately. He's ecstatic. Not only is Dot back, but she seems actually happy to see him.

*   *   *

Greg courted Dot as diligently and as gently as could be imagined. She was grateful. And profoundly relieved. Relieved to discover that she did have a life after David. That she would live again. That she would rise up from the ashes.

She was surprised how much they had in common. How much they had to say to each other. And inevitably, their conversations began to point towards two central truths: neither was getting any younger, and both wanted children.

She rented a nice little apartment with a pretty view of the city and started working at a local bank. They lunched together, dined together, rented movies together and slept together.

Greg was too tactful to talk about love. They had so much else to talk about! And so many plans to make!

20. The Solutionist

"HELLO MR. FINNEGAN, my name is Jango."

The man named Jango holds out his hand for me to shake. He's clean-cut to perfection and muscle-bound like a Commando tricked into wearing a designer suit for the meeting. His accent is Euro-speak. Austrian, maybe.

"Hello, Jango," I say, shaking his outstretched hand. There doesn't seem to be anyone else in the entire office aside from the receptionist at her desk in the front room. "So you must be the Solutionist?"

Jango lets out a fluttery dismissive chuckle as if the very notion he could be the Solutionist is jocular. "No, no, no, I am not the Solutionist. The Solutionist never meets directly with clients, of course. But he is listening to us as we speak."

Listening to us? I don't like that. Too contrived, dramatic and electronically eavesdroppingish for my taste, but what the hell. This guy is supposed to be the best. And prima donnas all seem to have their eccentricities.

"So, you got sort of a Wizard of Oz thing going, huh?"

"Ha ha, Wizard of Oz. Ya, ya, very funny."

I smile thinly.

"Please sit down. Something to drink?"

"No, I'm fine," I say.

We're in a penthouse loft with expensive minimalistic Zen ultra-modern furnishings. I sit in an aerodynamic-looking armchair, and Jango follows suit on a futuristic couch of some sort.

I'm anxious to get down to business to see if this is just a waste of time. After signing the contract to "make Max happy" I've been racking my brains as to the best way to go about it. I need a support team. The best money can buy. My research led me here, to this man who calls himself the "Solutionist" and charges enormous sums of money to achieve a certain goal, whatever that goal might be. He's fabled to have engineered escapes from maximum security prisons, to have expedited the passing of husbands, wives or unwanted business associates, to have found people who are missing, to have caused others to go missing, to have executed fabulously painful revenge schemes, and so on and so forth. He's supposedly *the* turnkey solution for those with a specific goal, a desire for discretion, and an unlimited budget.

Nothing in the office seems to shed any clue as to whose office it is. No logo. No shiny brass plaque. Nothing. Then I notice discreet holographic letters floating in the air spelling out "The Solutionist" followed by a strange-looking variation on the trademark sign indicating the letters "AZ." I point to the hologram:

"What sort of a trademark notice is that? I'm not familiar with it."

"So, this is maybe your first experience with someone in the Alternative Zone?"

"Alternative Zone?"

"Yes. You understand that we don't want to use the traditional system of courts and banks and things like that. There are a lot of us like this. So many that we have formed what is called the Alternative Zone or 'AZ'. It is all anonymous, so none of us knows who the others are. Completely untraceable."

"How does it work?"

"Well, if the Solutionist has a problem, for example, someone who is infringing with the trademark, or someone who won't pay. We don't file a lawsuit with the traditional court system. We file with the problem solving committee of the AZ."

"And then?"

"And then the problem is always resolved. Very efficient."

Hmm ... I don't much like the sound of that, but in deciding to come see the Solutionist I've already prepared myself to be stepping a bit into the underworld. Or "alternative world" as Schwarzy the PA might say. At least they're being upfront about it. But enough chatter.

"OK, Jango, tell me a little about how this works."

"Actually it is very simple. I am your facilitator. You tell me what is your problem and I tell you how much it will cost for the Solutionist to solve it."

"You're right, it does sound simple. So here's my problem: I must make a man happy."

I note Jango's brows furrowing. He evidently hasn't heard this one before.

"That is a very singular request, Mr. Finnegan. Please describe the individual to me."

"Middle-aged. Hugely wealthy, healthy, good looking ... but blasé and world-weary. He has everything a man could possibly want. Lovely wife. Every material toy money can buy. But he's not happy. He says he feels like he's lost the spark ... that somehow he's just lost interest. He's already done everything and been everywhere. He's had his fill of chateaux, boats, cars, women and all the other typical rich-boy playthings, so the Solutionist would have to come up with something truly special to make this work."

"What you say is very interesting. We have never had such a request before."

"So what's the next step?"

"Well, as you know, there are many ways to skin a bull."

I wince at the mix.

"So I will interview you now, to get all the information possible regarding this man. Then the Solutionist will decide if he agrees to take your case or not. If he agrees, then I will get back in touch with you to tell you how much it will cost to solve your problem."

At this point I'm not quite sure what to make of the Solutionist. But there's only one way to find out. And the clock is ticking.

"Let's do it," I say.

21. Blue Marble

HAVING NO IDEA what's in store. Having no control. Now that's a feeling that is very new to Max. He's always managed his agenda as if it were a precious commodity to be scientifically budgeted in dynamic real-time cost-benefit analysis. But right at this moment he's stepping onto his plane without the slightest notion where he's going. He wonders what's in store for him. For the past few weeks he's been subjected to a battery of medical tests and forced to follow rigorous physical training several hours a day. Whatever it is, he's looking forward to it.

Meanwhile, I'm busily preparing for Max's imminent arrival, along with Jango and a cast of others, all being paid handsomely for the privilege. He'll be landing at 05:00. As soon as he arrives he'll be whisked away and prepped for a truly unique experience: included in a team of Russian cosmonauts sent into orbit to repair a failing satellite. Such an event is unprecedented, and apparently cost the Solutionist a considerable amount of favors, not to mention the astronomical amount of cash I spent from the make-Max-happy slush fund to finance the project. The mission is military and top-secret, thus completely off the media's radar screen, exactly as Max likes it. Jango is pleased with himself, and thoroughly confident of success. I'm just crossing my fingers.

Once on the base, everything is military by the book. Max is sequestered with the other cosmonauts, training and preparing for the mission.

Jango and I follow the progress through a closed circuit monitor. What we see fills us with hope. Max has no trouble bonding with the other cosmonauts, and by the second day of training, he's become completely integrated into their team.

The launching is flawless. We watch as the rocket pushes through the Earth's atmosphere and out into the cosmos.

*   *   *

Out in space Max is having a blast. Surely one of the best times of his life. Everything about the experience is wondrous and new. The military aspect; his fear of failing at the beginning; then gradually his confidence building as he realizes he can actually add something valuable to the team. It is incredibly hard, grueling, round-the-clock work, and he's loving every second of it.

The mission consists of matching orbit with an ailing satellite and sending a cosmonaut out on a spacewalk to attempt a repair. With his mathematics background, Max is the systems monitor. He'll stay inside the capsule with two other cosmonauts monitoring the computer and managing the uplink interface with the satellite while one cosmonaut attempts the repair. If the repair is successful, and if there's enough time, Max and his mission-buddy, Vladimir, will suit up for a spacewalk during which they'll perform a series of tests and maintenance on the satellite in an effort to prevent a future failure.

We watch with the ground crew on the monitors at Mission Control. There are some very tense moments. But finally, after nearly a full day's work, the repair is a success. We all cheer and congratulate ourselves on a job well done. But every second in space is precious. And the men are not back home yet. Within minutes, Max finds himself putting on his space suit with Vladimir at his side. His heart races. He's actually going out there!

Outside the capsule, Max is not prepared for the shock of stepping into space. He had expected to be impressed, but what he sees and feels surpasses anything he'd imagined.

The majesty of actually seeing the Earth as it really is ...

It's staggering. Humbling beyond belief. The photos and simulations during his training didn't come close to capturing the actual experience. He feels as if everything has fallen into perspective. There, in front of him, is his home world. He stares, awestruck by the beauty, filled with an incomparable feeling of wonderment.

He'd expected that standing out here in the vastness of space would make him feel small, insignificant and disconnected. Like some errant electron spun off from its nucleus on the verge of being disintegrated in this infinite frigid vacuum that would instantly suck out his life if there were so much as a pinprick in his space suit. But strangely, the very opposite occurs. As he hangs there weightless in space, he suddenly feels deeply connected to it all. As if it really did all fit together. As if everything truly were joined into some immense pattern. All of us down there living out our lives on that beautiful blue planet spinning around the sun. All of us somehow connected. How? In what way? For what purpose? For one fleeting flash, it almost seems to be starting to make some sort of sense. But the notions swirl around him like shooting stars, burning out before he can grasp their meaning.

Meanwhile, back at Mission Controlsky, we're watching on the monitors. There's a monitor showing the view Max sees from a camera mounted on his helmet, and another showing Max's face. And then, as we watch, the most incredible thing happens. The staticky white background noise of the space walk is suddenly replaced with music.

The Mission Control team immediately whips into a frantic frenzy, fearing that some stray radio signal has corrupted the system.

But watching Max's expression on the monitor, I instantly know this is his doing. He must have slipped it into the ship's computer.

"It's OK," I say out loud. "It's Max's music."

The Mission Control director is livid. He screams in Russian. Space missions are not amusement park rides! This is deadly serious! But then, as he listens, his features relax ... "Tchaikovsky Violin Concerto," he says in a whisper, now staring at the monitors, realizing that the moment is truly marvelous. The Mission Control staff take the cue from their boss ... everyone goes silent.

From Max's POV Cam we all watch the Earth floating there in space as Tchaikovsky's violin reaches that magical crescendo where no mortal can listen without tearing up inside.

Then, without missing a beat, the music segues into Elvis' Jailhouse Rock. Max smiles wide. He grabs Vladimir's hand. And now, in violation of every rule in Mission Control military protocol, the whole room rises up in spontaneous applause as Max and Vladimir—for the first time in the history of humankind—actually *dance* in space, rocking and rolling, with the universe spread out before them.

*   *   *

After Max's return, I can't wait to get a chance to talk with him. Once the medical team is through with their tests, he emerges.

"Well, David," says Max, "it truly was magnificent. Thank you for arranging one of the most enjoyable experiences I've ever had."

"And?"

"And ... you're getting close. Nice, but no cigar."

I don't bother hiding my disappointment.

"You're going to have to reach further inside for inspiration," he says, looking into my eyes with that motivating smile of his. "I hope you haven't given up on me as a lost cause."

"Of course not."

"Good. And you're not going to rip one of my arms off are you?"

"I'm beginning to wish it were that easy."

22. The Drawing Board

JANGO SITS next to me. We're in an upscale wannabe bar in a largish Russian town. I catch our reflection in a mirror on the wall. I'd say we both look like shit. I take a thoughtful sip of beer to reconsider. Yeah, it's official. We both totally look like shit.

"So I guess we blew it, Jango."

Jango nods sadly into his beer. A Commando on the verge of tears. "This Max is a very hard nut to pick."

Ugh. But then, metaphors aside, I have to agree with Schwarzyknockoff on this. The task is not an easy one. The question is: *what next?*

Several beers later the question still hangs in the air. Thick as the ubiquitous cigarette smoke. Haven't they heard about lung cancer here? Jango is off in a corner, presumably strategizing with the Wizard on his cell.

My would-be-constructive mind racking has drawn a blank. Jango comes back with an upbeat grin on his face. Apparently his powwow with the Wizard has borne some sort of fruit. Expensive fruit, no doubt. "We have an idea," says Jango.

Of course I'm not surprised. Considering the cash that Jango and Ozboy have already harvested orchestrating this very expensive exercise in space age futility, I wholly expect them to come up with an equally expensive plan "B."

Jango sits down and begins: "Mr. Simon—"

"—The nut—"

"—Yes, we have maybe found a way to pick."

I wince. "Tell me."

"He said to reach inside for inspiration."

Drily: "I know, Jango. I was there."

"Yes, well then, the Solutionist has a very good idea."

"OK Jango, lay it on me."

*   *   *

I wander through the streets. Eyesore Soviet architecture is jumbled randomly with brave new starts at something striving for modern, yet for the moment falling miserably shy of anything remotely aesthetic. Decrepit Ladas vie for space next to shining luxury cars. Snowflakes fall. Swirling around virgin white until they touch the ground where they become instantly filthy black as pitch. Fitting. Right now I'm identifying profoundly with the black slush sticking to the soles of my shoes.

What the hell am I doing? I had more than a million dollars waiting for me in my account. And a great job on the Island. And I traded it all away for what? A chance to win the lottery? What was I thinking? How did I possibly agree to this charade? If I fail I'll be shipped off the Island in a heartbeat. Broke. Completely broke. One thing for sure, failures don't stay on the Island. And there's no way my old firm will give me my job back. I snubbed them, and that's that. I'll be back out there combing the job market without a dime to my name. But there's something else. Something worse. Something sordidly creepy about this whole thing. Maybe if I wasn't such a greedy jerk I could have seen it earlier. Something perversely Faustian. Grotesquely decadent. Like eating nightingale tongues or live monkey brains. What's wrong with this guy? It's all shamelessly hedonistic. And I'm a part of it. No, worse. I'm the circus leader. Unfuckingbelievable.

Or am I needlessly flipping out? I should calm down. Too many espressos compounded with beers whizzing through my veins. Sure, the whole thing is bizarre and perverse. But that's to be expected, right? A recluse billionaire on an Island full of nerds. Of course he's weird as shit. Of course it's perverse. But if I can sail off into the sunset with ten million in my pocket, then it's worth it, no? Hell yeah it's worth it! Dot and I'll be free as birds, forever.

The trick is to know whether I'm being played. He's smart. Real smart. Is he jerking my chain? Tricking me into being just another disposable minion that he'll discard when he's done having his fun, after taking back the money he pretended to give me.

Or is he sincere?

Anyway, the dice have been cast. It's up to me now. I've got to think of a way. I've got to pull this off. I will do this. I can't wimp out now. I will succeed! Whatever the cost.

... Whatever needs to be done.

23. From The Ancients To Auschwitz

TRUTH IS, I'D NEVER REALLY THOUGHT about happiness as a goal before. It just happened, or didn't. I guess I always just took it for granted. Just something that appears on the horizon like a rainbow when things go right in your life.

But this is different. This is business. There's a lot of money at stake here. Maybe the hotshot Solutionist with his metaphorically challenged sidekick will come up with the right plan, but maybe not.

I've got to take control. But how? How would *you* do it?

Back to basics. I ask Gwen to gather everything she can find on the subject of happiness. With her customary discretion, she doesn't bat an eye. Almost immediately the research materials start pouring in. I'm amazed at the volume. Who would have thought so much ink has been spilled over the pursuit of happiness? First there are the reams and reams of "self-help" books ... *The ABC's of Happiness, User's Guide To Happiness, Happiness 101, How To Be A Happy Lover, How To Inspire Happiness Around You, The Zen Path To Happiness* ... the list seems endless. Even such unexpected titles as *The Thief's Guide To Happiness, Making Your Gerbil and Other Rodents Happy, Happiness for The Sexual Deviant, Obesely Happy, Obscenely Happy*, and so on. And if you want more of that, you can actually consult online the *Journal of Happiness Studies* or the *World Database of Happiness* and scads more.

I cut through the "self-help" books like butter. Nothing even remotely applicable to Max's very special circumstances. The only thing I glean from them is the central, perhaps self-evident truth that everyone has to find his or her own unique recipe for happiness. Gee Sherlock, thanks for the newsflash.

But the Ancients. Just like always, they're awesome.

It turns out that a century or so after Socrates accepted the Athenian death sentence by drinking the cup of hemlock rather than walking out of prison through the door discreetly left open, Epicurus was focusing his philosophical musings on the subject of happiness. He figured the only path to happiness was through earthly pleasures. He was preaching "don't worry be happy" more than two thousand years before Bobby McFerrin or Bob Marley lit up their first reefers. As you can imagine, such a philosophy was wildly appealing. Maybe it was due solely to the magnetism of his philosophical ideals. Or maybe it had something to do with the parties. Anyway, it was well known in the third century BC that the best shindig from this side of Sparta to Damascus was chez Epicurus in his sprawling country mansion, *the Garden,* just outside of Athens. Fans came from everywhere. Face control was nowhere to be seen. Anyone who was anyone showed up at Epicurus' garden bashes, no matter how long it took to drive your oxcart there.

So this terrestrial questing for happiness through earthly delights was all well and good for the Epicurean party animals. But it presented a real burr up the butt of the Catholic Church stumbling upon the whole thing with a bit of a hangover after a thousand years of neglecting their classical studies.

And as they started dusting off and reading the ancient texts they realized they'd unearthed a time bomb. Why? Because the ideas were subversive, that's why. Think of it. You're in the middle of the thirteenth century and you're trying to consolidate power over

Christendom. And you've spent a hell of a long time during the early years, when the whole show was just getting off the ground, convincing everybody that there's no happiness in this terrestrial life and that you can only be happy in heaven.

Of course the Dark Ages was a pretty good time to convince the huddled masses that life sucked, because generally it did. So the Church had a no-brainer preaching that happiness could only exist in heaven, and they were the ones holding the roadmap and the keys to the Pearly Gates. Any happiness on earth was illusory—just a trailer for the real show to come. And of course you could only get into heaven if you stopped whining and complaining, paid your tithes, and worked constantly for your feudal lords. An entire population of peasants accepted their shitty life on the promise that the Hereafter would rock.

For the Church and nobles who needed vast amounts of manpower to cultivate their fields, build labor-intensive stuff like castles and churches, and serve and die in the armies, the whole thing was tailor-made.

But what about the ancient texts? What about those ancient philosophers with their implacable logic and seductive syllogisms? What about their claims that the only happiness is here and now? You can imagine that thoughts like these were more dangerous to the Holy See than armies of infidels. If the word ever got out, who would work the fields or go to battle? Such thinking could undermine the whole system and wreak havoc with the workforce. So the Church fathers kept all the ancient texts securely locked up and stashed away. Lucky for them, they were pretty much the only ones who knew how to read.

But eventually word of that sort always gets out.

Which brings us around to Saint Thomas Aquinas. For starters, he wasn't always a VIP saint. The road was rocky. His dad was the powerful Count of Aquino. So technically Thomas was in line to be a powerful count himself. But his timing was off. He was the youngest son of a big family, which means he wouldn't get diddlysquat until his older brothers were killed off. So at the age of five little Tommy was sent to study at the monastery with a standing order from Papa Count that he would grow up to become the Abbot, as was customary for budding counts-to-be. But the lad Thomas had ideas of his own. Rather than become the powerful feudal ruler of the monastery, he wanted to go out into the world and beg for his food in the streets as a poor friar. Go figure.

Naturally, as soon as his older brothers got wind of this, they did what any good bunch of siblings would do. They locked him up in the prison of the family Castle of Roccasecca, north of Naples. And in order to put him back on the straight and narrow, the brothers sent him a gorgeous young lassie to share his prison bunk. But Tom would have none of them apples. He spurned the fair wench and finally managed to escape those loamy loins and the bonds of fraternal love to make it to Paris, the then-capital of learning.

Despite what you might think, he wasn't such a great hit at school. His fellow students nicknamed him the "dumb ox" and the name stuck all through his doctorate program (but was jettisoned before sainthood). Maybe because he was an outcast student spurned by his classmates who wanted to distinguish himself in some spectacular way, or maybe not. In any event Tommy worked like a dog. He read everything he could get his hands on. And eventually he got his hands on the classics. As soon as he rolled out one of those Aristotelian parchments, he realized that stuff like that was just too good to keep locked up in the archives, like so many of the other ancient tomes already transformed by mice into little brown rice-sized pellets. But there was a problem. The problem was how on earth to get it into the curriculum. This was worse than trying to get a black kid into a white grade school in the South in the fifties. No way José. Tom realized that if the Ancients were going to get to play ball, they needed a serious makeover. And so he made it his mission.

Again, he worked like a dog: writing, reading, lecturing, convincing. And finally, with the angelic dexterity of a saint, Tommy performed the most extraordinarily adroit sleight of hand. He explained that what the Ancients really meant when they referred to happiness was not secular, earthly, physical happiness. No, no, no ... The Ancients were just speaking *metaphorically*. You know how they're always doing that. What they really meant was that by being true to the faith and following the Ten Commandments, good Christians could enter heaven, and that's where they would experience true happiness.

And thus a whole epoch of ancient philosophy was snuck in the back door of Western Civilization while the guy with the pointy hat was looking the other way. Sure, the plan was to graft all those slick toga-clad philosophies onto Church doctrine. But ideas have a way of wiggling out of their syntactic straightjackets and remaining true to themselves.

Once the floodgates of ancient thought were opened, there was no stopping the tide. The cat was out of the proverbial bag. The wine uncorked. Pandora was sitting on top of the box with a voluptuous, beckoning smile. It was time to rock and roll. The concept of happiness on earth before you croak had crept back into the party. And the world would never be the same. Obviously. For if you could obtain happiness on earth, why continue to painfully toil your life away as slaves to the ruling class? And thus the earthly pursuit of happiness was able to work its way into the mortar of those thick monastery walls and make them tremble from within. Those formidable bastions and towers that had withstood centuries of barbarian onslaught were quivering under the power of the *word*.

But forgive me if I paraphrase, misconstrue, misquote or completely miss the point. Pardon my clumsy Cliffsnotes rehashing. And any of you philosophy or history of religion jocks out there who really know this stuff, just cut me some slack, OK?

Anyway, I've lost the thread. Now clearly too tired to think ...

But wait a second. Did I say that young Thomas worked like a *dog*? Sorry, it just dawned on me how lame that simile is. I mean, have you ever seen a dog *work*? Ever? Lick his balls, chew through your slippers, drink out of the toilet or try to hump a houseguest's leg, sure. But *work*? How falsely misleading. I apologize and take it back. Makes you wonder how such clearly misguided images can creep into our culture and stick.

And while some stick, others just don't seem to make it. Take the concept of *telos*. For some of the Aristotelian groupies, everything had a purpose or *telos*. The only way to achieve balance, ergo happiness, was by joining an object with its specific telos. Some even went so far as to postulate that each individual human had a specific telos. Hmm ... Food for thought. And at the risk of abusing another canine metaphor, I'm dog tired and ready to crash. Just one last read before dozing off:

An ancient king, wildly protective of his only son, decided to shower him with luxury and preserve him from all sources of pain or suffering. The young prince grew up in the royal palace surrounded by young healthy and happy people. He knew nothing of sickness, old age or suffering. Whenever the prince insisted on voyaging out beyond the palace, the king made sure that only beautiful people lined the roads where the princely carriage passed. But despite the king's well-intentioned subterfuge, the prince eventually came into contact with an old work-weary peasant from the real world. The peasant spoke to him of physical suffering, of hunger and sickness, of the torment of watching loved ones suffer and die. The young prince was devastated. He realized that without knowledge of pain, all his feelings of happiness were purely artificial. He knew nothing of the real world. Nothing of true pain, thus nothing of true happiness. Nothing of truth at all. He decided never to return to his palace, and began wandering the streets in search of wisdom, begging for his daily food. The young prince grew into a man. He was later known simply as Buddha.

*   *   *

And my research didn't stop at books. I had the Solutionist put together a list of people who were reputed to be particularly happy, or for some reason had some special light to shed on the matter. The Solutionist accomplished this mission with great virtuosity, for the people on the list were from all walks of life, and were truly remarkable.

There was, for example, Mr. H—. I knocked at the door of his plain New Jersey apartment tucked away in the suburbs. He answered and we sat down in his small but meticulously tidy living room. He sat back in his chair like a ninety-year-old sack of bones in a short sleeve shirt and high riding trousers. He talked about himself while I wondered how he'd ever made it on the Solutionist's roster. As far as I could tell, his life was just a long string of misery and suffering. I let him ramble on while my thoughts wandered, and then honed back in when he started talking about his time in a concentration camp. Within seconds I was riveted, hanging on his every word:

"... One day, after the most terrifying year you could imagine, they took ten of us outside. Right outside the barbed wire fence of the main compound. They handed us each a shovel and told us to start digging. Of course we all knew what that meant, and so did everyone inside the camp. They could all see us through the wire fence. The ground was cold and hard, and we were in pretty bad shape, so the digging was slow. But then again, we weren't trying to go fast, mind you! It's funny how even at times like those, you still cherish every minute you have. Anyway, we all knew each other pretty well from spending time in the camp, and at that moment, as we dug together, we felt a very strong and special bond. We couldn't speak, or we'd immediately get hit by one of the guards. But even without words, just looking at each other, we were communicating, clear as day. I can still remember each one of those shovels full of dirt. Savoring each one. The sound, the smell, the feeling of the earth, the pressure against our muscles. None of us wanted to leave any of that behind. We were clinging to it dearly. Making it last. Every second. But eventually the guards decided that our hole was deep enough. They took away our shovels and got their rifles ready for the final step in the process. And that's when something wonderful happened. Without speaking a word, we all joined hands and started singing. It was an old and very beautiful traditional song. Everyone in the camp knew it by heart. We sang out very loud. At the top of our lungs. Of course everyone in the camp was staring at us. The guards were furious, but they didn't quite know what to do. We started dancing around the hole we just dug. Our arms joined together at the shoulders, singing out and laughing like we were at our bar mitzvahs. And as we danced we looked out at the others back in the camp. They were looking at us with such love and support and complete togetherness ..."

Mr. H— stopped talking and seemed to gaze into the distance, back into the faces of the people inside the camp. Hearing his friends singing as they danced. I watched him look into the past.

"What happened then?"

"The sound of the gunshots ripped into us. We kept on singing as, one by one, we fell into the hole we just dug."

Mr. H— stopped talking again, eyes far away, as if this were the end of the story.

"But, then ... how are you here?"

"Oh that!" Mr. H— broke into laughter. "Well, it seems the bullet that was supposed to go through my brain somehow glanced off my thick skull, knocking me unconscious but without any real damage. It was getting pretty late in the day, already dark. So the guards just left the hole uncovered, probably planning to cover it the next day with a bulldozer or something. I woke up before dawn, covered by the frozen bodies of my friends. When I realized I was alive, I checked to see if any of the others were still breathing, but they weren't. They were all cold and stiff as ice. So I crawled out of the hole and ran for my life."

... Mr. H— and I spent the rest of the afternoon chatting and drinking coffee. At one point I asked: "Is there some moment of your life that stands out as the happiest moment of all?"

"Oh yes. Without question. It was when we danced at the concentration camp."

"You mean when you woke up and realized you weren't dead?"

"No. Of course I was quite happy then as well. But the most beautiful moment of all was when we danced. We knew the guards were going to shoot us, and that we'd fall into the hole. But even so, we could look them straight in the eye and dance and sing. They had the power to torture and kill our bodies. But they couldn't touch our souls."

24. The Curious Demise Of Mr. Singh

I'M SITTING in the conference room with Max. We both sip our morning coffees. I have no idea why he called this early meeting, but I'm just about to find out.

"I'm afraid Mr. Singh is dead," he says.

"Dead?"

"Unfortunately."

"How?"

"In his sleep. He had a heart condition. Both he and I knew it would happen, sooner or later, and we'd already for some time made all the necessary preparations. As we speak, his body is being sent back home to his family in Bombay, where he'll receive the dignified funeral he so rightly deserves."

I nod.

Max continues, "Mr. Singh was a very loyal and a very good man." He seems to be studying my reaction as he speaks. "And aside from spiritual matters, the passing of Mr. Singh raises a very practical issue. One in which I believe you could play a decisive role."

"Me? What's that?" I ask, surprised.

"You see, among Mr. Singh's many functions, he was what I jokingly refer to as holder of the key to the black box."

"Black box?"

Max chuckles. "You've heard of interlocking trustee structures, haven't you?"

"Sure."

"Well, our system on the Island has a unique variation of such a structure in place. The key to the black box is nothing other than signature power over the structure. And I think you would be the best person to hold the key now." Max studies my reaction again and continues. "It's really only a formality. The structure is set up so that I retain full control over everything, but you would hold the corporate seal, so to speak." Max gets up from his chair. "But you're the brilliant lawyer, so you're in a better position to judge than anyone. I'll have all the legal documentation sent in here now so you can study it. I'll be back for lunch and we can continue our chat. OK?"

I nod.

"Good," says Max, walking out the door.

A few minutes later, a huge trolley arrives, stacked with documents, pushed by one of Max's secretaries.

"Hello, David," she says cheerily. "Here's some stuff to read. Do you want some fresh coffee with this?" I glance at the towering piles of paper and nod gratefully. Coffee would be good.

Over the next few hours, I delve into the hidden legal labyrinth on which the Island is built. Max has to be careful not to be a direct owner of Halcyon, for that would create all sorts of needless fiscal complications, not to mention jeopardizing the entire financial integrity of the structure if he were to become individually implicated in a lawsuit. In the past, a structure like Halcyon might have been set up through offshore companies. But of course tax authorities, blackmailers, or any good hacker can access all the information they want in the digital world. Anyone who thinks he can evade liability by routing funds through offshore entities is a complete fool in this day and age. And Max is no fool. Moreover, he isn't interested in evading taxes or liability illegally. Max's vision is completely different, far grander. Max wants the system to be conceptually perfect.

The Island is his creation, his baby, his brainchild. And he wants it to be able to function perfectly. Perfectly independently, perfectly legally, and perfectly airtight—all through structural creativity and innovation, not vulgar subterfuge.

And as far as I can see, he's accomplished his goal. The capital funds for the investment vehicles are structured through various cross-linked holding companies. The trick is to allow Max to control these entities, hence the funds, without actually owning them.

The crux of the system lies with the Trustee, who holds the funds *in trust*. Through a complex, yet seemingly foolproof system based on delegation of final authority through the codes in the black box, Max is effectively able to control the Trustee. So the black box really is the *key* to the Island: legally, figuratively and financially.

At lunchtime Max joins me in the conference room. A cartload of food is wheeled in with him. Max goes straight for a deli club sandwich, while I sample the finer morsels.

"So, what do you think?" asks Max.

"Well, I think it's very well put together. You have the legal benefits of a Trust, and yet you retain control over the structure. That's quite a feat. And from what I can gather, you don't own anything at all in your name, it's all held through the Trust."

"Exactly. I own absolutely nothing. Nothing in my name. Not even the shirt on my back. I think it suits my ascetic nature."

I smile.

Max continues, eyes serious and probing. "So, will you agree to be the Trustee?"

"Sure. But I was thinking ... I mean, maybe you'd want someone else. Someone who's been on the Island longer."

"You know, David, in my life I've had to make a lot of decisions. Sometimes very fast snap decisions based on little or no real data. And over time I've grown to trust my instinct. So I'm trusting my instinct on this one, and my instinct tells me I can trust you."

I nod.

"Good," he says, "then it's decided." He takes out a black rectangular metallic object and hands it over to me.

"So this is the black box?" It fits neatly in the palm of my hand. I turn it over. It seems hollow. "Am I supposed to open it? I feel like those apes at the beginning of *2001*."

Max is smiling. "In certain aboriginal tribes, when there occurred an important delegation of authority, the tribal chief would present the newly promoted warrior with a small box."

I keep searching for a latch or button. "So what did the aborigines put in their boxes?"

"The severed testicles of the deceased warrior."

My hands pull back as if the box just bit me. "Please tell me you didn't ..."

"No," says Max with a smile, "but I thought the symbolism was inspiring. Anyway, don't lose it. Inside are the access codes to the safe in my office. If I should get in some sort of trouble, then Larry Kramer, the lawyer behind all this legal stuff, will press a button on a gizmo he has in New York and the black box will open up to give you the codes you need. And Kramer has all the instructions. Let's give him a call."

Max punches a button on a remote console and Kramer's voice comes over the sound system like he's sitting in the room with us.

"Hi Larry."

"Hello Max, how are you?"

"Fine. I've got someone here I'd like to introduce to you."

"Great."

"His name's David. He's the most recent arrival. A lawyer too, and now he's the man with the black box."

"Nice to meet you, Larry," I say. "I just spent the morning admiring your handiwork. About ten thousand pages of it."

Larry chuckles. "Thanks. So, I guess we'll need to work together to draw up and sign the Trustee papers."

"I'm ready when you are."

"Well, there's a lot of paper, and a lot of issues to go over. It might be better if I come out to see you."

"Sure," I say.

"Actually," adds Max, breaking in, "I think we should be able to wrap it up with e-mails and phone calls. Don't you think?"

"Well, I guess so." Larry's voice tries not to sound miffed. I wonder what sort of tension lies beneath the subtext.

"Good. And how about Mr. Singh?" asks Max.

"Everything's going as planned. We had to make some pretty hefty donations to circumnavigate the standard procedures, but don't worry, the body will be there in time for the ceremony tomorrow."

"Excellent, Larry, then I'll be hopping on the plane now to pay my respects to the Singhs. Call me if there are any questions."

"Will do, Max. Nice to meet you, David. I'll send you encrypted copies of the first drafts of the Trust documents and we can take it from there."

"OK, Larry," I say, and Max hangs up.

I look over at Max. "Any particular reason you didn't want Larry on the Island that I should know about?"

"He's an off-Islander, David. A hired tool. There's no reason for him to be here."

I nod.

"And furthermore, like any tool, there comes a time when it has served its intended purpose and must be changed. I think Larry has run his useful course, and it's time we start looking for a new lawyer."

25. Lucky

MARCIE has exactly two smoking breaks of ten minutes each during her eight hour shift at Wal-Mart. Unlike her co-workers, she doesn't take her breaks in the air-conditioned "smoking room" with the cheery-colored (staff energizing) walls, the junk food vending machines, public interest billboard, staff complaints clipboard, coffee pot and incessant gossip.

Marcie takes her breaks by herself, rain or shine, out the back entrance, in the small utility parking lot by the dumpsters.

And today is no exception. When you step outside, the heat is like opening the oven door to see if the cookies are done yet. You can actually feel the heat waves colliding into your skin and entering inside you, like a microwave heating up a TV dinner. And sitting there, if you concentrate on the vibrating hum from the huge air conditioning units that refrigerate the happy shoppers on the inside, you can actually lose yourself in the hum. As if your brainwaves somehow fall into the same droning frequency of those huge electric fans and motors and thingamajigs whirring around, shutting everything else out like some cosmically meditational "*Om*."

She sits there staring at her un-puffed cigarette smoking itself. Self-consuming tobacco. Amazing to think that burning happens when something unites with oxygen. According to the Discovery Channel, each atom or molecule or whatever actually binds with the oxygen in the air and floats off into the atmosphere. Which is, when you think about it, incredibly beautiful and spiritual. Binding with the air and becoming spread throughout the entire world. How wonderfully Zen. And apparently, within twenty-four hours (or was that twenty-four days?) the molecules from a burning cigarette, or from your breath when you breathe out, are actually dispersed throughout the entire planet through the atmosphere so that chances are someone on the other side of the world, like in Australia or Zanzibar, would actually breathe in one of those very same air molecules. Put that in your pipe and smoke it.

But then, out of nowhere, breaking through the mechanical Zen background hum, a familiar noise bubbles up from her distant past. It's the low rumble of a classic Harley Davidson motorcycle. Too late to close out the thought and zap onto something else quickly before it can work its damage. Too late. Unseeing glazed-over eyes follow the Harley down the side road past the dumpsters and out of earshot. The memory is one of those that's been desperately trying to forget itself over the years.

Trying to cover its tracks as if it never existed, like some witness protection program for bad shit of the past. Stuffing itself down into an obscure brain cell well out of plain view. Out of sight, sure. But no matter how much you tiptoe around these things in the dark, sooner or later something works its way in from the outside and sets you off course just enough so that you step smack into it like a puddle of dog piss on the floor when you're wearing only socks.

And so, as it always does, the memory comes back with that same lurching stab inside. That same lurching stab concerning one man: *Lucky Hollister*.

It was during the spring, nearly summertime of her sweet sixteenth year, or sixteen *"and-a-half"* as she would proudly emphasize. Her mother tended bar at a local tavern, and often came home with one of the random late night clients. When the sounds woke her up she would turn up her stereo full blast till it was over. And she would get up early and slip out the door to school so she wouldn't have to see the face of whoever it was. So what if she arrived at school more than an hour before the bell?

She dreamed of the day when she could just ride out of town and never look back. And not just "dreamed" figuratively. She actually *dreamed* during the night about leaving. In those dreams she'd usually be rescued by some prince riding up on a great white stallion to sweep her away to live happily, or at least adequately, ever after.

And thus, the sixteen-year-old Marcie was lying on her back, with her head in the clouds, on an old wooden weather-darkened picnic table in the parking lot next to the Good Ol' Boy Tavern waiting for her Mom to get off on a break at work, when the noise of a classic Harley blasted its way into her consciousness, making her jump in terror.

She bolted upright and screamed: "What the fuck's wrong with you?"

The twenty-something guy on the Harley turned off the rumbling motor and took off his helmet, uncovering his curly Michelangelic locks. He smiled and said: "Hello there, Miss, I didn't see ya. I'm real sorry 'bout that." And they didn't need to say another word. She was already looking deep into his eyes and he was already developing a monster bulge next to his gas tank.

"My name's Lucky Hollister," he finally ended up saying with an accent so thick it made his last name sound like *holster*.

"I'm Marcie," she said, with love glowing in her eyes.

"You wanna go fer a ride?"

Her Lancelot was taking her on his steed! Almost fainting, she nodded "yes." She climbed behind him. The only thing separating her body from his was a few layers of fabric! He pressed against her with the Harley's accelerating g-force. He smelled like something she had never smelled up close before: a man.

She directed him to a park where she knew they would be left alone to admire nature. Thirty minutes later Marcie had given her flower to her knight in shining armor. By dawn they had made love so many times they'd lost count. They were so sore the next day they could barely walk. Marcie was on top of the world. She had found her prince! *Oh sweet sixteen ...*

They spent a few days frolicking. Far enough from town to avoid attracting attention. Checking into budget roadside motels whenever the fancy struck them, which, it turned out, was very often.

Lucky's idol was a man named Werner Heisenberg. Lucky's entire knowledge about Heisenberg and his work stemmed from an article he'd read while standing up thumbing through pornographic magazines at the periodical rack of a large discount department store.

To protect the sensitivity of the female shoppers, Lucky had devised a technique whereby he would shield whatever skin mag he was currently perusing with a respectable magazine like *Popular Science* or *Dirt Bike Weekly* when someone of the female persuasion walked by. It was during one of these furtive magazine maneuvers that his eye caught the title: *"The Heisenberg Uncertainty Principle"* in the periodical camouflaging the foldout of enormous boobs he'd been inspecting. Something about the article captured Lucky's interest. Perhaps it was the diagram of the electrons whizzing at the speed of light around the atom's nucleus. In any event, Lucky stood there and did what he *never* did. He actually read something. He folded back the Playmate of the Month, returned her to the shelf, and delved into the mysterious world of quantum physics.

When he finished the article, he realized he'd never be the same again. He was a changed man. Indeed, that brief moment of erect reading was all Lucky had needed to profoundly re-forge his worldview and adopt his new guiding philosophy of life.

THE SECRET (*of happiness*)

It was in the midst of one of Marcie's teenage-spawned metaphysical out-loud musings about the meaning of life that Lucky decided it was time to introduce her to his philosophic worldview.

"Well, baby," he said in that irresistible Rhett Butlerian drawl of his, "I'm a great believer in the *uncertainly principle.*"

"What's that?" asked Marcie.

"Well, baby," he said again, "according to the uncertainly principle, if a man knows how fast he's going, then he can't know where he's at." Lucky turned those puppy dawg eyes of his over to Marcie who was listening with great attention and a growing horniness. He furrowed his brow with intellectual sensitivity and asked her in the manner of a concerned professor: "You with me, baby?"

"I'm with you," replied Marcie, thinking more of his pelvic region than his interpretation of quantum mechanics, "but I'm not completely sure I understand what you were saying."

"Well," drawled Lucky with professorial patience. "Baby, think of it this away. The Hysenboom Uncertainly Principle governs all living creatures, and all men as well. And it's because of the uncertainly principle that when, for example, I'm riding my Harley, and I look down at the speedometer to see that I'm driving at a hundred miles an hour, by the time I look back up at the road to see where I am, well I ain't no longer at the same place, now am I?"

Marcie looked up from what she was doing with a wide smile of sincere appreciation. "I suspect you're right, Lucky," she said admiringly. Then she batted her eyelashes, finished unbuckling his belt and took him deep inside her mouth. After all these years she could still taste the warm gush of pungent salty cream.

It was in the café adjoining the roadside motel that Lucky first informed Marcie that he had to be riding up north for a spell. Marcie choked on her mouthful of banana pancakes and started crying. Eager to avoid a scene in a public place with a minor, Lucky slapped down enough change on the table to cover the bill and whisked Marcie away across the dingy parking lot to the motel room where she proceeded to cry her eyes out for hours.

Finally Marcie calmed down.

Several love makings and teary-hugged discussions later, they'd developed a plan. Marcie would stay behind to finish school while Lucky rode on ahead. On the last day of school, Lucky would pick her up, and they would ride off into the sunset to live happily ever after.

As the semester dragged on, Marcie thought about Lucky every second of the day and night. She was sure they would spend their lives together. And of course they would get married as soon as she was of legal age.

A few weeks before the last day of school, Marcie woke up with a tummy ache. She went to the school nurse and received some very startling news.

Later that day, she called the number that Lucky had given her.

"Lucky?" she said into the payphone.

"Yes, baby." Even from a gazillion miles away, that gorgeous voice of his made her tremble and quake all over.

"I got some really wonda'ful news."

"What's that, baby?"

"I'm so excited I can barely talk to tell ya."

"Take a deep breath, baby doll," he said with his voice that inspired such confidence and inner strength. With Lucky around, everything was always under control!

She took that deep breath.

"Now tell me," he said.

"I'm preggers."

The line remained silent for a few minutes that seemed to stretch into eternity. Then the automated voice of the telephone company broke in with a warning that her time was up. She dropped another coin into the phone and the automated operator told her she could continue her conversation for another ten minutes.

"Lucky?" she said. "Lucky?" She waited, but there was no sound from the other end. She waited the whole ten minutes before hanging up.

She tried calling back dozens of times, but each time she got someone different who said Lucky had left without telling anyone where he was going. "Ah, you know Lucky," they would say with a good-hearted chuckle.

At first Marcie would tell herself that Lucky must be on his way riding down to pick her up early. If she were away from home somewhere, she would suddenly become obsessed with the idea that Lucky might be waiting for her *at that very moment*. She would dash home to check if Lucky was there. Of course he wasn't.

She stopped going to school. What was the point anyway? And finally the day came. The last day of school. The day that Lucky was coming. She was up at dawn, dressed in her prettiest dress. The pastel yellow one with the little flowers sewn over the pleated front. It was raining, but that didn't matter. Everything she was taking with her was packed into a little suitcase scarcely bigger than a lunchbox. She sat outside on the street curb so she could see him coming from as far away as possible. This way she'd be able to spot him even before hearing the rumble of his bike. And as soon as he got there she would just jump right on behind him and they would zoom off together forever.

She waited all day, straining her eyes and ears for a flash of faraway chrome or the noise of his Harley. Finally, around midnight she decided he must have had some sort of a delay. Maybe a mechanical problem. OK, he'd be there tomorrow. She walked back inside, shivering. Her dress and hair soggy from the rain.

She waited every day for a week. She prayed for a miracle. Like those miracles she'd heard about in church. She loved those miracle stories. That's what kept her going back there by herself on Sundays, long after her mother stopped going. As far as she was concerned, it was the miracles that made the whole God thing work. Otherwise all the adoration and devotion just seemed too one-sided. But with miracles in the deal, she was all aboard. And so she prayed and prayed. If God was good for anything, surely he'd come through for her now!

But finally, as the summer days and her belly stretched on, she had to admit to herself that Lucky wasn't ever going to come for her.

When her Mom found out she was pregnant she screamed with the maternal sensitivity of an army drill sergeant: "You stupid slut, I didn't even know you had your first period!"

Marcie visited the free family planning clinic downtown. As soon as she saw the first ultrasound picture of her baby, she knew she could never go through with an abortion.

She would stare for hours at the black and white photo of the lima bean sized little person who had mysteriously taken up residency in her abdomen. No matter how many times she tried to convince herself it wasn't so, she was certain that the little lima baby had Lucky's smile. She would fold up the photo and stick it her pocket, only to take it out a minute later and see it there again—plain as the nose on your face: Lucky's smile smiling back at her. It was almost as if she could hear the little lima bean voice talking to her with Lucky's soft honey drawl.

At the clinic Marcie told them she wanted to keep the baby and raise her (it was a girl!) herself. But her mother refused to be the legal guardian, and with no consenting legal guardian it seemed that things were very complicated. As a minor, with no job, no money, and no place to live other than her mom's, there didn't seem to be any real choice about it.

They told her it would be better if she didn't hold the baby after delivery, and she agreed. They whisked the baby away before she even saw her face. All she heard was one small cry muffled by the heavy door as they left the room with her.

Left with her baby girl! Her own flesh and blood! Born through her love with Lucky Holster. Sweet Lucky with those puppy eyes and soft golden hair. Lucky! Our baby, Lucky ...

"*They took our baby!*" she screamed.

The nurse increased her dose of sedatives and she faded back into nothingness.

Before she left the hospital she filled out some paperwork in a daze. She glimpsed herself in the mirror, looking like someone in one of those war films with concentration camps. On the forms there was a box she had to check if she wanted them not to maintain the record of her maternity. She had to ask them what that meant, and they explained that if she checked the box, then no records would be kept that she had ever given birth to this baby.

The matronly nurse bent closer to her and said softly, reassuringly: "I think it would be best for you and the baby if you check the box. That way, all this remains in the past." Yes, that's what she wanted. She wanted this to be all so far in the past it would be like it never happened. Like things that happened to her when she was so young she couldn't remember anything. Like those baby pictures of her next to people and places she had entirely no recollection of. Yes, that's what she wanted. She nodded absently and checked the box.

It wasn't until she arrived back home, alone in her bed, in the middle of the night, that she realized the enormity of the box she'd checked. Sometimes it seemed to her that little box had somehow sucked in the most precious thing she had in life, and then closed it away from her. Inaccessible. Irreversibly. Forever.

During the subsequent years, Marcie often thought about that box. If she'd left it unchecked she could have found her baby. She even went back to the hospital and the adoption agency, but they said they couldn't help. The files with that box checked had been *destroyed* long ago they told her. There was absolutely no way to locate her baby.

Destroyed!

But Marcie knows that her baby is somewhere out there in the universe living her life, and thinking about her: her *real mom*.

She can't believe how much she loves her daughter. She scolds herself how stupid it is to waste so much love on someone she'll never see, never meet, never hold the hand of or comfort when she's afraid. Never share in her joys and sorrows as she grows up and goes off— the first time on her own—to college, where she gets good grades, graduates with honors and becomes a famous scientist.

And sometimes, out of the blue, she sees a girl about the right age with her same dimple, or the same way of holding her head off to the side when she laughs, or the same little furrow in her brow when she doesn't understand something. More than once Marcie actually ran over to the girl as if it were really her daughter. She'd stop in front of her with nothing to say—suddenly petrified. Of course the startled girls would react in any number of different ways. Most just stepped aside and moved on, taking Marcie for some sort of whacko. One girl flipped the bird at her.

And as for men, she decided she could just do without. In fact she decided she was far better off without. And the more she did without, the more she promised herself that she would never love again. Sort of an Alcoholics Anonymous thing. She figured that the part of her soul that could love had just dried up and fallen off. Like an umbilical cord or a stubbed toenail.

Sometimes she felt like she just wanted to burn every bridge in her life and then jump off the last one as it burned.

A clap of thunder snaps her out of her thoughts. She inhales that slightly sickly sweet acrid smell of the dumpster and glances at her watch.

She's already used four minutes of her ten-minute break. She stares out into the drizzling rain and cries quietly for the remaining six.

26. The Little Man At The Top Of The World

ACCORDING TO JANGO, this time we can't fail. We choppered out to a remote part of the Himalayan mountains. Only Max would be allowed to continue onward, chaperoned by a group of acolytes from the Temple up towards a remote outpost.

The Temple has existed right here in the same spot for as long as man has wandered the Himalayas, which is a very long time indeed. There is one Guru and a host of acolytes.

Every year many world leaders and other global VIPs ask to meet the Guru. But they are almost always denied. The Guru meets with only a few people every decade. Alexander the Great spent a night at the Temple. John F. Kennedy came twice. Charlie Chaplin loved it so much he believed it was the spiritual center of the universe. After Hemingway spent a night here, he told a friend he was going to write a book about a fish catching a man. Ghandi spent a week here, and so did Khadafi, right before his surprising decision to abandon his prior terrorist inclinations.

Everything is prepared. Max will be arriving later in the day. I decide to spend my free time roaming the Temple's sprawling winter garden. Although I've never been much of a gardening fan, I'm amazed by the beauty of the place. Outside it's freezing and covered with snow. Yet inside the garden it's a tropical paradise complete with birds, butterflies and every flower imaginable. There's a symphony of bird and insect song. The atmosphere is warm and moist. Bright jungle colors everywhere. I expect to see Simba or that skinny little kid from the Jungle Book dart out from behind a tree at any moment.

As I walk along a path I notice an old gardener bent down on his knees. He smiles and stands up, his head reaching barely to my waist.

"Your garden is beautiful," I say, thinking at the same time that the man probably doesn't speak a word of English. But I'm wrong.

"Thank you," says the gardener. "Everyone at the Temple works in the garden to help it grow. Maybe this is why."

I agree. And somehow, without any coordination or invitation, we fall into step together. As we walk along the path side by side, I can't help thinking there's something Yoda-ish about him. Or maybe it's the other way around ... maybe Lucas or Spielberg ...

After a few steps, the gardener asks: "So you are the boy who seeks the secret to happiness, yes?"

"Well, I don't know if I'd put it that way. When you say it like that it sounds a bit ridiculous."

"There is nothing wrong with ridiculous, especially if it works for you."

The old man looks up at me with laughing eyes and a magical chuckle. There's something deeply soothing and inspiring about him. We continue our walk in silence. Then I decide to ask the question that's gnawing at me.

"There is no secret, is there?"

The gardener laughs. "Of course there is."

"Really?"

"Of course. But everyone already knows."

"How can it be a secret if everyone knows?"

"Everyone knows, but very few believe. And it is the believing that counts."

"So what is it?"

"You must find this out for yourself. I don't know, but maybe happiness is like a kiss. You have to share to feel it."

I look at him quizzically.

"Just remember, sometimes there are no shortcuts," he says with an enigmatic smile.

And before I can blink, he turns and vanishes from the garden.

*   *   *

When Max arrives at the Temple, he's immediately snapped up by the acolytes and escorted outside to begin his trek. They have to reach the high outpost by nightfall, and don't have a second to lose.

The hike up is rigorous, even for someone in as good athletic shape as Max. During the last few hours, he's blindfolded and led by the acolytes.

When his blindfold is finally removed, he finds himself sitting in a simple wooden room, cross-legged on a small rug made out of some sort of animal skin. A fire crackles in the fireplace. Incense burning over the centuries seems to have impregnated the walls, giving off a deep and serene fragrance. In front of him the Guru sits cross-legged, smoking a pipe, looking at him with bright friendly eyes. Max is instantly struck by the man's intense energy, as if he's surrounded by some sort of powerful aura. He looks ancient, or rather timeless. Like he's always been here, exactly the same.

Max has met many charismatic people throughout his life, but no one even remotely comparable to this little man. Modern politicians these days are digitally re-mastered, with think-tank spins and rehashed sound bites. They don't need charisma, they have media consultants. But this man is different. He is the charisma of the Ancients. The force of character that could inspire a whole continent of followers, without mass media. A magical magnetism. Max doesn't say anything. He just sits there, basking in the blissful calm. And the Guru seems more than happy just to sit there as well, puffing on his pipe.

Eventually the Guru asks: "What are you seeking?"

"What makes you think I'm seeking something?" responds Max.

"You hike up in cold mountains and sit here all night long with old man. You are seeking something."

"OK, but promise you won't laugh."

The ancient Guru shakes his head. "No. That I cannot promise."

"That's what I figured. Anyway, I'll tell you. I'm seeking happiness."

The Guru laughs and Max joins in.

When their laughter dies down the Guru takes a long and prophetic puff on his pipe. "Maybe that is your problem. Maybe you cannot seek it. Maybe it must seek you."

Max bursts into laughter. "Don't you think that's a bit cliché for a guru of your stature?"

"You tell me you seek *happiness* and you are surprised that my *response* is cliché?" The Guru's smile sparkles and they both laugh until their eyes are wet with tears.

The old Guru takes out a wooden case with two glasses and a clear unmarked bottle. He fills each glass high to the brim. For the rest of the night the two men sit talking and drinking together. They talk of nothing and everything. Of the stars, of time travel, of dreams, of love, of how wonderfully some combinations can become greater than the sum of their parts like strawberries dipped in chocolate, like a man and a woman. They talk of suffering and cruelty and death ... of beauty and joy, of their favorite books, of that tingly feeling in your leg when you sit on it for too long ...

By sunrise they're as close as brothers.

As they stand there, side by side, looking out the open window at the sun coming up over the mountains, the Guru turns to Max and says:

"Some of the Ancient Greeks believed that everything and everyone has a purpose. They called this *telos*."

Max considers.

"You look doubtful," says the Guru.

"Everything and everyone?"

"Try me," says the Guru with a playful smile.

Max thinks for a moment. "What is the purpose of man?" he asks.

"To change for the better," answers the Guru. "Perhaps if you find your telos, then happiness will find you."

*   *   *

When I meet Max at his return to the Temple, I can tell the result right away.

"Sorry," he says. "The Guru is the most amazing man I've ever met. And this is one of the most fantastic nights I ever spent. But I'm afraid you're not done yet." He steps into his chopper and calls out over his shoulder, yelling to be heard above the noise of the rotor:

"On the right track, maybe, but not done."

The chopper takes off, leaving me standing there, mired in failure, deep in thought. I feel like the Scarecrow losing my straw. Like the Tin Man rusting from the inside.

Jango joins me.

"We blew it again, Jango."

"Are you sure?"

I nod. I'm sure.

Jango is clearly distraught. He pulls out his satellite phone and steps away for privacy, explaining: "I must tell the Solutionist."

Moments later Jango returns. "This has never happened to us before, but do not worry. The Solutionist always succeeds. He has agreed to meet with you in person to brainstorm."

But I'm on the verge of a profound and frightening realization: *I am about to fail.*

I can feel it. My time is running out. And one thing for sure: failures do not stay on the Island. Max will surely ship me off. I realize with a sickening feeling that I'm just about to lose everything I've worked for all my life.

I cannot let that happen!

And then suddenly I realize something else. Something that chills my blood. Max is one of the smartest men I've ever met. One of the most ruthless businessmen on the planet. The very first day we met he used my coke idea to make thirty million dollars. Shortly after that I agreed to this ridiculous "happiness contract" where I'll lose the million dollars I already earned if I fail to fulfill the contract. Maybe once Max made the thirty million dollars from my coke idea, he had no further use for me. Maybe Max never intended to keep me on the team, and this whole happiness farce is just a way for him to get some kicks, take back my million, and throw me out like a broken, discarded plaything ...

Maybe Max is playing me for a fool. Has been from the start. The way he plays the whole business world. Manipulating everyone around him. After all, it would be fair game, wouldn't it? It's dog eat dog. Survival of the fittest. Natural selection. The law of the jungle. I feel my eyes grow hard and cold with determination.

And my thoughts now focus on one fact: *I have the black box.*

I can take control.

Jango has been staring at the internal wrestling match reflected on my face. Now he clears his throat uneasily. Maybe he's wondering why my expression has suddenly taken on a harder edge ... something resolved and determined.

"As I was saying, the Solutionist has agreed to meet with you in person to brainstorm," offers Jango with a worried smile.

"That won't be necessary, Jango. You and the Wizard are fired."

"Did I hear you correctly?" he asks, stunned.

"Does a mouse shit in the woods?"

I leave him standing there, incredulous, as I step into my chopper.

I've made up my mind. I haven't come this far to lose it all. I'm not about to let those millions slip through my grasp. I know what I have to do.

Do I have the guts to do it?

As the chopper pulls away, banking over the mountain peaks into the clouds, I feel myself standing on the brink. About to do something I never would have imagined myself capable of.

In that split second I realize that a human being is capable of anything. It doesn't matter what you think you might do or not do before the opportunity is presented. When it's just theoretical we'd all take the high road. Of course we would. But when it comes down to really making the choice, it's only then that you can truly know.

And I know now: *I have to destroy Max.*

27. The Revenge Of Mr. Singh

FEDERAL PROSECUTOR NIKI CARBONE sits in his cramped office cluttered with files, eating an exceptionally good chicken Parmesan sandwich and reading a legal brief. He's short for his height, but has made up for it by working out every weekend since he was a teenager, and thus now boasts exceedingly well developed muscle tone and a hairy chest to boot.

As he chews and reads, he's careful not to let the thick Italian sauce splash onto his papers. But despite his caution, a long string escapes from his mouth, swings down like a cheesy Tarzan and slaps onto a pristine white page, instantly splattering it with a dab of that famous secret recipe tomato sauce.

"Fuck," he says at the splotch. He looks around for a paper napkin amongst the clutter of his desk. None in sight. But a letter catches his attention in the *in*-box. He grabs it, opens it, narrows his eyes, cocks his head, completely forgets about the sauce splotch, and reads:

Dear Sir:

If you receive this letter, then I have been murdered, and I am telling you this so that you may apprehend the man responsible for my death. His name is Mr. Max Simon. You will not be able to indict him for my murder, for he will have been far too careful for there to be any

evidence against him. You will, however, be able to indict him for
fraud, the proof of which I have enclosed in this envelope.
Sincerely,
Gupta Singh

Carbone sighs. Occasionally he receives these types of letters, and
the subsequent investigation into their veracity always starts the same
way, with a call to that prick Gomez. Carbone clicks his mouse and a
webcam view of Gomez pops up on his computer, eating a tuna
sandwich and munching on potato chips while thumbing through a
magazine. As always when Niki sees Gomez on his screen, he
immediately thinks to himself how truly ugly the man is.

Gomez's bored supercilious webcam voice says, "Yo."

"I'm sending you a letter. I need you to scan it for prints or
anything else you can tell me about it."

Gomez answers without bothering to look up at the webcam,
"Deviant sexual solicitation?"

"No."

"Murder threat?"

"No."

"Then I'll get to it tomorrow," says the bored Gomez, still not
looking up.

But Carbone is Gomez's ranking superior. He sighs, flexes his
powerful trapezoids, infuses his voice with the requisite menacingly
authoritative tone and says: "Gomez, just do it and get back to me in
the next hour, OK?"

"Fuck you, Carbone."

"One hour," replies Niki, clicking off Gomez's image so that the
view could go back to the soothing screensaver with the sailboat
gliding past that perfect desert island sprinkled with shortcut icons.

Niki takes out the documents from the envelope—the ones that are supposed to incriminate the murderer—and starts reading.

They're mostly financial printouts. But as he reads on, his eyes go wide with amazement, the way you'd picture an archeologist might look when he stumbles onto an ancient scroll he'd been searching after for ages.

"Christ Almighty," says Niki under his garlic breath. "Rich prick fucks up big time ... That's sweet. Very sweet."

28. The Fall

EVERY SUMMER WITHOUT FAIL, Monsieur Antoine Leparv hosts what is beyond question the most important jet-set party of the year, hence the dispensation with any adjectival modifier which could otherwise be deemed to diminish the paramount significance of the occasion. It is referred to by all simply as "*the* Party."

On this day, the wealthy and famous flood the local airports around Saint Tropez with their private jets hailing from every major capital on the globe. So many helicopters ferry the guests from their planes to the seaside Côte d'Azur villa that the skies are literally filled with them, looking like a swarm of little noisy bugs from afar.

For Mrs. Katya Simon, this is surely one of the most important events of the year. For Mr. Max Simon, this is indubitably one of the most insignificant. Mrs. Simon loves the party because all the most glittery of the world's glitterati are here. Mr. Simon hates it for the same reason. Mrs. Simon makes sure she is snapped in photos standing next to all the stars most in vogue. Mr. Simon makes sure he is as far as humanly possible from anyone armed with a camera.

As Max and Katya step down from the helicopter, there is already a host of delighted laughing guests spread out over the estate with drinks in their hands and rapt smiles on their faces.

The steadfastly mercantile (thus constantly changing) winds of fashion this year are blowing short skirts for the female youth and brightly colored ensembles of exceedingly expensive fabric equipped with extravagant hats for their elder feminine counterparts.

As the Simons de-chopper, Katya is immediately snapped up by Madame Antoine Leparv, the hostess, and whisked away into a flutter of insatiable social butterflies. Thus forsaken, Max is now free to do what he's done every year in the past: head straight for the bar, cleverly set up next to the ocean-view overflow pool.

Max is ordinarily not a drinker. It dulls his senses, and slows him down. But a night like tonight warrants being both dulled and slow. It takes the edge off how insipid he thinks they all are. In fact, if he drinks enough, he can almost get to the point where he doesn't begrudge the whole lot of them for wasting his time with their fatuous socialite inanities.

From the corner of the bar and his eye, Max throws back a shot of vodka and looks out at them. There they are. Exploding in uproarious laughter with their picture-perfect teeth. So carefree, insouciant, full of vigor and robust joie de vivre. *Le beau monde*, the planet's finest specimens, all collected here at this tiny juncture of supremely conspicuous, seemingly boundless wealth. Everyone is perpetually smiling or laughing, reveling in the pure Olympian joy and privilege of being amongst each other, the uncontested consummate winners of the game. Ah ... the heady ecstasy of it all.

The women kiss each other lightly on the cheeks with European chic. Careful not to smear their cosmetics. Wearing fortunes' worth of jewelry. Exchanging seemingly euphoric greetings, bursting into showers of toothy mirth. Mercilessly taking in every flawed detail in each other's appearance. Eager to segway into private groups with scathing gossip about out-of-earshot friends and acquaintances.

Off to the side, the young crowd, with their impeccable tans and orthodontically sculpted dentition, are busily affecting bored indifferent looks while complaining about parents, friends and school, in slouching grammatical constructions where superlatives like totally rule the day. But under those calm, cool, designer label, expensively groomed exteriors, they're up to their necks in the jungle. Locked in that relentless bestial struggle between the alphas and the betas. In poor war-ravaged villages scattered across the globe it may be waged by physical strength and courage. Here, the battlefield is fraught with good looks and cool scathing quips.

And the older men. Many from modest backgrounds who've fought their way up through the plebian masses with their bare hands and risen to these golden summits. Casting off first wives like rockets jettisoning their burnt out stages in their giddy ascent to the heavens. Now splendidly groomed, draped in astronomically expensive smart casual, they shake hands warmly or grab each other in manly bear hugs with enthusiastic back slappings and hearty laughs. Some parade their trophy wives or girlfriends—those incredibly young, gleaming-toothed, long-shanked, perfectly-tanned, expensively-bejeweled, flawless specimens of feminine sensuality. Others bunch about in tight masculine groups smoking cigars, pursuing animated conversations that tend to oscillate from golf to politics, while forever gravitating back towards either money or sex. Laughing so heartily at what they're saying. Who cares if they're speaking tripe? At these lofty altitudes of success, pure crap is intrinsically *à propos*.

In the midst of all this unbridled euphoria, Max is fully cognizant that he personally effuses all the social animation of a tapeworm. But he's profoundly unconcerned. This is just an evening to endure, as painlessly as possible.

Alone at the bar, he looks out over the Mediterranean. He's sailed out there, right past this very house, so many times. How he prefers the solitude of his boat to the confines of these socialite beehives! He downs a glass of vodka and absently watches some middle-aged movie star whose name he can't bother trying to recall hitting on some bedazzled young thing with a portentous décolletage who just can't keep her eyes and hands off him.

He downs another vodka and scans the crowd ... mostly bipolar. One half just money: the industrial tycoons, bankers, etc., and the other half showbiz: some with money, some terribly without. There are novelists, talk show hosts, actors, DJs, movie producers, pop stars, and flocks of young angelic models with their pearly smiles and long silky legs disappearing into dresses and skirts cut so short they may as well be belts.

A burst of laughter erupts as some enterprising guest impresses a group of fun-loving onlookers with an all-too-sure-to-be-ill-fated attempt to remove a glass from the bottom row of a champagne glass pyramid that two staff-members spent the better part of the night erecting.

Meanwhile, as Max slaps down another empty vodka shot, a very different type of helicopter is setting down on the lawn ... A French police chopper.

The seriously drunk, wired, or stupid figure the police chopper is an excellent prank of some clever *m'as tu vu* showoff socialite, and grin approvingly. But the sober, or otherwise intuitive, realize that something is definitely going down.

Throughout the decades that *the Party* has raged on with its annually opulent extravagance, a police helicopter has never dared actually *land* here. It just isn't done. There are limits to be respected after all.

Assistant United States Attorney Niki Carbone, the federal prosecutor, steps down from the chopper flanked by two French cops and the French prosecutor with whom he coordinated those exceedingly ball-breakingly complicated extradition procedures. As he looks around at all these beautiful people, he breathes in deeply, savoring the moment—this exalted moment of glory.

Sure, these assholes have money. But *he*, Assistant United States Attorney Niki Carbone, has something too. He has power. The power of a whole state. In fact, at this particular moment he is wielding the authority of a nation. The most powerful nation in the world. A grand jury that *he* convened empowered *him*, Niki Carbone from Houston, Texas, to step off this helicopter and exert the awesome power of the United States of America, right in the very heart of *their* world! This, he congratulates himself, is the stuff of legends.

He is exceedingly conscious of the stares. One by one the rich sonzabitches stop doing whatever it is they're doing to stare at *him*. Taking in his every move. And right now he's looking around. Peering into them. His powerful hunter's gaze is stalking its prey ... searching for *someone* amongst them. The suspense has them holding their collective rich breaths ... who would it be? And slowly, dramatically, he spots him. Sitting over by the bar. Prosecutor Carbone smiles. He's got him now. He walks slowly towards his prey. Nonchalantly, with a commanding swagger that captures the very power he feels coursing through his veins.

Max, meanwhile, has his back turned to the advancing posse, sitting at the bar, listening to the barman talk about the dangers of global warming.

Niki Carbone stops with a mighty smirk behind his unsuspecting victim. He towers straight and tall from the summit of his five feet five inches frame, bearing down fiercely on his quarry like a great warrior, or some legendary hero, defender of the weak, enforcer of justice, pouncing with terrible righteousness. His men, yes, *his* men (whatever their difficult to pronounce frog names might be) stand fanned out behind him in respectful deference to *his* unquestionable authority.

He clears his throat and says, exactly as he rehearsed it on the way over, "Mr. Max Simon, I presume." But the presumed Mr. Max Simon doesn't hear him, so intent is he on blocking out the party noise. The spectators smile. This part was definitely not in Niki's script. And it riles him big time. He notices one of his men actually smiling in evident amusement. It's high time to reassert his command. He speaks up louder, almost in a shout, with a strange crackle to his voice (also not scripted).

"Mr. Max Simon?" he barks.

Max turns around slowly to face the formidable wall of law and order glaring down at him.

"I beg your pardon?"

"Are you Max Simon?"

Max blinks at them. Surprised. "Last time I checked."

Chuckles ripple through the crowd. Pissing Niki off even more. He bridles a well-honed law enforcement glare.

"You'll need to come with me," he snarls.

"What?" responds Max. At this point he's merely befuddled, convinced that whoever these jokers are, they've simply made some sort of stupid administrative error.

"I said," (louder) "you'll need to come with me. You're under arrest." Niki allows himself an inner appreciative smile. His show is back on track.

Max doesn't move a muscle. Unperturbed. Like most barons of industry, throughout his tumultuous business career, he's experienced various scrapes with the law—over tax and other financial matters. And armed with the most expensive attorneys on the planet, he's always emerged victorious.

"What is this about?" he inquires, looking up at them with an amused half-smile over his vodka shot. Serenely unflappable.

"It's about me arresting you now. I'm bringing you into custody back to the United States pursuant to a warrant for your arrest where you will stand trial for fraud." Niki spits out the words with a vengeance. He scans the audience as if fulfilling a sacred mission to protect them all against the forces of evil, trying his best to look like he isn't looking to see how everyone is looking at *him*. Everyone! Everyone's eyes transfixed on *him*, wielding the mighty power of a continent.

Niki's old grandmother used to tell him how the Carbone family could trace its ancestry directly back to the Caesars. Niki had always assumed that that was just a crock of shit, but nevertheless the thought of his Caesarean ancestors would flash back through his mind every once in a while, especially at moments like this when he's wielding such righteous governmental authority.

Of course he spends the vast majority of his time behind his ragged old desk in that pitifully decrepit miniscule office of his, not to mention his tacky studio apartment that practically cries out "loser." BUT, all that is beside the point, and has nothing at all to do with the pure exhilaration he's experiencing at this very moment.

And the best is yet to come. Now he, Niki Caesar, will publicly humiliate this jet-set socialite freshly descended from his private plane. The ultimate *coup de grace*. Now he is about to read this prick his rights like a common criminal from the gutter in front of all his super-rich gossip-mag perfect-looking asshole friends.

And that's when Max stands up, towering dramatically above the short Assistant United States Attorney, which alas, was also not in the script. Max is calm and imposing, almost regal as he says softly, "I'm sure this is all some mistake. In any event, let's have the courtesy to discuss the matter in private, so as not to intrude on everyone's evening." He smiles warmly, but firm and commanding. The music has stopped. Everyone at the party is silent, drinking up the real life drama unfolding before them, and oh-so-thankfully happening to *someone else*.

By now all eyes have singled out Katya. For the past few moments she's not been thinking about the welfare of her husband. All she can bring herself to think about is whether he will have the social tact to leave quietly with the police without drawing attention to the fact that she has any idea who he is, let alone actually being *married* to him.

Still calm as can be, Max looks directly at his wife and says: "Katya, let's accompany these gentlemen. I'm sure this will all be over very soon."

Now this is beyond any shadow of any doubt, the worst moment of Katya's entire existence. She is so deeply humiliated that she feels it jab into her heart *physically* like a butcher's knife, or more like some long jagged rusty serrated spike that someone is twisting around in her aorta. As the crowd's eyes turn on her like ravenous locusts, she just stands there, frozen, in shock. She looks feebly around, as if through some magical spell she could get all these people—most of whom actually know her—to somehow be deluded into thinking that Max is addressing someone else, someone standing behind her, a bit off to the side. But this futile charade merely inspires a few snide smiles, so she gathers her strength and says in something akin to a cracked whisper, "No, you can go on ahead," as if her husband were dashing off to the opera or a dinner date.

Again the snide smug smiles ... *oh, the shame of it all!*

Katya's reaction causes a flash of pained disappointment on Max's face. But it's almost immediately replaced by a stoic frown. He's not about to let all these bloodsucking vultures have the satisfaction of knowing how much it hurts. So he smiles for all to see.

And of course no one has missed the slightest iota of the reality show transpiring *live* before their eyes. Niki laps it up, every luscious drop. And now it's time for him to step back out onto center stage.

"You have the right to remain silent. Anything you do or say can be used against you in a court of law." He pauses to make sure everyone can appreciate the majestic irony of what he's now about to say. "And, if you can't afford an attorney, one will be provided for you free of charge." Oh yes, he relishes, *this* is grand! *Free of charge* he said—to this rich fuck!! Wait till he tells this story back home!

Max stands there with an annoyed, yet nobly tolerant smile as the French officers handcuff him. Still smiling, radiating regal self-confidence, he says loud enough for everyone to hear, "It seems these gentlemen would like to have a word in private with me. I'm therefore afraid that I must miss out on the pleasure of your company for the remainder of the evening. Do carry on though."

Everyone just stands there and stares. And then, perhaps inspired by a vein of Gallic rebelliousness, or perhaps simply by solidarity for one's fellow man ... somewhere, someone starts to applaud Max's fine bravado in the face of adversity. Though ragged at first, the applause is soon taken up by nearly everyone.

Needless to say, Niki's euphoria evaporates instantly. *He* is supposed to be the star of this. And yet somehow, this rich prick has just robbed him of it! Unfairly upstaged him! The fucking nerve!

Without waiting for Niki to instigate, Max starts walking— actually *leading*—the French policemen flanking him towards the police chopper. As he does so, he motions to Niki with his eyes, and says to the French cops in perfect French: "When you see bastards like him, it's no wonder you guys can't stand Americans." Niki, of course, didn't understand a word of what Max just said. But even a dog knows the difference between being kicked and being stumbled on.

He glares at the smirking grins on the faces of the two French policemen ... as if they were actually on that prick's side!

"Laugh it up while you can, you rich bastard, 'cause you're gonna pay!" Niki promises himself.

29. Getting Away With Murder

THE RINGING WAKES ME. I glance at my Island Com to see Max's name flashing on the screen, notice that it's the middle of the night, and touch the screen to put the call on speaker.

"Hi David," says Max's voice as if he were sitting at the foot of my bed.

"Hello Max," I mumble with that woken-up slur.

"Can you believe it? Just like the movies, they only give you one call."

"What are you talking about?"

"I got arrested in France. They're extraditing me to Houston on some sort of fraud charges."

"Fraud? That's crazy!"

"Yeah. There's a fanatic prosecutor leading a wild crusade against me. But Kramer will straighten things out. I need you to make sure his team gets me home as fast as you can."

"Of course. I'll call Kramer now and hop on the jet to ... where did you say?"

"Houston. Texas. Probably something to do with the takeover of an oil company headquartered in Houston some years back. I can't think of any other reason. I've never even been there."

"OK, I'll get on the jet right away."

"Good. Tape a message telling the team what happened, and get on that plane."

"I'm on it, Max."

"I'll see you in Houston. Christ! My time's up—"

And the line goes dead.

I call Gwen. "What can I do for you, David?" comes her voice from the air. Despite the late hour she sounds as fresh as a daisy.

"Hello Gwen. Max got arrested in France and is being extradited. I have to meet with the lawyers tomorrow morning in New York before going down to Texas. I was thinking it might be helpful if you come along."

"When would you like to leave?"

"Just as soon as you can make a short video of me telling the team what's going on."

Moments later I'm taping the message. Short and to the point. I explain that Max has been arrested on charges of security fraud and that I'll be flying over to organize the legal defense. No cause for worry, just a matter of showing the prosecutor the errors of his ways. Otherwise, as far as the team is concerned, it's just business as usual.

Then Gwen and I are in the sky.

It doesn't take long to wake up Larry Kramer and get him on the phone. Kramer made his fortune by keeping Halcyon clear of legal snafus over the years, so getting out of bed for his main client is no problem at all. After a few hours arranging things on the phone from the air, everything is set up for a kick-off meeting at 6:30 a.m. in Larry's office where we'll meet with the whole legal team, complete any required research, and then fly down to Houston to start showing the prosecution who they're tangling with.

I catch an hour of sleep on the plane before we touch down, and then continue to nod off in the limo on the way into the City. By

6:25 we're at the posh Midtown building and on our way up the elevators.

Larry meets us at reception. This is our first face-to-face. Larry's a real New Yorker. Born and raised in a tough neighborhood in the Bronx, and now living the high life in Midtown. He looks every bit the quintessential high-powered corporate attorney as he shakes our hands, welcoming us to his firm. Through a glass wall we can see the team of associates already hard at work on Max's case in a large conference room. As Larry prattles on with small talk, I'm thinking to myself that if I hadn't met Mr. Singh that night in Cambridge, I would have been just like those tired-looking associates in their Wall Street suits and starched white shirts slogging through eighty-hour weeks.

We've come to the end of a corridor. "David, if you don't mind, I'd like to have a word with you in my office down the hall before we start," says Larry. Of course Gwen doesn't need to be told. She goes straight into the conference room to meet the associates.

Larry opens the door and waves me into one of the armchairs in the "salon" area of his corner office, over by a floor-to-ceiling window with a stunning view of the skyline. We both sit.

"I'm afraid something very strange has happened," he says, handing me a piece of paper with what looks like a short letter written on it. "It's an exhibit to the prosecution's case. We just got the file about an hour ago. No one on our side knows about this yet but you and me."

I start reading. It's the letter from Mr. Singh to the prosecutor accusing Max of murder and fraud. Larry watches my face turn a whiter shade of pale with every sentence, right through my tropical tan.

"I don't believe it," I say after reading it twice.

"Well, whether we believe it or we don't, it nevertheless raises some very serious issues for you as the Trustee for Halcyon."

"What do you mean issues for the Trustee? I thought the main issue here was how to get Max out of jail before lunch."

"Well," says Larry. Then he clears his throat, like there's something he needs to get out of the way.

I watch him.

"I'm not so sure it's that simple," he says.

"What do you mean?"

"Well ... before we continue, here's something we received for you." He hands me an envelope. "We don't know where it came from. It was delivered this morning with no indicated sender."

I look it over. As he said, there's no return address. Just an envelope with my name printed on it. I flash him a puzzled look and he shrugs his shoulders. "I don't know what it is, but given the timing, I'd bet it has something to do with all this. Anyway, I had security scan it to make sure it's not a bomb or something. It's just one sheet of paper. Do you want some privacy?"

I shake my head and open the letter to read:

Dear Mr. Finnegan,

I am very sorry that events have transpired forcing me to have this letter delivered to you. Unfortunately, if you are reading this, then I'm dead. I'm dead because Max Simon killed me to eliminate the only man alive other than himself who knows about his crimes. I know how he illegally siphoned funds to get his operation up and running, and I know how some of his most profitable ideas were actually based on illegal insider information and fraud, and I know that he murdered my predecessor, Jimmy Bradshaw, as part of his plan. This letter was delivered to you because you hold the "key to the black box." In Max Simon's system that "key" is in reality the key to your misfortune and

premature death, for Max Simon will choose his moment and then
murder you as well, just as he murdered me and my predecessor in order
to keep his secrets safe. Unfortunately for myself, my predecessor did not
warn me as I am now warning you. If you value your life, heed my
warning and stop Max Simon from striking again before it's too late.
Sincerely,
Gupta Singh

If there's any whiter left to go with my facial pigment, I'm totally
there now. Lips drawn thin, eyes wide with alarm, I hand Larry the
letter with a trembling hand.

When Larry finishes reading it he looks over at me.

"I can't believe it," I say.

"It's strange," says Larry, "but I have to admit, the pieces appear
to be falling into place."

I look at him like he's crazy. "What pieces?"

"Think about it. You being hired and groomed to accept the black
box, then Singh mysteriously dying ... And then the strange way Max
dealt with Singh's body."

"What do you mean?" I ask, looking more worried by the second.

"We handled the legal side for Singh's body. Max insisted that he
be flown out to Bombay immediately. We spent a fortune to bypass
all the usual formalities. You know, like a medical examination and
death certificate, eventually an autopsy. We did it for Max without
thinking twice about it. Hell, the body was probably still warm when
they put Singh on the jet. Max told us he didn't want any
administrative red tape. Now I'm beginning understand why."

"But I just can't believe it."

"I think you mean you don't *want* to believe it, but deep down
you're beginning, like me, to realize it's true."

Larry watches me shaking my head slowly in disbelief.

"Want some coffee?" he asks.

I nod. He pushes a button on a small remote control device. A moment later a secretary comes in, looking very staid and secretarial. "Two espressos, Doris," says Larry. She nods and disappears.

"Holy shit," I say in an effort to jumpstart the dialogue.

"My thoughts exactly," says Larry with an edgy chuckle.

"So what now, counselor? How do we break Max out of jail?"

Larry's expression clouds over again like a doctor with bad news. "David, we both understand that one fundamental difference between a *trust* and a *company* is that the Trustee has a very special responsibility with respect to the assets he holds in trust."

"What are you saying, Larry?" My voice is cold and dry.

Larry can feel the sweat pouring into the finely combed Egyptian cotton fibers of his impeccably starched white shirt. The next few minutes are going to have an enormous impact on his life. This is show time. He's about to take the leap. "Well, I haven't thought this completely through yet ... but ... hell, David, you're a lawyer. You understand as well as I do. Max set the structure up so that it's independent. Halcyon is the benefactor of the structure, not Max. And *you,* David, are the Trustee, with the keys to the black box."

I look at him like he's just announced that Max is really an extraterrestrial.

He locks eyes with me. But we both know we're not talking about little green men. He's cutting through the bullshit now. Straight down to the bone. To the marrow inside the bone. The air is charged. It's that critically recursive moment in the history of mankind where Brutus still had time to pocket his dagger, turn back home and climb back under the covers with Portia. When Benedict Arnold could have avoided crossing the line and becoming such a wanker. When Judas could still have called off that supper before it's too late. At this crucially crystalline moment Larry is choosing sides. Opting for the devil or the deep blue. Poised between angel and demon. Staring down the barrel of that age-old dilemma of right or wrong.

With Max he'd seen the writing on the wall. Max was getting ready to ax him. And that ax would have spelled out his personal catastrophe with a capital C. His entire firm is built on revenue from Halcyon. His life depends on these revenues ... his mansion in the Hamptons, his beach house on the Cape, his penthouse apartment overlooking the Park, the Porsche he bought his wife to distract her from his occasional marital strayings, his Maserati, his wardrobe, the astronomical tuitions for his kids to go to those snotty prep schools. Every atom of his lifestyle depends entirely on steady revenues from Halcyon.

It didn't have to have turned out this way. He would have been happy to continue on as the humdrum lawyer he was before Max found him and turned him into *this*. But once you climb on, you can't climb off. You stay on, clinging for dear life, or you get thrown off. But you don't just climb down on your own. You can't. What about the mortgages? And how the hell could you tell the kids that they have to go back to public school? You can't go back. And now, this is his chance to hang onto the golden goose ... or rather to trade the old goose in for the new.

"I'm saying that as Halcyon's Trustee, you're legally required to act in Halcyon's best interest, and right now Halcyon's interests are in severe conflict with Max's interests. In such a situation the Trustee is required to block off any *interference* ... to protect the Trust from any conflict of interest."

"Let me get this straight, Larry, as attorney of record for the Trust, are you instructing the Trustee what to do?"

"Yes I am."

"And what would those instructions be, Larry?"

"As Trustee for Halcyon you're under a legal responsibility to protect the Trust's assets until this whole situation can be sorted out."

The door opens and Doris steps in with two espressos on a serving tray. A welcome interruption. She serves us and disappears.

We drink our java in silence. The only sound is the aggravating scraping of Larry's spoon against his coffee cup as he turns the long-ago-dissolved sugar nervously around and around.

I break the silence, my voice icy cold. "Are you saying that you want me as Trustee to block Max off from Halcyon?"

"It doesn't have anything to do with what I *want*, or what you want, for that matter. What I'm saying is that I believe it's your legal duty as Trustee for Halcyon."

"Larry, come on, this is Max we're talking about. Halcyon is *his*."

"Technically, you and I know that nothing could be further from the truth. He didn't want the fiscal burden of Halcyon so he put it in an interlocking Trust, and therefore Halcyon isn't his at all. Halcyon is held in trust, legally, by you. And if you don't respect your mandate as Trustee, then you become legally liable."

"Yeah, but as Trustee, I take my directions from Max."

"That's true only up to a point."

Larry takes a thick document from his desk and hands it to me. It's the Trust Agreement appointing me Trustee over Halcyon. "Take a look at clause 43.1."

I read out loud: "The Trustee is bound by law to request for removal from the list set forth in Annex 43-A any individual that the Trustee deems unfit to provide directions to the Trustee as set forth herein, such request to be submitted as soon as the Trustee becomes aware of the situation prompting him to proceed with such removal. The Trustee's request for removal will become effective only if the Attorney of Record for the Trust concurs with such request." I stop reading and flip over to Annex 43-A. "Max Simon" is the only name on the list, of course. I remain silent for a moment.

"So you think I'm required to deem Max *unfit?*"

"For Chrissakes David, the man's a murderer!"

"Well, as far as I know he hasn't been tried, convicted, or even indicted for murder."

"Yeah, and he's not going to be. He's too smart. Gupta Singh is already cremated and his letters could never be admitted as evidence in a murder trial. You know that as well as I do. That's where the discretionary authority of the Trustee kicks in."

"You really believe Max killed Singh?"

Larry nods solemnly. "I'm sorry, David, I know this must be a terrible shock to you, but we have to face up to the evidence and act accordingly."

I don't answer right away. Larry studies my face, trying to gauge my reaction. I let the silence settle in, then ask, "So how do you think Singh managed to set all this up, with the letter to the prosecutor, and this letter to me?"

"He must have sensed the danger, and hired a lawyer or someone to get the letters properly delivered after his death. I guess Max didn't see that one coming. Singh might be dead, but he's one of the only people I know who ever pulled something past Max, even if it's only posthumously."

"So, Larry, what do you recommend?"

"Well, let's take it step-by-step. First of all, based on what I've seen, I've already come to the conclusion that I can't represent Max. I've always been attorney of record for the Trust. Now there's a clear conflict of interest between Max and the Trust. It would be unethical for me to represent Max. I could get disbarred for it. But you know that, David."

"Yeah, I understand."

"The second step is for me, as attorney for the Trust, to officially advise the Trustee by registered notification that I've become aware of circumstances that force me to conclude that Max must be removed from Annex 43-A so that he can no longer operate any control or beneficial status concerning the Trust."

"Are you sure about that?"

"Yes I am, David. And I feel duty bound to act on it."

"And what then?"

"As Trustee, once properly notified by the attorney of record that an individual should be removed from Annex 43-A, you must respond. Either you agree to remove Max, or we can take the issue to court on an emergency injunctive motion. And I imagine you know how that would end."

I nod. "And if I follow your advice and take Max off the Annex. What would happen to him?"

"He'd be cut off from the Trust."

"From the Island?"

"Yes."

"And all the investment funds?"

"Yes."

Larry's voice is calm now. He's placed his bets, chosen his side, angled his play and formulated his strategy. And now he's about to play his final card ...

"David, have you given any thought to what Mr. Singh says in his letter about the previous holder of the key to the black box being murdered as well?"

I shake my head.

"Well, perhaps we should give Sal a call. He's the one who informed me about it. Might be better to hear it from the horse's mouth."

"OK," I agree. I can feel my voice is rough and gravelly, like I'm trying to wake up from a nightmare.

Larry pushes a button. "Doris, get me Sal on the line please." A moment later Sal's voice comes on speaker. "Hello Sal, this is Larry Kramer. I'm here with David."

"Are you there, David?" asks Sal's inimitable voice.

"Yes Sal, I'm here."

"OK, just a second while I switch to a secure line."

A click and Sal is back. I ask, "Sal, what can you tell me about the person who had the key to the black box before Mr. Singh?"

"Before Mr. Singh it was Jimmy Bradshaw. He was recruited for the Island right out of law school."

"And where is Jimmy Bradshaw now?" I ask.

"He left the Island two years ago."

"And where is he now?" I pursue.

"That's the thing. I'm afraid I don't know. Of course we like to keep tabs on these sorts of situations, so we contracted out a few searches with some top-notch players, but they all turned up nothing. I searched too. He seems to have just vanished."

"Do you think Bradshaw is hiding somewhere?" asks Larry.

"Let me put it this way," answers Sal, "If the people I contracted can't find him, then he's no longer breathing."

Larry watches closely as the fear shows in my face. "Sal, I have another question for you," I ask with a tremble in my voice. "How many other recruits have left the Island?"

Sal hesitates a beat before answering, then says, "None."

I gulp.

Larry's watching me. He knew it was a winning card. The only Islander who ever left the Island is *missing ... no longer breathing,* in Sal's opinion.

My heart is racing. I can feel the beads of sweat on my forehead. I fumble for a moment with my coffee cup, then say, "Thank you Sal, that's all for now."

Sal hangs up. I don't say anything. Larry lets a few silent seconds tick past, then says: "Given the present circumstances, I think I should go down to Houston and explain the situation to Max without you."

But I'm shaking my head. "No way. I can't let you do that."

"Let me ask you something, David, have you thought about the alternative?"

I face Larry head on. "I hear what you're saying, Larry, but I can't do it. I can't betray Max."

"Do you have the black box?"

"Yes. Back at the Island."

"I think you should go back to the Island now. I'll activate the master switch here so that by the time you get back, you'll have access to the codes. You'll be in control of the Island and all the funds."

I don't answer.

"Listen to me, David. Max is a murderer. You don't have a choice. Just think what would happen if you ignored my advice, posted bail for Max, and helped him keep control over Halcyon. This isn't law school anymore. The stakes are real now. You got yourself into this. And now you think you can just stand up and walk away?"

"Yes, Larry. As a matter of fact, I'm thinking to myself right now that I *can* and *should* just walk away. What's stopping me?"

"I'll tell you what's stopping you. Wake up! *What do you think Max would do to you when he finds out you know he killed Gupta Singh and Jimmy Bradshaw? You think he'd just leave you alone?*"

Larry lets his words hang in the air. He's said his piece. It's time for me to put up or shut up.

I stand and walk slowly over to the window, staring out at the city that never sleeps. All those people out there bustling around. Going about their daily lives ...

"I don't have a choice, do I?" I finally say, still looking out the window.

"Not if you want to keep on breathing. It's you or him."

"If we did this, how would it work?"

"Simple. With Max out of the way, you run the Island."

"But how would you deal with ... Max?"

"I have some contacts down in Houston who can make sure he gets into one of those constant jail brawls and never sees the light of day again. Another unfortunate victim of our deplorable penal system. Happens all the time. We'll give him a nice funeral, and everyone moves happily onward."

I wince at the thought.

"It's the perfect cover. Completely untraceable."

"What about the rest of the team? What would we tell them?"

"We stick to the verifiable official truth: Max gets arrested. He has an accident in jail. End of story."

"And what about you, Larry? What do you get out of it?"

"Besides the joy of doing a good deed and keeping you from being the next victim on Max's list?"

"Yeah, besides that."

"Nothing extraordinary. Just keep paying my legal bills ... plus a discreet bonus of five million dollars wired to my personal account to thank me for the good deed."

My voice is hard and grim. I turn to face Larry. "We'd be murderers. Could you live with that?"

"No, David. He's the murderer. We're just helping along the wheels of justice so that a real cold-blooded killer will be punished for killing two of his employees. And at the same time you save your skin and take control of a multi-billion dollar empire. Now how hard could that be to live with?"

30. Bayou City

ONE FINE EVENING IN NEW YORK CITY in the early 1800s, two brothers experienced an extraordinarily fortuitous run at the poker table. Although there were strident accusations of cheating from the less fortunate players, such aspersions were never substantiated, and thus deserve no further attention here.

Following time-honored tradition, the two happy winners found their way over to Madame Jane's, which, though admittedly a bit spendy, was nonetheless considered by one and all to be the finest brothel north of the Mason-Dixon line. Heedless of the expense, the suddenly wealthy brothers indulged in what witnesses unanimously recall as a highly festive evening.

Such establishments are traditionally teeming with well-wishers anxious to help the newly enriched improve their station in life. And that night was no exception. It turns out that one of the ladies with whom both brothers spent a very enjoyable portion of the evening had a cousin who was on the verge of closing a most advantageous real estate transaction. And, provided it wasn't already too late, if the brothers moved very quickly, it might just be possible for them to acquire the real estate in question instead of the heretofore anointed buyer who did not share the good fortune of having stopped by Madame Jane's.

The brothers were no fools, and would not, in any case, tolerate being bested by this unnamed upstart who did not have intimate knowledge of the seller's buxom cousin, and thus, as far as they could reckon, was less well positioned to rake in on the fabulous real estate.

The brothers were ultimately successful in purchasing the entire tract of land, which, after a relentlessly whiskey-infused negotiation, turned out to cost exactly the sum that the brothers still had left from their card winnings, appropriate deductions having been made, of course, for that excellent time spent at Madame Jane's.

It was thus with an elaborately printed Deed of Title in hand, but no money in pocket, that the brothers awoke the next morning to prodigious hangovers, only the dimmest recollection of why they had ever entertained the notion of buying such land, and a deep regret for the money they no longer possessed. They weren't quite sure where the property was. But they did sadly understand that it was way the hell south of New York, and somewhere off to the left.

The immediate question for the fraternal entrepreneurs was how to raise enough funds to finance their lunch, as well as an expedition down to the great territory of Texas, where they figured they would found a thriving city (which of course would bear their name) and generally become wildly prosperous.

It was at this juncture that one of the brothers had the brainstorm of selling off portions of their real estate empire to aspiring settlers, the proceeds from which they would use to fund their expedition. In order to acquaint the prospective investors with this rare and marvelous opportunity, the brothers drafted a brochure which spoke longingly of rolling hills, wide open plains, fertile land, a nearby river, and abundant wildlife. Although the rolling hills, wide open plains and fertile land were pure extrapolations of good faith, the brothers distinctly remembered that the seller, all trace of whom had since evaporated, had clearly mentioned abundant wildlife, and something about water.

The enticing brochure worked its magic, and soon the brothers had sold enough of their land and collected enough settlers to embark upon their journey southwestwards.

The brothers set off two days before the settlers, in order to scout out the area. When they finally arrived at their property, they were understandably surprised. The seller had guaranteed to them that the property was close to water. What he had neglected to disclose, however, was that the entire property purchased was in fact *under* water, and was, to make soggy matters worse, actually situated on a terrestrial geographic indention fifty feet *below* sea level.

In respect to the seller's reference to abundant wildlife, if one were to include mosquitoes and alligators in one's definition of wildlife, then the seller was, on this particular point, right on the mark. It would appear that the presence of marshland actually situated below sea level presents the finest breeding grounds that nature has ever devised for the mosquito. By day the mosquitoes were ubiquitously omnipresent, voraciously attacking any pore so hapless as to be uncovered. But it was at night that the mosquitoes truly came into their own, traveling in veritable marauding buzzing clouds, engulfing any living creature in their path. As for the alligators, it seems that the brothers had, quite unbeknownst to themselves, become proud proprietors of the tract of acreage populated with the highest concentration of alligators on the planet.

The brothers of course immediately realized the enormous predicament that the swamplands presented. The settlers—less than two days away—would not be pleased.

But despite the undisputed amplitude of the disaster, the brothers could not help but be overcome by the beauty of the place. It was as pristine and pure as the world when dinosaurs walked unchallenged. It was a throw from the past. A little spot on the planet that time seemed to have forgotten. Insects and birds filled the air with melodic wonders. It was beautiful!

And thus, as the sun began to rise on their swampy fields, without a word, the fraternal pair sat down on a convenient tree stump, stoked their pipes, rested their weary limbs and gazed admiringly out upon the poetic beauty of their kingdom.

A few days later, when the settlers set eyes upon the marshland that was now their new home, and compared this with the description made by the brothers in the brochure, their disappointment was very great indeed. So great in fact, that they seemed wholly impervious to the natural beauty of the site. Within moments they had fed both brothers to the alligators, hence the sad result that history remembers them simply as "the brothers" and the city they founded does not, as they had so fondly intended, immortalize their name.

In dire need of a namesake, the settlers strategically elected to name their marshland after a celebrated general currently in vogue, a certain Samuel Houston, hoping thus to attract his benevolent attention and the desperately needed financial support to allow their swampy settlement to survive.

With little or no choice in the matter, the settlers set about draining their new land. They dug trenches and trenches and trenches, which soon evolved into what, for no good reason anyone can remember, came to be called *bayous*. They dug literally hundreds of them everywhere in an effort to drain off the water. By the sweat of their collective brow they ultimately succeeded in creating such a comprehensive network of them as to earn the coveted appellation: "The Bayou City."

Thus having gained some headway against the swamp, the settlers turned to the second most pressing problem: *alligators*. Every morning, for three hours, everyone—including women, children, retards and cripples—would fan out to shoot alligators.

Now although alligators today enjoy a somewhat violent reputation, the truth of the matter is that these big lizards are rather slow and lazy, and certainly no match for angry white folk with shotguns. Alligators became the settlers' staple. They ate alligator stew, alligator chili, alligator porridge and caramelled alligator dessert treats. They of course made alligator shoes and handbags, and one settler is even rumored to have worn alligator underwear. And so the alligators gradually reduced in number, and eventually developed the notion somewhere in those couple of bundled neurons that nature bestowed unto them as a brain, to move their reptilian colonies further away from the settlers' new homesteads.

As to the mosquitoes, it wasn't until the arrival of DDT and other elaborate pesticides that the Houstonians' war against the mosquito showed any sign of progress. Nevertheless, despite the noxious chemical warfare, it is safe to say that to this day the mosquito still holds the cards.

Of course Max's mind is far away from bayous and poker games when he steps off the airplane and walks down the ramp to touch the concrete terra firma of Houston. But within a millisecond he does experience an encounter with a Houstonian mosquito as one lands on his neck. Normally he would just slap it away. But presently he has his hands cuffed in front of him, escorted by two federal Marshalls from the plane to the waiting car.

And so the creature feasts his full of Max's blood and flies off, heavy with his crimson load. Vermin parasites sucking his lifeblood. It's the beginning of what would turn out to be a very long day.

31. Et Tu?

LIKE ALL SUCCESSFUL CORPORATE LAWYERS, Larry never goes to meetings without taking along an associate or two. The king needs his court, after all. But this meeting is different. Larry is flying solo. He doesn't want anyone to witness what he's about to do. This one's off the radar screen.

The guard leads Larry inside the prison. A shiver tingles up his spine when the heavy reinforced door swings shut behind him with that horrible clanking thud. He feels overcome by a crushing ominous feeling of oppression, as if *he's the one* that should be kept inside instead of just passing through. He shudders and follows the guard into a small grimy room with two metal chairs bolted to the floor.

He sits down. Nervous as hell. He's never had to face up to Max before. And quite frankly he'd just as soon rip out a thumbnail with a rusty pair of pliers. He smells his armpits. Despite the deodorant he's starting to sweat like a pig. At the sound of the door grating open he snaps his nose out of his pit. Did they see him sniffing himself like a mongrel?

The door swings open and there he comes: *Max.*

How strange to see the powerful Max dressed in orange overalls wearing handcuffs! How quickly this shit can happen! Unbelievable!

With a friendly nod in Larry's direction, Max sits down and holds out his hands so the guards can un-cuff him. The guards walk out of the room, but before leaving, the one with the keys turns towards Larry and says, as if Max were a wild beast, "We'll be right outside if you need us. Just push the red button." Larry glances at the big red button mounted on the wall, and nods stiffly at the guard. The door closes and Larry turns to face Max.

"You know, I usually hate seeing lawyers, but I must admit, I'm glad to see you," says Max with his trademark smile.

But something in Larry's expression strikes Max as wrong. "What's the matter, Larry, you don't like my orange jumpsuit?"

Larry's not smiling. "I'll get right to the point, Max. I'm afraid I can't represent you any longer."

This catches Max broadside ... completely by surprise. A muscle twitches nervously in his face. Larry stares at that small patch of twitching skin. He *never* saw that before! Max had always prided himself on never losing his nerve. Keeping an even keel no matter what adversity he was facing.

Max is furious. And suddenly very worried. Trying to hold his anger in check. Urgently scrambling to figure out what's happening. "So what's the problem, Larry? Are the millions of dollars I've paid to your firm suddenly not enough?" There's a sharp edge to his voice now. Pleasantries are over.

"It's not about money, Max. And it's not my choice. The indictment is against *Max Simon* as an individual. This is not a corporate matter. There is no mention of Halcyon in the indictment. Thus the current legal situation presents a conflict of interest with Halcyon Trust. And as you know, I've always been attorney of record for the Trust. So plainly speaking, I can't represent you as an individual in this litigation."

Max's powerful eyes hold Larry in their glare. "You're joking."

Under Max's stare Larry cringes for an instant, then regains his nerve, trying to hold on to the thought that he's not the one in the orange jumpsuit. "No, I'm not joking, Max," he says as calmly as he can muster.

"You know damn well there's no difference between me and Halcyon. Conflict of *interest* you say? The only conflict that interests me right now is the one that's keeping me in jail. And after all I've done for you, you son-of-a-bitch, that should be the only conflict that interests you. Are we clear?"

And now, for the first time in his existence, Larry stands up to Max. For as long as he's known him, Max has treated him as some sort of office clerk. And that's just changed. "No Max, we're not clear. This isn't a game, and Halcyon is not your toy. Halcyon is a trust that's governed by serious legal principles, and those principles cause me to be bound by both legal and ethical—"

"Spare me the legal bullshit, Larry. I made you. I can break you. I'm in trouble now, and I need you to help me get out of it. Afterwards, if you want to play legal niceties, I'll let you talk with my staff and you and your teams of associates can bill the hell out of it. But right now you've got one thing to do: *get me out of here.*"

Larry shakes his head. "I can't do it, Max. I'm serious. I can't represent you, and moreover, as attorney for Halcyon Trust, I can't even talk to you further because of the conflict of interest this situation presents."

"I am Halcyon, and you fucking know it. And you, Kramer, are an asshole, and I won't have any trouble replacing you." But as Max says these words, he suddenly has a terrible feeling. Like a vice grip clamping down on his chest. To make things worse, Larry is looking at him with an expression Max doesn't like one bit. It reminds him of a cartoon character's smile when something delightfully horrible is just about to happen to his nemesis, like an anvil falling on his head, or a stick of dynamite exploding right behind his back.

"I'm sure you won't have any trouble replacing me, Max. Which brings me to our next order of business."

Larry is wearing that damn anvil smile again as he hands Max the first of the two documents he prepared. Max takes it and reads. It's a consent settlement for divorce. Looks like Katya didn't lose a second. All he has to do is sign on the dotted line and his marriage is over. Just like that. He takes the pen and signs without a moment's hesitation. He already knew it. His marriage was over back at *the Party* in St. Tropez. This is just the paper formality.

Then Max snaps up the second document. Unlike the divorce, the second document takes Max completely by surprise. His eyes fly over the text, but after the first few sentences he already knows what it is. A resolution by the Trustee cutting him off from Halcyon. Cutting him off from the Trust! *From his life!* He feels as if the air is being sucked out of his lungs. An uncontrollable spasm shakes his body.

... The anvil has fallen.

Max boils with rage. This despicable lawyer has betrayed him. Then another jolt of fear ... *where's David?* His eyes rush to the bottom of the document, the signature line with ... *David's signature on it.* Of course! The coup de grace. Brilliant! The perfect con! How could he have been so stupid? He suddenly has trouble breathing. His throat is dry. The vice grip on his chest is crushing out his life.

"Where's David?" he manages to say, his voice cracking. But he already knows the answer.

"Mr. Finnegan is merely acting as a Trustee must act pursuant to the law. He too is barred from any contact with you because of the present conflict of interest. We're just following the law, Max. If you have any dispute with how the Trustee is running the Trust, you can challenge his actions in court. Of course, you'd have to have a pretty clean conscience before challenging us in court, and as Halcyon's legal counsel we'll be advising Mr. Finnegan on this issue."

"I bet you will, you money grubbing traitorous bastard."

"At least I don't kill my employees."

"What?" screams Max. "What did you say? What do you mean *kill my employees?*"

Larry lets out a snorting contemptuous laugh. "Very good, Max. You should keep up that innocent act of yours. I figure you'll need it."

Larry stands up to leave.

Max stands up too, ready to throttle him. But before Max can make a move, Larry has pushed the red panic button and the guards pour in.

"We're done here," says Larry, heading for the door.

Max lunges. Furious hatred twists his features. But the guards grab him first. He struggles, trying vainly to break free. Never in his life has anyone restrained him. Never has anyone stopped him from doing his will. His self-control vanishes. He lets out a wild cry. But the guards deal with far tougher animals than Max every day. Within seconds they pin him down. Larry leaves the room, taking a last glance at Max before the door shuts.

Max fights back. Struggling against the guards. But of course he can't break free. He's no longer in that universe of his where he can do as he pleases. Where he can crush people like Larry in an instant. He's now back on Earth.

Welcome to Earth, Max.

32. Business As Usual

THIS IS LARRY KRAMER'S FIRST VISIT to the Island. He flew straight here after leaving Max screaming and kicking in that Houston jail.

Before now, despite a decade of tending to Halcyon's legal affairs, Kramer had never even set foot on one of the corporate jets—*despite* the fact that his office had drawn up all the documents for their purchase. Kramer had never seen the Island because he'd never been invited. Because Max liked keeping his worlds separate. Hermetically sealed. Max considered him to be part of the "off-Island" world. Just another cog in the wheel that kept his perfect universe in order, mused Larry to himself ... Pompous murdering bastard. He's got it all coming to him.

"More coffee, Mr. Kramer?" inquires a very beautiful voice belonging to a very beautiful receptionist or secretary, or something like that. They seem to be everywhere on the Island ... beats the hell out of Doris.

Kramer flashes his best smile. "Sure, that'd be great."

He's sitting in an open conference-room-terrace overlooking the ocean. It's every bit as wonderful as he'd imagined. And since he's just been given a private office on the Island with a private jet at his beck and call, he's in seventh heaven.

"I guess you won't be needing that anymore," says Larry.

I follow his eyes to the black box sitting on the table in front of us. "Yeah, I guess you're right," I say. I reach over, pick up the black box and throw it like a baseball from the outfield. We both watch it sail through the air and plunge into the waves.

Remaining staid and lawyerly on the outside, Larry nevertheless betrays an inner smile as he watches the black box disappear into the ocean ... *The reign of Max is over!*

Larry speaks up. "Perhaps we should go talk to the team before they start letting their imaginations run wild."

I nod. "When is it going to happen?" I ask.

"You mean Max?"

"Yeah."

"Tonight. In his cell."

"You're sure it will look like an accident?"

"Completely. It happens all the time. Those jails are fucking cesspools."

I sigh. "Are you positively sure about this, Larry?"

"Positively. And stop thinking about it. We've been through it a million times. You don't have any other choice."

*   *   *

Virgil, Stacy, Vlad, Flo and the others are all assembled in one of the big conference rooms when Larry and I walk in.

They look worried.

"Hey everyone, this is Larry Kramer," I say. They all nod. "As most of you know, he's been Max's lawyer for a long time. He's come here to talk about what's been going on."

I sit down, and Larry takes over. "I'm sure you're all wondering about the ... situation." He clears his throat. Their eyes bore into him. "Well," he continues, "Max has been charged with federal fraud violations. We're perfectly confident that he will prevail against the charges, so I think that you can consider it all just an administrative screw up." He looks around at the faces watching his every move. Weighing his words, sifting. "Be that as it may, during the process Max will not be involved in any of Halcyon's business. He'll be taking a break. You know, laying low until this blows over. You can think of it as a sabbatical. I would also like to stress that all the allegations are against Max as an *individual*. None of the allegations implicate anything concerning Halcyon. In other words, it really doesn't have anything to do with you or your business. This, as you can imagine, is one of the reasons that Max must distance himself at this time. It's just good business sense. And it's crucial to the smooth functioning of the Trust. As the Trustee appointed by Max, David will be running Halcyon for now, so you should really just carry on as before. Business as usual." Larry clears his throat again and looks at the young smart faces. They make him feel self-conscious and jittery. "Any questions?"

"Why doesn't Max tell us himself?" asks Stacy.

Larry chuckles as if something about the question might be amusing. "Listen, I'm just the lawyer. I'm telling you what I know, and what I've been told to tell you." He chuckles again. "But you know Max. When he wants to contact you he will." Larry glances nervously over the faces. "Any other questions?"

They shake their heads.

I stand up. "Thank you, Larry," I say. Then to the team, "I'll show Larry out. In the meantime we should get back to work."

After returning from walking Kramer to the jet, I don't have the heart to go back and join the team. Instead, I head for an empty conference room and plop into a chair. I look out over the water. One of the Island jets comes into view, whisking Larry back to New York.

Good riddance, I think to myself. I'm starting to like lawyers less and less every day.

33. In The Bowels Of The Beast

A JAIL IS THE CITY'S UGLY HIDDEN UNDERBELLY. The festering boil on its butt. Try it. Take any beautiful modern city. No matter how affluent or sophisticated. Take a peek at its jail. You can't even begin to imagine until you step inside. The filth. The violence. The constant threat of being assaulted and raped. And with AIDS raging in the double digits ... well, you get the picture.

And here's Max. Lying on his back in one of the four narrow bunks bolted to the wall of his cell. The other bunks are empty. Ever since meeting with Larry this morning, he's been lying here, turning the situation over and over in his mind. Analyzing it from every possible angle. And now he's decided that any way you look at it comes down to one inexorable conclusion: he's screwed. Big time. How could he have been so stupid? His cocky overconfident arrogance has finally crucified him. Now with hindsight he can see it all as clear as day.

And so now what? What will their next move be? Now that they've put him here ... By now they've opened the black box. They have complete control of the Island and they've cut him off from everything. Island Security will make sure he can't contact anyone on the Island, and that no one can contact him. And of course they've cut off his credit cards and access to funds. But what next?

... And then, with a sudden jolt of fear, he realizes what's next. *Of course! This whole jail thing is just the setup!* As long as he's alive he's a threat to them. Their plan is excellent. Jail is the perfect setup to eliminate him for good. Now they're going to kill him. Without a trace. Without any possible suspicion that could boomerang back to them. He feels his entire body break out in a cold sweat. The bile rises in his mouth. He wants to vomit, but holds it back. He must retain his dignity. Try to calm down. Try to think—

—But what's that noise?

The lock turning. The door opening!

His heart skips a beat and slams into the pit of his stomach. His upper lip quivers uncontrollably. Stand up? Or stay on the bed sleeplike? Panic-stricken paralysis opts for the bed tactic.

Through closed eyelashes he watches the door open. In walk two huge men and a third smaller guy, all sporting the same orange overalls. The door swings shut behind them. Locking them in. Locking them all in here together!

Is this it? The execution squad? Or just the arrival of his cellmates?

He keeps his eyes closed. Pretending to be asleep. His heart pounds in his chest so loud it's a wonder they don't hear it.

"Say Snowman, we gotta neighbor," says the smaller guy through Max's semi-closed eyelashes.

"Fuck yeah," agrees one of the others.

Max feels them towering over him. He wonders whether it's time to sit up. Stretched out like this he feels horribly unprotected and vulnerable. Like a beached jellyfish. But at the same time maybe ignoring them and keeping perfectly still will work, like the safari leader said to act around marauding beasts during that last camping trip in the African bush. Or these might just be normal regular prison inmates. Not assassins. They might even become friends. A sort of

Shawshank Redemption thing. He can smell the visceral animal fear oozing from his pores. His pulse thunders in his head. Kaboom, kaboom, kaboom—

"You think he's sleeping?"

"Nah, he ain't fuckin' sleepin'."

"Yeah he ain't sleepin'. He's fuckin' playin' possum."

This cracks everyone up. Perhaps the safari strategy needs urgent revision. *What to do? If only this nightmare weren't happening. If only he could just wake up in his bed on his Island. Gotta keep calm!* OK, time to sit up. Slowly. Stretching like he's just waking up from some nice dream.

"Hello," says Max.

The three men cackle. Enjoying themselves thoroughly.

"Told ya he wasn' sleeping."

The smaller guy, apparent talker of the bunch, steps forward. "This here's Snowman." He motions to the huge muscle-bound giant. The white jolly carrot-nosed image the word "snowman" typically brings to mind has no business here. The man staring down at Max with a sadistic smirk is solid meat. Not the slightest bit jolly. He looks terrifying. The flesh and blood version of Max's worst nightmare.

"Hello, Snowman," says Max.

Snowman doesn't so much as nod. His eyes are deep dark pits of cold brutality.

Max feels the clammy sweat coating his body. *Must keep calm ...*

"Well, I think I'll try to catch some sleep," says Max with a friendly nod. He starts to lie back down like he's just hankering to doze off for a catnap.

"Not so fast, old man. Snowman here ain't finished talking to ya."

Of course so far Snowman hasn't said a word. But who's arguing with that? Max looks up at him. Trying at least not to appear petrified. Snowman's cohorts grin in anticipation of all the good fun to come.

"So you in the mood for some lovin'?" says the smaller guy. "Cause Snowman here likes you."

Max looks at them each in turn. Wearing his deadpan poker face, or at least trying to despite the quiver in his lip, now spreading to his cheek. So this must be it ... This must be the death squad sent by David and Kramer to finish him off.

"So what ya say, Gramps?" prods the smaller one. All smiles.

"No thanks," says Max, hoping the tough sort of Clint Eastwood edge he's trying to put on his voice will do the trick.

The towering men smile and chuckle like Max is quite the comedian.

Max nods along, hoping for the best. Then suddenly his world morphs into one of those fast-motion blurs we're so used to seeing in action films. Snowman's friends grab Max's shoulders while Snowman unzips his fly and pulls out what looks like a fire hose. Max tries to break free. He manages to stand up. Icy horror courses through his veins. He feels like a cornered beast. He struggles with all his force. He catches sight of some blurry mass speeding towards his face—too close to focus on—as a huge fist smashes into his jaw.

Pain blazes through his skull. He staggers backwards. They're laughing at him. Of course they are. Any one of them could easily overpower him. With three of them it's not a fight, it's a joke. Three monsters toying with their comically helpless victim.

And in the split second that Max tallies up the confrontational odds, he realizes he's at a terrible crossroads. A grotesquely macabre decision tree. What is happening? Have these animals been hired by David and Kramer to kill him, or is this just random prison violence? If they're assassins then he has no choice but to fight to the bitter end. But if these are just common jail brutes he still has a chance for survival. He could submit and live. No one in the outside world would know about it, after all. It would be a temporary ordeal of pain and humiliation. But then he would emerge alive and go on living.

His tormentors grin at him, enjoying the good time. And as he ponders his choice he realizes he doesn't have any idea what he's going to do. He's never thought about something like this before. As if his entire being has been stripped back to some pre-formatted version. On the one hand it makes logical sense to at least attempt to live. To bow down and suffer the indignity rather than be beaten into a bloody lifeless pulp. But then on the other hand ... he stares back at the three men.

These completely new thoughts buzz through his head, waking up parts of him he didn't even know existed. As he gazes into the eyes of his tormentors, he feels a strange adrenalin pumping through his veins. Something amazingly bestial. He's no longer answering to logic. Some subconscious circuit breaker has been tripped. He suddenly hates these men with all his force. A force he didn't even know he possessed. Of course the analytical intellectual Max realizes he doesn't actually hate them personally. He has nothing against the humans that must lie somewhere buried inside; he just hates what they represent. Hates the cruel evil automatons they've somehow become. But that's now beside the point. Now he's beyond all that. Now locked into this crazy tornado spinning so incredibly fast. And deep inside his own heart he's feeling this amazing surge of strength. As if every cell in his body is now pulling together as a team. As if the whole Maximus Simon show is now being played out here in this dirty smelly dark cell. The final bouquet, the ultimate curtain call. Who would have thought it would all come down to this? But now it's time. Yes, it might be time to go down, but he's decided he's not going down without a fight.

Without even thinking about it he opens his mouth and roars.

It's a roar straight from some jungle savannah in his prehistoric past. A powerful lion, erupting from the deepest recess of his soul. When his assailants hear the roar, it surprises the hell of out of them. They've never heard someone scream like that. And they're not easily surprised after all the shit they've seen during their screwed-up lives.

Accompanied by his battle cry, Max charges into them. Blindly. Hopelessly. Flailing wildly like an enraged beast. He feels another fist slam into his face. The crunch of teeth snapping off at the root. The blood in his mouth. He spits out a few of those magazine-smile teeth.

Adrenalin shunts off the pain. Only fear and rage now. Lashing out wildly. Swinging, kicking.

He hears the fists crunching into his skull, but it registers only as a cold numbness, as if this whole hellish nightmare was somehow happening to someone else ...

34. Ain't Dead Yet

FOR A BRIEF SECOND, Max has no idea where he is. Then it all comes flooding back. Washing in like a frozen tidal wave. Bringing it all home with a sickening stab to the heart.

He's here—in prison. Really. No waking up. This is it. Hideous images of the monsters attacking him last night flash before his eyes like a strobe. He blots them out and tries to take stock. His eyes are swollen almost shut, but he can see that he's somewhere else. In some other cell. A smaller one, this time with only one bunk. Lying on his back.

His head feels like it's been crushed under a steamroller. Slowly sitting up, every muscle is a jab of pain. But all the major body parts seem to be present and accounted for. No broken bones ... a miracle.

He runs his tongue over the torn holes and jagged stumps where his teeth used to be. His hair is matted and clumped with clotted blood. At various spots over his face and body are bandages with stitches underneath, so the prison doctor must have treated him.

Head pounding. What time is it? Never mind. The real question is how come alive? How is it possible? If Snowman and his jolly bunch were sent by the David/Kramer Show to snuff him out of the picture, then he shouldn't be breathing. Unless of course the fight was miraculously broken up by the guards before his assassins could finish him off.

... Or perhaps Snowman was just a normal prison thing, and the real killer will be walking through the door at any moment.

But his head is spinning far too fast to keep these thoughts together, much less make any sense of them. He's having trouble just trying to keep his eyes open and his mind switched on. He lies back down and curls himself into a fetus, letting himself sink back into blissful unconsciousness.

The sound of metal grating against concrete makes him bolt upright. The door to his cell swings open. A terrible pain rips through his chest at the idea of reliving the terror of last night.

He holds his breath as a huge black man steps into his cell. This guy is *huge.* One of those XXXXL T-shirts would be snug on him. Like those terrifying creatures he saw grouped together in the "recreation" yard when they escorted him into his cell. Huddled together like some sort of tribal herd listening to that dreadful techno-rap, speaking in that unintelligible southern ghetto patois, lifting weights non-stop, with muscles so huge they make Schwarzenegger look like a pansy.

But wait. This guy isn't wearing orange overalls. He's wearing some sort of baggy brown suit that looks like it was cut by Neanderthals with flint scissors. And he seems more like the deep fried, loaded-with-carbs-and-sugar type. In one hand he holds a folding chair, while the other hand clasps an old battered briefcase. The door slams with a jarring metal thud behind him.

Max watches as the man methodically unfolds the chair and sits. The chair strains under the weight. For a second Max wonders if it's going to collapse. But it holds. Now settled in, the man takes up his briefcase and looks at Max. Nodding at his bruised and swollen face. Returning his stare.

Whoever this guy is, he's not an assassin.

"Who are you?" asks Max gruffly.

"I'm Tyrone Jones, your court-appointed attorney."

Max looks at him with a scowl, like he can't believe this is happening to him. And in fact that's exactly what he's thinking. Ever since this whole nightmare started, he really can't believe this is actually *happening* to *him*.

He just can't believe it.

All his life he's been pampered. Everything he wanted, exactly how he wanted all the time. Always protected, surrounded by a bastion of loyal advisors and employees, sheltered from any legal difficulties by teams of highly paid attorneys.

And now he feels like a cornered beast. No, he doesn't just *feel* like a cornered beast, he's actually *become*, for all practical purposes, a cornered beast. Kept in a cage, treated like an animal. Waiting to be executed.

On top if it all, to ice the cake, it appears that this Mr. Tyroown, or whatever the hell his name is, is now supposed to be his lawyer! How could this be happening to *him?*

"You're wondering why I'm so fat, ain't ya?"

"No," replies Max. It's true that Max is wondering how that huge girth could possibly lodge itself on the comparatively small chair that must cover only a minute portion of the surface area of either of those monstrously enormous butt-cheeks. But more to the point, he's already decided he's better off defending himself than teaming up with this jumbo-sized clown, and now he's simply formulating the best response with which to shoo him off like a colossal fly. "I'm wondering if you went to law school," he says, looking Tyrone straight in the eyes.

Tyrone can't believe his ears. *Who is this honky asshole?*

As a court-appointed social services lawyer, or "public defender" as he prefers being called, Tyrone has come into contact with about every brand and variety of two-footed scum and lowlife on the planet. But this one seems to be of a species he hasn't run into before. He's tempted to just get up and walk out of there. To leave the cocky white mothafucka sitting there in his orange overalls. He could go straight to the assignment magistrate and get this buttmunch cracker reassigned. Yeah, reassigned to some white guy who works as a public defender for this shit pay, despite the fact of his whiteness and therefore relative ease of getting a real lawyer job, which should give you a pretty good idea of how shitty a lawyer *he* would be.

But Tyrone reminds himself that he chose his job to defend those poor bastards caught up in the system who needed defending. And this cracker with an attitude needs a whole lot of defending real fast before he finds himself at the wrong end of a lotta pointy sticks. So, true to his ideals, Tyrone doesn't stand up and leave. But he doesn't roll over either. "What'd you just say?" he asks.

But Max is in no mood to mince words. "I was just wondering if you went to law school," he replies, deadpan.

Tyrone returns his stare. "Yes I did, Mister ..." glancing into the turd-brown government file he's holding, "uh ... Mister Max Simon. Yes, I did go to law school."

Tyrone stares at him, amazed. Fascinated. This asshole's a real piece of work. Truth is, Tyrone is no novice to insults. In fact, you could say that Tyrone is a seasoned expert in the world of insults and ridicule—both spoken and unspoken. It's the unspoken variety that stings the most. Those stares that tell you they're thinking foul thoughts about you, but leave you guessing as to the specific target of their contempt. Race? Class? Physical appearance? Open scorn at the rampant obesity? Hilarity at how his bulk engulfs and spills over chairs?

It is thus most likely Tyrone's vast experience on the recipient end of humanity's venting of bile that enables him to sit there calmly. And unlike some of the public defenders who defend humanity's impoverished downtrodden across the nation, Tyrone does not work as a public defender solely and uniquely because he can't land a higher-paying job. Tyrone works as a public defender also because he knows that otherwise the poor slobs caught up in the system who can't afford an attorney are 100% certain to get royally reamed.

If you have the funds to hire a team of hotshot lawyers like O.J. Simpson, then the system lets you walk (at least the first time around). But with a court-appointed attorney who doesn't give a rat's ass about yours, then you're screwed. Reamed to the bone and then some, no matter what you did or didn't do somewhere back at the beginning of that long chain of events that ended with you sitting in jail waiting for your day in court. And so Tyrone sits there, looking at Max, wondering how exactly he wants to react.

"Listen, I don't need your shit," he decides to say. "And I ain't the one dressed up in the fuck-me-in-the-butt orange jumpsuit. But before I get up and walk outta here, I'm gonna tell you, just in case you don't know, what's going to happen to your sorry mothafuckin' ass. After I leave here, you're gonna eventually be put back into a cell with some other prisoners. And of course you're gonna be considered a white mothafuckin' bitch 'cause you ain't exactly the type who already spent time in the joint. Which means you gonna experience every kinda fucked up abuse known to man, and I ain't gonna paint the fuckin' picture for you, 'cause I think your imagination is probably doin' a pretty good job of that right now. And maybe you'z innocent, but you see, the system don't give a fuck. When you in the system, the system fucks you over so bad before you even get to trial, that it don't matter if you'z innocent as the fucking Pope, you're still fucked. So, Mr. Buttmunch Cracker, I wish you good luck."

Tyrone gathers his briefcase to leave.

Few people in the world have ever been able to shake Max's confidence. Yet, at this moment, Max has never felt so terrified and defenseless in his entire life. And whatever Max's character flaws, it cannot be said that he lacks the capacity for lucid self-critical analysis. And thus, as Tyrone concludes his soliloquy, Max has already completed his emotional 180-degree pirouette, and is now reconciling himself with the incongruous fact that Tyrone is, at this precise moment, his greatest ally.

Max stares at him for a second and smiles. "Sorry. I've been having a very bad day, and I suppose I'm a bit edgy."

Tyrone stares intently into Max's eyes for a good long time. Max returns his stare, and the two just sit there, in silence, looking into each other's eyes, trying to figure each other out.

As Max stares at the huge man, he decides he likes this Tyrone after all. "Mr. Jones," says Max, "upon careful consideration, I would be deeply honored if you would represent me as my lawyer."

Tyrone keeps on staring for a beat, then bursts into laughter. "You are one strange mothafucka," he says.

"I'll regard that as a compliment."

"Good," says Tyrone. "Now let's get down to business. By the looks of you, I'm thinking you don't have a clue about how the system works. Right?"

Max nods.

Tyrone is reading the file. "Hmm ..." he says at last.

Max watches him read. "So?"

Tyrone looks up at Max with a different eye. He's just read the file for the first time. And it turns out Max isn't your usual humdrum indigent defendant.

"So, Mr. Simon it looks like you're one lucky mothafucka."

"I don't know what they taught you in that law school of yours, but could you tell me what part of being locked in here with a bunch of rapist killers who want to murder me makes me *lucky?*"

Tyrone laughs. "The report says the guys who did your dental work were hired to kill you and make it look like just another prisoner getting fucked by his friends."

"Well I guess they're right."

"So I was saying you're lucky 'cause the prison guards saved you before you got your ass killed. And that doesn't happen too often around here. Usually they're pretty good at getting the killing done before the guards get there."

"I guess for once in my life my big mouth saved me."

Tyrone squints his huge eyes at Max. "You say your big mouth saved you?"

"Yeah. I roared."

Tyrone laughs. "Now I've heard of some strange shit in my time ..."

Max laughs with him. "I did. I actually roared like some wild beast. I think everyone in the whole prison heard me."

"Well. It worked. It saved your ass, and they've even put you in the *program*."

"The witness protection program?"

"Naw. Shit no. In the witness protection program they're really interested in keeping you alive because they want your testimony, so they do all sorts of shit for you like giving you a new name and relocating you and protecting you and shit."

"So I won't get that?"

"Hell no! They don't give a fuck about you 'cause you ain't a witness, you're just a prisoner. They just don't want you to get whacked in their prison. So they seal the file so no one knows where you are and they let you out on bail so if you get whacked outside it's your own fucking fault and no one blames them."

"OK, I get the idea."

"That's why you got such a nice pad to yourself here, and why I can probably get you out on bail today."

Max's face lights up. "I can get out today?"

"Well, you're going to have an emergency bail hearing this morning. If all goes well you'll be able to walk out of here and not come back until your case goes to trial."

"And if things go badly?"

Tyrone shrugs. Max winces.

"Now tell me, you got some money to pay bail?"

"At the moment, I'm afraid I don't have anything."

This surprises Tyrone. He'd been betting on a very different answer. "Let me get this straight. Before you got arrested, you had money, right?"

"A few billion."

"Fuck! Really? No shit? A few *billion*?"

"About ten billion."

"Fuck me!"

Max nods. Like some sort of synchronic gesticular duet, Tyrone falls into a perpendicularly opposed rhythm with Max's nods, shaking his head in disbelief. "Well fuck," he finally says to sum it all up.

"Yeah. They have me pretty good. My structure is set up airtight as an independent entity. I didn't own anything in my name. Nothing. They turned the structure on me. I didn't see it coming. But it's just as airtight as I built it. It won't be easy to get back in. And by now they've fixed up the legal side so it's as if I never existed. I was so damn sure of myself, I didn't even bother setting up a safety net."

"Fuck."

"Yeah. Hubris I guess."

"What?"

"Never mind. For all practical purposes, at the moment I'm broke."

"OK. Anyways, your record's clean, and they think someone's trying to whack you, which they don't particularly want to happen here in jail before your trial, so I think I can get the court to keep your passport and let you out on recognizance."

"That would be great."

Tyrone looks down at his turd-brown folder. "But I got something I need to ask you first."

"What?"

"Who the fuck is Gaptan Singer?"

"Who?"

Tyrone takes another look at some document in the folder to fine-tune his pronunciation.

"Gopta Sing," he ventures again.

This furrows Max's brows. Tyrone studies his reaction. He's accustomed to his clients lying through their teeth to him about their heinous deeds, and has acquired a certain skill over the years of sifting the wheat from the bullshit.

"What are you talking about?" asks Max, with what Tyrone concludes to be sincere bafflement.

Tyrone reaches into his file and hands Max a copy of the letter Mr. Singh wrote to the prosecutor, now appended to the indictment as an exhibit.

Max reads the letter, his hands trembling with rage.

"So who was he?" asks Tyrone.

"Gupta Singh," replies Max. "He was my oldest and most faithful employee."

Hearing it pronounced right prompts Tyrone to glance back at the name. "*Gupta?* Shit. What was he? Chinese or something?"

"Indian. From a very old and noble Indian family."

"So why'd you kill him?"

"I didn't."

Tyrone stares at him, still skeptical, but ready to be convinced.

Max frowns his eyes at Tyrone like he's missing the obvious. "Of course I didn't kill him, Tyrone. Singh was like a brother to me."

Max reads the letter again. His eyes burn with a deep fiery glow, then suddenly shine with enlightenment.

"It's *him*. He set the whole thing up."

"Either I'm a rat's asshole, or you're lookin' like you just figured out something."

Max looks at Tyrone, eyes still flaming. "You're no rat's asshole, Tyrone."

"Tell me about it."

"*He* did it. He framed me and stole everything. He wrote this letter to the prosecutor with falsified documents making it look like I committed fraud. And he tricked that stupid-ass greedy lawyer into excluding me from the Trust. And by now he has the codes to the black box so he's taken control of the Island and cut me off from my money and anyone who could help me."

"Who is *he*?"

"*He* is David."

"Who the fuck's David?" asks Tyrone, watching the anger burning in Max's eyes.

"David is someone I trusted. And he betrayed me."

"Well, that sorta shit happens," observes Tyrone with a philosophical nod.

"That's true, Tyrone. And when something like this happens we want revenge. It's all perfectly natural. Perfectly human. Very Count of Monte Cristo."

"Say what?"

"I was referring to David."

"What about him?"

"I'm going to kill him."

"You shittin' me?"

"No. I'm not, Tyrone. *Lex talionis* ... eye for an eye, tooth for a tooth. He destroyed my life, and I'm going to destroy his. He won the first skirmish. But it's not over yet. I'll bide my time. And when I strike it will be lethal. I have nothing to lose. I'll look him in the eyes. Into his traitor eyes, and I'll kill him."

*   *   *

The courtroom is modern and functional. With all the charm of a post office. The judge is in her fifties with eyes like a pair of shotguns.

Because Max has been put in the *program* following his attack, his entire file is sealed and the courtroom is cleared of everyone but the Marshalls and attorneys. The court clerk calls out the case: "United States v. Maximus Simon" and Max is led by a Marshall into the courtroom, over to the Defendant's desk and seated next to Tyrone, who smiles at him with an upbeat wink.

Max notices Niki Carbone sitting at the prosecution table.

The judge looks out over her reading glasses. "Would counsel please approach the bench?" Tyrone and Carbone step up to her.

"Hello," she says in an absent monotone without looking at them, reading the file. "Mr. Jones, do you represent the Defendant, Max Simon?" She looks down at him from the bench.

"Yes, I do, Your Honor," says Tyrone.

"And, Mr. Carbon, I see that you oppose the motion at bar." The judge pronounces his name like the element from the periodical table.

"Yes, Your Honor, the Government does oppose the motion, and it's Carboné, Your Honor."

The judge looks over her spectacles straight down at Carbone. Her glare says that she has a very full docket to get through and doesn't care the slightest how he pronounces his vowels. She peruses the documents in front of her. Carbone is about to speak but puts a clamp on it when he sees the judge purposefully turn to face Tyrone.

"Mr. Jones, does your client possess any assets, or have the ability to pay bail?"

Tyrone shakes his head. "No, Your Honor, he doesn't."

Carbone scoffs theatrically. The judge looks over her glasses at him again, clearly not a big fan of his brand of theatrics. "The prosecution has something to add?"

"Your Honor, the Defendant is very wealthy. He probably has assets hidden all over the world. When he was arrested, he was at this party for billionaires in this huge mansion in the south of France. He's clearly a flight risk, and I would urge this Court to hold him without bail."

Behind them, Max Simon, (the creature they're talking about as if he weren't there) sits at the defense table flinching at the thought of going back to jail.

"Mister Carbon," says the judge, "do you have anything to submit in evidence to substantiate what you've just asserted?"

Carbone bites his tongue. "No, Your Honor."

The judge continues, "Does the Defendant have a criminal record?"

"No, Your Honor, but—"

"Has the Defendant ever evaded the jurisdiction of this Court before?"

"No, Your Honor, but—"

"Mr. Carbon, are you aware that the Defendant was assaulted during his first night in custody?"

"Yes, Your Honor."

"And are you aware that the warden and the Marshall's office have filed a report concluding that the assault was a coordinated attempt to kill the Defendant?"

"I read the report, Your Honor, but—"

"You wouldn't want Defendant to get killed in pre-trial custody, would you Mr. Carbon?"

"No, of course not, Your Honor."

The judge looks at the lawyers with an expression that says her decision has been made. "The Defendant will be released on his own recognizance. In order to protect the Defendant against further attempts on his life, the Defendant's file will be sealed and kept confidential. This Court hereby orders that the Defendant be remanded to the U.S. Marshall for processing. Defendant's passport shall be confiscated, and notification filed to prevent Defendant from leaving the jurisdiction."

The judge turns to face Max. "Please step forward Mr. Simon."

Max does as he's told.

"Mr. Simon, because you do not have the financial ability to present bail, this Court will release you on your own recognizance. That means you have to keep in contact with the Federal Marshalls. When you have a court appearance, you must appear in court. If you violate any of these requirements, or if you are arrested on any matter prior to your trial, then you will be remanded into custody immediately. Your passport will be kept by the Court. Do you understand this, Mr. Simon?"

"Yes, Your Honor, I understand."

"Very well then." She pauses to look at the papers on her desk and says: "Next."

Max smiles. Tyrone looks at him with a big grin, patting him on the shoulder.

Niki Carbone glares at them as if this were all a concerted personal attack to besmirch his reputation.

Max is elated. *He's free!* He can't believe it. He's actually going to be able to walk out the door!

35. Out Of The Frying Pan

AT THE PRISON EXIT there's an ATM set up with a prison guard stationed next to it. Apparently Max isn't the only one to mosey out of jail without a dime in his pocket. He nods pleasantly to the guard, takes out his wallet and puts a credit card into the slot. But he already knows what's going to happen. And yes, exactly as he thought, the machine keeps it, with a blinking warning "CARD CANCELLED" on the screen. He tries his other card. Ditto.

Congratulations David, he mumbles to himself ... looks like your preparation has been thorough. I wouldn't have expected anything else from you, after all. So you win this round. But it's not over yet. You took my Island and my money. I didn't see it coming. I was stupid. Careless. Arrogant. I made the oldest mistake in the book. I trusted you. But in my misfortune, I've just been dealt a lucky card. I got out of Snowman's little playdate alive. You missed the perfect chance to obliterate me. Which means now you're scared. You're scared because you know I'm coming after you. I don't know how yet, but I'll be coming after you—

"Hey Frankenstein, you gotta get going."

The guard's voice snaps Max out of his Monte Cristolian musings.

"Yes, of course," he says to the guard, who's looking at him like he's the scum of the earth.

And so Max steps away and proceeds outside, limping through the successive guarded gates, and out through doors into the blinding sun of the real world.

His eyes are purple and swollen nearly shut. Every step is a symphony of pain from his aching joints.

His thoughts turn back to basics. Bottom line is he's flat broke. Like most billionaires, he never kept cash on him. There was always some staff person around to pay for things. After all, he hadn't planned on needing any cash. He'd planned on leaving the party in a helicopter, getting on his jet and flying back to his Island. So much for those plans. Of mice and men and all that crap. It all seems so long ago, already so far away, so much in a different world.

The air is blistering hot. Nothing seems to move. Not even a piece of trash or old plastic bag stirs in the wind because there is no wind. Three taxis are parked on the opposite side of the street, waiting for people like him from the prison. The drivers are chatting together, squatting in the shade of a tree. They smile at him.

"Hey Missa, you wanna taxi?"

"No thanks," says Max, "due to an unexpected financial setback, at this moment I prefer to walk."

The men smile. "Velly hot fo wok," offers one.

"I'll be fine, thank you," says Max, walking off as they look after him, shaking their heads and commenting in their language. He wonders for a moment what they're saying.

The sidewalk seems to stretch on in either direction until it dissolves in the heat waves like some old western movie. Left or right? Same difference. Everything is mindlessly flat. A car whizzes by every few minutes. But other than that, there's not a soul in sight. Houstonians are apparently not much for urban strolls. Can you blame them? It's desolate, ugly, humid and scorching hot. Granted, they don't usually build prisons in the nice parts of town. But surely if you walk straight ahead long enough you end up somewhere.

As he walks, he suddenly realizes he's smiling. Smiling with those ragged gaps where his teeth used to be. But it's not the aesthetic quality of his smile that's noteworthy. It's the fact that he's smiling at all. In fact, considering his present predicament, he's tickled pink to picture himself smiling. He's thinking there's probably some maxim out there that would capture the moment perfectly. Something about how when you've been caged with a bunch of monsters waiting in line to ream out your guts, just being able to walk outside free to wander where you choose with a face full of broken teeth is heavenly. In any event, one thing is certain: if you're ever feeling depressed about the state of your life, try spending a night in prison. It's a foolproof way of snapping everything back into perspective. Put that in your self-help books.

But enough existential chatter. He needs a plan. Analysis. His mind churns the problem as if he were formulating a business strategy in a corporate takeover ...

So it looks like Snowman and his bunch really were assassins, and the gang rape angle was all PR spin. Charming. And now that the first attempt missed the mark, the David/Kramer team will be out there hiring contract killers to finish up what Snowman botched. The *program* will cover his tracks enough to get a head start on the next wave of hitmen, but only a brief head start, like some wild animal released from a cage while the hunters eat their lunch.

His thoughts race through his options ... Of course he can't contact anyone he knows. David will have the Island Security team maintaining surveillance. Contacting someone from his past life would be walking straight into David's trap. He'd be dead within the hour.

He's completely cut off from anyone who could help him. So he has to do this from the outside, alone. If he still had his millions he would simply hire a team of mercenaries to attack the Island and take it back by force. The whole thing would be over in a matter of days. But without any money, the problem is far more complex ... he'll need to find mercenaries who will fund an armed takeover of the Island in return for a huge payment when they succeed. It won't be easy to find such entrepreneurial souls in that line of work, but it's feasible.

OK, so the basic Edmond-Dantesque-Monte-Cristo premise is indisputably clear. And it would all be so easy with some cash! But without any money, Max suddenly realizes that the immediate logistics are a bit murky, as in frankly opaque. Revenge is an expensive business. For example, how on earth to get down to Central America (or wherever it is one looks for a group of mercenaries) without any money? And what to do for food? Or shelter?

He continues walking. Every once in a while he turns a friendly enthusiastic face and an outstretched thumb to a passing car. But he soon concludes he has more chance of finding a snowball on the sidewalk than getting picked up by a passing car.

It's so hot his clothes cling to him like a baggy wetsuit. The salt from his sweat burns into his countless open wounds and stitches. He's drenched and thirsty and tired, and every muscle and joint in his body hurts. What a hellhole of a city! Don't they refer to this place as the crotch of America? Anyway, if they're referring to the chafing, they've got that one right on the mark. His suit wasn't exactly designed for long hikes in subtropical climes. He's chafing like a camel in heat.

But he trudges on like Lawrence in that spectacular film. He ponders for a fleeting second the other scene from the film bearing such a strong parallel with what happened to him in jail, and then blots it from his mind. He'll never be able to sit through an enjoyable screening of Lawrence or Midnight Express ever again. That's for sure. And something else for sure is that up ahead appears to be a strip mall. Not as in strip joint, mind you. But as in one of those particularly American phenomena whereby a coagulation of replicated carbon copy chain stores crops up periodically along a highway where you'd least expect it. He accelerates his trudge to a more canter-like gait. He can already make out the signs. A slew of fast food outlets: McDonalds, Subway Sandwiches (God knows what marketing genius though it was clever to associate food with the dirty noisy underground transportation system), Pizza Hut, Taco Bells, and a host of others. Along with gas stations and convenience stores overflowing with things to eat and quench your thirst.

The first business establishment is a 7-Eleven. Max is not typically a fan of junk food bought in a local convenience store, but as he looks in through those picture windows, almost everything looks deliciously good. Hunger and thirst are indeed the finest condiments. Even those brightly colored frozen drinks swirling around in those refrigerated machines look absolutely delicious. At that moment he'd take them over a 1975 Cheval Blanc or even a '61 Chateau Latour. He looks longingly at the rows and rows of cold drinks. And the juices! Oh how wonderful a cold glass of apple juice would taste! Why, even the Gatorade looks divine.

A beat-up clunker wheezes into the parking lot with the windows open for air conditioning and parks sloppily between two spaces right next to where Max is standing. A woman wearing short-shorts and a leather halter top displaying a stupendously successful muffin effect steps out of the car clacking gum, swinging keys, jiggling hips and somehow smoking at the same time. She waddles past Max and into the 7-Eleven. And then, you know what she does? As Max watches through the window, she buys a bag of donuts and a six-pack of cold beer. Now Max was never much of a beer drinker or a donut fan, much less the dubious combination thereof. But as she strides back out of the store towards her car, past him toting that sack, he would trade a million of his old Max dollars just to sit down and share the meal with her. Problem is, of course, he doesn't have *any* old Max dollars. All he has is his gap tooth smile. And since there's no harm in trying ...

He steps up to her as she passes him towards her car.

"Excuse me Ma'am, I'm terribly sorry to trouble you, but I was wondering if—"

She glances at his bloated face and missing teeth, cringes, looks quickly away, and actually speeds up to get to her car. She puts her sack in through the open window, climbs in and drives off, glancing over at Max like he's some sort of revolting pariah.

The cashier, a big man in his mid-forties dressed in a cheery-colored polyester 7-Eleven uniform with Elvis Presley sideburns and a neck as thick as a good-sized tree, is staring at him through the window with a large grin, obviously having enjoyed the scene.

Max feels ridiculed. He feels small and weak and insecure. And he's profoundly surprised by these feelings. The *old* Max would have cared nothing at all for the opinion of the Muffin Woman or the 7-Eleven clerk. Max marvels to himself how fast all this can change. Impervious and invulnerable one moment, then suddenly, a twist of fate and he we are cringing and begging. We walk through our lives thinking certain givens are actually given, but they're not. Not in the least. It's all fleeting. It can all disappear in a heartbeat. Health. Wealth. Reputation. Everything. That's what he's thinking as he watches the 7-Eleven clerk eyeing him with evident disgust.

There's no one else in the store. The clerk's skilled eye has already determined that Max isn't going to be buying much of anything. That he's just another bum who should get the fuck out of the store before he stinks it up requiring a mega dose of that air freshener spray thing kept handily behind the counter. Max registers the man's hostile smirk. It's funny, if you think about it. Before his arrest, Max was the type of man that this clerk could never ever meet in real life.

Their worlds simply had no intersecting points. And if, by some amazing happenstance, the clerk could actually have come into contact with some billionaire like the *old* Max, he'd be fawning all over him. They always do in the presence of such vast wealth.

But right here, right now, it's a completely different picture.

... "I'm sorry to bother you," ventures Max. "But you see, I've run into a little spot of bad luck, and I was just wondering if you would have the kindness to lend me enough money to buy something to drink. If you give me your address, I will send you payment in the mail."

The clerk just stands there for a moment staring. Enjoying the show. Drawing out the pleasure of seeing an inferior human being begging for something from his obviously superior self. After holding out the pleasure as long as he can, he guffaws with gusto.

"You crazy? I wouldn't give *you* my address," he says with that particular inflection to his Dixie drawl that can only be achieved after many years devoted to chewing tobacco. "And I ain't gonna give you no free food. Why don't you get a job and work? Shit, I work my ass off. Don't come in here begging to me." He reignites his caustic guffaw as Max walks out the door and back into the street.

*   *   *

Max notices a large store down the road and walks towards it. It's a Wal-Mart. During his entire existence, Max has never been in a Wal-Mart or any other type of discount department store before. People like Max just don't do Wal-Marts unless they're buying up a franchise chain. But now, as he steps through the automated glass doors, he feels as if he's stepping into the Promised Land.

Never has air conditioning felt so good. After the blazing heat of the street, this place is a veritable sanctuary. An ecosphere of creature comfort. An island of pleasure. He goes straight to the water fountain and drinks what seems like a gallon of ice-cold water. It's amazing how good water tastes when you're really thirsty! It reminds him of those scenes in various books and movies where the protagonist has come riding across the desert dying of thirst to finally arrive at an oasis. And the feel of this cool air! What luxury! Even that hideous background music is welcome. He smiles to himself as the irony strikes him again. How everything is truly relative. Gravity might keep us stuck to the ground, but it's relativity that reigns supreme.

With nowhere to go, he's in no rush to leave. He decides to wander the aisles, soaking up the delicious coolness of the air.

He walks past a counter of wristwatches on display. In his past life, watches were one of the many outward trappings of wealth. His peers would casually spend hundreds of thousands of dollars on watches. In his bedroom on the Island he had a special cabinet for his many watches, outfitted with tiny motors to keep them painstakingly rotating in a scientifically-designed pattern of motion so that their astronomically expensive automatic movements would never die down. And yet these watches on display, many for less than $100, all accomplish the same functions just as well. Who's the butt of that joke? Certainly not the Swiss. They're laughing all the way to the bank. Theirs too, of course.

In his previous life he'd practically never set foot in a store. Any store. Not even the most exclusive star-studded boutiques of London or Paris could lure him in. All his clothes were either tailor-made or purchased for him by his army of PAs, who also took care of procuring all other material needs. He actually laughs out loud at the thought of now wandering Wal-Mart aisles, falling headfirst into the cliché. Sounds like a tabloid title or Reader's Digest special: *Man Appreciates Simple Things In Life After Near-Death Experience.*

THE SECRET (*of happiness*)

What is it with him and clichés? Has he got some genetically programmed cliché-esque chromosome? But then again, why fight it? After all, you can run and hide all you want. You can individualize, originalize and uniquilize to your heart's content. But in the end the pure distillate remains. Our common humanoid denominator. And stripped to its bare sinews and Wal-Martorian ligaments, the clichés capture it all perfectly. You can dress it with fancy psycho-socio terminology wrapped up in archetypes and Freudian heuristic reflexes, but we all know we're talking about the same thing, just pimped up to make it palatable to our intellectual sensitivities and viable for topical doctoral theses. So cliché or not, right now, just walking down a Wal-Mart aisle feels good. It feels great. To wander air-conditionally. Without bars, without being afraid of being attacked or raped.

And as he spins out these lofty reflections he concludes that the day is turning out just fine. Despite, of course, being broke, without a passport, looking like an escapee from a Halloween horror set, under indictment for fraud, just conned out of ten billion dollars, nearly beaten to death and gang-banged, arrested at a People's Party, and presently being pursued by hitmen.

He watches the Wal-Mart shoppers choosing stuff to buy. Just like they do every day. Homo sapiens Wal-Marticus. The families arguing. The young couple debating whether they really have enough to buy this toaster when they could, after all, just keep on toasting their toast with the broiler in the oven. The kids playing hide and seek. The young machismo Latino sales clerk with the tightly trimmed mustache and rolling gait hitting on every female who passes by. The guy with the beer gut, bushy sideburns, red and white bulging checkered shirt cut off at the shoulders mentally undressing every young girl over the age of twelve who wanders into his field of vision as he waits for his wife to finish choosing a pair of XXXL panties.

Max watches as a teenager selects something or other from the cosmetics counter. She appears to inspect herself in the mirror while furtively glancing around and quickly slipping a tube of lipstick into her purse. Oh no! She can't do that! She's crazy! Max looks around. He'd better do something quick. He hurries over to her.

"I don't mean to be meddlesome, Miss, but there are security cameras everywhere in this store."

She jumps back in fear and surprise. "Are you like, an undercover cop?"

He shakes his head.

"Oh. Good." She calms down, then adds, "Cause if like you were, then I would say your makeup looks, you know, real good."

"Makeup?"

"Yeah, the bandages and busted up face."

"Why would an undercover cop want to call attention to himself by disguising himself with bruises and bandages?"

"Uh ... I don't know. Maybe a good/cop bad/cop thing."

"How would that? ..." he begins, but then decides to abandon the budding Socratic dialogue and just smile instead.

"So ... like, who are you?" she asks.

"I'm nobody, but if *I* saw you, then you can bet that you're on camera, and if some security officer is doing his job, they've seen you and they're going to nab you on the way out, unless you're very quick."

She looks around suspiciously, suddenly feeling the eyes of Big Brother bearing down on her like laser beams. Then looks back at Max.

"And I don't want to interfere, but you should really stop stealing before it gets you in a lot of trouble. You look like a smart nice girl. You don't need this."

"Thanks, man," she says and starts towards the exit.

Max nods, "Don't mention it, but aren't you forgetting something?"

"Oh yeah." She takes out the lipstick and puts it back for the cameras as if she'd just been perusing, and simply decided not to buy it.

*   *   *

There are many things that Marcie hates about her job at Wal-Mart. She hates the neon lights that make her face look like something you'd find in a swamp or a dumpster and *way* older than she feels inside.

And she hates having to be so fucking nice to the customers when they're being complete assholes, which, sadly, is surprisingly often. Much more than you would think. As if Joe Blow American actually gets off on being rude to Wal-Mart clerks.

And she hates sucking up to the huge amount of people—basically everyone—hierarchically above her in the Wal-Martian pecking order who could get her fired in a heartbeat. And she hates being considered by everyone working here like she's some anti-social loser freak. And she hates the ever-present constantly repeating muzak. And most of all she hates herself for still working here after all this time. For wallowing in her own whatever it is she's wallowing in and not going back to school or getting a better job or doing something meaningful with her life. Like sailing off to Africa to feed the starving orphans with AIDS or saving the whales or polar bears or emus or some other Discovery Channel species getting the short end of the planetary stick at the moment between commercial breaks.

But she doesn't hate everything about her job. For instance, she likes getting her paycheck and being able to pay her bills. Even though it seems like it's calculated to be just enough to stay alive, yet just a step or two behind. Always having to run to catch up. Her credit line always maxed out and the bills always being paid late, timed down to the last second before financial disaster. It would be so great *for just once* to have a little safety cushion. But hey, a lot of people are far worse off. Be thankful for what you got.

And most of all she likes when she's working the registers and actually connects with someone. Of course that doesn't happen very often. Mostly never. Most of the people she checks out are either talking on their cell phones, arguing with their kids, or just ignoring her. Just looking right through her like she's not there. For some reason most people somehow think that a cashier doesn't really exist as a real person. Like she's just an extension of that robotic laser reading thing going blip blip blop bleep while it scans the prices. But every once in a while she connects. And that's great. Sometimes it's just a smile, or a shared look, or some comment about something. But you feel it when you connect. And that makes the day worth it.

And she hates re-stocking, which is what she's doing now, just as she's done so many brain numbingly repettttatttttive times before. But look—something's just caught her eye—What is that guy doing? Oh yuck! This middle-aged guy is hitting on that girl. That teenager! Fucking pathetic. Why are men so fucked up? He's dressed up in this fancy looking suit, but he looks like a truck rolled over his face. Two black eyes and teeth like a jack-o'lantern. Fucking pervert. She must be, what? Fifteen years old at most. He walked straight up to her and is now totally freaking her out. Why are men so gross?

The girl says something to the pervert, puts back the lipstick she was going to buy, and walks away. Going straight toward the exit. Of course she's taking off. Poor kid. That's the sort of shit that can totally screw up a kid. That fucking pervert!

Marcie's thinking she should go straight over there and kick him in the nuts. Yeah, sure, like she'd really do something like that. You're all talk, but you can't do the walk.

* * *

Clyde, the Wal-Mart security officer currently on duty, is completely engrossed.

The actual usefulness of a security guard at a Wal-Mart is an exceedingly rare and wondrous thing cherished by any guard raised on action films and video games.

Nothing to do with real criminals or anything dangerous of course, but adolescent shoplifters (especially cute young girls), vagrants, or maybe even a boisterous drunk. Those are choice instants in the security guard's otherwise excruciatingly boring job description.

And at that very moment Clyde is replaying one of the security cams. The one with the perfect angle on cosmetics. And he's spotted a thief at the lipstick display. He has a clear shot of her taking the product and slipping it into her purse, but then this dumbass guy customer moves into frame, blocking the view. And then, infuriatingly, she takes off.

Clyde jumps into action like Robocop. He barks into the walky-talky with a litany of rogers, copys and other jargony syllables he's picked up from a lifetime of TV, telling two of his deputy underlings to meet him at the entrance. He checks that his gun is in his holster, adjusts his Dirty Harry shades and proceeds SWAT-like out of his office towards the exit to make sure he apprehends the perp before she can flee the scene of the crime.

*   *   *

Max watches as the lipstick thief reaches the exit. She walks straight out and vanishes. He continues browsing through the aisles. A few moments later he sees a security guard burst into view near the exit. Two other guards appear. They're looking around for someone. Max smiles ... *don't bother, guards, she's long gone by now.*

*   *   *

Marcie watches Clyde and some of the other guards playing cops and robbers at the entrance. Clyde's wearing those stupid comic book state trooper glasses of his. Makes him look like a fly. What are they doing? Looking for someone? Ah, they're giving up. Of course. That full minute of action must have been exhausting. Gotta hurry back to the box of donuts.

Before working at Wal-Mart she'd always thought that the thing about cops and donuts was just a malicious class pejorative cliché. But that too turned out to be perfectly true. No matter what time of the day you go past the lounge where the security guys hang out, there are always donuts. She smiles to herself. She always smiles to herself when she finds a cliché that proves itself true.

Oh gross, here comes the middle-aged pervert with a beat-up face in a fancy suit. Should trip him as he walks past. If he continues his present trajectory he'll walk directly into target zone at "T" minus three seconds. OK, all she has to do is sticky outy her footy and he'll go flying. Maybe break a hip. Yeah sure, talk's cheap. But go ahead, do it for once. Just do it. Let karma really happen.

She watches as the pervert walks past her. Now's the time to trip him! Do it! It's now or never!

But of course she doesn't. Of course she doesn't have the guts. Karma doesn't happen. Not like this anyway.

He walks straight past her. Un-tripped by her totally gutless foot. He's probably prowling for some other teenager to hit on.

And here's Clyde sauntering up to her.

"Hey Marcie."

"Hi Clyde," she says with a tone clearly tailored to cut off any further conversational forays.

"You want to catch a movie this weekend?"

"No, Clyde," she says absently, still keeping an eye on the pervert.

Clyde follows her gaze. "What you looking at?" he asks.

Hmmm ... maybe Clyde can be of some use after all. "See that guy in the suit with the fucked up face?" She points to Max, wandering away down the aisle.

"Yeah."

"I've been watching him going up to teenagers. I think he's some sort of pedophile pervert. Why don't you check him out?"

No words could make Clyde happier. This is a golden opportunity to look cool *and* display his sensitivity to women's issues both at the same time. After this he's figurin' Marcie is gonna be doing more than just a movie with him this weekend ... He flashes her a debonair wink and walks towards the pedophile pervert, rolling his shoulders like Clint used to do before he became so intellectual.

Clyde, of course, can feel Marcie's eyes on his back. He can even imagine her hands groping to pull down his fly. He accentuates his saunter in a way he figures must surely look tough and completely in control of the situation.

Marcie watches. She wonders why Clyde is walking weird like that. Probably got some disgusting disease on his testicles.

Clyde overtakes Max and says authoritatively: "Excuse me, sir."

"Yes, officer," says Max, startled by Clyde's sudden and inexplicably overzealous appearance.

Like a schoolboy who didn't prepare for a test, Clyde suddenly realizes he'd been thinking about how cool sex with Marcie was going to be, and hadn't given a thought as to what he'd say to this guy. So he goes for an old classic line, highly useful in most all impromptu situations: "Can I see some ID?" he says with a perfect cop voice.

"Why would I need to show you ID? Am I being accused of committing some crime?" answers Max.

"Well, not *accused* per se. But a complaint has been formulated."

"*Formulated?* What's that supposed to mean? Against me? What kind of a complaint?"

Clyde was never great at improvising, and you can't just walk up to someone—even one who's face looks like shit—and say, "Hey, this chick who I wanna bang thinks you might be a pedophile." Nothing in the Wal-Mart security guard informative imitation leather black binder of which he'd read certain portions comes even close to addressing this sorta shit.

"A complaint concerning your sexuality."

"My what?"

"About you maybe being a sexual predator."

"Are you serious? Who would say something like that?"

Clyde looks back to find Marcie, but she sensed the way the wind was blowing and retreated into the aisles out of his field of vision a moment ago, just in time.

Max follows Clyde's gaze and sees no one.

Clyde turns back to face Max. He feels a bit awkward now without his star accusing witness to back him up, and decides that he should toughen up a bit and just get this asshole outside where he belongs. Anyways, it's clear he's just a fucking homeless. Good thing about the homeless is you can fuck around with them without worrying about it. It's not as if he's going to file a complaint with the manager.

"Listen, Mister, I'm going to have to ask you to leave."

"Because some undisclosed random person said I'm something I'm not?"

Clyde stares at Max while trying to process the sentence he just heard. He's pretty sure he got the words right, but not exactly clear on what they mean lined up like that. For a second he wonders how to answer, then just decides to skip over this shit and cut to the chase.

"Because it's my job. Now are you going to go easy, or am I going to have to assist you?"

Clyde escorts Max towards the exit. The glass doors open and Max steps out into the sweltering parking lot.

"Thank you, officer," says Max. "I'll take it from here."

Clyde smirks at him through his sunglasses. "Now don't you be coming back in here," he says.

"Wouldn't dream of it," says Max. He steps away from Clyde and starts walking off.

After Wal-Mart, Max keeps on walking down the street.

Cars whiz past. A steady flow now. He's hot, tired and hungry. He feels caked and sticky with filth. The last time he washed was on the Island before getting into his jet to fly to St. Tropez. He would do anything for a shower. If only he had a little money he could check into a hotel and get cleaned up. Get his thoughts together. Get something to eat.

It's all been happening so fast, he hasn't had time to think it through. The arrest. Getting attacked by those monsters. Getting released.

And now?

... That's just it, *now what?*

36. Screw Up

I'M OUT ON MY BUNGALOW TERRACE eating breakfast while the sun rises over my island paradise. I wish Dot were here. I miss her terribly. No matter how hard I try, I can't drive her from my thoughts. Even when I'm successful in banishing her from my mind for a full day during work, I can never get through an evening without seeing, hearing, smelling, or thinking of something that reminds me of her.

And the more I think about the whole situation, the more I realize what I have to do if I want Dot back. I have to. It's either that or lose her. And in that split second as I look over the ocean I make up my mind. I'm going to do it! I'm actually going to take the plunge. I'm going to fly over to Portland, sweep her off her feet and propose! And suddenly, with my mind now made up, I feel a wave of happiness wash over me. I look across the table at the empty chair and can already imagine Dot sitting there, smiling back at me, my lovely bride.

The buzz of my Island Com shatters the magic of the moment. I pick up and hear Gwen's voice: "Larry Kramer on the phone for you."

"Thanks Gwen. Switch us over to a secure line."

Larry's voice sounds forebodingly apologetic: "I don't know how to tell you this, but I've got some really bad news."

"What?"

"It's Max. He escaped."

"Escaped? How is that possible, Larry? You said you had this under control."

"I know. I'm really sorry. My guys promised me it would be taken care of ... and something went wrong."

"What could go wrong? He was defenseless in prison."

"I know, I know. I still can't believe they fucked this up."

"So what do we do now?" I ask.

"We find him. And this time we won't screw it up."

"Put as many guys as you need on it. Expense is no issue. We need to find him and do the job properly this time. No excuses."

"Don't worry, I'll get it done. He's got no money, no passport, and his face looks like it was used as a football. He can't get very far."

37. Harsh Reality

IT WAS THE BEST OF TIMES, IT WAS THE WORST OF TIMES, or so Max just figured.

In his past life he'd always faced up to every challenge, and had always emerged victorious. And of course winning is habit-forming. Accomplishment breeds accomplishment. The momentum of success and the ease of wealth carry you forward with confidant acceleration towards the next crowning achievement. So Max just naturally considered that losing the Island and becoming homeless was merely a passing impediment. A hurdle in his path. Simply the nadir of that Dickensian curve before rising up in habitual, time-honored, classical triumph. He just assumed he would soon devise a plan to get things back on track. Absolutely certain he would shortly be wreaking his revenge on David and reclaiming his Island.

But he was wrong.

He was completely wrong about what life on the street would do to him. Although a man of great wisdom and experience concerning the jungle-world of business survival, it turns out that the real world of actual physical survival in the jungle of the streets is a whole other kettle of fish. He was utterly unprepared for how a human spirit becomes broken down and battered on the streets. Washed away like dogshit in the gutter in the rain.

He had always known, of course, that there exists a group of people who survive and live out on the streets. The *homeless*. We all know that. We see them in every city. We just don't want to think about it. It's a bothersome reality. A niggling pebble in our societal slippers. When you're comfortable in your own house, thinking about the homeless puts a real damper on your evening. A cold draft up your cerebellum.

And Max's past billionaire life is so far removed from the harsh reality of the streets of the real world, it might as well exist in a different dimension. In a completely different universe.

Homeless. As Max turns the reality over in his mind, he quickly realizes there's nothing Jack Kerouacky or even remotely liberating about it. He catches himself wondering what the dictionary says. Probably something like it's an adjective meaning "without a home or permanent place of residence." But that's about as accurate as saying a concentration camp is where people went to camp out and concentrate. When a person is homeless, he's not just without a home, he's cast adrift. While the rest of the world keeps spinning, he's stuck dead in the water. He can't work ... no one's going to hire him because he's dirty and he stinks. Every day he becomes dirtier, stinkier, lonelier, and more depressed. One step closer to just lying down and pulling the plug from the sheer misery of having disappeared from the planet even though he's still stuck here. Physically stuck, but socially zapped off the grid. The rest of humanity hurries on as if the homeless were completely invisible. We all do it. After all, how on earth could we possibly enjoy our cozy homes if we're thinking about the homeless?

Max had never really thought about them. Certainly not in any concrete, tangible manner. But necessity makes for strange bedfellows. And now, suddenly, he has to figure out how they *live*.

How do they eat? Where do they sleep? What do they do during the day? And most of all, how can he escape from their world?

After being escorted out of Wal-Mart by Clyde, Max wanders through the city. He's never been so physically uncomfortable in his entire life. The scorching sun feels like it's baking him alive, broiling him in the marinade of his own stinky sweat. And his head and body ache horribly from the Snowman ordeal. It's been so long since he washed he reeks like a pig.

So he wanders. Wondering what to do. He figures the best thing would be to talk with some other homeless people to find out how they do it. He spots a lanky fifty-something man standing out by a dumpster behind a rundown warehouse. He has a long thin face, a scraggly beard, and a nose that's been broken enough to make it look like it was stitched on from someone else. Max walks up to him and says: "Hello."

"Hey," says the man.

Max is about to introduce himself, but remembers just in time that he's on the run from hitmen. "My name's Fred," says Max.

"Hey Fred, I'm Jeff."

"Nice to meet you, Jeff."

Jeff nods.

"So, Jeff, I'm new to this. I was wondering if you could help me out with a little information."

Jeff looks at him. Sizing him up. "Is this your first night?" he asks.

"Yes, it's my first night, and I was wondering, actually, about ... well, about everything, in fact. Where do people sleep? How do they eat?"

A sort of wise-old-sage look has crept into Jeff's face, underscored by the zigzagging white scar marks across his nose. "I used to be a high school teacher," he confides.

Max nods.

"Yeah. Wife divorced me. Took everything I had. I was so depressed I thought I would die. But I didn't die. I just started drinking and got fired. At first I thought it was just temporary. You know, like everybody thinks at first. I thought I'd get my shit together and get another job. I thought that for a good long while. Until one day I woke up and realized that it didn't work like that. This here's a one-way street."

Jeff looks at Max until Max nods again to keep up the narrative flow. He's wondering how he can steer Jeff away from existential biographical philosophy towards more relevant practical information, such as where he could find something to eat.

"So you're thinking it's just a spell of bad luck. Well it ain't. It's more like one of them roach motels. You know, how you check in but you don't check out?"

Jeff is looking at Max again, studying his reaction. Max takes the cue and acknowledges his full appreciation of the pesticide/auberge metaphor with an approving nod.

Jeff continues. "Anyways, you're checking in now. So you might as well forget everything you ever knew about life before. Now you don't exist. You've become shit. You think you're still alive, but you're not. You're just excrement. Just a piece of feces hanging around until the world flushes you down the toilet. Waiting till you disappear. And you *will* disappear. Sooner than you think. Soon you'll start coughing, or having heart spasms, or something else wrong with you. Even if you're healthy right now, just wait and see how you'll be after eating out of dumpsters for a while. And then you'll just die out in some field or in some shelter. Or they'll pick you up during the night and take you away to some hospital for homeless where you won't ever come out of. That's what always happens. Don't think you're special. Once you're here, there's no way out. Unless you believe in miracles. You believe in miracles, Fred?"

Max stares at him, wondering for a second who Fred is, then remembers. "No, I guess I don't really believe in miracles," says Max.

"Yeah. Me neither."

Max feels an uncontrollable urge to walk away and keep on walking as fast as he can. To get out. To get back into his own world where such crazed prophecies have absolutely no relevance to his life. Despite the heat, he shivers.

"So where do you think I could sleep, or maybe get something to eat?"

Jeff eyes him and spits out a brown-colored glob. "That depends," he says.

"On what?" asks Max.

"You got any money?"

Max shakes his head.

"Not even some small change?"

"No."

Jeff nods like he was expecting as much. "Well, if it was a few hours ago, then you could line up and hope to get a cot and a meal at the shelter. But it's too late for that now. So you ain't got much choice. If you had some money or something to eat you might find some people who'd sell you something and have yourself a real dinner and a place to sleep. But if you don't have any money at all, then you're better off just finding somewhere no one can see you, and hope you don't get bothered none. And then tomorrow you can go out and do the streets for change."

Max nods.

"And if you're hungry you can work the dumpsters. There's always stuff in the dumpsters. Sometimes the restaurant dumpsters can be really good. But be careful. You don't want to be digging in a dumpster that's in someone's territory. They don't like that. And you want to stay clear of the cops. Them motherfuckers will beat the crap out of you just for kicks."

"Thanks for the advice," says Max.

"Sure thing," says Jeff, watching Max walk off with a feeble wave.

Max wanders on.

The last thing he had to eat was yesterday's prison meal, which he barely touched. Every time he passes a dumpster he's tempted, but he doesn't stop. For some reason he's not quite ready to take that leap, despite the growls from his stomach.

Around midnight, he finds a secluded spot in an abandoned lot. He takes off his suit jacket, hesitating as to whether to spread it on the ground, or use it as a cover.

He decides to go for the ground, spreads it out, and lies down. It's hot and muggy. Clouds of mosquitoes swarm over his entire body. He begins by swatting and twitching, but soon gives up. They cover him with bites. He dozes off for a few minutes, only to wake up scratching wildly, covered with miniature fire ants. He strips off his clothes and picks the ants off one by one. He shakes out his clothes. Examines them for remnant ants and then gets dressed again. He searches for a new spot, this time hopefully not in fire ant territory. Finally, scratching like a flea-infested dog with eczema at every painful step, he finds a new spot and dozes off. But the slightest sound snaps him awake out of fear of being molested.

He gets up with the sun. Exhausted, miserable, and ravenously hungry. He walks across the abandoned lot and towards a convenience store called "Stop & Go". Even at this early hour there is a steady coming and going of clients, hence, no doubt, the clever appellation.

He observed yesterday that the vast majority of street beggars equip themselves with cups to receive the change, undoubtedly designed to ease the donor's discomfort by avoiding any risk of hand-to-hand contact. So Max fishes an old paper coffee cup out of the trash and chooses a strategic spot to attract the attention of clients on their trajectory between vehicle and store. All very scientific.

An hour later, Max concludes that begging is much harder than one might think. Most potential donors ignore you completely. They come out of the store, holding their purchases, walking towards their cars. And when they see you it's as if they've just spotted a hostile incoming on their radar. They look as far away as possible, quicken their step, and make for their car in hopes of avoiding an encounter. And if they do actually have to cross your field of vision, they look right through you as if you don't exist. As if you've just disappeared from the face of the Earth. Become a ghost. A ghost-like nuisance. A vermin. A parasite.

And of course you can't blame them, really. It's annoying to be constantly nickled and dimed like this on your way to your car. It's the system that's out of adjustment. These people walking to their cars pay their taxes. They shouldn't have to deal with guilt-inflicting problems like this. There just shouldn't be homeless on the streets begging. That's the problem.

At the very top of any community's list of priorities should be providing some sort of minimal safety net for those in need. There's certainly enough money in the economy. Anyone who's ever had money or been in a position of power knows this. It's simply a question of priority. Choosing between allocating public funds for a new football stadium or a low-income housing development should be self-evident. Only a minute portion of the national budget would be more than sufficient to completely solve the homeless problem. It's perfectly obvious. But then Max realizes that it never seemed obvious to him before. Back when he was a billionaire he never gave it a thought.

After two hours of early-morning panhandling, Max has amassed enough capital to venture inside. The clerk eyes him like a leper. Max is surprised at how expensive everything is. It turns out that a few hours of loose change gathering barely produces enough for a coffee and a bun. After concluding his purchase under the hostile stare of the cashier, he steps back outside to eat his breakfast. He can't wait.

But once outside he sees that another homeless man has taken his spot. A scrappy looking thirty-something man with an abundance of tattoos, a T-shirt cut off at the sleeves to show his sweaty biceps and hairy armpits, a pair of mean eyes, and two dogs on a single leash.

"Excuse me," begins Max, "but I'm afraid I was here before you."

"Fuck you, asshole. Get the fuck out of my sight before I rip off your nuts and feed them to my dogs," says the man with the dogs.

Max smiles at him like an old friend who just invited him over for dinner. "It's crazy how they look at you, isn't it?"

This causes the man with the dogs to look confused. "Who the fuck you talking about?" he says.

"The store clerk, the people walking to their cars ... everyone." Max gives the man with the dogs another warm, friendly smile. The man stares at Max for a moment, and suddenly his aggression disappears.

"You got that shit right," says the man with the dogs. "It's like we're fucking monsters or something."

Max nods in agreement.

"Hey man, sorry about taking your spot. You can have it back."

"No, that's fine," says Max, "I should be moving on."

38. Tying The Not

I'M NERVOUS AS HELL as the jet lands. A Rolls is waiting at the Portland airport with a huge bouquet of flowers and an engagement ring. The flowers occupy half the back seat. Perfect. They're gorgeous.

Apparently Dot has moved out of her parents' house into an apartment. As the Rolls rolls towards her apartment, I stare into the diamond engagement ring. It's beautiful. Finally the car stops and I get out. So jittery my knees are wobbly.

It's drizzling, of course.

I cart the huge bouquet of flowers with me over to Dot's door. I never realized flowers could be so heavy. I ring the bell and wait. No response. I ring again. The flowers weigh a ton. It's Saturday morning. Dot shouldn't be working. Where could she be? I ring again but there's no response.

I decide to wait. In fact, I'll wait all day and all night if I have to. Right here in the drizzle. Imagine Dot's reaction when she comes home to find me standing in front of her door, cinematographically endearingly drenched, holding a float-load of gorgeous flowers and a diamond ring! But after about an hour waiting in the rain I concede that it wasn't such a keenly inspired idea after all. I return to the Rolls and wait inside, soaking those fine leather seats.

Three hours later, the wool/silk mix of my sodden suit is starting to smell seriously gamey. For the past hour I've been putting off calling Dot's parents, but there doesn't seem to be much choice. I dial. The number comes automatically. It's never changed after all these years. I must have called it a million times. Those long hours on the phone ... "You hang up first. No, you first. No, you first. OK, let's do it at the same time. One, two, three."

Then, before anyone can answer at the Peabodys' residence, I think better of it and hang up. This is not a conversation for the phone. I have to do it in person. I direct the driver, and a few minutes later we pull up in front of Dot's old house.

I walk up the path through the scrawny front lawn. Everything looks terribly worn and decrepit. Pa Peabody's ancient golden retriever meets me halfway with a series of happy welcome barks.

"Hey Gandalf, how you doin' old buddy?"

I push the doorbell. It's strange to hear the familiar fake Big Ben mall-sounding chimes again. The door opens, and there stands Pa Peabody, with Ma Peabody hovering nervously behind him. They look mad as hell. An American Gothic thing going on without the pitchfork. Mouths drawn tight. Eyes dark and reproachful.

So I of course try to sound as upbeat and chipper as can be. "Hello there! You two look great. I was just hoping I could see Dot for a moment."

"She doesn't want to see you, David."

"Well, I realize that, but it's very important. I really need to see her. What I have to say will be quick, and then if she wants me to go away and never come back, I will."

"She's not here."

"Could you tell me where she is?"

"She took a week vacation."

Shit. This certainly wasn't in the plans. "Could you tell me where she went?"

"I don't think so, David, you really should leave her alone now."

Despite myself I look inside, to the TV room where I used to spend so much time with Dot necking on the sofa when we were lucky enough to have the room to ourselves, or watching TV when we weren't. I look back up at Ma and Pa Peabody's faces. They've been like family since I met Dot in grade school. All that love during all those years now replaced by this cold, horrible, awkward resentment.

It's amazing how fast these things can change. I want so much just to tell them that I'm sorry I mucked things up so bad. That I've come back to fix it all, and that everything will soon be fine ... set back to the way it used to be when we all loved each other like family ... to the way it's supposed to be. I imagine myself blurting this out, after which we all fall into one big giant hug like in a Friends episode, and Ma Peabody goes back into that familiar kitchen off the den and makes me a hot chocolate with those little marshmallows floating in it just like she used to. And Dot will come home and we can lounge on the sofa with our legs intertwined and make out. Maybe rent a movie later or go out to Nemo's for pizza.

... But of course I don't say any of this. Instead I ask, "Will she be back next week?"

Pa Peabody nods ever so slightly. "We have to go now, David," he says.

I nod sadly as they shut the door on me.

I wonder where Dot went. It's not like her to just go away. Maybe some church retreat or something. I'm not quite sure why, but for some stupid reason I tell the chauffeur to drive back to her apartment.

When we arrive, I grab the flowers and get out of the car. What are they? Made of lead? Still without a clue as to what I'm doing, I walk over to Dot's door and just stand here. Schlepping the whole misconceived botanical travesty like some FTD-flavored nightmare. Don't ask me why. I just stand here as if waiting for some sort of inspiration.

Of course none comes. Instead, I take the flowers and pull them out of the bouquet, bending down on my knees, spreading them out in front of the door like some deranged freak.

*   *   *

Dot and Greg return from their trip in high spirits. It's been a great week. Sort of like a pre-elopement practice honeymoon. She goes on ahead to their apartment while Greg unloads their suitcases from the car.

When she arrives at the door, she stops dead in her tracks.

It turns out that the cold drizzly weather of Portland provides optimal climactic conditions to leave flowers outside on someone's doorstep. The flowers are beautifully arranged in front of the door. You can still read the message clear as day. Like an alien sign left in a farmer's field, the flowers spell out:

"I♥UD"

... *their shared signature* from all those secret love notes they used to pass to each other in school.

Still unloading the suitcases from the car, Greg glances over at Dot. Strange. It looks like she's doing some sort of frenetic native dance in front of their door. Stomping about and kicking violently. And what is she standing in? He squints to see. She seems to be standing in a huge heap of leaves. Spreading them all over the place. Kicking them away. Bizarre. Who would dump leaves there in front of their door?

She keeps kicking until the flowery remains are completely scattered.

Inside the apartment she runs into the bathroom. She can't let Greg see her like this. She steps into the shower so she won't have to feel the tears as they mix in with the warm water. But strangely enough she can still taste them, as if they're running down her throat, inside. She stares down at the water pouring off her body. Swirling down the drain, faintly red from the blood from her ankles where the rose thorns scratched through her flesh.

After her shower she sits down on the closed toilet lid with her hair up in a towel turban. A knock on the door makes her jump.

"You OK in there?" comes Greg's worried voice through the door.

"Yeah, I'm fine. I'll be out in a minute."

Her hands are still shaking, but she's calmed down enough to do what she's decided to do. She pulls out her phone and writes a text message:

Dear David. It's over. Please stop trying to contact me. You've chosen your own path now. Without me. If I keep following you without thinking about me I'll just disappear. I can't let that happen. You've made your choice. Please leave me alone now.

She reads it over about a dozen times and then deletes it. Letter by letter. Her face is sad but determined. She has to cut this off. Once and for all. Like some gangrened limb holding her back. She thinks for a moment, then writes:

Stop stalking me. You didn't want to include me in your decisions, so I had to cut you out of my life. That's why I haven't read any of your messages or letters. You don't exist for me anymore. You hurt me too much. I never want to see you again. Never!

She doesn't even read it over. Just wipes away a tear and pushes "*send.*"

39. Quitting

AS MAX STRUGGLES through the next few weeks living on the street, he gradually starts admitting to himself that there might have been a grain of truth to what Jeff said about the roach motel.

Suddenly, everything has become excruciatingly difficult. Just trying to get enough to eat is a monumental challenge. Begging turns out to be a full time activity that barely yields enough food to keep you going at sustenance levels.

And the dumpsters raise a whole other host of problems. First, the good ones are squatted by some sort of homeless mafia. And if you get lucky enough to locate an unclaimed dumpster in which you find something edible, you can hardly help wondering what hideous disease incubates inside. Whose saliva are you sharing from that last bite before whoever ordered it decided not to finish it? How many viruses are teeming invisibly, ready to hatch? The filth, the stench ... all crawling with maggots and flies and rats.

Everything becomes problematic. Everything we normally take for granted. For example, you can usually find a secluded enough spot to urinate. But defecating is another matter altogether. You can't just go anywhere. And you can forget about washing your hands afterwards. And oral hygiene? Without a toothbrush and floss, he feels like his mouth has become a sewer. At first this bothers him. The thought of his teeth—or what's left of them after Snowman— sitting there rotting in their own food-caked saliva slime ... But then, gradually, as the yellow gunk builds up, you get used to it. And bacteria-by-bacteria, you just stop caring, or even noticing the foulness.

The entire day is spent just trying to survive. How to get enough spare change to buy things to eat? How to find the right dumpsters that can yield some food? How to find the right place to sleep for the night? He's spending less and less time thinking about how he can reconquer the Island. In fact, with every day on the street, the idea of actually seeing the Island ever again grows further and further away, as if the whole thing was just a chapter from some other person's life. A prequel back-story that just doesn't line up anymore.

Yesterday morning he woke up with a terrible cough and crushing headache. And his skin seems to have developed some strange rash covering him with oozing, infected sores. He stayed out a bit later on the streets begging, so as to hopefully save up some change to buy some medicine, but by the time he arrived at the shelter, he was of course too late to get a cot. The line seems to be getting longer every day. He would have to start lining up right around noon to be admitted inside.

So he sleeps out in the vacant lot over by the meat processing plant. Although "sleep" is not exactly the word. Between his coughing and itching all over, the discomfort of the ground, the incessant bugs buzzing and biting, and the fear of getting molested, he spends the night dozing lightly and waking every few minutes. His body feels completely broken. He's never felt so miserable and exhausted. He doesn't even have the energy to think about David, or revenge anymore. It's as if he's just stopped caring, as if his mind has just stopped thinking, just given it all up ...

After one of these fitful dozes he opens his eyes. It's not quite dawn yet. He's about to close his eyes again when he hears a voice that makes him jump.

"Hey," says the voice.

Max looks up. The voice belongs to a bald man with a long beard pushing a shopping cart filled with various clothes and bags. The man and the cart have just stopped in front of him. The man holds his head cocked a bit to the side like he's sizing something up. He smells like stale sweat and rancid piss, and his face is flaked with dirt.

"Hello," says Max.

"I've been watching you," says the man.

"Is that so?"

"Yeah."

The man looks relatively harmless, so Max doesn't feel threatened. Strangely enough, even after being woken up like this, Max actually feels grateful for the company. He hasn't spoken much to anyone recently.

"Why are you watching me?"

"Oh, I watch the newcomers. Especially the green ones."

Max chuckles at the thought of being *green*, but the chuckle merges into that nagging cough. The man with the shopping cart watches intently as Max hacks and wheezes. He seems to be nodding his tilted head as though confirming his suspicions.

When Max manages to stop coughing the man holds out a hand. The pores and wrinkles of the man's hand are highlighted with grime that's long since merged with his natural pigment. His fingernails are thick, ragged and yellow, with rims of caked blackness. Max takes his hand and shakes.

"Everyone calls me Bald Bearded Guy."

Max smiles with a nod. "Pleased to meet you, Bald Bearded Guy."

"Likewise," says Bald Bearded Guy.

Max wonders whether he should introduce himself as well. Ever since being on the run from the hitmen he hasn't given out his real name to anyone. He just makes up some name on the spot if anyone asks. But usually no one asks. Anonymity just seems to come along with being homeless as an included bonus. But the present pause seems to be requiring a name. He toys for a moment with a descriptive character-driven handle so as to fall into step. But nothing comes to mind other than "stinky unshaven depressed guy with missing teeth." So he just settles for: "I'm Fred."

Bald Bearded Guy tilts his head another degree, then smiles, displaying a few brown stumps of teeth through the matted tangle of his beard. He sits down next to Max, reaches in the pocket of his grimy suit jacket and pulls out a small bottle of whiskey. He holds the bottle delicately, unscrewing the cap with great reverence. He winks at the liquid first, puts the bottle to his lips, takes a long deep gulp and holds out the bottle, as age-old tradition requires.

Max takes it, noting the bubbles of spittle along the rim. Of course he'd like to wipe the bottle clean before drinking, or even better, he'd like not to drink at all, but he rightly senses that would be a serious breach of protocol. The whiskey burn as it goes down. He never liked hard liquor before, but it feels wonderfully good right now.

"Well, Fred," says Bald Bearded Guy, "like I was saying, I've been watchin' you since you came in."

"And what have you seen?"

"I seen a lot. And I seen that you're getting mighty tired of all this shit. So I said to myself: Bald Bearded Guy, I think this gentleman might be needing your services. So here I am."

Max looks at Bald Bearded Guy, tilting his head a bit as well in order to get parallel with him. "And what services would those be?"

Bald Bearded Guy laughs. "What kind of services do you reckon?"

"I have no idea," says Max, then adds jokingly, "I don't suppose you can get my old life back for me?"

Bald Bearded Guy explodes into laughter, and Max joins in, trying to suppress the cough that breaks through the laughter despite his efforts.

He takes another swig and hands the bottle over to Max who gladly takes another as well.

"I can't give it all back to you. But I can give you a little part of it back."

Max is all ears. What in God's name is this man talking about?

"Remember how it felt when you would be sleeping in some nice bed thinking nice thoughts all comfortable and clean and feeling good?"

Max smiles. "Yes, I do remember that."

"Well, I can give you that feeling. You'll have that nice happy feeling, and then you'll go to sleep and you won't ever have to wake up. Won't ever have to feel sad, or depressed or angry anymore. Won't have to go out begging for food anymore, or feel afraid someone's going to attack you for your money, gold tooth, or your shoes, and you won't have to cough or feel your head ache, or your skin itch, or anything."

Bald Bearded Guy is grinning. In his outstretched hand he holds one red pill.

Max looks at the pill. The little red oblong pellet forms an impressive contrast with the man's creased and filthy palm.

Never in his life has Max ever contemplated what he is contemplating now. In fact never had he even contemplated contemplating such a thing. Every minute used to be so precious. And now every minute just seems painful. What's the point anymore?

Hope?

Hope for what? Be realistic. What's the real chance of actually getting down to Central America, or wherever, and finding a group of willing mercenaries before the hitmen track him down? With no money and no passport? Hardly probable. Maybe it's time to just call it quits. He's never been a quitter before. But perhaps it's better just to face up to reality. It was a good run. But now it's over. Give it up before it just gets worse. Why draw out the misery? At some point it's just checkmate.

Bald Bearded Guy watches Max thinking for a long time. He can imagine all the things Max must be thinking about.

And after a few moments lost in his thoughts, Max looks over at Bald Bearded Guy. He's decided: he reaches out for the pill.

But before he can take it, Bald Bearded Guy closes his hand into a fist. Max smiles. Of course. Nothing's for free. If there's one thing he learned as a businessman, and relearned over and over again since he's been homeless, it's *that*.

"I don't have much," says Max, letting his hand fall to his side, rummaging in his pocket and pulling out all his money ... a few dollars.

Bald Bearded Guy looks at the money and frowns. "That's not gonna do it," he says. "Keep your cash. It ain't near enough."

Max just sits there. Feeling incredibly tired. The more he thinks about it, the more he wants that pill. Of course he could just jump off a bridge or a tall building for free. But strangely enough, it's not the same. He wants those last minutes of peace. Of feeling good and normal, one last time. Not the terrified feeling you must have while throwing yourself off a bridge. No, come to think of it, it's definitely the pill he wants. And now he notices that Bald Bearded Guy is eyeing his shoes.

"I'd bet you're about a size ten," says Bald Bearded Guy.

Max nods and looks down at his shoes. They're caked with mud and grime, but you can still see they're beautifully hand-made Italian.

"Yeah, I thought that the first time I saw you and I noticed them shoes. They're mighty nice shoes. I'm a size ten too. Really more like nine, but ten would do the trick. What do you say? You wouldn't be needing them where you'd be going."

Max smiles. Without a word, he unties his shoes, removes them for the last time in his life, and holds them out. Bald Bearded Guy takes them and points to Max's socks. Max slips them off as well. Bald Bearded Guy removes his tattered pair of tennis shoes and they trade.

Bald Bearded Guy spits on his new shoes and buffs them with a rag from his shopping cart. Max watches as he puts on the socks, slowly, and then each shoe, methodically with great appreciation. He stands up and takes a few steps with a beaming smile gazing down at his new acquisition.

"Italian, huh?"

Max nods.

"So, Bald Bearded Guy," asks Max, "what keeps *you* going? Why don't you take one of your pills?"

"Are you crazy? This is the best business I've ever had. My life was really fucked up before I got this business started up. Now I'm on easy street."

Max smiles at this, and slips on the reeking tennis shoes. They feel gooey on his bare feet.

"You ever heard of Bottleneck Hill Park?" asks Bald Bearded Guy.

Max shakes his head.

"Ride the Montrose bus out of town and ask the driver where to get off. When you get there you'll see a hill. It's mighty nice out there. Almost sort of like the country. Climb up the top of the hill. It's best at night. You can see all the purty lights, like Los Angeleez. I figure that's probably one of the best places. A lot of my clients go there. Seems to work for them."

"Thanks for the advice."

"And here, take these too," he says, holding out a few small white pills. "It's for the cough. Might as well feel your best on the way out."

"Thanks," says Max, taking the pills.

"All part of the service," says Bald Bearded Guy, standing and starting to push off his cart. "Nice knowing you, Fred, and thanks for the shoes."

Max watches Bald Bearded Guy walk away. He's so tired he doesn't feel the least bit of regret.

He's sure he's made the right decision as he trudges over to the bus stop, his feet shifting nauseatingly in the goo with every step.

40. Caught Dreaming, Again

THE CUSTOMER ON THE TV MONITOR checking out at the cash register is holding out a handful of bills. He's a stocky man in his thirties with a John Deer Tractor cap on backwards and a scruffy beard.

He keeps holding out the bills, but for some crazy reason, the cashier isn't taking them. She seems to be just staring out into space like she's in some sort of trance. The John Deer customer holding the bills looks at the customer in line behind him with an expression that says the cashier must be out of her gourd. He waves the bills in front of her again, but she still doesn't react. Then he grins, shrugs his shoulders, pockets his money, and walks out the door, carrying off his purchases without paying for them.

The Assistant Manager's stubby finger pushes *pause*, and the TV monitor freezes on the image of the cashier—Marcie Rogers—staring into space with a whimsical, faraway look in her eyes.

"Would you like to see it again, Miss Rogers?" asks the Assistant Manager's voice from behind his desk.

"No, that's OK." Her voice is small and distant. She sits there, staring at herself frozen on the monitor like some sort of wax zombie gazing into another dimension.

"Well then, Miss Rogers, could you explain to me what happened?"

She peels her eyes away from looking at her zombie self and says: "Well, Sir, I must have just had a lapse."

"A what?"

"A lapse. You know, a lapse of attention."

"Thank you," he says. His voice is hard and sharp, clearly intended to show Marcie that he's no fool, and is not going to stand for any more of her antics. "And by the way, I know what a *lapse* is, I just don't understand how you can have something like that while you're supposed to be working at your cash register." He pauses dramatically. "Do you realize how bad this looks for the Wal-Mart image?"

"Yes, Sir, I'm really sorry, Sir." Voice oh-so-soft and compliant.

"And do you realize how dangerous this could be? Do you? That man walked off with more than a hundred dollars worth of Wal-Mart property, but he could just as well have reached in and taken your entire register."

Marcie nods in complete submissive agreement. "It won't happen again, Sir, I promise. And if you're worried about the registers, you could transfer me out to the aisles."

The Assistant Manager tsk-tsks with his tongue and shakes his head slowly to accentuate how profoundly troubled he is by the incident. She's already well aware of her Manager's propensity for melodramatics. But this time, with a horrible sinking feeling in her stomach, she senses she's really up the proverbial creek.

"Please, Sir." Her eyes plead like the swashbuckling cat from Shrek.

But the Assistant Manager keeps shaking his head. "Quite frankly Miss Rogers, your behavior has always been, rather ... shall we say, unsatisfactory. Subpar ... You've already had a few of these *lapses* as you call them."

Marcie's thoughts scramble. She can't imagine what she'll do if she gets fired. Just thinking about it gives her this sickening nauseous jab-like jolt in her stomach. It would be a disaster. But it's not going to happen. No way. She's always been able to hang on to her job before. This is no different. No reason why this should be any different. Everything will be fine. She just has to keep saying she's sorry *Sir*, and everything will go back to normal.

She glances at the clock on the wall. *It's already time for her to get back to her cash register!* OK, enough of this wasting time, she has work to do! Customers' chosen articles to check out. Misplaced items to re-shelve. And anyway, she's already three months behind on the rent. She couldn't possibly get fired. She just couldn't.

"Please, Sir," she begs, "I really promise everything will get better, it won't happen again. I'll do any—"

Her words are cut off by a knock at the door. "Come in," says the Assistant Manager, with a smile. Like he's expecting whoever it is.

And in walks Sally Epstein!

Oh no!

Marcie's heart sticks in her throat. That bitch! She's the regional human resources manager, called in to provide an official corporate presence when staff is fired. Oh God, please don't let this happen ...

In the past, Marcie has always talked herself out of bad situations like this one in the nick of time, at the last second. But with Sally here she's a goner ... completely screwed. Already signed, sealed and delivered. They're only going through the motions now. She's *already* fired. As the realization sinks home, Marcie feels her limbs growing cold, as if the blood can't find its way there anymore, and her head feels suddenly full of some heavy liquid that's somehow causing her to lose her balance and her train of thought. She grips the sides of her seat to keep from tipping over and braces herself for what's about to come.

Sally the bitch is saying hello to Pizza Face, smoothing out her beige paisley skirt with a plastic smile, layers of makeup and those eyebrows of hers plucked out and drawn over. Now what was wrong with the real eyebrows in the first place? Why pluck them out just to draw them back in? Well, FYI you look like a fucking cartoon character. Yeah go ahead and sit down in that chair that had *already* been placed there behind the desk next to Pizza Face. *Aha!* So it had all been planned from the start.

"Hello Miss Rogers," says Eyebrow Plucking Bitch.

Marcie nods and mumbles, "Hello." She knows she should be focusing on the moment, concentrating on fawning, ass-kissing and the like, but despite her efforts to remain on point, she finds herself zapping through the inventory of stuff she owns that she could possibly sell to be able to pay the rent. She's already sold the TV and the stereo. For only a fraction of what they were worth too. It seems you always get screwed when you try to sell stuff. How about the furniture? No way. Get serious. She bought most of it from Goodwill in the first place. It's not worth a dime.

Why is her mouth so dry? Like it's full of sawdust, or pencil shavings, or that dusty gravel by the dumpster out back where she takes her coffee breaks. Strangely, she feels a wave of nostalgia at the thought of her dumpster coffee breaks. If only this wasn't happening! If only she wasn't being fired, then she could still go on those breaks. Two of them a day! Ten precious minutes each! The possibility of still being able to take those breaks seems suddenly like heaven. A heaven of peace and security. As long as she has her breaks that means she has her job, and that means she could at least pay the rent.

But it's all crumbling now. Peeling away her insides as it crumbles. Like one of those demolition things she saw on the Discovery Channel where they put dynamite, or some kind of explosive, in key parts all over the building and then blow it up with a very specific timing so that the whole building caves in on itself in one choreographed cloud of dust in slow motion. And then they show it in reverse, the exploded building miraculously putting itself back together with all the dust, each speck of it, fitting right back perfectly into place. If only she could do that now. Un-explode it all. Go back and make it right. Get her job back and start over. Start the fucking day over!

"Miss Rogers, we're sorry to inform you of this, but your very poor performance over the past year has forced us to terminate your employment with Wal-Mart."

The bitch is actually nodding along as Pizza Face talks, glancing over at him sideways now and again to show how much the whole Wal-Mart universe is pulling together here on this as a team. But why the hell did she sell her car? If only she still had the car, then she could sell it now and get another couple of months in her apartment. That would give her enough time to get another job. But she did sell it. To pay for that stupid private detective who said he could get the records back from the adoption agency. What a fucking con artist he was! But then it was her fault for believing him. How gullible can you get? She told him that the adoption agency said that the records had been destroyed, but he just nodded like they always say that and explained to her that if you have the "proper connections" you could get the information. "Really?" she said. She was almost crying she was so happy. He kept saying he'd done it many times before. And that with his "foolproof system" there was no reason why he couldn't get the name and address of her little girl so they could be reunited as a family. She was so happy and so excited. Thanking him over and over as she handed him all her rent money plus all her savings and the money from the car. And then, a few weeks later she received the letter in the mail informing her that despite his "diligent attempts, it was impossible to recover the records." She kept calling him for a while, but his secretary always said he was out of the office. And when she went to his office to see him, the secretary said the same thing. But still, she was the dumbass for believing him and giving him her money. And anyway, none of that matters anymore because now *this* is HAPPENING.

For a second she has the inane feeling that maybe it's happening to someone else. Like the figure of Marie Antoinette she saw at the wax museum with the guillotine blade just inches above her bare neck—so lifelike! She can almost feel the coolness of the blade as it first touches your skin. Then slicing in like butter. And the warmth of your blood as it squirts out in pressurized spurts. And that sudden dizzy weightlessness as your head rolls over into the basket. Apparently you can even keep on thinking for a few seconds, your eyes looking up, blinking at the clouds scudding across the blue sky before everything goes black—

"Miss Rogers? Miss Rogers? Are you listening?"

They've stopped droning on and seem to be expecting her to say something.

"—Uh … yes, of course," she says.

"Well, then can you answer our question?"

She can't for the life of her imagine what the question is. She feels like one of those animals on the road right before getting run over by a car. Staring into those blinding white lights getting brighter and brighter, not knowing what to do, and closer and closer *until* …

"Yes," she mumbles.

They look at her with patronizing expressions saying that "yes" is just so *not* a valid response to whatever question they're asking. They nod knowingly to each other like they've got some little private joke going, and the bitch apparently re-asks: "Miss Rogers, we need to know whether you prefer to receive your severance check in three weeks according to our standard procedure, or whether you prefer to settle for an alternative amount today?"

Marcie stares at them for a moment. She tries to swallow away some of the pencil shavings and gravel. "How much would I get in three weeks?" she asks. Her voice sounds like it's coming from someplace far away.

Pizza Face looks down at some papers and says with a solemn but hugely generous corporate glossy tone, "One hundred and thirty-four dollars and eighty-six cents."

Marcie blinks. There's something suddenly horribly wrong with her stomach, causing her to be on the verge of letting out a huge fart. She focuses her energy on keeping the gas securely locked inside, leaning ever so minutely to the side to let a bit seep out to ease the pressure without any noise.

"But you owe me more than that ..." Her voice trails off.

"We of course had to deduct the money from your prior salary advances, as well as the money that was stolen by the customer during your *lapse.*"

As he says the word "lapse" he provides finger quotes, glancing sideways at Sally with a fun smug grin. "And there were some administrative charges connected with the back-audit of your work performance, plus of course the deductions that we needed to make for social security and tax purposes." He pauses with a falsely indulgent smile. "And of course the good news is that you'll probably get a social security refund mailed to you from the government later next year."

Marcie blinks again, and tries to swallow. She had expected more. Much more. This won't even begin to cover ... she can't even think about it. A jolt of electricity zaps into her gut. She's about to faint. Or worse. She tries to swallow again and says, "And if I sign and get the money today ... how much do I get?"

Pizza Face consults his papers and puts on an extra upbeat expression as if something he's just discovered in there makes the whole situation eminently reasonable and acceptable after all.

"That would be fifty two dollars and ninety one cents ... which of course represents the amount needed to be retained as per corporate policy in order to defray the costs of yada yada yada ..."

Fifty bucks! Fuck! That won't even begin to ...

Marcie feels like crying. If only she could just lie down for a few minutes and cry, and then go to sleep! The paper shavings in her throat must be mixing in with the gravel, bunching all together. That must be what's making it so hard to breathe.

She closes her eyes for a second to catch her breath. With her eyes closed she imagines Pizza Face looking at her with that smug grin. Actually grinning at her misery!

And that's when, from somewhere deep inside of her, she hears a voice. The voice seems to be singing. Something strong and pure and crystalline and spiritual and empowering. It resonates with her *true* self, not this Wal-Mart cashier train wreck of a human being.

And as she listens to the voice she feels herself grow strong and stand up. Standing up tall she resolves that she will take this abuse no longer! She doesn't need to take this shit! She has her self-respect after all. She looks Mr. Assistant Overbearing Asshole straight in the eye and says loud and clear for everyone to hear:

"Fuck you Pizza Face!"

Instantly the Assistant Manager's expression loses that self-satisfied sadistic smile. He starts stammering in contorted rage, but all that comes out of his mouth are some toilet-like sounds. He looks over at Plucky Bitch for support, but she's just staring at him, speechless. So he just keeps on stammering as Marcie storms out of there.

Right on out of there!

She's won! Sure, they might have fired her, but she salvaged her dignity. *She is Marcie Rogers!*

"Miss Rogers? Miss Rogers?" The voice brings Marcie back. Back to where she's still sitting in that molded plastic chair *again,* with her sweat drenching her, overpowering her deodorant, sending little droplets running from her armpits down to her thighs.

Assistant Pizza Face is smiling at some private joke with Sally. He's holding out some papers. Something Marcie is supposed to sign, already prepared for signature on a convenient clipboard. And he's folding a fifty-dollar bill with some change, which he puts in an envelope and seals with his big gross tongue.

And before she realizes it, Marcie is holding the clipboard with the pen cleverly attached to it by a string and signing on the blank next to the date declaring that she has received the money in settlement, that she has no legal claims against Wal-Mart or any of its employees ... and that she will not presently, or in the future initiate any lawsuit, legal action or other administrative procedure against Wal-Mart or any of its ... blah blah blah blah in small print that she doesn't even bother reading.

She just signs, without a word.

Then takes the envelope, silently.

She stands up, steadies herself on the back of the chair for a second, and walks slowly out the door.

41. Getting The Message

EVER SINCE I LEFT THE FLOWERS on Dot's doorstep, I've been waiting. If I leave my phone unattended for a second, or take a shower or swim, I immediately check it again on getting out. I must have checked it a hundred million times. I know Dot is going to call as soon as she sees the flowers.

I'm sitting in my bungalow when it comes. My face lights up with joy. Dot has sent me a message! The first one since that disastrous last phone call with Sveta and those Brazilian girls. I quickly shut that terrible memory out of my mind and think instead about how happy Dot must have been when she saw the flowers in front of her door. Of course it would have been better if she'd been at home so I could have given her the ring and pop the question. But no matter. Now that she's back in Portland, and actually communicating with me, I can hop on the jet and be with her tonight. It's going to be perfect!

I click open the message and read.

Perhaps no one is ever prepared for this type of shock. As I read the message my world caves in. Ever since I sent her the letter from Max's yacht, I was sure she was waiting for me. Still a bit angry perhaps, but nevertheless waiting for me to come back so we can go off and live happily ever after. Just like we'd always planned.

I knew she received the letter because the special courier confirmed delivery. But I never imagined she wouldn't read it ... *I* would never do something like that! Of course, with hindsight, if I'd really stopped and thought about it. Really put myself in Dot's shoes for a moment, I might have realized that's exactly what Dot would do. After all, when Dot makes up her mind, that's *it*. She follows through. Always. Just like her Great-Great-Granddad Peabody who kept marching his tired family across the whole North American continent to get to the other side, despite the crying babies and the pleading from his wife to please stop and settle down every time they passed through a town. And if Dot's really made her mind up to leave me, then that's final.

My first impulse is to jump on the jet—to go see her and try to win her back. Try anything to convince her. But after an initial enthusiasm for the idea, I read her message again and realize the complete and utter futility. Dot has decided. Worse! She probably decided long ago, probably on that first night I left Cambridge, after the drunken Brazilian girl telephone call. *Ugh!* She never even read my letters! Can you believe? Never even read them!

As the realization sinks home that I've really lost her, lost her for good, I begin feeling that the world has suddenly become a very cold and cruel place. Glacier ice cold. My best friend, my childhood sweetheart, has just disappeared from my life, leaving a terrible gaping void. An emotional vacuum.

I'm stunned. Paralyzed. I cancel everything I'd planned for the day and just sit there. Kicking myself mentally over and over for being so stupid. How could I have let this happen?

I sit marinating in my own sadness, stewing in my deception and pain. This terrible feeling of loss and guilt and gloom. And as the sun turns red and sinks into the sea, my despair reaches some sort of critical mass. I've arrived at the inevitable conclusion that I must put Dot aside and move on. She's already moved on. I have to do the same. I have no choice. Dot has chosen for both of us. But how? How does someone get over something like this? How do you get through the pain? The sadness? That horrid black hole where your heart used to be?

42. Stacy

VIRGIL ARRIVES at one of the Island's many rocky cliff-like promontories overlooking the ocean. He drove a buggy here, alone. Just as Stacy had so mysteriously requested the very second he came back to the Island for a few hours before heading back to work on a project in Russia.

He can see her now in the moonlight, standing off by the cliff's edge. He steps out of the buggy and walks over to her.

"What's going on?" he asks.

"I just wanted to talk."

He looks around, hands upturned, eyebrows raised, questioning the necessity of meeting way out here ...

"In private," she offers in response.

"You're such a drama queen."

She shrugs.

"So what's up?"

"Max."

"Ah, yes ... Max. Our fearless leader run amok."

"What do you make of it?"

"Nothing. Nothing *to* make."

"But don't you think it's all very weird?" she pursues.

"Of course it's weird. Christ! The man set up a paradise island for whiz kids to make shitloads of money. He lives like some whacked out Robinson Crusoe and socializes only with us, his minions. I mean, as far as I can see, everything he did was weird. So he gets arrested and takes a sabbatical. It all seems perfectly within the same parameters of weirdness to me."

"I don't know. Something about it rubs me the wrong way."

"Yeah, that's because something always rubs *you* the wrong way, Stacy."

"Cute. But I'm serious. I mean, first Singh mysteriously vanishes in the night, and then the new kid on the block, a.k.a. your pal David, becomes the Trustee, and then Max gets arrested and disappears, without even bothering to contact us directly. And I've checked the Net, and police reports, and everything else. After the arrest in France, there's no trace of Max out there. I had someone check into it in Houston and he drew a blank. He thinks the file might have been sealed by the court. If you ask me, I smell foul play."

"Well, good thing no one's asking you. Talk about an overactive imagination and too much time on your hands ... And what are you suggesting anyway? That David killed Singh and then framed Max, and then maybe killed him? Or maybe it's Max pulling the strings on some kind of gigantic charade? Or maybe there are extraterrestrials behind it all?"

"As much as I appreciate your condescending sarcasm ... I mean, shit, Virgil, I don't know. Aside from ruling out the extraterrestrials, I don't know what to think. I just feel that the whole thing's a bit strange. I think we should be keeping our eyes open and trying to figure out what's really going on. There's a lot of money at stake here. Anything's possible. I don't know ... maybe Singh isn't really dead. Maybe he's blackmailing Max and setting us all up."

Virgil scoffs and shakes his head sadly like he's dealing with a mental case. "You heard Larry Kramer explain the situation. What more do you want? Or is Max's trusted lawyer for the past decade in on the conspiracy too?"

Stacy shrugs her shoulders like it's possible.

Virgil rolls his eyes with a sigh. "So, Nancy Drew, because I'm David's friend, you figure it's worth pumping me for any inside info."

She nods. "Pretty much."

"Well, I'm sure that David is just following corporate procedure. After all, Max set this whole thing up so that it'd keep on spinning by itself. Independently. He always told us that. And he always talked about taking a sabbatical."

"Yeah, well I still think it's strange he doesn't contact us. Maybe we should try to find him just to make sure he doesn't need our help."

Virgil laughs. "You think Max needs *our* help?" He smirks for emphasis. "*Hello* Stacy, this is Max we're talking about. If Max wanted to contact you, he would. He hasn't, so he doesn't. Have you ever seen Max when he wasn't perfectly in control of everything?"

Stacy doesn't answer.

"Well?"

"No."

"Well then what else do you want? Maybe Max is pulling some kind of a stunt. Who knows? But whatever's going on, you can bet Max is in control. So why don't you just give it a rest?"

"I don't know, it still seems weird ... And what about David? What did he tell you?"

"Exactly what he told everyone else. That Max is taking a sabbatical, just like Kramer said."

Stacy is staring at Virgil in silence. A long hard stare.

"What?"

"Well, how about you, Virgil?"

He scoffs. "How about me, Stace? How nice of you to ask. I'm doing mighty fine, thank you."

"You are, after all, one of the best positioned to pull something like this off, if you wanted to get rid of Max."

Virgil pauses a moment. Changing gears. Guard now up. Eyes suddenly wary. Battle stations drawn. "Not any better positioned than you," he notes.

"Tsk tsk tsk Virgil. Spare me the patronizing theatrics. Of course you're better positioned than I am. You've got access to David. He's the *key*, so to speak."

Virgil nods, upping the ante. "OK, I'll concede you that. But being less well positioned certainly doesn't prevent someone from doing it anyway, and then inviting me here to seed suspicions of foul play thus throwing me off her trail when in fact she's orchestrating the whole thing."

"Not bad, I admit. However, unlikely, given the fact I have no access to David and his black box."

"Which is of course exactly what you'd say if you're in cahoots with him. And the common knowledge that you think he's a twat would create a most effective subterfuge. Or perhaps David is merely the *object*, and you're the one setting him up in league with ... let's say Singh, for instance."

"I like it. Now suppose it *is* me, with Singh or David or even Larry Kramer, then what would I do next?"

"You'd try to persuade me that it wasn't you."

"Exactly. But when I realize I can't persuade you—because you're just *too* clever—then what?"

Virgil glances behind. Somehow, during their conversation, Stacy has maneuvered him around so that he's now facing her, his back to the cliff—dropping straight down for hundreds of feet onto sharp rocks and pounding surf. All she would have to do is push him off ...

"Well, Stacy, if you were convinced that I knew it was you, then logically you would have called me here to dispose of me by pushing me off this charming cliff. However, that assumes you're physically capable of doing it."

Stacy's laugh rises above the muffled roar of the surf pounding into the rocks below. "Come on, Virgil. Someone as insightful as you surely realizes that my physical capabilities are completely irrelevant. Since this would all be part of a carefully composed plan, I'm either physically capable of pushing you over the cliff, or I've come equipped with a suitable weapon to achieve my objectives ... You know, something I could just whip out of my pocket at the right moment."

She smiles, and reaches slowly into her pocket.

Virgil glances behind him at the surf pounding below. The white foam glows in the moonlight.

"It seems we've reached a bit of a checkmate, haven't we? At this point, if it really is me, then either I have the physical means to push you over, in which case I will, or I have my hand on a weapon, in which case I'll pull it out of my pocket. In either event, if it *is* me, then it's curtain time for you now, isn't it?"

"Unless of course you've misjudged your physical capacity, thinking erroneously you could push me over, when you fact you can't."

Her smile changes flavor. She withdraws her hand from her pocket, slowly. Virgil's eyes follow her hand, straining to see ...

He breathes a sigh of relief to see the hand come out of her pocket empty. Then, looking up at her face, he's surprised at how ferocious she now looks. Standing there in her trademark army fatigues, her eyes gleaming defiantly in the moonlight.

"So, Virgil. Now you're wondering whether I'm just a nerd, or a nerd with a black belt."

"You're not a black belt, Stacy, you're just a pain in the ass."

"Them is fighting words."

And with that, she lunges, knocking him to the ground.

43. The Slippery Slope

MARCIE STANDS THERE THINKING THAT she's right now smack in the middle of a crock of shit-bad-luck. The type of shit-bad-luck it seems she's so skillful at getting herself right smack in the middle of. As if she were bestowed with some God-given talent for fucking up her life.

For the past week she's been receiving these day-glo colored letters stuck up on her door that cry out in loser capital fluorescent-fuck-you-font: "EVICTION NOTICE." And every day she's been telling herself she should go back to Accounting and beg for another salary advance.

Of course she's already way beyond maxing out her allowable Wal-Mart company policy salary advances. But if she'd flirted with that douchebag in accounting she could have maybe swung another one. That's what she *could have* done when she was still an employee. But of course you CAN'T get a salary advance if you don't fucking work there anymore, can you, fluff-for-brain? What hurts even more is the thought that if she had flirted for an advance *before* she'd been fired, then she could have hung on to all that extra money. Can you imagine that? The screaming injustice of it! Just one fucking day earlier and that money would have been hers. So sweet! Makes you want to barf, and goes to show once again that Ben had it right that you shouldn't put off till tomorrow what you can do today. Even if the thing you have to do today is degrading and disgusting, well, just fucking do it, like it says in the Good Book.

There are so many things that didn't go right. The list is probably endless. Like that eight turned on its side. How could any mortal be so fucking pathetic? Never mind, that's a rhetorical question. Well, bottom line is there's nothing left to pay the landlord. Nothing. But seriously, do they really evict people in this day and age? It sounds so nineteenth century ... when people used to work in the mines, or on the railroads all the live-long day. But nowadays they must have laws against that. Come on, taking away someone's home and throwing them out so heartlessly on the street? Just for a few dollars? That would be so unfair, so inhumane or un-human, whatever the word is. Especially 'cause the bills were always paid. Always ... just need a little more time now to get another shit job.

In fact, it's really not even a question of money. Just time. So, when you look at it that way, they couldn't evict you. Not just over a matter of time. They give you maybe an even bigger warning envelope with an even larger pathetic loser font in maybe another shade of day-glo. Think of it rationally. There's not just the orange. There's fluorescent green and fluorescent yellow. What a waste not to use those other perfectly nice shades. No, seriously, they don't really throw you out. Like on the street. It must be set up like the "empty" mark in a car. Even after you're completely in the red with the blinker blinking, you know you still have some gas left in there. It must work like that. It would only be fair ... At least that's what she's thinking as she walks along the sidewalks looking for places to go in and ask for a job.

She combs the city on foot and by bus, filling out endless employment applications. Every place she tries wants a reference from her last employer, which, needless to say, poses a calamitous problem. When she fills in the application forms she makes up stuff to put in the line marked: *last employment.* Like she was on a "leave of absence," or "travelling in Europe." And sometimes she even tells the truth. All with about the same result. Those she lies to suspects she's lying, and those she tells the truth to call Wal-Mart and never get back to her, evidently not wanting to hire someone who got fired from Wal-Mart based on whatever nice things Pizza Face has to say about her.

If you ever want to feel really low and depressed, try walking around getting refused one after another for every possible shit job imaginable. Try feeling that no one on this fucking earth gives a pig's fart for you, or thinks you're even capable of flipping a fucking burger.

Of course she knows she'll *eventually* land a job. This is America after all! But the problem is that she needs one quick. If only she'd kept current with the rent, then she'd have a few months ahead of her to get another job and fall back on her feet. But after the private detective thing, she just couldn't seem to catch up. Every month it got worse, and now she's more than three months late.

The text from the eviction letter runs through her mind with that same sentence she read over and over about how if she didn't pay within five working days, she'd be evicted. Maybe "five working days" could be construed as five days after she'd found a job and started *working* again ... ha ha ha, not even funny. A million times she's already combed through her stuff to see if there is anything else she could sell, but there isn't anything left anyone could possibly want to buy. Certainly nothing that could raise enough to pay rent. She just needs a job. Desperately.

Sometimes as she walks along she tries to buck up her self-esteem. She tells herself that she'll soon be moving on to bigger and better things. But the whole façade collapses microseconds later ... *"Get real"* her rational realistic self screams at her. Where could she possibly move on to? To bigger and better failures that's where. On to uncharted, newly discovered personal shortcomings. Where the fuck's your self-esteem? No self-esteem! None whatsoever. Lots of other selfs, if you're looking. Self-pity, self-doubt, self-loathing, do-it-yourself. But no self-esteem. Self-tolerance perhaps, but that's as good as it gets. Oh Christ! Stop wallowing. Onward now. Towards new disappointments! After all, why the fuck should it change? Why should things start turning out good? How did everything get so screwed up?

Without realizing it, she starts taking special note of homeless people in the street during her constant rovings in search of work. She'd always averted her eyes before, like everyone else. But now she can't help staring at them directly. Morbidly drawn to them. And every time it's as if she can put them on rewind and see them in their past lives. How they were *before*, usually not too long ago, back when they were real people living in society with real jobs, real places to live, and sometimes even a real family. The fall is so fast and so hard! All it takes is to get behind on the rent, and then without a home, a telephone and a place to get washed up in the morning, you have no chance of getting back on the happy wagon. You're offline. Off the grid. Hanging around only out of inertia until the hardship of being homeless wears you down and finally disposes of you.

And then something happens that changes everything in her life.

It happens.

She's walking home in the dark after a long hot day of not finding a job, when she first sees the people standing on the sidewalk around a pile of stuff. Before she can get close enough to tell for sure, she already knows it's her stuff. She recognizes the oversized backrest of her favorite armchair, the one that looks like an upside down smiley face. How strange to see her stuff, *her living room*, out on the lawn.

Her world collapses. It seems that somehow her insides have become scrambled so that none of the parts fit together the way they used to. Her vertebrae melt, her skull shrinks like a perforated water balloon, and her lungs no longer seem to be connected to any way to get air. Humiliation and fear have taken physical, palpable form, squashing her like a beetle on the pavement, just hard enough to crush all but the last trace of life, jerking and twitching in randomly futile disconnected spasms.

She can feel the crowd around her, pressing in. Feasting on that shamefully coveted human delicacy: the misery of others. Ravenous. Staring. Secretly thrilled that it's happening to someone else—*not them!* Whispering. Excited by the gruesome spectacle. Greedily drinking in the grisly gore of her public desecration. She feels the weight of their stares on her as she herself stares down into the ground to avoid facing them. Numbed, groping somehow to resurrect enough of her old self to figure out what on earth she's supposed to do next.

Normally, if she were still at home, she would sit in her favorite armchair, the only piece of furniture she took when her Mom moved up north with that gross guy who used to look at her with those creepy eyes. But somehow the thought of sitting in her favorite chair out here seems impossible. She lets her head droop and sits down in another chair, frozen. Keeping her eyes low enough so she can't see the people staring at her.

She doesn't really have a plan. Or even a clue. What do other people do in circumstances such as this? Most, she figures, go to stay with a relative or a friend. Of course she doesn't have any relatives to speak of. And for the life of her she can't think of any friend she could call. Now how pathetic is that? A wave of terror washes over her.

She thinks about what happens to a bike in her neighborhood if you leave it outside for the night. Even if you lock it up, by morning the wheels and the seat are gone. There are carcasses of bikes all over her neighborhood, their rusting metal frames like mangled animals, still solidly (and so uselessly!) locked to some signpost or fence, with every other piece of hardware stripped away, never to be ridden again, condemned to perpetual inutility.

Who does that to those bikes? It must be those gangs of young kids she would glimpse sometimes, always skulking about, there on the peripheral edge of your vision, moving off before you can get a clear look, like packs of adolescent wolves. Her mind zaps for a second on what they could do to *her* during the night, but she quickly blots out the thought. But too late, the panic has already begun swirling around in her stomach. Her teeth start chattering a little, which confuses her because it's real hot outside. But she needs a blanket anyway. She rummages around in a box, pulls out a blanket and wraps it around her like a poncho, beads of sweat pouring down her face.

She notices that the crowd has thinned a bit. Just a couple of kids from the apartments, an old lady, a man in a suit stopping to stare on his way from his car, and this older sinister-looking guy staring at her. She can feel his eyes unwinding the blanket and peeling off her clothes. She shudders.

She wonders what she could have done so wrong to deserve this. Or maybe it doesn't have anything to do with deserving something or not. After all, no one said any of this was going to be fair. But still, wasn't there supposed to be some sort of safety net? Something to catch you when you fall? Something to give you just a little break? A second chance? Back in school she never thought she could end up ... *here*. Here at the bottom. The very rock bottom. She looks at the boxes stacked randomly around her. With everything she has in the world in them.

... Then she sees *them*.

Them. A jolt of fear hits her like a punch in the stomach. There they are. Right on the edge of her vision. It's too dark to see them clearly, but she can glean their oversized-tennis-shoed shadows skulking about like ruthless predators closing in on her.

If she ever needed a miracle in her life it's now. *Please let there be a miracle! Please!*

She sees the shaggy tail of Mr. Biggles, the stuffed cat her Mom gave her for her seventh birthday, dangling out of one of the boxes. She reaches over for him, takes him out and hugs him tightly. His little cat face with its reflective eyes always looked so incredibly real.

She coos to Mr. Biggles in a reassuring way. Keeping her eyes down to avoid *them*.

They wouldn't rape someone with a cat, would they?

44. The Meet

FELIX AND ROSA RODRIGUEZ ARE WALKING BACK from the grocery store. The Rodriguezes don't have a car, unless you count the Ford Pinto still up on cinder blocks in Felix's sister's garage. Felix has been fixing it up himself ever since he bought it years ago for a song. But Rosa certainly doesn't consider it a car, being as it's never once driven anyone anywhere since they've owned it. Who would have thought it takes so long to fix a Pinto? Of course it doesn't help that Felix's good-for-nothing brother-in-law always has some football game on with nachos and beer. It is thus partly because of the Pinto situation, partly because of his natural machismo, and perhaps most importantly due to his deep devotion to his wife, that tacit tradition has appointed Felix entirely responsible for getting the groceries from the store to their apartment. Often he finagles some friend or relative to loan him a car or drive them back. But sometimes, like tonight, he's stuck just walking on those feet the Good Lord provided for him.

Despite the fact that the sun set a while ago, it's still hot. Felix is carrying so many grocery bags he wonders if there's a place for him somewhere in the Guinness Book of Records. You know, back in the section for the stupidest dumbfuck Latino tricked into carrying shit by his wife.

"What you got in here, Rosa? Bricks?"

Rosa smiles inside with a theatrical scowl on her lips. She's walking about ten steps in front of him, swinging her knock-off handbag and singing softly. Truth is, she loves these grocery walks.

One of those rare moments in her life where she feels that the scale actually shifts for a short while over to her side. She'd never admit it to anybody, but in a weird sort of way, she thinks the whole thing is very romantic. After all, her man is providing for her while she walks ahead, leading him home, protected by his manliness. She'd secretly choose this over a ride in a Pinto any day. She learned long ago that you gotta grab happy moments any way you can. Grab 'em on the fly wherever they come from. Often in the most unexpected way, it turns out.

"I don't know, why don't you ask your Pinto?"

Felix answers with a throaty groan, just as Rosa knew he would. She feels a flush of pride at her husband's strength. All those grocery bags must weigh a ton!

But hey ... up ahead, off to the left, on the apartment complex lawn, she sees something weird.

"What's that?" she says. It looks like a pile of furniture and boxes stacked together. At first she thinks it must be someone moving in or out. But then she notices the people staring at the woman sitting in one of the chairs wrapped in a blanket with her head resting on her chest. It reminds her of a western lynching in one of those old Poncho Villa films on late night TV.

Felix follows her gaze. Shit. The furniture. The boxes sealed with that red striped tape and orange day-glo stickers. An eviction. Another one. Like when they kicked out that guy Bernie with his little girl after his wife died. Fucking capitalist pigs. It always makes him want to puke when he sees this sort of shit. With all the money they make off poor people, you'd think they'd have a little heart sometimes before throwin' someone out on the street. But they don't. Always the same fucking thing. He wished he could talk to the guy responsible. He'd tear his fucking head off.

"Don't look," he says to his wife.

But they both look. The way they'd look at an accident on the side of the road or some gut-wrenching TV mini-series drama.

Suddenly Rosa recognizes her. It's the clerk from Wal-Mart! The nice one. What was the name on her tag? Mary or Maria? Something like that. She stops walking so her husband can catch up to her.

"It's the girl from Wal-Mart."

"Who?"

"You know, the girl who works at Wal-Mart."

Felix frowns. He has no idea who she is. He squints to try and see better, but can't tell if it's the girl from Wal-Mart or some bum from who the fuck knows where. Anyway, if his wife thinks she works at Wal-Mart, she probably does. Lots of people work at Wal-Mart, so what?

"Come on. Let's go. This shit gives me the creeps."

But Rosa isn't moving. She's staring at the Wal-Mart girl.

"I think her name's Maria," she says. As if this could have anything to do with the fact that she's stopped walking and keeps on staring.

Felix shakes his head and continues walking ... the packages aren't getting any lighter.

"Wait. We can't just go and leave her here like this."

Felix stops dead in his tracks and turns to face his wife. "What you mean?"

"I mean we can't just leave her."

Rosa is looking at him the way she looks when she wants him to do something he doesn't want to do ... Not a good look.

"What you expect *me* to do?"

"Go over and ask if she needs help."

"Of course she needs help. She just got evicted."

"Well then we should help her."

"How?"

"We can invite her to come stay with us for a few days."

"Are you crazy? Why us?"

"Because no one else is helping her. She wouldn't be sitting there like that if she had someone to help her."

Rivers of sweat pour down Felix's skin as he tries to work his mind around his wife's logic. He looks over at the person. She's sitting in one of the chairs. Not moving. Head slumped down. Probably asleep. He doesn't like at all where this seems to be going. Their apartment is much too small to be taking in strangers. But Rosa's always had this Mother Teresa thing about her.

"Felix. I ask you one thing. Would you want her to do this for us if it was us sitting out there without a home? Huh? Would you?"

Felix scowls and turns away from the laser glare of his wife's altruistic pupils.

Rosa pursues. "Remember the Good Samaritan?"

Ugh. Felix always feels like he's cornered when Rosa invokes scripture. How are ya supposed to fucking argue with God? It always seemed like an unfair move. Sweat pours over his body like the river Jordan.

"What would we do with all her stuff? The Good Samaritan didn't have to deal with a truckload of furniture did he?"

"Ask your Pinto."

"Rosa ..." he pleads.

"Put the groceries down and go over and talk to her," says Rosa.

Felix puts down the groceries. But it's not to go over and talk to the evicted Wal-Mart person. He has to put his foot down here. Somewhere. Hopefully not in the dogshit that seems to be multiplying lately wherever he puts his foot. But if he's learned anything, it's that putting your foot down with Rosa starts with a hug. Without that you might as well stick your foot up your ass for all it's worth, 'cause she won't budge an inch. But with a hug anything's possible. He walks over to her with one of those smiles and tries to take her in his arms, but she pulls back.

"Don't you go trying to hug me to shut me up!"

But he gets his arms around her and holds. He whispers in her ear. "I know you want to help her baby, but we can't go taking in everyone we see on the street. We only have one room in our apartment. Where's she gonna sleep? And what if it's a trap? What if we take her in and during the night she opens the door for some guy who comes in and kills us while we're asleep? That sorta shit happens all the time. Listen to me baby. Let's go home now, OK?"

She lets him hold her. His strong arms feel good. Finally, she nods. He kisses her neck and releases her. She doesn't look back as they walk to their apartment. Why is everything so unfair? Just because there's like some ten billion in one chance that she's got some sort of boyfriend killer. How is that fair? How does that make any sense? Why would the Good Lord set things up like this? Letting her suffer like that while so many bad people, like all those criminals and mafia guys and pornographic kingpins or whatever they're called ride around in their big shiny new cars taking drugs?

Why is everything so out of balance? When you're poor you get screwed. Even by the poor people who want to help you. But that can't be right! Why would God let that happen? There's something wrong with all this. It doesn't feel right.

There has to be something to do ... to start trying to fix it all. But what?

* * *

Max walks along in Bald Bearded Guy's tennis shoes with an exceedingly unpleasant squishy sound at each step. He can actually smell their putrid stench all the way down there on his feet. He's been taking his time wandering across town, spending his last coins for coffee and junk food along the way.

It's dawn. The sun's barely up, and the sky is still a bit dark. He walks past the Wal-Mart and across the street. His last bus transfer should be right at the end of the block. As he walks down the sidewalk in front of a sprawling low-income housing development, he notices a strange clump of furniture slightly off the sidewalk to the side. There's a woman sitting in one of the chairs. The scene looks like some sort of urban shipwreck. Like a personal homemade terrestrial version of that Delacroix painting hanging in the Louvre.

What a terrible situation. Forced out of your house. With nowhere to go. Surrounded by your furniture. Soon this poor soul will be living on the street, and he knows how terrible *that* is. And he can imagine it's even worse for a young woman. Perhaps he can help her?

After all, he has nothing else planned. He'll be taking the pill tonight, but until then his agenda is completely clear. The woman seems to be asleep. But the sun's coming up, so she'll soon be waking up. Waking up to her terrible reality. What will she do? She'll need help. He might as well see if he can be of some assistance.

"Excuse me, miss," says Max.

The voice startles Marcie from her fitful semi-sleep. She nearly jumps out of the chair, ready to fight off whatever rapist, murderer or thief might be harassing her. It takes her a few moments to focus. The missing teeth, puffy bluish bruises around the eyes ... Then she recognizes him:

The sex pervert from the Wal-Mart!

The sight of *him*—of all people—standing there in front of her, causes her to let out a very shrill scream.

Max takes a step backwards, fanning his hands out in front of him. The way you might in front of an enraged dog.

"You sick pervert," she says. Even as she's saying it, she can't believe she actually is. Christ! She's alone with some serial killer, and she's insulting him? And what's that terrible smell? She panics, spots her high school softball bat sticking out of a box, and grabs it. And before Max can react, she whacks him. The bat deflects off his arm enough to hurt, and then spins through the air. He steps back, rubbing his elbow as she brandishes the bat menacingly.

"Get away from me you fucking pervert, or I'll split your skull open like a pumpkin."

Needless to say, this was not the reaction Max had expected. She raises the bat again, and he turns and walks away, very quickly. Squish squish squish. Not even looking back.

"And don't come near me again or I'll call the cops!" she yells after him.

Marcie watches to make sure he gets the hell away from her. She sees him walk to the bus stop, get in a bus, and disappear down the road.

And now, with smelly pervert dispatched, the real horror of her situation clamps down on her. It's daytime. What is she going to do with all her stuff? For a few hundred bucks maybe she could find some storage company. Yeah, but even so, where could she get that sort of money? Nowhere. It ain't gonna happen. Her stomach grumbles. She would love a coffee. If she were back in her apartment she could toast up an English muffin with butter and jam and eat it while reading a good book. The thought suddenly makes her want to cry. She sits back down to try and help fight back the tears, but they manage to break through.

A large truck, like one of those moving trucks, pulls up to the curb right in front of her. Surely it's a coincidence. Surely it doesn't have anything to do with her. Right? Just some family moving in or out of the apartment complex, probably. Probably happens every day. Every morning, just like this.

But the man with the beer gut and greasy ponytail who steps out of the truck is looking straight at her. Why? Another thin wiry guy with tattoos all over his spindly arms and various metal shit pierced into his face in a way no sane mortal should ever consider decorative steps out of the truck as well. They snigger together and walk towards her. She grips the bat.

"Hey, check it out. The chick's got a fucking baseball bat," says Wiry Tattooed Guy, holding back Ponytail, who just laughs.

"Watch it man. They can be dangerous," insists Wiry. "Danny told me one of 'em bit him once. On the arm. Fucking bit him!"

"Yeah well Danny's a pussy," says Ponytail under his breath, "and speaking of, look at this chick! Check out those jugs. I'd like to have her biting on me." The two men cackle over their wit.

Meanwhile, Marcie is petrified. What do they want? What are they whispering and laughing about? She stands up with the bat cocked like she's ready to knock a homer over the fence.

Ponytail speaks up. "You can put the bat down, ma'am. We ain't gonna hurt you or nothin'. We're here from the City."

Marcie doesn't move a muscle. Like being from the *city,* whatever the fuck that means, is supposed to make her feel warm and friendly. "What do you want?" she says through clenched teeth. Bat still in battle position.

"Well, ma'am," continues Ponytail, "like I said, we're from the City. Is this here your stuff?"

"I wouldn't be sittin' here if it wasn't my stuff. What's it to you?"

"Well ma'am, like I said, we're from the City Sanitation Department, and the thing is that you ain't allowed to have no personal effects out on the public streets ... so we're gonna have to move 'em off."

Marcie feels like she just got kicked in the stomach. They're going to take away her things! Sanitation Department? Fuck! Everything she has in the world is right here. And these clowns are going to take it all away like it's just some heap of trash!

"My stuff is on the *sidewalk*, it isn't the *public street*," she blurts. Then she adds with a slightly conciliatory tone, "So it's OK, right?"

This seems to stump Ponytail for a moment. He's never heard that one before. He turns to Wiry, who steps up to the plate:

"Sidewalk or street. It's the same thing, ma'am. You ain't allowed to have your stuff out here like this."

How can he say that the *sidewalk* is a *street*? It's most definitely not! Any idiot could see that. Even one with all that shit pierced in his face. Can't they see the difference? Can't they give someone a break? How can they be such heartless assholes? Anyway, gotta change tack quick here. She piles on the amicable overtones with a friendly Mr. Rogers' neighborhood expression to go with.

"Guys, you got it all wrong. I'm just moving into an apartment, and I'm waiting for the movers to get here."

This causes Ponytail to nod and Wiry to smile with a tangled array of yellow teeth. They're back in the saddle now. *This one* they *have* heard before, hundreds of times. Ponytail reasserts himself. "Well, ma'am, we can see the eviction stickers on your boxes, so it's purty clear that this just ain't your reglar movin' situation."

Marcie glares at Ponytail. "You know, mister, I'm not having such a great day right now, and if you take one more step towards me, I'm going swing this here bat at your fat ugly face, and that might just make me feel better."

Ponytail stops short and Wiry stifles a chuckle. But they're pros after all. They can't be flustered by this bat-swingin' bitch with an attitude. Wiry takes the lead, "Ma'am we really ain't here to pick a fight. And I'm mighty sorry about your situation, but the City can't let you leave your personal effects out on the public ... uh, sidewalks. It's against the law."

"I only got evicted last night. Only a couple hours ago. How did you guys get here so fast? It's barely even daylight."

"The eviction guys tip us off," says Wiry.

Ponytail scowls at him. Somehow saying it like that puts them in a bad light. Like this is something else other than two guys working for the City just trying to do their jobs.

"Fucking bastards," seethes Marcie.

"Yeah they are," says Wiry.

Ponytail scowls again. Wiry has clearly come under the spell of those jugs and is about to start sucking up to her.

"I'm talking about you," says Marcie. "No one makes you come out here at dawn to harass people. You two pricks are the bastards."

"Listen ma'am," says Ponytail. There ain't no need to be callin' names. If you'd like to have your personal effects put in storage, we can have that done for ya. Otherwise, we'll just have to remove them 'cause we can't let them stay out here like this."

The word "storage" ignites a spark of hope for Marcie. Of course storage! These guys can help her! She can just put her stuff in storage for a while. She'll get some sort of job today. Get an advance on her paycheck. Rent another apartment, and go get her stuff out of storage later. This whole nightmare can get fixed. She's gonna pull this one out of the nosedive!

Marcie's expression morphs into friendly mode. "Wow, you mean it? You guys can put my stuff in storage?"

Wiry nods his yellowy smile. Ponytail too lets the corners of his mouth float skyward. "Yes ma'am," confirms Ponytail, "we can arrange for storage, if that's what you want."

Marcie feels a surge of relief. She almost feels like laughing she's so relieved. Everything's going to be OK. All's well that ends well.

Her features are friendly now, like some frazzled, but otherwise completely normal everyday person from some completely normal neighborhood. Just dealing with something that could happen to anybody, right? It's not as if she's a total and complete loser. She's not like some homeless person after all.

"Storage. OK. Yeah, storage would be great. I just need a few days to arrange some things, and then I'll come get my stuff, OK?"

Wiry and Ponytail are smiling now. They're both thinking about a story they heard some of the guys at work tellin' about how one lady was so grateful about the storage thing that after they loaded the furniture they all climbed into the back of the truck and closed the doors and partied.

"OK then ma'am, if you'd like us to take care of the storage we can do that for you, all you need to do is sign the form."

Ponytail is holding out a clipboard with some papers clipped on it. Marcie takes it with a huge smile and starts filling out the form. Name, number, etc., and then her eyes skip to the part about the *cash deposit* ... Oh no! Her stomach ties into a knot. Hope deflating like air from a balloon.

"I'd have to pay something if I want to put my stuff in storage?"

"Yes ma'am. There's a two hundred dollar deposit that we'd have to collect in cash."

Marcie feels her world caving in again. She's suddenly dizzy and faint and weak.

"And if I don't pay the deposit?"

"Well, ma'am, without the cash deposit, we can't put your stuff in storage."

"What would you do with my stuff?"

"We'd have to take it to the dump."

Marcie feels an icy cold wind enter her skull. The terror is coming back. The panic beginning to clutch at her throat again. "Is there any way you guys can put my stuff in storage and I'll come by and pay the deposit later. You know, like this afternoon?"

Wiry and Ponytail shake their heads in unison. "I'm afraid we can't do that, ma'am. City regulations won't let us."

Suddenly something snaps inside. She can actually hear it snap ... like some kind of poultry-like wishbone connected to her innards. All the fight leaves her. She barely has the energy to stand up any more. She wishes she could pick up the bat again and swing. Swing at something. At anything. It doesn't matter. But she can't. In fact, she doesn't even feel like standing any more.

What's the use? It's over. Her head and heart feel somehow dislocated and disjointed. She hands the clipboard back and swallows hard. "I guess I won't be using the storage after all."

Ponytail takes the clipboard. Wiry studies his shoes. "We're real sorry ma'am," says Ponytail.

But she doesn't respond. Her eyes have gone empty. She walks silently over to the hedge and sits down cross-legged on the grass. She watches the two men loading her entire universe into the truck.

Everything she has in the world is disappearing into that truck. She thinks to herself that she should go over and take some of her stuff out of the boxes. She should at least save something. Like a blanket or some clothes, or underwear, or some towels or a toothbrush, or Mr. Biggles. Save Mr. Biggles before he disappears forever!

But for some reason she can't bear to let these thoughts stick in her mind. Like just thinking them would make it all become more real, rather than just some sort of terrible nightmare that's not really happening. After all, this can't be happening, right? How can it? It's not supposed to be like this. So terribly unfair. So not like what it was supposed to be ...

THE SECRET (*of happiness*)

Then, before they even finish loading the truck, she stands up and walks away, in a daze. Without looking back.

45. The Hill

AFTER MARCIE LEAVES PONYTAIL AND WIRY, she wanders randomly around town for a while like a zombie. As if her mind had gone completely blank. Like some giant synaptic circuit breaker was just switched off. She can't register the fact that she's now actually *homeless*.

A bag lady! Without even a bag! She can't bear to think about her situation ... to face up to her new reality ... how to start begging in the street ... how to start looking for some sort of a shelter to spend the night ... how to survive.

All the fight inside of her has disappeared. She doesn't want it anymore. None of it. She's numb all over. Beyond numb. As if something had curled up and died inside, leaving just a walking shell. Like one of those hermit crabs but without the crab.

She just wants to close her eyes and disappear.

And now she's sitting on a park bench staring into space. She's been sitting there for a long time. A foul odor catches her attention. She looks up to see a man standing in front of her. An old bald man with a long beard pushing a shopping cart full of filthy-looking crud.

"How do you do, ma'am," says the man. "I couldn't help noticing you, and I was thinking to myself that you just might be in need of my services."

*   *   *

Marcie climbs the hill.

It's not the pastoral idyllic setting she was conjuring in her mind as her final terrestrial sendoff, but it will do. Beggars can't be choosers and all that.

It's already dark, and of course she doesn't have a flashlight, so she moves slowly. Navigating by the glow of the urban haze reflecting off the canopy of smog ... celestial navigation, Houston style. She spots a secluded patch of shrubbery that looks like a perfect place to lie down and disappear, and starts walking towards it.

She steps into the shrubbery and takes a leap backwards, as if she just walked into a rhinoceros. She can't believe her eyes!

There he is! THE SEX PERVERT!

Again! Sitting right there in front of her with those missing teeth and bruised eyes.

"Are you stalking me?" she blurts.

Max looks at her incredulously. "Are you stalking me? I was here first!"

"No. Of course not! Why would I be stalking you? You're the pervert!"

Max can't for the life of him figure out what on earth this young woman is talking about. Or why she insists on calling him a pervert. But there's a far more pressing issue he'd like to address, "You don't have that bat with you, do you?"

Marcie suddenly feels very vulnerable, and quickly hides her hands as if she were holding the bat behind her back. "Yeah, I've got it."

But he sees that she doesn't. "I'm sorry, but you must have the wrong person," he says with a gentle smile, hoping to tone down the encounter.

"No, it's you. I saw you at Wal-Mart last week sexually harassing a young teenager."

"I'm afraid I don't follow you," he says patiently.

"Last week at Wal-Mart I saw you go up to a teenage girl who was trying to buy lipstick and harass her."

He stares at her for another non-comprehending second and then remembers the lipstick girl he rescued from being caught shoplifting. He imagines how the scene might have looked to a third-party bystander, and bursts into laughter.

Marcie watches him laugh. There's something in his laughter that makes her think twice about this whole pervert thing. But she saw what she saw, and remember that Silent Lamb guy? Lester Hannibis or Cannabis, or whatever. If you met him on the street you'd think he was charming too.

"I see how you might have the wrong impression. In fact, I saw the girl try to steal some lipstick, and I warned her about the surveillance cameras so that she could rectify the situation before running afoul of the security guards."

Marcie thinks this over. It's possible after all ... And he certainly doesn't *sound* like some creepy pervert. In fact, he sounds really nice. With this perfect speech kind of accent. The way you'd expect some professor or someone to talk in a movie. She never knew real people actually talked that way. But still, gotta be careful.

"Why should I believe you?"

"Did you see the security guards at the entrance looking for somebody right after I talked with the teenager and she left the store?"

Oh my God, *he's right!* She did see that moron Clyde with his cast of idiots looking for someone at the entrance. Shit! He must be telling the truth after all. And he sure has beautiful eyes. Even in this light you can tell.

"Oh my God! You're right. I'm really sorry I called you a pervert."

Max smiles. "Don't worry, I probably would have thought the same thing myself if I'd seen it all from your perspective. Fair mistake. No harm done."

"And I'm sorry I hit you with the bat."

"That's OK. I must say, you're pretty good with that bat. Do you play professionally?"

She blushes. She can't believe she's fucking blushing like she's at the school prom. "No, I played a little in high school. I really liked it. Though it's just softball, not baseball."

"I see," he says, "well, you should keep up the sport."

"Yeah, I know, it's really important to exercise." And now she really can't believe she just said *that* ... Here she is, homeless, up on a hill where she's come to kill herself, talking to some still possibly rapist/pervert, though most probably almost for sure really not after all, probably just a stupid mistake. And meanwhile she's touting the merits of physical education? Thankfully, his voice interrupts her internal self-flagellating soliloquy.

"So what brings you out here?" he asks.

She hesitates. Not quite sure how to answer. "Uh ... a friend, sort of a friend of a friend told me that this was a very nice place, and I should come and check it out."

"Come *here?* To check it out?"

"Yeah. You know, might be a nice place to go ... jogging or something."

He glances around at the hill covered with patches of sinister-looking shrubbery. About the last place in the world anyone would want to jog.

She rolls her eyes with a self-conscious Annie Hall laugh. "I guess I'll be crossing this place off my jogging list."

But Max wasn't born yesterday. "Bald Bearded Guy?" he asks.

"What? No! I mean, no. Not especially ... bald, or with much of a beard, or anything."

But it's too late to cover up. Her eyes say it all. Then her features change. She pulls the plug on the lie and smiles. A real smile that lights up her face.

"So ... you too, huh?" she asks.

He nods.

"Bummer," she adds.

He smiles with a resigned shrug.

A silence settles in.

"I suppose that's a bit of a conversation stopper in most circles," he observes.

They share a smile. Then she winces. "What's that terrible smell?"

Max suddenly feels like a kid wanting to blame the dog for his own flatulence. But at times like these you just have to face the music. "I'm embarrassed to say that I didn't have any money to pay Bald Bearded Guy."

"What does that have to do with the smell? It smells like a dead cow."

He points down to the tattered tennis shoes.

"Oh my God! Those are *his?*"

Max nods sheepishly.

"That's so gross!" She bursts into laughter. One of those uncontrollable joyous laughs. Max joins in. She's laughing so hard she sits down, not far from him. When the laughter dies down she pinches her nose.

"You can't stay in those."

"I don't really have a spare pair with me."

"Well, you're better off barefoot then in those. I have some handi-wipes in my purse."

A comfortable intimacy has sprung up between them. She pulls a packet of handi-wipes out and hands it to him. "Come on, what are you waiting for? Get them off and get yourself cleaned up before I puke on you."

Max decides that getting cleaned up is an excellent idea. Living in the street he's grown accustomed to his rank odor, but the idea of actually cleaning up a bit, even if only with a handi-wipe, is an unexpected luxury.

He takes off his shoes. Marcie doesn't hesitate a second. She grabs and throws them as far as she can.

"You won't be needing them ..."

"You're right." He takes the handi-wipes and washes his feet and face and hands. It feels absolutely wonderful.

"Better?" she asks.

"Much."

"Good ... Are you hungry? Because I sort of splurged on the way over here and bought some stuff to eat. I mean, you can't take it with you, right?"

"No, you can't," he laughs.

"Do you like chocolate-dipped strawberries?" she asks.

Nothing could surprise him more. As he told the Guru on the mountain, strawberries and chocolate are one of his favorite combinations. "Yes," he says, "I like them very much."

"Well, good then." She smiles and sets out the basket of strawberries. "And could you open this?" She hands him a bottle of white wine and a corkscrew. He opens the wine.

"We don't have any glasses. I wasn't really expecting anyone for dinner. You don't mind drinking out of the bottle?"

He shakes his head. She hands him a chocolate-dipped strawberry, and when he bites into it the sensation that floods over him is completely unexpected. It's as if all his taste buds are suddenly on overdrive. Bursting with feeling. His mouth lights up like there's a party raging inside. The combination of the chocolate with the strawberry is absolutely heavenly. There's also some other fruit and a wedge of cheese and some bread. It's all divine. Max realizes it's terribly cliché for his last meal to seem like the best one ever. But there you have it.

As they eat their picnic and chat, a question burns in Marcie's mind. She can't stand another second without asking it:

"So ... did you already take yours?"

Of course he knows exactly what she's asking. He's been wondering the same thing about her. "Yes," he says, "I took mine about thirty minutes before we met."

"Me too," she says. "About the same time."

They both sit in silence. Now that they've talked about it ... actually said the words and acknowledged the fact, it suddenly seems more real.

Imminently, terrifyingly real.

"Do you know how long it's supposed to take?" she asks.

"I have no idea," answers Max. "It's my first time."

She laughs. But it comes out nervous and scared. "Do you feel anything yet?"

"No. Just maybe a bit tired, and relaxed."

She lies on her back. Looking up at the stars. "Lie down, Max. It's beautiful."

He lies down next to her, and has to agree. The stars are beautiful. He's looked up at them so many times. From Himalayan mountain peaks, from the deck of his boat in the South Seas, from so many beautiful places across the globe. He's always loved looking at them. He misses them already. This morning he was ready to leave it all behind. But now he's beginning to wonder if he made the right decision.

As he stares up at the stars, Marcie starts talking. At first just nervous small talk, but then she starts talking about herself. Opening up. Opening up like she's never done before. This is her last chance. Her last chance to say all those things she's wanted to talk about all her life but never could. And as she talks, he listens. He hangs onto every word, entering into her life. He's listening so intensely he feels as though he's reliving it all with her.

She talks about growing up alone with her mother, though mostly alone. She talks about her "lapse thing" where sometimes it seems she just blacks out for a minute or so, even though she's still there. And she tells him about Lucky and about giving her baby up for adoption, and about how after that she never really felt any love for anything or anyone, as if she had somehow used it all up.

"Do you think that's possible?" she asks.

"How do you mean?"

"That you can use all your love up, and then just not be able to feel it after that?"

"I really don't know," is all he can say, because he really doesn't. He lies there looking up at the stars wondering about all those countless questions he doesn't know the answers to, and now never will.

And she tells him how she was evicted because she couldn't pay the rent.

And as he listens to her he becomes infuriated. Enraged that her precious life could be destroyed for lack of a few dollars. After all the money he's spent in his life—hundreds of millions on completely useless things! The world is so screwed up!

He's about to say something, but Bald Bearded Guy's pill starts to take command. They both feel terribly drowsy. It's become impossibly hard to talk. So they lie quiet. Next to each other. They can still think, but their muscles no longer seem able to move.

Max's thoughts wander back to the Guru. The Guru knew all along. Max was searching for his telos. His purpose. Hidden inside the whole time. And as he lies there looking up at the stars he senses he's at this very second just about to experience an encounter with another Greek word: Epiphany. (As if those guys thought of everything.)

Of course he'd read about people who'd supposedly experienced epiphany, but he never really believed in it. Just another part of the legend. Another trick in the PR arsenal. Bells and whistles to attract the masses to the box office, like digitally enhanced special effects. But now Max has no doubt about it. He's dealing with a bona fide epiphany ...

Did the ape realize what was happening when she picked up that stick and the thought occurred to her for the first time in planetary history that she could actually use it as a tool to prod the anthill, or extract that yummy goo from her ear? Did she realize the epiphanic majesty of the moment? That nothing would ever be the same on her planet ever again? Did she realize that from that second onwards one species would dominate her world because of what she just figured out? That she had just created the first tool ... the first in a long line soon leading to toaster ovens, automobiles and cell phones. Or was she clueless? Just randomly picking up the stick, jabbing it in, and noticing she could scoop out and lick off those tasty ants more efficiently than with her bare hands?

Now, those same feelings of unity and purpose that swirled beyond his grasp when he was on the space walk are falling into place for Max. He suddenly understands that there *is* something he can do to make this a better world! Everyone can do it. It all makes such perfect sense now that he sees it!

He laughs out loud. At the irony. He's always believed that life's ironies far surpass anything fiction could dream up. And now his very own life is proving the point. If only he'd realized all this before he'd decided to swallow that damn pill! Then he could have put it into practice. Now that he's found his *telos*. Specifically tailored for him. Why didn't he realize it before?

Why? Is the whole thing set up so you can't spoil the punchline because you only get it when you're breathing your last breath? You don't get to know until it's too late to make any difference? Is that how this works? The ultimate jest? To hear the joyous shriek of "Eureka" on your lips just as those lips are silenced forever? To see the bliss of nirvana in your eyes right before they're closed for eternity? That can't be right!

But now the pill is entering into its final phase. Taking over. Turning off his cerebral stage lights one by one as the crowd heads toward the exits after the show. His inner voice sounds like one of those old vinyl records played at half speed. Like the computer in *2001*, "Daisy Daisy ..." At least at this final last moment he's found his telos. He resists the urge to think: "better late than never." But just the same, he figures it's probably true. Like all the other clichés turned out to be.

He feels himself slipping away. What a terrible terrible waste ...

Then Marcie's voice breaks through. Sounding like it's coming from a million miles away ...

"What do you think will happen?" she whispers.

"When we're ...?"

"Yeah."

"I think it will be like when we're sleeping. We just won't wake up."

"No pearly gates or burning pits of fire?"

"No, I don't' think so. What about you?"

"I don't know. I grew up with the pearly gates and pits of fire stuff. It sorta clings to you. 'Specially now."

Max nods. Or at least tries to. But his head barely moves.

"Are you scared?" she asks.

"Yes."

"I'm really scared." She moves closer to him. "Can we change the subject?"

"Good idea," he answers, but the words are barely a whisper.

"I'm feel so cold," she says with a shiver.

"Me too."

She moves even closer to him and takes his hand in hers. She can feel the spark of warmth. The last warm point they have.

"Will you regret anything in particular?" he asks.

She hesitates before answering, "Yes ... And what about you? What will you miss?"

"I'd rather not say."

"Oh come on. You have to," she urges.

"You go first," he says.

"Why should I?"

"Because I asked you first."

"No, I asked *you* first," she says slurringly, thankful for the childlike game taking her mind away from the icy horror of what's happening. "No wait! I know! We'll both write it down and hand it to each other at the same time."

He nods, or tries to. "Do you have pen and paper?"

"I think so." She roots around in her purse for a moment and produces two pens and an envelope. The other side of the envelope is printed in boldface: "Eviction Notice." She shrugs with a sad smile, tears the envelope in two and hands one half to Max with a pen.

They both fumble with the pen, but finally manage, with great difficulty, to write one word. They each fold the paper and exchange sheets.

"Wait," she says.

"What?"

"On the count of three."

They lie on their backs looking up at the stars.

"One, two ..."

She stops counting. They can hear each other breathe. The stars are beautiful ...

"Three."

It's excruciatingly difficult to open the piece of paper. Hard to move at all. Their eyes can barely focus. And in that last second they both read the same word.

The last word in their minds before slipping away into unconsciousness ...

... *you.*

46. Cliffhanger

IT ONLY TAKES STACY about five seconds to pin Virgil down. She does it with the fluid expertise of a martial artist. Straddling him effortlessly. His arms are pinned behind his back, his head dangling over the cliff's edge.

"I guess you're a pain in the ass *and* a black belt," he says.

"Flattery will get you nowhere, Virgil."

"OK, so where does this leave us?"

"Well, from my angle it leaves *you* a bit hanging. As for me, I now have the choice of throwing you over ... or not."

"Yeah, I get that part. I mean mathematically."

"Of course you do. Well, now that we're no longer hypothetically wondering what I *can* do to you, we've consequently removed all the dynamic unknown variables from our equation. The formula is now perfectly linear, thus allowing you to solve it and determine in the next few seconds whether it really is me pulling the strings behind Max's disappearance. Let me give you a clue. I'm going to count to three. If you're still breathing when I'm done, then it's not me."

Virgil smiles, as sarcastically as he can muster given the present configuration.

"One, two, two and a half." She pauses, smiling down at him pinned helplessly to the ground, holding his arms at the breaking point. One false move and *snap*. The waves crash and roar below. "Don't you always love these spots in stories?" she sighs. "You know, the place where the hero swoops in to save the day."

"Yeah, I love that."

"But that's not going to happen here, is it Virge? I guess when you get right down to it, that's the difference between real life and fiction, don't you figure?"

"Does this mean you're done counting?"

She shakes her head. "No, it doesn't. I'm still not out of fractions."

"Wait a second."

"Yes?"

"What if we're the ones running the show in cahoots *together*."

"And we just staged this little cliff-side extravaganza to throw off the clowns who're spying on us."

"Exactly."

"Watching us right now."

"Indeed."

She seems to consider for a moment, then shakes her head. *All part of the show?* All she has to do is release her grip and he'll plummet down to be splattered on the rocks below. Food for the fish.

"Nah, that'd never fly. No one would ever believe I'd team up with a scuzzball like you, Virgil."

Virgil is smiling. Stacy looks strangely beautiful in the moonlight, sweat beads glistening on her skin.

"Are you sure about that?" he asks.

She lets the question hang in the air.

47. You Don't Know How Lucky You Are, Boys

I HAD MAX'S OFFICE CLOSED and sealed off. Of course if I wanted to, I could take it over for myself. But I don't want to. Instead, I set up my office in one of the conference rooms.

All is going swimmingly on the Island. The team is happy. With Max out of the picture we're making even more money than before. I'm running the show as a real team. No more secrets. No more big boss calling the shots. We analyze strategies and vote on actions together as a team. It's as if we're functioning like a collective collegial brain made up of individual synaptic whiz kids. And the result is fantastic. Spirits are up. Profits are up. Nothing seems beyond our grasp.

And now we're riding the wave of a particularly interesting deal. Virgil cooked up the idea and developed it with Flo and Vlad. The basic concept is simple. After the collapse of the Soviet Union, the major industrial and natural resource assets: metals, oil, coal, etc., were all snapped up by the oligarchs. That we all know. But agriculture remained dormant. The oligarchs were satiated with retooling the industrial infrastructures, and the multinational corporate agricultural developers didn't dare venture into such unchartered territory. To make matters more dicey, the land is still held by the local "cooperatives" left over from Soviet times. The only way to acquire the assets is to take control of the cooperatives, which basically means buying huge chunks of land along with the people, whole villages of them, virtually cut off from the rest of the world.

Virgil and his team have been over there for some time working on the project. And now I'm flying to Moscow, where I'll meet Virgil, change planes (for some reason) and then continue on with him to the farm.

As the door of the jet opens, I hear a band playing and see Virgil standing there with a cinematographically-inspired welcome wave, surrounded by a hundred or so people of all ages dressed in folk costumes. Those who aren't singing are playing some sort of boisterous band instrument, and those who aren't either singing or playing an instrument are dancing. And you wouldn't believe what they're playing. Singing out with all their heart and a heavy Russian accent:

"Well the Ukraine girls really knock me out, they leave the West behind, and Moscow girls make me sing and shout, that Georgia's always on my my my my mind, I'm back in ..."

Down on the tarmac I'm met with a bevy of beautiful young ladies who embrace me in welcome. After making it through the welcoming committee I'm whisked into a long black Soviet-style limo with Virgil.

As the limo drives us somewhere, Virgil hands me a shot of vodka. "Welcome, comrade," he says.

I hold up the shot, at the same time noticing that Virgil is holding his glass a bit low. "What's wrong with your arm?" I ask.

"Oh nothing," he says, rubbing his shoulders as if they'd been bruised from some sort of fierce bodily combat.

Whatever, I shrug and lower my glass with a puzzled grin. We clink and drink, sputtering a bit as the crystal clear fluid works its way down.

"Don't you think you may have overdone it a bit with the fanfare?"

"Not one iota. I need to acclimatize you. Where we're going now you'll feel like you've voyaged back in time. Back to Pushkin or Dostoevsky. It's outrageous. Our farm is about the size of Rhode Island. And living on it are thousands people, who go to our schools, who live in our houses, who farm our land. They go to our hospitals when they get sick, and are buried in our cemeteries when they die, which is fairly often because the medical services really suck."

"How feudal."

"Yowza bro'. We are indubitably lords and masters now."

"And all those people at the airport singing and dancing were from our farm?"

Virgil waves away the casting detail. "Actually, they're from a Moscow dance troupe. But the real McCoy is even trippier. Completely authentic. It's a gold mine. With no resources to speak of, their production is at about 10%. So we rebuild the schools, stock the hospitals with medicine, pay them all a decent salary, and what have we created? The most loyal and motivated workforce on the entire planet! We'll raise product quality with better machinery and fertilizers and multiply production by ten. Not only will we cash in on the crops, but price per acre will skyrocket."

"Sounds great, but why are we changing planes?"

"Oh that."

"Yeah."

"Well, there's not exactly an airport nearby, and rather than go to the nearest airstrip and then drive forever on bumpy roads, I've developed a more efficient system."

"I'm not going to like this, am I?"

"Well, considering your general dislike of heights and cool stunts, not very much. But from the standpoint of pure PR and commercial image, I'm sure you're with me a thousand percent. You see, these people love a role model. The *in* thing is to be young, rich, adventurous and successful. And dude, you don't even need to be handsome. It's the balls that count. There's a real action hero cult here. We're just giving the crowd what they want."

But I'm wondering if I can grab a train instead, and am about to quiz him further concerning my travel options when the limo stops and we're ushered out through some sort of security zone and lead off into a military cargo transport by muscle-bound guys in combat fatigues.

We're barely inside before the props start and the plane begins rolling. The noise is deafening. I have to yell to make myself heard: "So I guess this is the surprise, right? We have to finish the trip in this deathtrap of a plane?" Virgil sort of nods, and since it's really too loud to talk comfortably anyway, we both settle in on the military cots prepared for us and fall asleep.

About two hours later, it's time. Virgil wakes me up, and I instantly don't like the look on his face.

"I have a bad feeling about this."

"Don't worry, bro', here's the deal. When we get over the farm, we'll jump out and glide right down, nice and easy."

I groan. "You know I hate this X-treme sports channel type of stuff."

"I know you do, Kemosabe, I know. But it would be so lame to just drive up like everyone else. And we shave hours off the trip. Anyway, you don't have to do anything. Just close your eyes. We're jumping double, and I've done it a million times."

THE SECRET (*of happiness*)

Virgil is already starting to get into his flight suit, which of course we're wearing Bond-like over our business attire. Meanwhile, a soldier helps me into mine, and before you know it we're all suited up, strapped together, and ready to go.

The back of the cargo bay opens up, just like in the movies.

I'm trying to convince Virgil to just head back and land and drive in like normal reasonable risk-averse people. But you really can't hear anything over the noise of the engines and roar of the wind with the cargo doors open. And the ultimate soldier guys currently pushing us into position aren't listening anyway. And before I can say another recalcitrant word everyone is giving the thumbs up (except me) and Virgil is running out the hatch with yours truly in tow.

Of course the chute opens perfectly as they always do. And even I have to admit, as soon as the initial panic wears off, that this *is* a breathtaking entry. The horizon stretches out forever, the fields and forests are frosted in white powdery snow. And as we get closer, I hear the sound of a band. Thousands of people assembled to welcome us. But the ground sure is coming up very fast—

"Just don't break your leg or something lame like that. It would totally blow our superhuman image," yells Virgil in my ear over the rush of the wind.

"How 'bout if I barf?"

Virgil's eyes show true alarm. Fear for his reputation is striking straight into his heart. "Please wait till we get unbuckled," he pleads.

But I'm already moving my mouth like Linda Blair in The Exorcist. Virgil winces and looks away, calculating the seconds to touchdown, and hoping it happens before I can puke on him. Actually, between you and me, my stomach feels fine, but the opportunity to freak Virgil is too good to pass up ... tit for tat.

And somehow we manage to land without a hitch. The band plays joyously. The crowd cheers as we step out of our flight suits wearing our impeccable business garb underneath.

The local dignitaries swarm to curry favor with the new power structure: *us*.

Handshakes, embrassades, toasts ... The band plays on. Random snowflakes fall charmingly. Just enough to add a wonderful snow-globe airport souvenir touch. We climb into a motorcade leading an official military-style parade through town. Sitting there surrounded by the most important local officials, waving to the cheering masses, Virgil and I feel like great kings coming home to our loving people.

And best of all, we're making everyone happy in the process. I know this sounds cheesy, but we are. Honest Injun. With a wave of our magic money wand, we're multiplying these people's income off the charts in comparison to the kommunalka farm down the road. Joy floats in the air like clouds of confetti as the motorcade winds its way through the throngs of cheering crowds. They love us. A truly win-win situation. Everyone's happy.

*   *   *

And perhaps no one is happier than Vladimir, the leader of the local government, who's right now sitting at the head of the VIP gala table flanked by Virgil and me. We're in the central meeting hall, a huge wooden structure where everyone gathers for weddings, funerals, political stuff, parties, and basically any excuse to drink, dance, sing and fool around.

Hundreds of people are squashed into chairs around wooden tables. The band plays merrily. Massive quantities of food abound. I'm amazed at the phenomenal amount of things the Russians choose to pickle. There's of course all the run-of-the-mill stuff, like pickled cucumbers, green tomatoes, mushrooms, cauliflower, mini-corn and pigs' feet. But that's only the beginning. Just overture. The Russians are the artistic Christos of the vinegar world. No pickling challenge can resist them. Eggs, rutabagas, whole chickens, pig ears, crayfish. Anything you can possibly imagine can be pickled by these guys. But no time now to go down the list because the band has stopped playing in mid-note, just as it does every time Vladimir stands up with his glass raised high for another toast.

He's a huge bear of a man with sparkling blue eyes and a bushy head of sandy grey hair. Since the beginning of dinner he's already launched into more than a dozen of these toasts, often in conjunction with someone in the crowd designated with great honor to complete the toast along with him. Somewhere between ten and twenty I lose count.

As explained by the interpreter, most of the toasts are variations on the theme of Virgil's and my magnificent benevolence and wisdom, or the great beauty of Russian women, or some crafty mixture thereof. At the conclusion of every discourse, the entire room stands up and downs another glass of vodka, slapping the empty shot glasses on the table with an amazing noise. Which of course is the cue for the band to segway into another swinging Russian song. Now and then the whole drunken throng joins in with the lyrics and the very timbers of the vast hall vibrate along in karaoke unison with flurries of heel-slapping thrust-kicking acrobatic folk dancing.

Throughout the evening, Virgil and I are treated like royalty. Or better ... like super heroes, or rock star demi-gods. Streams of VIP well-wishers hug us along with heartfelt unintelligible compliments.

And of course there are the girls. Countless beautiful girls. Each bubbling over with unbridled enthusiasm to take us out for a spin on the dance floor and wander off somewhere more discreet to further explore their inner beauty. Needless to say, Virgil is ecstatic. I, however, much to Virgil's consternation, prove to be a big disappointment. I'm not sure what it is. I don't want to come off as this prude sort of weenie jerk, but somehow I'm just not interested right now. I know that Dot has completely blown me off, and that I'm totally free to frolic. But I just can't get in the mood.

To tell you the truth, what I'd really like is just to be able to see Dot again. I'd like to be sitting here next to her laughing at Vladimir's jokes, swirling her around the dance floor, going out for a romantic walk in the snow ... But STOP. I'm digressing like a pathetic loser, so pardon me as I slap myself, pull my chin up, and get back on track. In short, I embarrass Virgil by declining one sublime girl after another. Of course Virgil's voracious appetite makes up for me, sampling them all. Right now he's being escorted away by two gorgeous best friends both named Sasha.

Finally, my repeated disinclination prompts an inquiring beauty to look at me reproachfully and whisper something in Vladimir's ear, causing Vladimir to glance over at me and knit his abundantly bushy brows. I don't have to be a genius to realize I'm the object of abject inquiry.

"Vladimir?"

"Yes, Daviosh."

"What is she saying?"

"Nothing. The girl is saying nothing."

"Vladimir, tell me what she's saying about me."

Vladimir reluctantly admits, "She's wondering if you like maybe boys instead."

I shake my head. The girl shrugs her lovely shoulders, unconvinced, and wanders off.

"It is no problem you know ..."

"What?"

"If you like instead boys, there are many—"

"No!"

"OK OK," says Vladimir with laughing eyes.

"It's just that I have a girlfriend, or rather I had a ... Never mind, it's complicated. A long story."

"*Da ... da ... Ya penyemayo*, I understand," he says. "It is question of philosophy maybe. Let us go outside for walk. Yes, you want walk outside?"

Ah ... the Russians. If I had to peg them into a grossly over-generalized cultural stereotype, I would have to go with these last two elements: girls and philosophy. That's what seems to make Russian guys tick. And alcohol and money, of course. Anyway, Vladimir and I put on our coats and walk through the village in the snow. The sound of the music grows fainter, punctuated by the soft crunching of the snow under our feet. The glow of the party lights twinkles in the distance.

The walk is beautiful. The snow shines magically in the moonlight with that inimitable midnight glowy incandescent blue. We gaze up at the stars and discuss pseudo intellectual notions in broken vodka-enhanced English.

Standing next to each other, peeing into a snow bank, Vladimir looks lovingly over at his brand-spanking-new fully-optioned Porsche Cayenne that came along with the welcoming package concocted as part and parcel of Virgil's commercial strategy. Zipping up his fly, he says:

"Daviosh, you know why communism could never work?"

I shake my head.

"Communism could never work because people just really like to own stuff."

48. Look Homeward, Angel

IT'S TIME for me to leave Russia and get back to the Island. I'm about to climb on the jet when a limo roars up and screeches to a Miami Vice stop right in front of us. Out steps Virgil in his boxer shorts with a blanket wrapped around him toga-like, hair and eyes testifying that he's only half-awake.

"Yowza bro'."

"Hey Virgil."

"I think it's a good time for me to head back too." He starts shuffling towards the plane, lids half-closed.

"Actually, I was thinking of swinging over to Portland and visiting my folks. I haven't seen them in ages."

"Now that, my friend, is a capital idea. Mind if I tag along?"

"Of course not."

And we roar off into the skies. Virgil sprawls onto one of the couches, wrapped in the blanket.

One of the pleasures of the private jet is being able to eat whatever you want exactly the way you want when you want. In keeping with Virgil's theory that every moment of life is far too precious to waste, he customarily has the chef comb the countryside for local delicacies while the plane is on downtime. Or comes up with some other amusing diversion. But there's always something. "So did you check out my surprise yet?" he inquires, eyes still shut.

"What surprise?"

He pushes the "call" button and a new stewardess enters. She's stunning. Even by Virgil's extremely strict standards. I wave and say,

"Hi, who are you?" In response, she lights up with a gorgeous smile that nevertheless conveys her embarrassment of clearly not understanding squat.

Virgil performs the introduction with his rudimentary Russian, "David, meet Nastya. Nastya, this is David."

We shake hands and Nastya goes back to the galley.

Virgil is sitting up in the couch, still be-togaed in his boxers, beaming. "Great, huh? During the weeks I was down there on my own, I organized this cooking contest throughout the entire farm. There were literally hundreds of contestants. First prize was $10,000. That's a veritable fortune down there. It turned into one of the biggest and most prestigious events in local history. And I was the jury panel."

"*You* were the panel?"

"Yup. I figured there was more intellectual freedom that way. And so, over the past weeks that I've been down on the farm, every night for dinner one of the contestants would serve me a meal, some having travelled for days to get there. Sometimes the whole family would come and cook, the grandmother, the mother, the daughters ... oh my God, those daughters ..." Virgil's eyes bask in blissful memory. "All the meals were terrific. It was basically impossible to choose."

"So what did you do?"

"I awarded a whole lot of first prizes."

We laugh. Nastya comes in holding a tray.

"And Nastya here is one of the happy prize winners," says Virgil, smiling at her as she serves us. "And today she's prepared her famous borscht with handmade dumplings."

Given the superlative nature of Nastya's other visible qualities, I'm highly dubious concerning the meal to come. But when I taste the borscht I have to admit that my suspicions are wholly unfounded. If borscht is the star of soups, then this is a supernova. The dumplings are exquisite. Each one a different shape molded by Nastya's expert fingers, and a slightly different taste according to the time spent in some secret marinade.

"Look how happy she is," comments Virgil. "Last week she was a poor peasant, and this week she's the richest girl in her village and the first one to step on a plane and travel outside Russia. She's become a local celebrity ... happiness incarnate."

Virgil is glowing. Enjoying the wonderful borscht, now philosophically on a roll ... "Humans. We never cease to amaze. I actually saw this documentary showing how if you take random photos of poor people and compare them with similar random photos of rich people, the poor people are actually smiling 300% more than the rich people. Now these are photos taken randomly while the people are doing the same everyday things: working, eating, talking, walking, buying stuff, washing, etc. And they don't know they're being photographed, so their smiles should be a representation of what they're truly feeling as opposed to the photo-op smiley faces that the affluent wear at fashionable parties."

"So you're saying that poor people are happier?"

"Hell no! I'm not saying anything. But the authors of the documentary made an interesting point. They said that humans have biologically evolved to feel happiness as a relative emotion. In other words, happiness is the hormonal response to a realization that something is good. In evolutionary terms this pushes the organism to strive to better its condition, which of course is the name of the evolutionary game. For Cro-Magnon this worked perfectly. The happiness he procured eating a good steak next to a roaring fire motivated him to evolve towards making the proper tools to kill animals with good steak meat and to master fire-building techniques, thus improving his skillset and his capacity for survival. That's pretty much where the documentary stopped, but that's where I started thinking that if you extend the logic to our world today, the evolutionary variables remain much the same. The poor man will strive to better his condition. And here's the catch: ironically, the poorer a man is, the higher the delta function would be."

"Uh ... come again?"

"Well, if happiness is an evolutionary mechanism triggered by the relative difference between two emotional states of subjective contentment, then wealth becomes inversely proportional to the mathematical potential for experiencing such relative change."

"Which would explain why the poor are smiling more often."

"Exactly. When you're dirt poor living in some hovel, just not being sick, or having your malnourished kid not be sick is such a blessing that of course you smile. When you're starving, cold and in pain, the simple creature comforts that the more affluent take for granted become unparalleled luxuries: a good meal, a roof over your head ... all causes for supreme happiness. However, take that same man and give him the money and resources to get what he wants all the time and the math is completely different."

"So according to the theory, in the case of the rich man, the evolutionary cards are stacked in the other direction. If happiness is produced by closing the gap between what you want and what you have, then the wealthy, by virtue of their own wealth, have already narrowed the gap, thus reducing at the same time their possibilities of happiness."

"Bingo." Virgil smiles approvingly. "And, did you ever think about how all religions throughout the world extol poverty and warn against the evils of wealth? You know: easier for a camel to go through the eye of a needle than for a rich man to enter the kingdom of God ... The meek shall inherit the Earth, etc. Buddha walked away from being a prince to become a beggar. I mean sure, that one religion gets it wrong, or even that most get it wrong is one thing, but could *all* religions unanimously be off the mark? Extolling poverty and a simple life is perhaps the one point on which all religions agree. How could they *all* be wrong?"

"True. Unless of course it's not a question of being right or wrong. Perhaps the reason religions promote the virtues of poverty is because the various religious doctrines were formed with substantial influence from the wealthy ruling class with vested financial, social and political interest in keeping the poor at their station in life tilling the fields or working in factories instead of vindicating redistribution and starting revolutions."

"Exactly!" exclaims Virgil, holding up two full vodka glasses. "Take your pick, is it vodka theorem number one, or number two?"

I close my eyes, take a random glass, and we down the shots.

*　　　*　　　*

When we touch down in Portland, a gleaming Rolls Royce is there on the tarmac waiting for us. We climb in and start driving to my parents' house. I decide against calling first, opting for the surprise.

When I ring the doorbell and my parents see me standing outside on the doorstep in that trademark Oregonian drizzle, they can't believe their eyes. Mom is so happy she starts crying. Before long Uncles Liam and Billy arrive with their teeming broods of kids and the "Welcome-back-David" party is raging.

At one point during the party I'm able to break away and find myself alone in my old bedroom with Dad. There's my old model airplanes ... there's my collection of old coins ... all the books I read as a kid in the bookshelves ... my magic trick set that I used to spend hours with practicing in front of the mirror. And there's the bed I grew up in, where my parents used to read me bedtime stories, where I'd have nightmares and wet the sheets, where I would cry when I was punished, vomit when I was sick, and where Dot and I would sneak in for those wonderful moments during those rare times when my parents left the coast clear.

Dad's looking at me. I return his look, but for some terrible reason, we can't get our silent communication going. It's always worked before. Something must be out of alignment. Out of whack. Dad seems edgy and nervous, fumbling around for the right words to say, when we never had to find any words before.

"You alright, Dad?"

"Yeah, I'm alright, but how about you? You're the one I'm worrying on."

"Don't worry, Dad. I'm good."

"You sure, son?"

"Yeah, Dad. I'm good."

Of course Dad's not buying it. "Well, that's fine son," he says without believing a word. He looks off to the side and nods uncomfortably.

A silence sets in. But not the good kind. A painful, awkward silence. The first that's ever come between us.

"Dot's moved back here," says Dad.

Her name hits me between the eyes like a missile shot from one of my model planes dangling from their nylon strings.

"Yup. Moved back right after you left. Hasn't been out much though. Spends a lot of time alone in her room. I guess she took it all pretty hard."

I can hear the tears in Dad's voice. He always loved Dot like a daughter.

"Yeah, well ..." My voice trails off because I can't find a way of ending the sentence with anything that could ever possibly make any sort of sense. Every time I think about Dot I feel like there's a dagger stuck in my heart. The only way I can find to stop the pain is to block her out. To chase away the thoughts. To pretend she never existed. Now expert at these mental gymnastics, I zap Dot out of my mind. Instead, I notice that the wallpaper is peeling in places. In fact the whole house looks drab and shabby.

"Dad, I'd like to help fix up the house a little bit." I realize as the words leave my mouth that this isn't the right phrasing. And I know I have to be careful here. I'm treading on highly touchy turf.

"What do you mean, son?"

"Dad, look, I have more money than I know what to do with. I'd really like to share some with you and Mom." An almost imperceptible microsecond of a scowl flashes across Dad's face. *Shit*. I was afraid of that.

"Thank you, son, that's mighty generous of you, but we really don't need any help. Everything's fine."

The door to my room bursts open with Liam, Billy and Virgil laughing and lugging beers. Dad stays for one quick toast and says he'd better "git" going downstairs.

As soon as the door closes, Uncle Billy instantly produces a joint. Uncle Liam clearly approves. Virgil laughs, but I shake my head like I always do in these sorts of situations.

"Aw c'mon, David," goes Uncle Liam.

Then Uncle Billy has a brainstorm: "I bet you've never gotten high, have you David?"

They all look at me like I'm being accused of high treason.

"Well ..." I begin a feeble denial, but my face reads guilty as charged. They all laugh.

"Never got high," marvels Uncle Billy. "It's unacceptable. You're like a marijuana virgin." More laughter by all.

"Yeah well, getting stoned was for the guys who didn't need the good grades as much as I did. In fact, I'm sure at college my stellar

GPA was simply due to the fact that the other kids were smoking all the time and we were graded on a curve."

The Uncles and Virgil take long puffs and pass the joint to me as if I had agreed. I stare at it like it's the devil, which makes everyone laugh even more.

"I don't know, guys."

"Shit, David, you ain't got a test tomorrow, do ya?" scoffs Uncle Liam.

"And I think you can spare some of that grey matter now," smiles Virgil. "Go ahead, lighten up."

"Well, maybe a bit ... just to see."

I reluctantly take a hit as everyone claps.

It turns out that a second puff is easier than the first, and the following ones happen automatically. Soon the four of us are laughing up a riot at nothing in particular. We pull out my vintage video games, the ones I used to play when I was a kid, and laugh until our stomachs ache. This, of course, eventually inspires us with an overpowering urge to pay a visit downstairs to the Finnegan kitchen.

Music blares happily. Uncle Liam's and Uncle Billy's kids have taken over the party and are horsing around laughing. When they see me coming down the stairs they immediately switch off the stereo and start chanting: "Ray Ray Ray Ray Ray." I modestly refuse for a few minutes, to make them beg. Then, amidst a joyous roar of applause, I pull out my shades, sit down at the piano, shoot the keys, and burst into my traditional impersonation of the Genius.

After a few encores, Virgil, me, and the two Uncles move into the kitchen like a swarm of locusts. We first eat all the cookies, then attack the potato chips, dips and pretzels. I marvel that (although I'd never noticed it before) potato chips and cookies in Oregon taste worlds better than any place else.

And as we chomp through every bit of junk food in sight, and even scarf down the stray celery and carrot sticks, Uncle Billy mentions offhandedly to me, "You know, Dot's moved back here."

"Yeah, I know."

"Why don't we go over to her place and say hello?" suggests Uncle Liam.

In my ordinary state of mind I would immediately recognize the utter foolishness of such an undertaking. But presently I'm not quite sure what to think of it, and for some reason I'm feeling particularly charming and clever at the moment, which, I figure, would assist me in dazzling Dot ... And isn't that exactly what's needed after all?

"That would be cool," offers Uncle Billy in between pretzel chomps.

"Who's Dot?" inquires an extraterrestrial voice. We all turn to see Virgil wearing a Darth Vader mask and a pair of hockey gloves he must have found lying around my room.

"My old girlfriend."

Virgil experiences, at that moment, the beginning of a coherent argument voting against the proposed Dottonian visit, but the thought vanishes before he's able to organize it into anything resembling a sentence, so he just says wheezingly: "Do not underestimate the power of the force."

Everyone laughs and continues to munch. Uncle Liam comments, "Yeah, seeing Dot. That would be cool."

And repetition being the powerful ideological tool that it is in such circumstances, we all gradually agree that the idea is a mighty fine one indeed.

We climb into the Rolls with the waiting chauffeur and start driving. On the way we sing. Armed with the battery-operated keyboard from my room, I can play along with basically any song we can remember, or at least partially remember, for it appears at such times that everyone becomes possessed with a proficient capacity to recall small fragments of uncountable popular songs. And so we start off singing something from the Blues Brothers and halfway through segue into a Rolling Stones or Beatles tune degrading into an AC/DC screaming contest and back again.

Destination attained, we spill out of the Rolls, amble over to Dot's door and ring the bell. Standing in the drizzly light from the porch lamp we grin happily at each other with the pure fun of it all. Even Virgil grins under his Darth mask. "May the force be with you, Padawan," he says.

When Dot opens the door, the first thing I see is Greg Maloney standing behind her. And behind Greg, my eyes focus on the romantic candlelight dinner table set for two.

The sight of that candlelight dinner overpowers me like nothing I have ever seen before. I stand there. Blinking like a moron. Nauseous. Hoping the image will disappear when I close my eyes. But it doesn't. If anything, it becomes even brighter and more precise—seared permanently into my brain pixels forever.

Greg fucking Maloney!

Uncle Liam, Uncle Billy and Darth have gone completely silent, all looking at me. Greg, in the background, is looking at me as well. And Dot stands there. Barring entry at the door. Looking straight into my eyes. Her lower lip is trembling and her eyes are turning red around the edges. I realize at this precise moment that she is truly the most beautiful woman in the universe. *My* Dot! My Dot who I've known forever. The only one I could ever love.

"Hi Dot," I finally manage to say.

"Get out of here, David! I told you not to come back here looking for me. But you never did listen to *me*, did you?"

Then she shuts the door on us.

Just like that.

49. Drowning Sorrows

I STARE AT DOT'S CLOSED DOOR for what seems like an ice age. Men might disagree on most everything from religion to beer brands. But all would sadly agree here. If there are a few salient moments in a man's life where he truly realizes how completely he's screwed something up, standing in front of a slammed door in the drizzle with your girlfriend on the other side of the slam with another guy and an intimate dinner setting is definitely one of them.

Virgil puts a hand on my shoulder. "Come on, man. Let's go."

We drop Liam and Billy off in silence, and start driving back towards the airport.

I stare out the window as we drive. Everything on mute. We pass by my old high school. Meanwhile, Virgil's roving eyes are focusing across the street on a glaring neon sign boasting "Captain Nemo's Pizza."

"How about a pizza?" inquires the munchies-inspired Virgil.

But I don't even hear the question. Right now I feel all dried up and shriveled inside. I can't actually think directly about Dot or that terrible candlelight dinner. It's just too painful. For now there's a protective shell around what happened tonight. Shut away like some pulsating container of nuclear waste. Of course it'll all be back to haunt me soon, but for now it's cordoned off at a safe perimeter.

Instead, I'm thinking how weird it is to be driving in front of school in a Rolls Royce. Never back then would I have ever dreamed I'd someday drive by school in a Rolls, or drive anywhere in a Rolls for that matter. Just goes to show you how when you project yourself into the future and think you know where you're going, you really don't know squat.

Then, strangely, as we roll along, I suddenly feel like I've somehow come unstuck from time ... looking out the window I actually *see* myself—my high school self—walking along the street. There I am, clear as day, strolling down the sidewalk with my scruffy pubescent joke of a beard, my tangled hair and my Che Guevara T-shirt. What a dork! My intellectual-cool façade looks preposterous. I don't blame the jocks for picking on me.

And who's that running up? Oh my God. It's Dot. She looks so young! So incredibly young. Just a kid! We both do. We *are* just kids. She's so happy to see me. She twirls around in the dry fall leaves, kicking them up so they swirl in the air like butterflies. Pure joy! Despite the fact that I'm a total nerd. But she looks great! So innocent and vibrant. And so thrilled to see *me*. My God. She's running. Running into my arms like some scene from an Oscar-winning romantic comedy starring us. She's accelerating. Dropping her books and jumping towards me. Oh no! I'm not gonna fall under her weight, am I? She's thin and light, but I look like such a friggin' wimp. I'm not even dropping my books. Like not letting my books fall to the muddy ground is more important than catching her. Christ! What a dweeb! I'm actually worrying about my schoolbooks! OK, finally, there I go. Dropping my books just in the nick of time. And there she goes, in mid-air. She flies into my outstretched arms. So far so good. Except for my ridiculous lopsided grin, everything else is prime. Now we're at that critical 1/100th of a second where we can either meld dreamily together for a perfect wrap, or finish in the bloopers bin. Knowing me I'll drop her. But no! I wince under the weight, almost lose my balance but manage to stay on my legs. *Yes!* I catch her. She clasps her legs around me. Her beautiful smile exploding with happiness.

She kisses me wildly. She's so incredibly in love she would do anything for me. Anything. It's written over every inch of her. Her every cell beats with the pure undeniable fact that she's truly in love with me without any conditions. Without any boundaries, without any ulterior motives or designs. Just pure love.

Oh no! Lord help me. I'm starting to spin around! Clearly ill-conceived. Didn't I know that in those type of rotating 360° shots the actors aren't turning? It's the dolly grip turning around them. The world turns around them, dammit, not the other way around. But there I go, Mr. Coordination. Tripping over my own damn feet. We both go sprawling on some guy's front lawn that hasn't been raked for ages. Leaves all over. But oh ... it's wonderful. That fantastically magical, completely unique fall leaf smell. She rolls over onto me laughing. Smothering me with a kiss. What a fantastic kiss! So in love. A real kiss. A completely in-love kiss. Unlike anything else in the world! It seems like it's been so long. Eons, in fact, since I felt a real kiss like that.

But what's she doing now? Pulling away for a second. My lips are ready, waiting for the next blissful kiss, eyes closed ... But what is she doing? Stuffing a leaf in my mouth! A big dirty leaf. I spit it out, and we're both laughing and yelling, and I say she's gonna be sorry, but then she squeals. I first think she's squealing in mock fear of my impending counter-attack, but I see her pointing to the leaf I just spat out of my mouth. On the backside is the smashed remains of a slug. She bursts into laughter as I gag on the thought of having just eaten the missing half of Mr. Slug. Then I grab her and kiss her. She tries to avoid the slug-flavored kiss. But I get her lips and go for a wet sluggy French smooch. At first she fights it, then gives in and starts kissing back. "Slug's not half bad," she says—

"Earth to David! What about a pizza?"

"What?"

"A pizza. I'm starved."

I'm having trouble getting back to the present, and am still totally wallowing in my misery, so a weak nod is about all the enthusiasm I can muster. But that's evidently enough for a hungry Virgil, who tells the driver to pull into the parking lot.

Located across the street from the high school, Captain Nemo's has been the local hangout for as long as anyone can remember. The walls are covered with a mixture of Jules Verne aquatic knickknacks and sports trophies, photos, old uniforms and other memorabilia from my venerable high school alma mater. We take a seat at an empty table.

Virgil immediately seizes a menu, but I'm just staring at the walls. Soaking up the blast from the past like a time-capsule detonated aftershock.

"Don't you want to look at the menu?" asks Virgil.

"Are you kidding? I know the menu by heart. I used to come in here constantly."

"That was a while ago. Maybe it's changed."

Without even touching it, I glance at the menu. "Nothing changes here."

"Suit yourself." Virgil shrugs and continues his gastronomic perusal.

"Wow. Being here is very weird. I feel like I've travelled back in time."

The waitress comes over. I order my classic Nemo's Special Sub and Virgil goes with a Giant Squid pizza and a side of 20,000 Leagues salad.

I don't know what comes over me, but I start narrating as if I'm Rod Serling:

"I was sitting over at that table." I motion to a table over in the corner. "Just minding my own business, eating a slice of pizza and drinking a Coke doing my homework. It was my senior year in high school. I was sporting my newly grown peach fuzz beard with a scruffy look about my hair. In other words, I didn't consider myself a geek at all. More of an artistic intellectual type. But such distinctions were lost on Jimmy Kazinsky."

"Who's Jimmy Kazinsky?"

"He was this big jock. Played on the football team. Screwed all the cheerleaders. Dumb as a post. Anyway, Jimmy and two of his friends, Bobby Fields and Frank White walked in, right through that door over there. The place was full. All the tables taken. I glanced up from my homework to see them shuffling towards me. Instantly I knew I was in trouble. I nearly peed my pants. So Jimmy, Bobby and Frank stood there towering over me, wearing confident smirks. 'Hey nerd, this table's reserved,' says Jimmy. I can still feel the shot of adrenalin pumping through me.

Of course by this time everyone in the joint was looking at us. Hoping a fight would break out. Naturally I wasn't going to fight them. I'd be flattened with one punch. But it was the perfect moment for a clever quip. Just like in those films where the underdog captures the crowd's favor with his razor sharp wit. The scene was set. I actually came up with a few good lines which would have worked perfectly. But you know what? I couldn't get up the balls to speak. Can you believe that? I was such a wimp that I didn't even dare open my mouth.

So what did I do? I cowered. In front of all my peers, I cowered. I mumbled 'OK'. Just 'OK'. No sarcasm, not the slightest clever trace of defiance, just a completely submissive 'OK'. And as everyone watched, I gathered my books, my Coke and my half-eaten pizza slice to vacate the table. My hands were shaking. Not from fear, because at this point I'd completely capitulated, so I knew they weren't going to hurt me. No, my hands were shaking from shame.

Did you know your hands can actually shake from shame? Anyway, I could feel everyone's snickering eyes on me as I gathered my stuff to leave, dropping my pizza slice to everyone's amusement in the process. I scooped up the mangled pizza and slunk over to sit at the bar. Trying to ignore the smirks and laughs of the other students. My face was as red as pizza topping. I must have played that scene over in my mind a million times. It still makes my cheeks burn."

Virgil nods sympathetically and says, "I'm gonna go pee."

"Straight back and to your left. Picture of Captain Nemo on the door."

After taking a left at the back of the room, and thus out of my line of sight, Virgil whips out his cell. He pushes the speed-dial for Sal.

"I need you to rustle up a party with some of David's old high school classmates. Their names are Jimmy Kazinski, Bobby Fields and Frank White. They weren't close friends, more like class bullies, so they might be a bit surprised when you call. But my guess is they don't have anything better programmed in their lives than watching the tube, so they'll probably jump at the chance to come and drink for free. Emphasize the booze and whatever else it takes to get their butts here as soon as possible. And tell them to call and invite any other friends in town from high school. Sort of like an impromptu class reunion."

The food comes, and of course our sensamillian mind frame makes it all taste scrumptiously delicious. We're well into our wholesome meal when three guys walk in the door.

When I see them walking towards me, I almost choke on my sub. But the panicked thought that my high school traumatism is about to be reenacted only lasts a ganja-boosted microsecond. Reality kicks in and I realize with glee that the tables have turned. Oh how they've turned! Jimmy is now sporting a beer gut just a tad shy of obese, and his face is all bloated like Jabba the Hut. Bobby is thin and pasty looking, and Frank looks like a caricature portrait of white trash, complete with tattoos, rotten teeth, white trash haircut and white trash clothes.

After an awkward moment of handshakes, virile back tappings, and introductions to Virgil, we all sit down.

"Well shit, how long has it been, David?"

"About eight years."

"Well shit, eight years!"

"Yeah."

"Well, you're looking good," says Jimmy.

"Thanks Jimmy, you guys look good too," I lie.

"So how you been?" asks Bobby.

"Oh you know, keeping out of trouble," I answer, with a suddenly re-acquired down-home accent that makes Virgil smile. "How about yourself, Bobby, what have you been up to?"

"Well," says the pasty-skinned Bobby, "I got a job down at the mill in accounts receivable."

"Nice."

"It's OK."

"Married?"

"Was. But that didn't work out. So now I got alimony and child support."

The waitress arrives and Virgil orders beers and pizzas for everyone. He discreetly hands the waitress a $100 bill and tells her to make sure the beers keep flowing before any of the pitchers can go empty. Her eyes light up at the sight of ol' Ben Franklin and she promises that everything will be perfect.

It turns out that Jimmy works selling used cars and Frank is helping his brother out with his struggling deep-sea fishing business.

We nod politely at the picture Jimmy hands around from his wallet of his obese wife and their two plump girls.

I stare into the photo. "Wow, is that Marlene?"

"Sure is," replies Jimmy.

"You married Marlene the cheerleader?"

"Yup, sure did," affirms Jimmy with a swig of beer.

"Wow," I repeat. And this time I'm leaving the *wow* right where it is, completely justified by the incredible sight of how those eight years have transformed one of the hottest fillies at school into the Pillsbury Dough Girl.

And as I look up from the photo, in comes another group of my classmates. It seems that the Rolls Royce in the parking lot has not gone unnoticed. Captain Nemo himself is out in the lot with Mrs. Nemo taking pictures posing next to it. And having arrived in a Rolls, it appears that we are very hot items indeed.

By now word of the party has gotten out, and soon there are far too many classmates, party crashers, and general well-wishers to be contained at a table, so Sal organizes with the Nemos and the diplomatic support of ol' Ben to have the whole place closed down for the private party.

The music blares. All-you-can-consume pizza and pitchers of beer everywhere. Off to the side, Virgil watches as my old classmates gush and fawn over me, just like he'd planned. And of course he's completely right on the mark: when you're down in the dumps, a little ego boost never hurts.

Mingling with the crowd, Virgil soon makes the acquaintance of Sid, one of my old classmates who opted to eschew the lumber, fishing, retail, insurance and used car industries, which otherwise account for the livelihood of pretty much everyone else in the room. Electing to tread the high road, Sid has gone into business for himself in what he describes as a para-pharmaceutical supply service. Virgil promptly purchases Sid's entire inventory, and instructs him to make the rounds and see to it that everyone has everything their hearts desire, courtesy of the house. Sid is only too happy to comply.

And I, in a world premier, actually decide to let myself go completely with the flow. And the flow is flowing wildly. By eleven o'clock a very happy Captain Nemo confides in Virgil that this is the best bash they've ever had. Like at those VIP showbiz parties, Sal has installed me at the large alcove table in the back. Classmates nudge and elbow their way to get as close to me as possible. At one point, Sid's at my side. His professional advice is two of the little yellow pills and one big snort of the white stuff.

I have to yell into his ear to be heard above the roar of the music and the crowd. "You sure this is OK?"

"It's better than OK. It's fucking stellar. I take twice that every day, and right now I must have at least five times as much pumping through me. And I feel awesome."

So what the hell. With a devil-may-care shrug, I follow my schoolmate's advice.

Incredibly quickly the chemicals kick into gear and I soar into the stratosphere. Suddenly I've become the roaring party animal I'm totally not. I'm actually dancing on top of the tables playing air instruments like a rock star.

And then, in a break between sets, I find myself sitting very snugly next to Kelly Abbot. Unlike most of her peers, she's somehow avoided that apparently natural local propensity to morph into the Michelin Girl. Back in school Kelly was a real bomb, and of course a cheerleader, and of course she wouldn't have given me the time of day back then. Now she's divorced. From across the room, I notice Virgil watching her sitting next to me. Of course she's not anywhere close to the level of the beauty goddesses Virgil frequents on his weekend forays, but for a normal person, she looks just fine. Virgil watches her maneuver closer and closer. And next thing you know she's got her tongue down my throat.

This neighborhood of Portland is not exactly the most swinging spot on the planet. In fact, it's probably one of the least. Truth be told, nothing even remotely as interesting as this impromptu reunion has happened here for ages. And it is thus with the relish and gusto behooving such a once-in-a-lifetime event that the guests now party down. Being re-united after all these years with one of their classmates who's become a millionaire infuses them all with a surge of adrenalin and self-importance. *They're this guy's friend!* A real live VIP. A millionaire who drives around in a Rolls Royce! Even those who are normally tame and subdued on a drab daily basis are letting it all hang out now. They're going wild. Partying like there's no tomorrow.

Around midnight a consensus forms that the festivities are ripe for a small contingent of die-hard partiers, a bona fide fiesta commando group, to break off from the main pack and go out for a spin on Frank's brother's deep-sea fishing boat.

A short drive later the core party-strike-force regroups on the deck of the boat. There's Ned and his wife. Ned was my best friend back in high school because we were both dorks. He sells computers now, has two kids, and seems to be a completely normal sort of guy. And there's Craig, who's become a gloomy bachelor with a comb-over, goggle-like glasses and that same lisp. He has some sort of insurance-related job and rarely lines up more than two words in a conversation. Tim runs what used to be his dad's pet shop and Brad sells caskets over the Internet to funeral parlors. And of course there's Kelly Abbot and Jimmy and Bobby and Frank and a couple of their buddies and assorted girlfriends and tagalongs.

A white stretch limo pulls up to the boat and out step a few party girls hastily recruited from God-knows-where through Sal's inimitable network.

As they exit the limo, the joyous crowd roars with applause and catcalls. Meanwhile, another car under Sal's direction is unloading enough food and beverages to get from Sodom to Gomorrah and back again.

The boat is spacious and perfectly adapted to wild partying. Frank decides that under the particular circumstances it'd better if they borrow the vessel without actually informing his brother, the owner, who's probably sleeping by now anyway. Why wake the poor guy?

And thus we intrepid mariners cast off our lines and head out across the Columbia Gorge. Standing side by side at the prow, Virgil and I admire Sal's masterful artistry. He's patched an iPod into a powerful amp and speakers so that the appropriate music blares joyfully. Several chilled beer kegs have been rolled aboard, as well as untold gallons of hard liquor.

The night is pitch black. The typically incessant drizzle has been put on pause. The moon is either hidden behind the clouds, or has some other excuse for not showing up. In any event, the boat is enveloped in a seemingly four-dimensional expanse of dark inky nothingness. Frank is at the helm, and despite the alcohol coursing through his veins, says he could drive the boat with his fuckin' eyes closed.

As we chug down the Columbia Gorge, there's not the slightest breeze or wave. The water's as flat as a mirror. An opaque black mirror.

The party rages. The ship looks like one big floating frat house on Friday night. Lights blaze. Liquor flows like the river. The party girls mingle. None of the guys have ever had such lovely girls paying them so much attention and finding them oh-so-interesting. They're in guy heaven.

And, for those of you who don't know it, one exceedingly fine feature of many nautical VHF systems is their ability to double up as a loudspeaker, which of course is useful when calling out to a nearby fogbound vessel, or alternatively for addressing a boatful of hammered guests. It just so happens that Virgil is feeling particularly eloquent, and it is thus with great oratorical flourish that he takes to the mike. Sal kills the music, and after that classic burst of intro feedback, Virgil's voice blasts out:

"I just want to thank you all for being here tonight."

—Roars of applause.

"And you might not realize it, but just being here is an amazing feat."

—More deafening applause.

"In order for that to have happened, the Earth needed to cool to just the right temperature so many millions of years ago. And there had to be just enough CO_2 and other gasses in the atmosphere, and just the right mixture of amino acids in that primordial soup."

—Nonplussed white noise with no applause.

"And then when your ancestors got tired of being single-cell slime, they had to go through an astounding series of genetic mutations over millions of years with various combinations of beaks, flippers, scales and feathers before they developed into homo sapiens. And then your direct ancestors managed somehow not to get squashed by wooly mammoths or eaten by saber-tooth tigers or burned at the stake as heretics ... So do you realize the odds against you being here? Well the odds are incredible, but you made it. And I'd just like to say: *congratulations* to one and to all."

There is complete silence where the applause should be when Virgil stops orating. The crowd trades stoned puzzled looks.

Someone is heard to mutter: "Man, that's some intense shit." A few straggling claps and coughs here and there.

"I guess that went well," says Virgil with a happy grin as he hands me the mike.

Me to Virgil: "Thankz for warming them up for me."

Me to the crowd over the PA: "Now you all remember why you ztayed away from me in high zchool, right?"

—Uneasy chuckling.

I continue: "And I jez wanted to zay, it'z really nice being back in Portland."

—Wild hoots and hollers wash over the vessel. I smile and raise my hands up like the MC at a rock festival.

"Because Portland rocks," I yell out, just like Mick Jagger would.

—Insane applause.

"And zo lez paaaarrrtyyy!"

—Deafening roars of claps and cries and hoots and hollers.

Sal segues back into the music with DJ virtuosity and everyone parties like never before.

Frank is steering up on the fly bridge when Virgil and I join him. One of the party girls has taken an evident shine to him, but steering the boat is clearly distracting him from full appreciation.

I decide to help him out. "You wan me to take ze helm zo you can take care of your friend here?"

"You know how to drive thiz?" asks Frank.

"Of courz!" I answer with a confidently assuring seamanlike scoff.

Virgil gives me a sidelong glance, but Frank is already moving off to the corner with his friend.

"Since when do you know anything about boats?" asks Virgil.

"I drove Max'zz."

"A fucking sheep could drive Max's with all the computer overrides. You just *felt* like you were sailing. You could have been watching a video. You do realize there's no computer guiding you here, don't you?"

But Virgil's words fall on deaf ears. I'm so chemically inspired at this point I'd happily volunteer to fly a MIG over enemy territory based on my adolescent hours behind the stick of a PlayStation.

"Don' zurry, I fine," says I with a huge nautical grin.

Virgil nods, still doubtful, but content to go with the flow.

... Can't be too hard to drive this thing, after all ... He gazes into the stars ... "It's so amazing," he muses out loud.

"Yeah," I agree.

"What?"

"Whatever you were about to zay."

"Oh. Yeah. About time travel. How if you ever want to travel back in time, all you have to do is look at the stars. Their light spent hundreds or thousands of years coming here. So when you see a star twinkling, you're really seeing a twink that actually *–led* hundreds of years ago, maybe while Christopher Columbus was sailing around. By now it might have turned into a supernova or burnt out into a black hole. And if right now, some creature living on a planet orbiting one of those stars is looking at the Earth with a powerful telescope. They won't see *us*. They'll see the guys building the Pyramids or Stonehenge. They won't see us on this boat for hundreds of years after we'll be dead and buried."

I nod in solemn appreciation. We feel the beauty of the night philosophically wrapping us up like a Gortex blanket, or a California roll, or a Gortex roll in a California blanket. Whatever, it's heavenly.

"Hey Virge. Can I azk you kweztion?"

"Yowza Dave. Fire away."

"You think I'm gonna get Dot back?"

Virgil reflects a beat before answering, sensing that lucidity isn't exactly the ticket that's called for here.

"Maybe, I guess."

I smile. "I know I will. Zomeday I will. 'Coz we're zoul-mates and we're meant to be together." As I affirm the certainty of this obviously highly unlikely event, I note pleasantly that for some reason right now I just don't feel in any way constrained by the usual concerns for realistickness.

"OK bro', just concentrate on steering the boat," suggests Virgil.

"You're right. And thankz for the party."

"Don't mention it."

"No, I mean it, man."

"Yeah, well ..."

The moment is bursting ripe with cumbersome, yet loftily-intended nautical poetry. The moon casts its alluring glow over the mystically inky water ... Call me Ishmael, and that sort of stuff.

"I love zailing. I really feel the elementz. You know what I mean?"

Virgil nods. He's feeling it too. The gentle breeze of intoxicated joy bubbling up the brainstem. It's brilliant.

And as Virgil and I thusly commune with nature, the teasingly rocky shoreline of the Columbia Gorge sneaks mischievously up on us.

SUDDENLY, a horrendous sound of smashing and splintering wood shatters through the music and laughter. The boat stops dead in the water, lurches to one side, and starts to sink. The guests go sprawling and start screaming or both.

I turn towards Virgil, "Thiz zuckz."

Frank appears, buck naked, eyes wide in terror, his rubber-coated virile member dangling in the wind like a shrink-wrapped sausage.

"What ze fuck'z going on?" he shrieks.

"I think we hit zomething," I respond. In fact, the astute and sober observer would remark that we're less than a stone's throw from shore.

"Oh fuck!" yells Frank, running from the fly bridge, sausage flailing. He slips down the stairs and sprawls, balls akimbo, from the fly to the main deck.

"Ouch," comments Virgil.

But Frank quickly scrambles to his feet and runs towards the bow amidst the chaotic cacophony of a boatload of frantic screaming.

Amongst the scrambling passengers, Jimmy's huge naked self scuttles into view wearing only a U.S. Coastguard-approved life preserver and his undies. Apparently he'd accepted a dare to jump in the water, and was stripping down to his shorts to cash in on the bet when the crash occurred. Virgil and I wince at the nightmarishly psychedelic vision of those jiggling folds of aspirin-white flab against the orange day-glo vest jostling gelatinously in the rush for safety.

Craig and Brad sit philosophically on deckchairs smoking, calmly contemplating the pandemonium. They thoughtfully compare the present situation to that great scene in Titanic. "Except in the flick no one was naked," observes Brad.

"Which is just another poignant example of how art falls so dramatically short of reality," adds Craig, demonstrating that he is in fact perfectly capable of communicating in sentences, while at the same time providing needed support to the oft-neglected Mr. Ed approach to life.

Sal appears at our side, habitually unruffled. "Don't worry," he says, "we can walk ashore."

"What about the boat?" I inquire.

"Totaled."

By now the screaming hysterical guests have begun to realize that this is neither Poseidon Adventure nor the Perfect Storm, and that the boat has safely settled on the bottom of the riverbed, tightly stuck onto the outcropping of those sharp rocks that tore through the wooden hull like an ice pick into a Twinkie.

With the realization that they're not going to drown comes great mirth and merriment. Someone starts singing the Gilligan's Island theme song and everyone joins in, with a hefty dose of laughter at the mention of the millionaire—what was his name? Oh yeah: Thurston Howell the Third.

Meanwhile, Frank is inconsolable. He's screaming at the top of his naked lungs: "Fucking zhit! Fucking zhit! Fucking zhit!"

Virgil turns towards Sal. "Do we have enough cash in the plane to cover this?"

Sal nods. "Yeah, I'll take care of it."

Virgil and I watch admiringly as Sal grabs the shrieking Frank and whispers something in his ear that has the immediate effect of calming him down.

"One very cool thing about being rich is that problems like this are simply not problems," notes Virgil philosophically.

Serendipitously, we chanced upon an exceedingly beautiful place to shipwreck. Sal loses no time in demonstrating how we can all walk to shore in the waist-deep water. He builds a huge bonfire and before long everyone is festively roasting hot dogs and marshmallows.

We're singing around the campfire when the sound of a helicopter makes itself heard.

"Ssshhhzzhzzhhz" say many, as the throbbing noise grows louder.

"What the fuckzz that?"

"It's the fucking copz."

"No zhit! You think?"

"The copz?"

"Must be the fucking copz!"

Then Sal lets out a piercing whistle—one of those two-fingered jobs—and everyone freezes. "Calm down people. It's not the police. It's our chopper, coming here with a little gift for Frank." A few moments later the hired helicopter lands on the grassy knoll. The pilot walks towards Sal and hands him a black leather briefcase from the jet.

Everyone watches in suspense as Sal walks over and hands me the briefcase. Then I ceremoniously walk towards Frank. With all the stately decorum of those final award scenes in the early Star Wars episodes, I stand in front of Frank and say: "I zorry I drove your boat on the rockz, zo with thiz you can fixz it or buy a new one."

I open up the briefcase, displaying stacks and stacks of money, certainly enough to repair the damage. Everyone starts clapping and Frank straddles me in a huge bear hug. None of the guests has ever seen stacks of cash like this anywhere other than the movies, so of course they all crowd around. Everyone's yelling and laughing, excited like kids, snapping pictures of themselves around Frank sitting down cross-legged in the grass with packets of money piled over him.

By dawn, everyone has dropped off to sleep, including Virgil and me. Sal wakes us both, and we climb into the waiting helicopter.

It is time to go, cognizant of that universal axiom holding that in such situations, things which look delightfully humorous and cool during the night, tend to look a whole lot less so in the morning.

*　　*　　*

As the jet takes off, I watch Portland zoom away from me, getting smaller and smaller behind the tail-wing until it doesn't even exist! Gone! Behind! Left behind with the whole cast of them!

What have I done? I travelled gloatingly back in time to lord my wild success over my hapless classmates. Is the whole thing sick? Hedonistic? Narcissistic? Perverted? Well, it's certainly not pretty. Clearly not one of my finer moments. But nonetheless hugely gratifying and sublimely, shamefully human.

The remnant molecules from last night are most assuredly still swirling through my synapses ...

Just then, out of nowhere, like a stray boulder launched from a subconscious catapult, the image of Greg Maloney slams into the side of my skull. It feels like a complex chemical formula with multiple convoluted components ... frustration and sadness and regret, and longing and deception and ... anger. Yes, anger is by far the easiest one to get a handle on. Some sort of an equalizing common denominator. I don't even have to decide whether it's at myself, at Maloney, at Dot, at ... fuck it all! The rage runs through me like a bolt of electricity. Like the Incredible Hulk during one of those green transformation sequences, or someone stepping out onto the highway and getting smashed by a Mack truck at sixty-five miles per hour, bouncing along the asphalt, tumbling at high speed under each of the eighteen or however many wheels they have, a bloody pulp ejected from the last wheel as it barrels away. So fuck you, Maloney! Fuck you fuck you fuck you, for slamming the door in my face and having a fucking candlelight dinner. (Even if it was technically Dot who shut the door) ... but she wouldn't have done it if you weren't there. *That* I'm sure of. Yeah, I'm sure. But that's not the point. The point is, the fucking point is that ... I'm not even going to think about the other stuff you're doing with her ... no, the point is ... well fuck you, fuck you completely ... yeah, the point is that I should have rammed my fist down your fucking throat is what I should have done. So you can just fuck off. The both of you.

Ahhh ... I feel immensely better after having so rigorously worked through the logic of the situation.

Speaking of logic, I reach into my pocket and pull out a little plastic leftover baggy from Sid of what could easily pass for flour.

"Whoa team, don't you think you'd better go easy on that stuff?" comments Virgil.

I grin and look at my watch. "It's still the weekend," I say with a lopsided conspiratorial wink. And though Virgil cannot dispute the factual accuracy of my retort, it clearly appears from his disapproving expression that he is, for some reason, questioning the direct causal relation to the underlying premise. What's more, I can see he's about to launch into some sort of formalistic challenge to my proposition.

"Yowza dude. Wake up! We had a good laugh, and now it's time to throw that shit away."

I hesitate for a micro-second. But my cognizant self has climbed back into the cockpit and taken over the stick. Of course he's right. I toss the baggy into the trash where it belongs, and stare glumly out the window at the clouds streaming by.

50. The Grapevine

DOT FREELY ADMITS THAT she's not the greatest driver in the world. It doesn't have to do with her attention span or any sort of mental oversight. On the contrary, when she drives she's completely concentrated, organizing and focusing her thoughts intensely on her task. It's the unexpected things that throw her for a loop. The things she hadn't figured into the program.

For example, the cat this morning on the way to work just jumped out of nowhere. There was no way of foreseeing that. And of course she had to swerve to avoid hitting him. And of course it was her luck for the tree to be right there where she was swerving. None of *that* was in the program. Anyway, this isn't the first time she would touch up a car after one of her automobilistic mishaps. She had already done it on David's old wreck of a Volkswagen many times.

Greg's car is green. A sort of overripe avocado green. Which explains why she's now in the spray paint aisle of the local department store scanning through the available cans of green. All she needs is a little bit to cover the dent from that stupid tree. The trick is in finding the right shade. She knows from experience that the wrong choice—even if only a fraction off—will spoil the whole effect and draw attention to the problem rather than camouflaging it. Like so many things in life, it turns out.

She's stooping down to compare two contending color choices when she hears some women chatting behind her, in front of the light-bulb display. Still crouching, she sneaks a quick look over her shoulder. It's Susan McNulty and Becky Ledford, two girls from high school. *Ugh*. About the last thing in the world she feels like now is small talk with old classmates. But if she stays crouched, and just lets them pass by, she can probably finesse it. After all, they look terribly absorbed in their gossiping. Without really trying to listen, she overhears bits and splotches: "incredible ... awesome ... Rolls Royce ... really cute ... David Finnegan—"

David? Why are they talking about David? Instantly she's all ears. Susan is talking about some party last night with ... *David?* Starting off at Nemo's? Everyone from school? He was kissing Kelly Abbot? Impossible! David wouldn't be caught dead kissing Kelly! And a boat ride ... with strippers? And drugs? David? No way! They're lying. Lying through their teeth. How dare they!

Susan and Becky leave the light bulbs and start wheeling their shopping carts down the aisle. Dot is livid. She remains crouched down, with her back to them. They walk their carts right by, without taking any notice of her. She's so mad her upper lip is trembling. So are her hands. How dare they talk about David like that! And then, suddenly, she stands up staring straight at them. They both recognize her and stop talking, realizing she must have overheard. Dot glares. Becky looks embarrassed, but that tart Susan actually looks amused. Not LOL amused, but clearly enjoying slandering David in public, right in front of her!

"Hello, Dot," they say, uncomfortably.

"You should have the decency not to tell your filthy lies out here in public."

Becky just looks more embarrassed. But Susan is half-trying to hide a mocking smile. How dare she! Dot is so mad she's trembling even more. She's never hit anyone in public before. In fact she's never really hit anyone at all before, except for that horrible morning the last time she saw David. But as she stares at Susan's mocking little face, her hands and brain go on some sort of uncontrollably enraged autopilot. She wants to lash out with a slap, but her hand is holding the paint can. Without actually even thinking about it, as if in slow motion, she sees herself popping off the plastic cap and pressing down on the spray button.

Susan screams as the green cloud envelops her.

Dot throws down the can and bolts out of the store, leaving Susan behind, screeching, with her face now as green as Shrek.

On the way home Dot stops by a convenience store to buy a pint of ice cream. The kind with whole globs of cookie dough in it. She picks up an inexpensive set of two spoons as well. Turns out you can't buy the spoons individually. They're only sold in pairs. Of course they are! How else could they spoon together? They made no sense apart.

She drives to a small park down the street where she parks Greg's car. She takes out the ice cream and attacks, ready to eat the whole pint.

She sits there eating and focusing on keeping her mind blank. Staring emptily out the windshield. It starts to drizzle. Big surprise. She watches the tiny specks of rain cover the windshield. Then the screaming image of the avocado-faced Susan flashes into her mind and she starts laughing. At first it's a silent inner laughter. Then it spills out and she begins laughing hysterically out loud. And as she laughs she thinks back to what Susan had said about David. She thinks of those things he must be doing with other women and her laughter merges seamlessly into tears. She cries for what seems like a very long time. Long enough for the rest of the ice cream to melt.

*   *   *

That night, in bed next to Greg, she stares at the ceiling. She's been staring for hours. She needs closure. It's time. She'd already decided she needed to cut David out of her life for her own survival. She just needs to take this last step. She wakes Greg up and tells him she thinks they should get married.

Greg is thrilled. He's puzzled why she looks so solemn and sad. But he doesn't want to ask questions. He takes her in his arms and holds her tight.

51. Hollywood

EVER SINCE VIRGIL saw Dot shut the door on me, he's been real thoughtful about drumming up fun excursions to cheer me up. And I admit I'm a bit psyched about tonight's celeb party. After all, you grow up seeing them in movies and on the covers of those stupid gossip magazines in the grocery store checkout lines, and the thought of actually hanging out with them is exciting. Hobnobbing with the stars. Of course on the exterior I'll have to play it down. Cool. Otherwise I'll pass for a total chump.

Virgil's been a regular at these types of parties for the past couple years, so he's gotten to know most of the big names. Right now he's sleeping on one of the couches and I'm stretched out on the other. Our jet's about to touch down at a small private airport outside Hollywood.

We land. The Rolls is waiting on the tarmac, of course. There's the usual pomp and ceremony from the welcoming airport staff as we walk out of the jet and into the Rolls. We're both dressed like any normal college kids on any campus ... jeans, faded T-shirts. In a practice-honed effort to grab every minute of sleep to enhance partying capacity during the night, Virgil stumbles along yawning like a sleepwalker. Our grunge seems weird in contrast to the uniformed clean-cut employees treating us with such extreme deference. The liveried chauffeur holds the door of the Rolls open like we're royalty. I guess I'll never get used to that part of this whole thing. In any event, once in the car Virgil immediately flops back to sleep and even I nod off on the way.

We wake up in front of S—'s house, our host for the evening. It's one of those sprawling Hollywood mansions with a backlogged tangle of expensive flamboyant cars outside, and an army of valets trying to cope. It's S—'s birthday. A bigwig movie director who's made tons of box office hits. We've all seen his stuff. He's a legend. And all the brightest stars have come out to shine tonight, even those who didn't feel like it. I guess in this town there are some people's birthday parties you just can't miss.

And don't think for a second that money can't get you in the inside loop. Maybe there are some circles you can't buy your way into. Like literary or other intellectual self-sufficient groups. But showbiz needs money to stay alive. Lots and lots of money. Money is the blood coursing through showbiz's veins, along with a lot of other chemicals, of course. Anyway, Virgil has thrown around enough cash, partied with enough of them, invited them out on enough rented yachts with enough free coke and other recreational activities for them to all call him "buddy." And apart from the few superstars, the vast majority of them don't have that much money, and are more than happy to hang out with someone picking up the tab. And unless you're inside the clique, you're outside. Hermetically outside. They hang out amongst themselves, party amongst themselves and marry amongst themselves. It's a status thing. But of course we all know that. We get that much from the gossip magz.

It turns out that Virgil has invested in various films, and thus is treated with the great respect inherently due in the film industry to anyone at all—regardless of race, creed, sex or links to suspected criminal activities—with future potential to shell out more cash. And as Virgil's pal I'm able to bask in his limelight.

We've only been here for an hour or so, and I've already been hugged and slapped amicably on the back by almost all my childhood heroes. There's the guy who made all those magnificent sci-fi flicks.

There's that incredibly funny comedian, who, ironically, isn't funny at all in real life. Practically all the hot women stars I used to fantasize about when I was a kid are here. And of course everyone's doing the same thing people do at any other party. Drinking, laughing, ass-kissing, flirting, story-telling, maneuvering, losing track of an idea in mid-sentence, spurning, complaining ... you know, just like normal.

And now we're chatting with a famous director, a producer and two A-list actors. All male. Virgil is discoursing poetically over something Darwinian, something about how us guys shouldn't feel guilty about not wanting to cuddle.

"You know how afterwards, when she's feeling cuddly and you're feeling like taking a shower or slipping out the door?"

"Yeah," we guys all nod.

"Well stop feeling bad about it. It's not your fault. It's programmed into you."

"Wow," say we guys.

"In evolutionary terms you've accomplished the mission. Think about it. Cavemen who possessed genes inciting them to cuddle were exposing themselves and their offspring to greater danger. Constant vigilance was the ticket to survival, not post-coitus cuddling. You can't protect your family against a marauding mammoth if you're spooning. The genes that had you up cocked and ready as soon as possible to continue to procreate and protect the species were of course the most likely to survive and replicate. So the cuddly spooning types were slowly but surely weeded out over those millions of years. The successful caveman was the one who was immediately back out there hunting, gathering and chatting up the other caveman chicks. So we shouldn't feel bad about the way we are. It's who we are. Genetically wired right into us. No shame about it."

I smile, watching Virgil be Virgil.

"No shit," say the actors.

"Fuckin' A," says the director. "This is so radically topical."

"So intrinsically pertinent," says the producer.

"Very high concept."

"Where'd you get it?"

"From a book," says Virgil.

"Let's option it."

"Totally."

"It's like a post-modern multi-allegorical prehistoric cross-cultural metaphor."

"We'll bookend it with awesome FX."

"We can get B— W— for the non-cuddly caveman."

"And W— S— for the cuddly one."

"You think a black caveman could work?"

"Absolutely."

*   *   *

At some point the alcohol and other chemical levels surging in the vast majority of the guests' bloodstreams conjugate with the loud music to render coherent conversation impossible. Communication, of course, becomes heightened without the barrier of language as the party shifts into that classic phase where even stupid shit sounds hilarious when you yell it unintelligibly over the techno bass reverbs into someone's ear. Makes you wonder how many would-be great thoughts have been maimed beyond recognition by trying to force them into actual words.

Somehow the swimming pool has become full of suds. People start jumping in. Assuredly not in the mood for an aquatic adventure of the sort, I wander downstairs. Following the sounds of uproarious laughter, I chance into the gym. It turns out that the gym is outfitted with a huge one-way glass mirror looking straight into the side of the pool, under the waterline. Suds float, so seen from below, the view is crystal clear: an aquatic tangle of limbs and torsos thrashing about as the clandestine voyeurs laugh it up hysterically.

I'm feeling predictably blue and depressed as I meander away from the gym. Now I'm not exactly the nosy type, but give me a break. This is my first time in a real Hollywood mogul's house, so I'm naturally not opposed to a bit of discreet exploration—don't tell me you wouldn't do the same. And if anybody nabs me snooping around, I'll just say I'm looking for the john. That's thinking ahead, homeboy.

Down the corridor is a side room. I snoop over to it. The door's half ajar. I peek in. Nobody inside. It must be some sort of downstairs study/storeroom. Framed posters of our host's great box office hits cover the wall. I've seen them all. Every single one. An overstuffed couch. Books piled up willy-nilly. An old foosball table, some sports gear, and look! There's a piano. Sweet. I glance around to make sure the coast is clear. It is, so I step in, close the door and beeline it over to the keyboard. I open the cover and blow off the huge coat of dust. It's a bit out of tune, so I opt for a blues, where out-of-tuneness is a plus. I sit there playing for a while, quietly so as not to attract attention.

This is exactly what I needed to get past that wave of sadness I was feeling. I'm better now, and am already thinking about going back up to join the party when I hear a voice behind me.

The voice is singing. An intense, rich, haunting voice. She's singing the blues I'm playing. Making up the words as she goes along. I know that because I'm improvising the tune from scratch. But her lyrics fit in perfectly. Like magic. How can she do that? And her voice! Her voice is absolutely amazing.

She sits down next to me on the bench and I look over at her. Oh my God. I can't believe it. It's her. It's actually *her*. I'm not much of a People follower. But I know she recently came out of nowhere to become a superstar sensation. She somehow brought jazz and pop and country altogether and rolled them into gold record after gold record hit. I love her stuff. And here she is sitting next to me.

I smile. Trying not to look too goofy as I recognize her and scoot down an octave, shifting to a walking bass line and rhythm riff so she can solo if she wants. And boy does she. Pure virtuoso. Simple, straight by ear and straight from the heart. Then she glides into that slowly accelerating dueling banjos thing. I answer and we're soon dueling the ivories, accelerating at every chorus.

In the grand finale cadence I actually get up the courage to sing with her. I sound like crap, but with her voice taking the lead it sounds great. We roll the turn-around over and over, modulating to the minor and laughing as we go. My bass walks up and her treble wanders south. Our hands meet around middle C and sparks are flying.

She's staring into my eyes. We keep on playing. A minor blues now. No lyrics, just those wondrous throaty sensual notes mixing together like they're made to fit that way. Our hands are crossing over each other, our fingers sometimes pressing down the same note. But it sounds great. Somehow it all comes together wonderfully.

We hold the last note till it fades away, replaced now by the dull thudding bass reverb of the party music from upstairs.

She's looking straight into my eyes with a smile. A beautiful mischievously playful smile.

"Hey," she says.

"Hey. My name's David."

"Hi David."

She knows she doesn't have to say hers. She's just looking at me with those gorgeous eyes.

"I was just thinking ..." I say.

"Yeah ..."

"That I'd like to ask you for something."

"For what?"

" ... For some happy news."

She looks at me, puzzled for a fraction of a second, then just smiles and turns away. "I'll bet you're going down to the sacred store, aren't you?" she asks.

I borrow a nod from James Dean. "Well, I heard the music there before."

"You saw the man?" she asks.

"Yeah. He said the music wouldn't play."

She cups a hand to her ear. "Do you hear that?"

"Children screaming."

"Lovers crying."

"And poets dreaming."

She breaks up laughing. Cocking her head. (Now why does that sound *dirty?* Sometimes I guess we all have our minds in the gutter.)

And now she's sizing me up. (*See?* That sounds dirty too).

"So, uh ... are you like some super rich guy?" she asks.

Instead of answering I just laugh.

"Sorry. I guess that sounded pretty awful. I didn't mean to be rude. I mean, at these parties you're like either real famous or real rich. And sometimes both. And 'cause I've never seen you before, I was guessing you're just rich. Anyway, the reason I was asking is that I just got this feeling. I mean, I was just wondering if you've always been rich, or just *recently* ... you know." She suddenly turns flushed and embarrassed. "I'm sorry. That all sounded really stupid. Just forget I said anything. Maybe I should just go now. *So* stupid."

"No. I get it."

"Yeah? Really?"

"Yeah. I totally get it. And the answer is *recently*. Completely totally recently."

She looks glad ... "I knew it."

"Why? Do I look nouveau riche?"

"No," she chuckles, shaking her head, then merging into a nod. "I mean not in a bad way. But kinda ... Yeah, in a good way though."

Still on the keyboard, her bass hand has found its way lightly on my treble.

"So how 'bout you?" I ask.

"Well, a few years ago I used to hand-wash my panties every night to save laundry money."

"And now?"

"Forbes."

"Gotchya. No more panties soaking in the sink or drying in the shower."

She's smiling and shaking her head. "Remember what it was like to fly on normal airplanes with other people, or buy your own stuff? And do your own laundry and your own dishes?"

"Yes I do. And it's really easy for me to remember because I've been rich only a very short time, even in dog minutes."

"Me too. So where do you live?"

"On an island."

"Private island with jets and yachts and stuff?"

I nod.

"OK, one of those. I get it. So how's that going for you?"

"It's good. I mean it takes some getting used to, but yeah, yeah, it's great."

"So why are you down here by yourself playing a sad song?"

"Oh that ... well, I guess I ... I guess that's a bit hard to explain."

"OK," she says, but she's not waiting for an explanation. She's looking into my eyes. We're still on the piano bench. Our hands are touching. She starts pressing a chord. A soft sexy chord. My fingers find notes as well. They blend together beautifully.

Still playing, she leans over and kisses me. A magically wonderful melodically-infused kiss. When our lips part, I can feel the gravity or whatever it is pushing us back together. I know she feels it too.

"It's getting late," she says.

"Yeah it is. Do you want to go back up to the party or something?"

"No. I'm really tired, and I got a gig tomorrow, so I should get home. But ..."

"Yeah?"

"I, uh ... live pretty close by. If you want, you could, you know, come over ..."

I look into her eyes.

"So? What do you say?" she asks.

To myself I'm thinking that this is the first kiss I've ever had with any girl in the universe other than Dot. But that's clearly not an answer to her question ...

... Or is it?

52. Silencing Dissent

BACK AT THE ISLAND, sitting at my desk in my bungalow, I think about the party last night. And of course I'm thinking about the girl I met. Hmm ...

Then my mind flashes back to the rumors I've been hearing that certain members of the team are growing uncomfortable. I can feel a rising suspicion brewing amongst them. Perhaps it's inevitable. After all, an Island full of geniuses is not an easy thing to manage.

Suddenly, my bungalow door bursts open. I look up, surprised to see Stacy standing there. She walks straight towards me with an accusing glare in her eyes.

"I think you have something to tell me, David."

"What are you talking about?"

She laughs mockingly: "Ha ha ha."

"What's the matter with you Stacy, you're acting very weird."

"What's wrong with *me?* What's wrong with you is more like it."

I stare at her, a non-comprehending look on my face.

"Max told me what you did. What you're doing. He sent me here to stop you."

"Now, now, Stacy. Just calm down. Why don't you take a seat and we can talk about this." I am calm and composed. "Would you like a drink?" I ask. And as I say these words, I discreetly reach into the drawer of my desk and pull out my gun. In one smooth movement I raise it, aim at Stacy, and fire.

Stacy collapses on the table like Rocky Raccoon. Her face is a twisted mix of surprise and pain. I watch her still twitching, wondering if I'll need to fire another shot to finish her off ... Probably.

She moves again.

I aim, but before I can fire a second shot, Stacy draws a gun—aiming point blank at me. Straight at my head.

Her blood-smeared face smiles at me as she pulls the trigger.

I feel the bullet graze my left cheek. A close shave! She missed, but I won't. I smile and aim, this time straight for her heart.

53. The Flying Pan

BOTH MAX AND MARCIE open their eyes at the same time right before dawn. Neither had expected to ever open those eyes again. You can imagine their surprise when they realize they are: (1) alive, and (2) clasped together in a tight embrace.

"Hi Max," says Marcie. And then she kisses him. They would both remember this as the best kiss of their lives.

They feel as if they've been bonded together. No need to talk about last night, or the miracle of waking up alive. No need to say anything. Looking deep into each other's eyes and beyond, they just know it.

Then Max's stomach rumbles loudly.

"Would you like to go get some breakfast?" asks Marcie.

"I would love some breakfast. But I'm afraid I don't have any money."

"I have about twenty bucks left," she says, "and I know this really nice place. It's close by. My treat."

They sit up, rubbing their eyes in the rising sun.

"What a beautiful day," says Max.

Marcie nods. She's looking at his bare feet. "You need some shoes."

He agrees. "You remember where you threw them?"

She points. "Over there somewhere."

Max gets up. "I'll just follow my nose."

*　　*　　*

A small mechanical bell rings with a wonderfully inviting tinkling sound when you open the door to the Flying Pan. Jaycee, the matron, likes the bell because it announces the arrival of each customer, like those courtly heralds in fairytales when a nobleman or princess enters the ballroom. Lee, the patron and devoted husband to Jaycee, likes the bell because it warns him the moment a customer steps into his establishment, so he can size him up and determine whether he's the sort likely to cause any trouble that would need recourse to the Taser or a call to the cops. And thus, at the top of the door to the Flying Pan, the little bell lives its double life, merrily sounding out each customer's arrival. A festive herald for some, a security watchdog for others.

Upon first stepping into the Flying Pan, most new customers do somewhat of a double take, glancing back at the sign to make sure this place is supposed to be a café. Truth be told, it looks a bit like someone's house transformed into a kind of half-café, half-bar. Early on in the Flying Pan's existence, Jaycee noticed that the café business, although moderately gainful by day, was horribly lacking by night. So the breakfast tables migrated to the window side in order to make way for the long bar that Lee constructed on the wall side.

As Max and Marcie enter to the clinking of the bell, Jaycee materializes to greet them. She's short and round, like Aunt Jemima from the maple syrup bottles without the bandana. "Howdy," she says. She sits them down, pours them coffee and scurries back to the kitchen.

They order breakfast and Max wonders why the place is called the Flying Pan. Of course Pan might be a reference to the ancient Greek god with the legs and horns of a goat and the head and torso of a human. Or perhaps it's a metaphorical allusion to a winged kitchen utensil ...

THE SECRET (*of happiness*)

As Max muses over the etymological mystery, his hand strays into his pocket, where he's surprised to feel a key. A lone key. Not on a key chain. Just a key by itself. He pulls it out and looks at it. At first he can't imagine what lock it fits into. Then it strikes him. It's the key to his Miami house. What's it doing in his pocket? He hasn't been to Miami in ages. But then, come to think of it, maybe the last time he was wearing this suit he was in Miami ... The key must have been stuck in the jacket lining.

And that's when, suddenly, the idea hits him.

"Marcie, I just had this idea."

"Tell me, Max."

"It's sort of crazy ..."

*   *   *

Jaycee carries the phone and sets it down on Max and Marcie's table. The extension cord drapes over the bar and dangles over the tables and chairs. Max thanks her and dials.

"Hello, Tyrone, how are you doing?" says Max with a voice so upbeat it could belong to the guy singing Zippity Do Da.

"Who the fuck is this?"

"Max Simon."

"Max Simon? Who the fuck? ... Oooh shit! Do you realize what fucking time it is?"

"When you gave me your card, you said I could call you anytime."

"I meant after breakfast."

"I just need a minute."

Tyrone sighs, exhaling a surprising volume of air you could hear even over the phone. "OK. What's so important to call me so fucking early?"

"I have a business proposition for you."

"Oh, fuck. Why don't I like the sound of that?"

"Because you're an overly suspicious cynic, Tyrone, that's why."

"Like you should talk."

"Just hear me out."

"I'm listening."

"I need to borrow your car."

"My car? Where you going?"

"Miami."

"Miami?"

"That's right. I'll be back in a few days."

"Max, I know you ain't going there to go surfing."

"Tyrone, as far as you're concerned I'll be driving to Miami on a vacation. Think of it as a ... a road trip."

"Sure, a road trip that has something to do with you violating bail by going out of state and whacking that kid who stole your money."

"No one said anything about whacking."

"Yeah, you going fishing?"

"You might say that. And I'll pay you handsomely."

"Handsomely? What the fuck does that mean, Max? How good-looking we talking?"

"How much would you like?"

"Shit, I don't know. Ten grand?" Tyrone says it as a joke, so obviously too much that it could never be taken seriously.

"OK," says Max.

Tyrone is silent for a moment. "Fuck. You serious?"

"Perfectly serious, Tyrone."

"My car ain't worth ten Gs, Max."

"I realize that, Tyrone, but exceptional circumstances call for exceptional measures."

"You wouldn't fuck me over, would you?"

"I wouldn't dream of it."

"Like you wouldn't be taking off with my wheels and never coming back, wouldy'a?"

"No. I'll be back in a few days. I promise you. But there is one other thing."

"What?"

"I'll need you to advance some money for expenses as well."

"Fuck."

"Some money for gas, a new pair of shoes, change of clothes ... food. Don't worry, I'll pay it all back."

Tyrone is silent for a moment. Then, "Oh fuck, Max. I guess I have a soft spot for you, and for the ten grand. OK. Come on over and I'll give you my car and some cash. You still got my address?"

"Yes. Thanks, Tyrone. We'll be over right away."

"We? Who's *we??*"

But Max has already hung up. Marcie has been listening to the conversation and is wildly curious.

"We're going to Miami?"

"Yes we are."

"A road trip. Cool."

Max is just about to explain to Marcie what this whole Miami thing is all about, but Jaycee arrives at that moment with their orders. And one whiff of that lovely breakfast immediately chases all other topics from the table.

* * *

"Just one thing," Max asks Jaycee as she arrives to clear off their plates. "I was wondering. Is the name *Flying Pan* an allusion to the ancient Greek god?"

Jaycee laughs heartily. "Oh my word no," she says. "It's on account'a when I met my husband Lee—the Chinaman standing over there—and we cooked our first meal together. Well, that's when we had our first fight. He kept asking me to go fetch the 'flying pan', and I didn't for the life of me know what he was talking about. He kept repeating: 'Flying pan dammit! Flying pan!' and getting all worked up and red in the face the way he does." She chuckles at the memory. "He got me so plum mad I wanted to hit him over the head with it. I guess that's when we fell in love."

*   *   *

When Max and Marcie walk out of the Flying Pan, the sun is beginning to rise. They amble over to the bus stop where they'll catch the bus that will take them over to Tyrone's house to pick up the car.

Max is still smiling at Jaycee's story. The walk feels great. He remembers how, as a young man, whenever he arrived in a new city (in those days before he'd seen them all) he would make sure to get up well before sunrise and walk the town. Paris is spectacular in the early morning. Before the traffic starts, with the cobbled streets just like they were hundreds of years ago. Wrapped in that trademark Parisian damp morning air with a nip of chill to it. The café waiters arranging the tables out on the terraces with their habitual bad humor. That incredibly delicious smell rising out of the boulangeries as you pass on the street. The unparalleled taste of a croissant and espresso. Or Cairo, with the wailing voices of the mosques calling the faithful, the mixed smells of spice and fruit and urine and meat and diesel fumes and coffee and cardamom all wafting together. Every city, even the most touristically undesirable ones, even the industrial and ugly ones, come into their own in some way in the early morning.

Even such a disjointed and unappealing city as Houston can muster a certain charm in the early hours of the morning. Before the cars take over the streets. Before the sun bakes the asphalt so hot you can fry an egg on it. Before the loud chirping cicadas crawl back into their holes to hide from the scorching day.

It's true. At moments such as this, as the sun rises, before the sprawling population wakes up, the big ugly polluted metropolis it has become still has a trace of the magical land that seduced the two brothers when they first laid eyes on her that sunny morning sitting on that stump, puffing away happily on their pipes, gazing out on the simple beauty of it all.

54. Guilty Conscience?

STACY IS STARING STRAIGHT INTO THE BARREL of the gun I'm pointing at her.

I pull the trigger.

My shot goes off: BANG and—

—I bolt up in bed, covered in sweat from the ghoulish nightmare.

I get up and walk over to the kitchen for a glass of water. Then I go to my desk drawer and open it.

I stare at the shiny black metal of the pistol for a few seconds. It's exactly the same gun that I used to shoot Stacy in my nightmare.

That's probably what gave me the nightmare. That plus maybe a smidgen of guilty conscience.

Anyway, it's stupid to keep the gun here in the desk. It was in Max's safe. Max's gun, I assume. This afternoon I took it out to look at. Holding it in my hand ... thinking about whether it had ever been fired before. And if so, at whom? By Max? Has he shot or killed someone before with his own hands? But stop. These are not good bedtime thoughts. I should watch an old flick to get my mind on something else. Princess Bride, or something like that.

And the gun should be locked up properly. I pick it up and put it back in the safe where it belongs.

My thoughts are jumbled. My head aches. I feel like shit. Like someone is trying to get into my brain, to read my thoughts.

Well, I've never been big on communing with some self-styled omniscient narrative presence, and you can bet your ass I'm not going to start now.

So get out of my head. You can't judge me.

Not yet ...

55. IKE

KRAMER SITS NEXT TO THE PILOT. I'm sitting in one of the two passenger seats behind them. The other seat is empty. We're flying so low over the crystal clear water I can almost make out the clown fish lounging in their anemones.

A small island appears in the distance. The seaplane flies over a coral atoll, banks off a row of coconut trees and into a small lagoon-like cove completely hidden from prying eyes by a series of low hills. Since time began, its naturally secretive topographical configuration has predestined the cove as a hot spot for those seeking discretion. By the seventeenth century the cove was a teeming Mecca for pirates, contraband runners, slave traders and other assorted riffraff from around the world.

And through it all the *Bar* has been there. The *Bar* has no name. No need for one. For like everything else at this exact spot on the planet, it operates on a need-to-know basis: everyone who needs to know where it is already does.

Our seaplane touches down and sails right up to a floating pontoon attached to the Bar built entirely on pylons over the water. Kramer and I get out of the plane and walk in.

A huge midnight blue parrot greets, or mocks us perhaps, as we enter.

A tall lanky man with curly blond hair, a particularly long nose and a sardonic grin sits at one of the tables tucked in the back. It's him. He fits the description perfectly. We make eye contact and sit down across the table from him.

"I'm Ike."

"Ike?"

"Yeah."

"Like in Eisenhower?" I ask.

"Nope. As in *I...KE...iLL* you."

Ike bursts into self-appreciative laughter. I grin along to be civil, but I'm really not in a ha-ha kind of mood. Kramer laughs heartily.

When he's done laughing, Kramer hands Ike a thick manila envelope. Ike opens it and his grin goes from sardonic to truly pleased. It's the big wad of bills inside that makes him happy. Then he looks at the photos. "Is this the target?" he asks, pointing at the photo of Max.

Kramer nods. "And in the envelope you have all the information you need to plan the ... uh—"

"—Surprise party?" Ike explodes into another burst of laughter.

Kramer laughs with him.

My already thin smile narrows further.

Ike smiles at me, "What'sa matter, mate? Cat got your tongue?"

"No, it's just that ... I thought you'd be ... different."

Ike laughs like that's the funniest thing he's heard in a long time. "Oh yeah? Bald with a bar code on the back of my neck like that movie?"

Kramer shakes his head and winks in a discreet effort to urge me to stop spitting in the soup and start rolling along with the friendly island ambiance.

But I continue obstinately onward. "No. Just a bit more ..."

"What?"

"Serious."

Ike laughs like I'm doing stand up. "It goes with the job," he says. "In my line of work I meet people who think they have decades to live. They're spending their time worrying about some stupid little

day-to-day shit, and suddenly I show up and it's lights out. Game
over. It sorta puts things into perspective. Any second your time can
be up, so why waste it worrying about shit with a fucking frown on
your face. Know what I mean, mate?"

I still look unconvinced while Kramer nods along enthusiastically
to show how much we're now all getting along like old school chums.

"Well, Ike, the person who recommended you said you had a
perfect record," offers Kramer.

"That'd be right. I've never missed a hit," says Ike. He grins wider
and starts knocking on the side of his head with his fist. "Knock on
wood, right?"

Kramer nods along with a big friendly grin.

"I gotta sorta résumé," confides Ike, leaning forward with a
winking whisper, "Wanna see it?"

"A résumé?" asks Kramer.

"Well, truth is, mate, I have it tattooed. After every confirmed kill
I tattoo on another mark." He bursts into laughter. "Good thing I
have a monster size cock or I'd have to retire soon!" He says this loud
enough for the waitress to overhear, then adds softer, "Yeah. Got a
lot of practice over in Bosnia and Serbia, you know."

I shudder at the thought.

"So any specific way you want it, mate?"

"No. Nothing exactly particular. Just dead would be fine,"
responds Kramer as if he were ordering a deli sandwich.

"Whatever you want, mate."

I increasingly dislike this Ike, but then again, I'm not shopping
for a drinking buddy. This is business, I'Ike it or not, and I still have a
few logistic concerns to address. "This man has," I explain, "a certain
grudge against us. In fact, I suspect he'd stop at nothing to kill us. So
we'd like you get to him first."

Ike cocks his head. "He knows you wanna ax him?"

I nod.

"Wait a second there, mate. This is new. You didn't tell me the target knows he's got a contract on him."

"What does it matter?"

"It matters a whole fucking lot. It doubles the risk. He knows someone's coming for him, so he's doubly careful, and he's trying to get me before I get him."

"Yeah, but the guy's a middle-aged financial math whiz geek with no passport and no money. And you're a professional killing machine on a huge expense account. So I'm thinking you don't have too much to worry about."

Ike is shaking his head. "He might be old and nerdy, but he's fighting for his life, and he's pissed at you, and he's smart. Which makes him very motivated, and a helluva lot more dangerous than you might think. I want double."

I look Ike straight in the eyes. "How about I pay you *three* times as much if you do the job right."

Ike grins. "Ike likes that."

56. Road Trip

FOR MAX, the drive from Houston to Miami is like a dream. A great wondrous dream. The kind you want to mentally record, so you can play it over and over again in your mind. He feels like he's reliving some sort of wild and crazy devil-may-care outlaw romantic life that he, of course, never actually lived in the first place. The Max now zooming along the highway at the wheel of Tyrone's beat up old car with Marcie sleeping next to him on the passenger's seat with her beautiful head resting on his thigh is light years away from the serious, studious, solitary, already business-driven Max at Oxford.

With Marcie he feels completely different, without being weighted down by any past. Reinventing himself like some underpaid WGA-hack rewriting a character in a screenplay.

And Marcie turns out to be the perfect companion for a road trip. They sing songs out loud with the radio blaring, play guessing games to wile away the miles, and eat stacks of pancakes with sides of crispy bacon in the middle of the night at roadside dives.

They drove nonstop from Houston, and are now entering Miami. Once in Miami, Max can navigate with his eyes closed. He used to come here often on vacation as a child with his parents, and then less and less after that. Almost never after marrying Katya. Miami was off her map of the *in* places to be.

The long hours of driving gave him time to think about his plan: his telos. And the more he thinks about it, the more he feels consumed by this new mission. Convinced, like all the Magellans and Christopher Columbuses who have come before him, that he is on the right course. That he is headed in the right direction. That the winds of providence are on his poop.

"Max?"

"Yeah."

"Did you just say something about your *poop?*"

He glances down at her sleepy eyes waking up in his lap. "Who me? No, I don't think so."

"Yes you did. You were mumbling under your breath. Like you have been for the past hundred miles or so. But I distinctly heard that last bit. Are you sure you're OK?"

"Yeah, I'm fine."

"I don't know ... Sounds pretty kinky to me."

Max smiles. The sun sets as they drive over the causeway, past the cruise ships. He takes a left to avoid South Beach, heads further up north a bit, and then down a side road opening up to a waterfront dock where a few dozen fishing boats are lazily moored. Marcie notices that all the signs are in Spanish. In fact everything's in Spanish. The whole scene looks like it's torn out of some off-road guidebook to Cuba or some forgotten Hemingway yarn.

It's dark by the time they pull up to the dock. Max turns to Marcie. "I think you should stay here. I'll be back in a moment."

"Why can't I come?"

"We're trying to be discreet. An attractive young woman on the docks is not exactly discreet. I'm just another ugly middle-aged fisherman."

Given the lack of air conditioning, she keeps the window down. Discreet or not. The air is heavy with fish. Countless years of cut-up fish goo soaked and sun-baked into the coarse cavernous grains of the weather-darkened wooden pier. The flies buzz merrily, feasting on the smorgasbord of body parts, juices and entrails of previously-ocean-dwelling creatures smashed and scattered about the pier in all possible stages of putrification. Here and there bare-chested or torn-T-shirted men cater to assorted fishing-related chores involving various combinations of noisily moving heavy stuff around, splashing water, cursing in Spanish and sipping beers.

She watches the seagulls squawk and bicker over who gets to sit on the higher wooden pylon thing or who eats this piece of discarded fish gut, trying to gobble it down before it gets snapped out of your beak.

It's so hot the fish smell seeps into your pores with a semi-viscous coating that would be great if it repelled flies and mosquitoes instead of apparently attracting them. A staticky Rolling Stones tune dribbles out the open window of a bait shop.

Now that the car is stopped, it's even hotter than when they were driving. Although it helps a bit that the sun has gone down. Somehow the fish smell makes it feel even hotter.

*   *   *

Marcie can't believe it. They're on a small speedboat actually zooming along on the water like in some film. Max is driving the boat like a movie star, except of course for his teeth.

This part of Miami is like a jungle paradise sprinkled with small islands interconnected by bridges and canals colonized by millionaires with big boats and bad taste. And Marcie is absolutely thrilled. She watches the gaudy mansions glide by, hypnotized by all the ostentatious wealth.

Max has driven boats through here hundreds of times. He weaves through some more canals, out towards a bay and over to a peninsular promontory.

Eventually he throttles down, and the boat settles back into its wake like they do when you cut the speed. Without any lights (in blatant contravention of Coastguard regulations) they're virtually invisible.

"See that house over there?" he asks.

"That's where we're going?"

"That's where we're going."

"Oh my God!"

She stares wide-eyed at the mansion nestled in the trees. It's the most beautiful thing she's ever seen in her life. Like some fairytale chateau on the ocean. With a huge swimming pool.

"I can't believe there are actually people who live in houses like this. That would be the greatest thing in the world to have a house like this. I'd be so happy, I'd never leave. I'd sit out at the pool, and then wander inside. Maybe make some tea and come back out to the pool for a swim. Look at it, Max. Isn't it beautiful? It's like in those magazines!"

Max smiles at Marcie staring dreamily at his house. But now is no time for banter.

"Are you ready for this, Marcie?"

"Completely."

"Let's do it."

Max reaches into his pocket, pulls out two nylon stockings, and hands one to Marcie. "For the security cameras."

Marcie frowns. "You really should have let me plan out this part. I would have gotten us good masks like in Point Break. That would have been much cooler. You could have been Nixon or JFK or anyone you wanted."

"We'll keep that in mind for next time."

They share a Bonnie and Clyde grin as they don their stocking masks.

Max cuts off the engine and glides the boat over to a small dock. He's planned every detail as rigorously as he would have planned the hostile takeover of some corporate entity in his previous life. He jumps onto the dock holding a Nike athletic bag and a jerry can, with Marcie following close behind. They creep behind the shrubs, looking out at the house.

They're now up at the gate, where a sign reads: "Property of *Halcyon Holding Company*. No Trespassing." Max pulls out the lone key he found in his jacket pocket. If the locks have been changed they might as well turn around and go home. They'll never get through outer perimeter security without the key. They hold their breaths ... The key fits perfectly! Just as he thought. Even someone as prudent as David wouldn't change the locks on all the many properties owned by Halcyon on the off chance there'd be a stray key in his suit jacket.

But now they have to move fast. Max scans the area to make sure no security guards have seen them. So far, so good. He leads Marcie over to the garden shed where the lawnmowers and other landscaping equipment are stored. Marcie keeps her eyes peeled for any guards.

Crouching down behind the shed, Max opens the jerry can and inserts a rag, which immediately becomes doused with gasoline as the fumes fill the air. His movements are fast and precise. All the energy and diligence he's applied throughout his business life are now being focused on the task at hand. He pulls out a lighter, lights the end of the rag protruding from the open jerry can as if it were a fuse, and heaves the can through the window into the shed. Instantly, as the window breaks, an alarm shrieks into the night.

Max and Marcie duck behind the shrubs, giving them the cover needed to run back to the house. The alarms are deafening. They run from the shed towards the main entrance, careful to stay out of sight. Lights in the house start turning on one after another as the guards spring into action.

Marcie's never been so excited in all her life. She's living a real adventure! She even forgets how scared she is. She glances back at the garden shed as they run away, expecting the whole thing to explode in a spectacular close-up shot with the blast propelling them forward as they make their getaway, stylishly blowing their hair a bit without burning them. But the real thing doesn't happen like in the movies at all. Funny how that is. There's no explosion. First just a small glow. Then the visuals come back online, just without the pyrotechnics. There's a little pop like something small blowing up, and the shed windows start to glow as if there were a party going on inside. Then moments later the whole thing stars flaming like a real blaze. Ah there it is, now it's more like you'd expect on TV.

The alarm screams into the night. The fire is now blazing, lighting up the night sky. They watch a handful of security guards scramble towards the flames. With the fire roaring, the sirens blaring, and all the guards rushing over to the garden shed, there's not much chance anyone will notice them.

"What now?" asks Marcie with a partners-in-crime whisper.

"We run to the entrance, use the key to open the door, grab the painting, and get back on the boat."

"Sounds good."

Max smiles at her through his stocking. The next step is critical. In order to get from the shrubbery to the house, they'll have to sprint across the lawn, about two hundred feet in plain view.

"Now!" says Max.

They run to the house, and reach the front door. Max pulls out the key and guides it key towards the lock. They both breathe a sigh of relief as the door opens.

He leads her inside and straight over to the main salon. Enough light from outside filters in through the windows for them to see clearly. But Max doesn't need the light. He knows the house like the back of his hand. It hasn't changed since he used to spend summers here when he was a kid. And come to think of it, he really likes this place. He wonders why he didn't spend more time here over the past years.

He moves straight for the far wall.

Meanwhile, Marcie is gawking. "It's so beautiful!"

"Come on, we only have a few moments."

"God, they're *so* lucky to have a house like this. It's perfect. Don't you think?"

But Max is already racing over to the painting. Of course it's still hanging on the wall right where it was the last time he saw it. He never really liked it. It's a book-sized ultra-modern collage resembling a series of splotches that look like squashed pumpkins by some famous painter whose art quadrupled in price as soon as he died. But it was a good investment and should be worth a lot now.

Max unhangs it.

"Wait! That's it? That's what we came here for?" asks Marcie.

Max nods, wrapping the painting in a towel and sticking it into the Nike bag.

"You gotta be joking!"

"I assure you it's worth more than all the other stuff combined."

Marcie shakes her head skeptically.

Suddenly a light comes on in the next room. They duck behind the sofa. The sound of voices and footsteps draws nearer. *Did the guards spot them?* Marcie grabs Max's shoulder. Gripping tight with fear.

A security guard enters the salon. If this were a film Max could just stand up and hit him from behind with a lamp or some other heavy object and he'd collapse conveniently unconscious so they could get away. But of course that never happens in real life either.

A voice calls out from down the corridor: "What the hell are you doing? Let's get out to the fire."

A security guard, presumably the one who turned on the light in the next room, steps into view. He's only a few feet away. If the alarm weren't shrieking he'd probably hear them breathing.

"I thought I saw something in here," says the guard, peering around. All he has to do is take another few steps behind the sofa and he'll see them! He takes a step.

"Come on, let's go," calls the other voice from the corridor. The security guard takes one more look around and turns to leave.

Ooof! Max and Marcie breathe a sigh of relief.

They run out the door, back to the boat, and jump in. The garden shed is blazing brightly at the other side of the property. A siren from an approaching fire truck blends into the alarms.

Max guns the throttle and they zoom away. Marcie stands next to him at the wheel, leaning into the acceleration. Her face is glowing with the excitement and adventure of it all, sprinkled with the salt spray.

"That was great, Max. We did it!"

Max nods. All smiles.

He looks back over his shoulder. They're far enough away. He switches the navigation lights back on and slows down ... now just a weekend boater out enjoying the night, like he'd done so many times in his past life.

He looks at his house dwindling in the distance. The firemen must be doing their job, because the glow of the fire is dying down.

*   *   *

Max and Marcie stand at a roadside pay phone outside an International House of Pancakes. Max has just dialed Tyrone's number.

"Hello," says Tyrone's voice.

"Hello, Tyrone."

"Max. That you?"

"Yes."

"Thank God. I was worried. Is my car alright?"

"Perfectly alright."

"Good! What about you and the girl? You guys OK?"

"We're fine."

"Well where the fuck are you?"

"Still in Miami."

A pause ... "But you're coming back, right? You're not going to jump bail and keep my car are you?"

"No, Tyrone, we're already on the way back. Just stopping for something to eat."

"Oh yeah, where you eating?"

Max glances up at the sign, then says: "International Pancake Place."

"IHOP. Excellent choice. When are you guys getting back here?"

"Soon. But first I need your help again."

"Fuck, Max. I give you my car. I loan you money. Who am I? Mother fucking Teresa?"

"It's about your ten thousand dollars."

"Oh. Now we're talking. You got it?"

"Yes, but right now it's in the form of a communal share in a small painting that I'd like to sell. It's worth a lot of money. And since you've spent your entire career defending criminals, I'm hoping you might know someone who'd like to buy it."

Tyrone snorts. "Fuck, Max. Do I seem like the Christie's type? I ain't no fucking art dealer. So NO, I don't know nobody who wants your fucking painting. And I can't get involved in that type of shit. Fencin' your hot fucking painting. We shouldn't even be talking about this shit over the phone. I'm a lawyer, Max, not a fucking fence."

"Ask around, Tyrone. I'm sure with all your connections you can find someone who's ready to take this painting off our hands for a small fraction of its real value. The artist is well known. Anybody in the business will be able to understand its value immediately."

Silence.

"And I guess I don't get my ten grand till you sell this thing, right?"

"That's right."

"You sure it's worth ten grand?"

"Much more than that."

Tyrone sulks a minute telephonically. "OK, I got a friend who knows a guy who knows someone who maybe does this sort of shit. Call me back in a couple of hours and I'll try to set it up. But I ain't promisin' anything."

*   *   *

It turns out Tyrone had no trouble finding someone to buy the painting. Just as Max said, the artist is famous, and an expert easily certified it's authenticity. They only received a fraction of its real value. But for a stolen painting sold on the fly, that's not bad at all.

Of course payment is in cash. In those nifty little bricks of Ben Franklins weighing ten grand apiece. Max hands Tyrone a 10-G brick and then dumps the rest into the Nike bag.

Transaction profitably consummated, they climb back into Tyrone's car. Tyrone at the wheel, Marcie shotgun, and Max in back with the Nike bag.

Before starting the car, Tyrone looks fondly at his two passengers. With an extra ten grand in his pocket, he's very pleased with how the whole lend-a-car-to-Max thing worked out. He's decided that they need to celebrate. "You know, you two dress like shit," he says. "Let's go buy us some new threads, and then I know a place where we can get the best barbecue this side of the fucking Alamo."

The three of them enjoy themselves like teenagers out on the town. They go from shop to shop, Tyrone leading the way, laughing and trying on and buying clothes. And when it comes to barbecue, Tyrone proves to be as good as his word. They end up celebrating late into the night.

After the celebration, Tyrone drops Max and Marcie off at a random discreet roadside motel, and drives away. He's smiling like Louis Armstrong. The evening was great, and the Ben Franklin brick has significantly increased his annual revenues. All in all, he considers himself to be a very happy man.

57. A Few Days

MAX AND MARCIE ARE NOW lying tightly intertwined in their motel room. They've been here for days. Staying blissfully in bed, ordering pizza and Chinese food in. Telling each other stories and laughing at the old reruns on TV.

Max still hasn't told Marcie anything about himself. He hasn't even told her that the house they robbed used to be his. He's afraid to break whatever wonderful spell he's come under. And he's not ready to face up to the fact that there's surely an army of hitmen combing the planet for him. He prefers, for the time being, to stay like he is: anonymous, without a past. Without connecting back the dots.

But of course Marcie is curious. And eventually she asks:

"So what's the deal with you, Max?"

"What do you mean?"

"Well, you know, the normal stuff. Like what's a good looking middle-aged guy who talks like a professor and walks around in a hand tailored suit with missing teeth and two black eyes doing robbing some rich guy's house and stealing a painting?"

"Well, when you put it like that ..."

"So who are you, Max?"

"You might say I'm just your typical Wal-Mart shopper."

Marcie laughs. Come to think of it, she doesn't really care. She knows all she needs to know about Max. "OK, Mr. Typical Shopper, what now? What's the plan?"

Truth is, neither wants anything more than to stay right here together, where everything is just perfect.

"How about we just stay here like this for now."

"That's the best plan I've ever heard." She pulls him closer "... *the best*."

They laugh and crawl back into heaven under the sheets.

*　　*　　*

"Max?"

"Yeah."

"You remember when we were on the hill?"

"Every second."

She smiles, remembering too.

"Well, right near the point when I was falling unconscious, I heard you say you found something. You kept repeating over and over *'my telos, my telos.'* What did you mean?"

"It was something a wise old man told me. It means *purpose* in ancient Greek. And it all came together for me when you were telling me about your life."

"*My* life?"

"Yes, your life, Marcie."

"That still doesn't tell me what your telos is."

"That's true."

"Well, tell me."

"How about if I show you instead?"

"OK. Should I shut my eyes or something?"

"No. But I need you to give me a few days."

"I guess I can do that."

*　　*　　*

Max walks through a vacant lot. He's peering right and left, clearly looking for something or someone. He recognizes the sickly sweet borderline nauseating smell of the nearby meatpacking plant in the air. There's a few homeless people scattered here and there. Some look up at him for a moment and glance away. He smiles at them, knowing that they've already decided, based on his clearly-too-clean-to-be-homeless attire, that he must be an undercover cop or a social worker of some sort. He doesn't recognize any faces, and is about to leave when he hears a voice from behind.

"Hey Fred, you looking for something?"

Max turns. Behind him stands Bald Bearded Guy wearing Max's spit-shined Italian shoes.

"Hello. Actually, I'm looking for you."

"I don't get many repeat customers."

Max laughs. "No, I don't suppose you do."

*   *   *

During the next few days Max comes and goes from the motel room at various times, disappearing for hours without offering any explanation, completely absorbed by his project. Marcie wonders what he's cooking up, but he insists on keeping it all under wraps. "You'll see soon enough," is all he says, with a twinkle in his eye.

Meanwhile, Marcie has never been happier. What more could she want? There's plenty of money in the Nike bag. When Max is out doing his telos thing, whatever that is, she just wanders around, feeling happy. Browsing in stores or going to the museums she never went to before. And when Max is back in the room and they're together, well ... then everything is just perfect.

58. It's Time

I'M SITTING ON MY BUNGALOW TERRACE, staring out at the ocean lit up by the moon. I sit here often. Right now Virgil is sitting next to me, trying to convince me to go with him to some wild party on a neighboring island.

"I'm telling you bro', this one's gonna be totally awesome, even on my Richter scale. Serious. You can't blow it off. It's gonna be epic."

"I don't have to skydive in or anything?"

Virgil shakes his head, all innocent-like. "Honest."

"I don't know. I think I'm just going to stay in tonight."

"Stay here? And just sit there?"

"I like just sitting here."

"Yeah, but *hello*, now you can do whatever you want. Use your imagination. If you want a snack in Paris, we skip down to the jet and a few hours later we're strolling under the Eiffel Tower. If you wanna go to a Rolling Stones concert backstage and the party afterwards, just call Gwen and it happens. If you want nightingale tongues on a bed of caviar served by naked virgins, just call Gwen."

"You're right. I'm going to make the call." I pick up my Island Com.

"Gwen?"

"Yes, David."

Virgil listens intently, hoping to be impressed.

"Could you have a bowl of cereal sent over?"

"The usual?" inquires Gwen.

I'm about to go for the usual, but Virgil's presence inspires me to take a walk on the wild side. "Surprise me." I look over at Virgil and ask, "You want some?"

Virgil hangs his head in shame for me, shaking it enough to decline my cereal offer. "That is so lame," he says, standing up. "Well, I'm going to the party, with or without you."

"On second thought, I'll roll with."

Virgil flashes me a smile with two thumbs up. "Meet you at the bird in an hour."

I nod as Virgil walks out my door and over to his bungalow.

I'm planning on resuming my thoughtful gaze over the ocean until my bowl arrives, but the Island Com rings instead. The screen says it's Kramer. I pick up.

"Hello, Larry."

"We found him."

"Well it's about time. Where is he?"

"Hiding out in a motel room."

"Hang on, I'll patch in Ike."

I press a button on the Island Com, and after a few rings ...

"Ike here."

"It's time, Ike. Kramer will tell you his location."

"You got it, mate. Consider your pal Max to be a problem of the past."

"Good. Just don't fail."

"Don't worry, I never do."

59. Telos

MAX COMES BACK to the motel room and leads Marcie outside where a taxi is waiting. They drive over to a Starbucks.

"Want a coffee?" asks Max.

"Sure," says Marcie, impatient to see where this whole telos thing is leading.

Max tells the taxi driver to wait for them and opens the door for Marcie. They walk inside, order, and sit down in a secluded cozy nook with two overstuffed armchairs.

"Now I'm going to tell you a story," says Max.

"A once-upon-a-time sorta thing?"

"You might say that."

She sips her latte, "I'm all ears, Max."

"Well, once upon a time, there was a taxi driver named Bernard, but everyone called him Bernie."

"The guy who drove us here?"

"No. This was a while ago. Remember, I said once upon a time."

"Got it. Bernie. Go ahead."

"Well, Bernie wasn't exactly the most handsome guy in the world. His nose was fat and squashed. He wore coke-bottle thick glasses that were always sliding down so that he was constantly pushing them back up. And to make matters worse, his hair started falling out during his senior year in high school, coinciding with a significantly increased rate of stuttering and massive weight gain. So you can imagine how much of a hit he was with the girls. He spent prom night in his room alone playing video games."

"Not exactly Prince Charming."

"Right. And though he was far from stupid, his painful shyness and bothersome stutter made everyone just assume he was, so he ended up adopting majority opinion. After high school he needed rent money, so he started working various minimum wage jobs, waiting for that day when he would save up enough to go back to school. He finally ended up working as a taxi driver. The days and months and years stretched on without ever saving up enough for college until the very idea just sort of faded away by itself. He lived alone in a small studio apartment without any real friends. Thus Bernie had etched out for himself what most people might be tempted to call a rut. But that was fine with Bernie. His life was monotonous, but not unpleasant. His job was tolerable. He could pay the bills. And since he'd already accepted the idea of never finding a woman who wanted him, he no longer even had to deal with that painful disappointment. It just became a fact of life, like a receding hairline or global warming. In sum, Bernie had reached an acceptable equilibrium. *Then*, one day, in one-split second, everything changed for him."

"He got in a car wreck?"

"No."

"Good. 'Cause that would really suck."

"One day, a day which started out like any other day, a woman opened the door to his cab and stepped in. She was yelling profanities into her cell phone as she slammed the door. So without even seeing her face, Bernie was already of the opinion that she was just another one of those all-too-frequent, obnoxious, foul-mouthed, cell-phone-screaming, door-slamming variety of clients. But when he glanced up into his rear view mirror and saw her face, it was suddenly as if the world had stopped spinning."

"Was it his twin sister separated at birth?"

"No. But as far as he could tell, it was the woman he'd been searching for all his life but had already given up trying to find. It was one of those genuine thunderbolts of love at first sight, if you know what I mean."

"I know exactly what you mean."

"So she gave him the address of her destination, and he wanted to say something debonair and seductive, like *I'll take you anywhere you want to go, gorgeous.* But all he could do was stammer.

"She watched him stammer. She saw his thin hair, his thick glasses that kept sliding down his fat nose, and his general obesity. She almost shuddered, she was so repulsed by his ugliness. Of course Bernie could feel the rejection instantly. His cheeks burned with humiliation and fear, but he forged ahead. He put the cab into gear and started driving, and as he drove he started telling her a story."

"Another story?"

"Yes."

"Inside this one?"

"Yup. You're thinking of Hamlet."

"Not really."

"OK."

"But it's a pretty cool. Do you want a bite of this muffin?"

"Thanks. Good muffin. Shall we get back ..."

"Of course."

"So Bernie started telling about how when he was a kid he went to see this Gypsy Fortune Teller. He paid the ten dollars and the Gypsy asked him what he wanted to know about his future. Now the woman in the backseat was surprised that this ugly driver had suddenly launched into telling her some kind of story. She was on the verge of telling him to just mind his own business and drive, but something about him changed her mind. She hung up her cell phone and started listening. So Bernie kept on with his story ... He explained how when the Gypsy asked him what he wanted to know about his future, he instantly responded that he wanted to know who he would marry. The Gypsy took one look at him, glanced into her crystal ball, and said that he'd marry a girl who was terribly ugly, who'd lost most of her hair and who wore thick glasses that kept sliding down her fat nose. The young Bernie sat there in shock. Devastated. This was a terrible blow to him. A heart crushing disaster. He sat there on the brink of tears, thinking about his bride-to-be. And then he said, with all the seriousness in the world, that such an ugly girl would be a terrible shame because she'd be sad and bitter. He looked straight into the Gypsy's eyes and said it would be much better if he could take her place ... if he could be the ugly and fat one so that she could be amazingly beautiful, like an angel.

"The Gypsy looked at him for a few moments as if considering. Then she said that she could arrange that. But that it'd cost one hundred dollars. Well, a hundred dollars was a lot of money for the young Bernie, but he didn't hesitate a second. The next day he rounded up all his savings, returned to the Gypsy, paid the money, and left—a very happy boy.

"Now, all the time that Bernie was telling his story, the woman in the back seat was listening.

"Then he looked at her through rearview the mirror, and he said: *'Later, when I grew up enough to think back about that Gypsy, I always just thought I wasted that money. But now I see it was the best money I ever spent.'*

"The woman in the back seat felt like she'd just been struck by lightning. She looked into Bernie's eyes through the rearview and was suddenly looking way beyond all that cellulite, way beyond those thick lenses and straight into his soul.

'My name's Bernie, what's yours?' he asked.

'Skylark,' she said.

'*That figures,*' he answered with a soft smile.

"He would have courted her for weeks and weeks without daring a first kiss, but she had other plans. She told him to drive to a new address: her apartment. Bernie made the U-turn, and they spent the rest of the afternoon together in her bed.

"Nine months later Zoey was born. She was light chocolate brown just like her mom, and Bernie was delirious with joy. They lived simply and happily together in Skylark's small apartment.

"A couple weeks before Zoey's seventh birthday, Skylark fainted at work. They rushed her to the hospital, but the cancer had already spread too far. Bernie and Zoey spent Zoey's seventh birthday party together, alone, silent, just the two of them. The funeral was still fresh in their minds and they couldn't bear to be around anyone else.

"At first it looked like Bernie would come through it all in one piece. Zoey kept him afloat, or rather, like the survivors of a shipwreck cast adrift at sea, they were keeping each other afloat. But then one day while Zoey was at school, Bernie ran across a photo of Skylark laughing. He stared at the photo for a while, and then just lost it. Right over the deep end. He drunk himself into a stupor and totaled his cab. He was fired, and his license was revoked. And from that moment on, the spiral down was sickeningly fast and merciless. Without a job Bernie quickly fell behind on the rent. Their meager savings had already been wiped out with Skylark's medical bills, so there really wasn't anything left as far as a safety net goes.

"Before he knew it, they were evicted. Zoey came home from school one day to find her stuff packed into boxes. She burst into tears, and nothing Bernie could say could cheer her up. '*It's your fault,*' she shouted at him. '*If Mommy were here, this would never have happened.*'

"What could he say to that? He bowed his head in pain and shame. For the next few weeks they moved from shelter to shelter, trying to get by. Trying to keep Zoey in school. But it was a hopeless battle. Being homeless alone is hard enough. Trying to get by with a young child is simply impossible. One day some social workers from Family Services showed up at the shelter and took Zoey away. She screamed and cried and kicked to escape. She yelled out at the top of her voice for her daddy to save her, but they took her away. And with her they took the last shred of Bernie's heart. He drank himself senseless and ended up in the streets. And out there on the streets, well … we both know how that goes."

"Why are you telling me this?" asks Marcie with a choked voice and tears in her eyes.

"Follow me," answers Max. "I'll show you."

They walk out to the waiting cab. Both still thinking about Bernie and Zoey. They drive for a while in silence. Marcie notices that Max doesn't even have to say an address to the driver, so this must have all been planned out beforehand. The taxi stops at a side-street alley behind a row of storefronts. They get out of the cab and Max leads her down the alley lined with dumpsters. They walk for a few moments, then stop.

A homeless man digging in one of the dumpsters looks over at them. Marcie is surprised to see that the man recognizes Max. He climbs down from the dumpster and walks towards them. He doesn't offer his hand to shake, realizing of course that no one relishes shaking a hand that's just been foraging in garbage.

"Nice to see you," says the man, looking at Max and shyly avoiding Marcie's eyes.

His head is a scruffy mess of bare scalp and thin hair, and his skin hangs off his frame like it's a couple sizes too big.

"Hello Bernie," says Max, "I'd like you to meet my friend, Marcie Rogers."

Marcie's eyes grow wide as she realizes who he is.

"Nice to meet you, Miss Rogers."

"Likewise, Bernie."

Marcie studies him. He's a wreck. He looks like that Gollum creature from those Hobbit movies. She turns to Max and is surprised to see that he's smiling with excitement. There's something definitely brewing.

"So, Bernie, I've got some very good news for you," says Max.

Bernie's eyes light up through his coke bottle glasses.

"Really?" he says.

"Yes," says Max. "Very good."

Bernie starts grinning as wide as Max, and Marcie looks at them both, wondering what's going on.

"Why don't you come with us?" says Max to Bernie.

"Where?"

"You'll see."

They all three get in the cab. The taxi driver must have been forewarned by Max, because he's lined the front seat, where Bernie now sits, with those big dark green plastic garbage bags.

Inside the cab with the doors shut, Bernie's foul homeless smell invades the air. The driver makes a face like he's about to puke and rolls down the window, preferring the hot fresh-air to air-conditioned Bernie stink.

They drive for a few minutes. Despite questions from Marcie and Bernie, Max refuses to provide any info. They stop at a modest apartment complex and get out of the cab. Max holds out a key to Bernie.

"What's this?" asks Bernie.

"The key to your new home."

Bernie looks at Max, speechless. So does Marcie. Neither can believe their ears. Max breaks into that wonderful laugh of his.

"Are you serious?" asks Bernie.

"Yes," laughs Max. "Now go on and take the key." Max puts the key in Bernie's hand and starts walking down the path leading into the apartment complex. "Come along, let me show you where it is. You need to get washed up and into some new clothes."

Bernie's new apartment is small, but comfortable. There's a room that Max has already set up for Zoey, with a child's bed and some stuffed animals.

When Bernie comes out of the shower shaved and dressed in the suit Max had bought for him, he looks like a new man.

Max and Marcie whistle and laugh in admiration, and Bernie stands there, his eyes filled with tears.

"This is a miracle," he says. "I don't know how or why you guys did this, but it's a miracle."

Max is smiling. "Come on," he says. "We just have time to stop and get your hair cut before picking up Zoey."

"My God!" says Bernie. "Is this really happening? Are we really going to see Zoey?"

"Not just *see* her. Pick her up and bring her back. It's all worked out. This apartment is yours. You now have full custody of Zoey. You two can start over again where you left off."

Despite his shyness and awkwardness, Bernie grabs Max in a huge hug. When he breaks away his cheeks are wet.

"Now let's go get my girl!" he cries out.

*   *   *

Max had arranged everything with Family Services. He'd leased and paid for the apartment in Bernie's name, and deposited enough money in Bernie's account for them to live on until Bernie could find a job. So Family Services was thrilled to release Zoey. It was extremely rare that a parent is actually able to come back and reclaim a child.

As they pull up in the taxi, they can see Zoey already waiting in the parking lot with a social worker sitting next to her. When she sees her father step out of the cab, she screams for joy and starts running to him.

Max and Marcie stand off to the side. Bernie kneels down, arms outstretched. And Zoey runs. She runs as only a child can run when jumping into the arms of a loved one. There's nothing else in the world like it.

If there existed some sort of meter for measuring joy, then it would be pegging off the charts right now in this parking lot, like a Geiger counter at Chernobyl. If happiness travelled by wave, then this would be a tsunami.

As Max and Marcie watch the miracle take place before their eyes, they're both feeling the exact same thing. It's magically wonderful. Like Livingstone must have felt when he first set eyes on those magnificent falls before they were called Victoria. Like Leonardo when he brushed on that last dab of color and saw her smiling back at him. Like Albert when he woke up that morning just knowing that energy really does somehow equal mass times the speed of light squared. Like the sun when she looks out and sees the planets spinning around her so incredibly perfectly.

They both realize, right then and there, as they watch little Zoey fly through the air into the outstretched arms of her dad, that they've just met their telos. Miracles can happen. It's up to us.

It's our choice.

... *They can happen if we make them happen.*

*　　*　　*

"Who are those people?" asks Zoey, peering shyly out from her dad's arms at Marcie and Max standing next to the taxi.

Bernie thinks for a second, then responds, "That's Aunt Marcie and Uncle Max."

"Wow! An aunt and uncle. I didn't know I had any! That's great!"

"Yeah, it is great. So, honey, let's go home now, I want to show you your room."

"My room? My very own room?"

"Yes, your very own room."

Zoey squeezes her dad even tighter. Then, she says, "Can Aunt Marcie and Uncle Max come over to our house for dinner?"

"Of course they can."

"You know, Dad, I think I must be the luckiest girl in the whole wide world."

*   *   *

Later that night, after their impromptu dinner together, while Marcie is telling Zoey a bedtime story, Bernie and Max sit at the kitchen table.

"I could never repay you for this, Max."

"Actually, you can, Bernie. You can help me out with a little project I'm working on."

"Anything. You name it."

"Let's go for a walk and I'll explain."

Marcie hears the front door close after putting Zoey to bed. She looks through the window to see Max and Bernie talking about something outside.

She can't hear, but she can tell they're talking about something very serious.

She's never seen Max looking so serious.

THE SECRET (*of happiness*)

And Bernie is nodding his head gravely, as if he were taking some sort of solemn oath.

60. The Bayous

MARCIE AND MAX DECIDE TO WALK back to their motel room after leaving Bernie and Zoey. They feel as if they're walking on air, strolling along the fluffy clouds.

"How did you do it, Max?"

"It was very easy. Insanely easy. Of course I really didn't know what I was even trying to do at first. I just had this crazy unformed idea of trying to help someone who needed it. So I wandered around, and I immediately found dozens of opportunities. All those people living out on the streets. An old widow without any family whose pension ran out. Someone like you who had just been evicted. So many nice everyday people needing a little helping hand. A couple hundred dollars here, a couple thousand there. That's all it would take to completely change those people's lives, to create a miracle for them. And as I was walking around the vacant lots, I ran into our old friend Bald Bearded Guy. I asked him for the next person on his list, and he told me about Bernie.

"How much money did it take?"

Max winces.

"You didn't!"

He nods with a sheepish shrug.

"It took the whole Nike bag?"

"Well, not the whole thing. But most of it."

"We're broke?"

"Pretty much. All but this. Here, you keep it."

He hands her a few bills.

"Well, this'll keep us in a motel room and fed for a few days, but we're going to have to come up with some way to make some money soon or we'll be back out on the streets."

"Don't worry, we'll think of something."

Marcie throws her arms around him. "I love you, Max."

They stand there holding each other.

"Everything's perfect," she says softly, only for him.

Max is just about to respond when he sees something in the distance. Something that causes him to dodge behind a parked car, crouching down and pulling Marcie down with him.

"What are you doing?" she asks.

"Someone's at our door."

"The maid?"

"Unfortunately, it's definitely not the maid."

She shrugs. He cranes his neck around the bumper of the car.

"Well, can you see who it is?" she asks.

"I can't see anything ... Wait. Oh no ... It's *him*."

"Who?"

"The hitman."

"*Hitman?* Why would there be a hitman at our door?"

"He's trying to kill me."

"You never told me someone is trying to kill you."

"I suppose it never came up."

Marcie glares at him. "I'm going to look. He's not searching for me." She tries to get a look at him without being seen. "It's a tall man with curly blond hair, a long nose and a gun in his hand," she says.

"What's he doing?"

"It looks like he's picking the lock. Now he's opening the door and going inside." Marcie looks at Max. "So what do we do now?"

"*You* stand up and walk naturally away without looking back. Go check into another room and I'll contact you when it's safe."

"What are you going to do?"

"I'm going to run. I don't want to be here in about two seconds when he realizes I'm not in there and comes out looking for me."

"I'm staying with you, Max."

"No you're not."

"Yes I am. I grew up here. I know the neighborhood like the back of my hand. I can help you hide." Max is about to argue with her but she grabs his hand and starts running with him in tow, squat-sprinting behind the cover of the cars.

And not a second too soon ...

Ike steps out of Max's apartment. Looking pissed. He'd been planning on an easy hit, an early dinner and a quiet night in bed with a good DVD. A classic. Something Oscar-worthy. Maybe Titanic. And he doesn't like it one bit when his plans get derailed. His eagle eyes scan the perimeter. He catches sight of Max and some girl just about to disappear behind the far wall of the building. He would have preferred to do it nice and clean inside the apartment, but what the hell, he's got one clear shot before they run behind the wall. He has to take it, even if it's a bit messy to work out in the street like this. But he's cool and calm. At this range he can't miss. Max is as good as dead, and he's as good as in bed with that flick. He raises his pistol and squeezes the trigger.

Max and Marcie run like the wind. Like their lives depend on it, experiencing for the first time in their earthly existence the full portent of the metaphor. And as they run they hear that ominous *phweet* sound, that sound most of us have only heard on film, the sound of a pistol shot with a silencer. And almost instantly a car windshield shatters next to them as the bullet buries itself harmlessly into the driver's seat headrest of a parked Toyota Corolla.

Christ! They're being shot at! With real bullets! Max grips Marcie's hand even tighter. They share a worried but adrenalin-stoked look as they turn the corner behind the building, out of Ike's line of fire.

They've made it! At least for now. They were shot at by a professional assassin, and yet they're still alive! Running for their lives. Struggling for survival. They might be dead in a few minutes when the hitman catches up to them. But for now they're alive!

Meanwhile, Ike is amazed to see the windshield shatter and Max keep on running. He's amazed because he never misses a shot like this one. He looks at his gun with an annoyed puzzled expression, like a star tennis player scowling at his racket after missing an easy lob. But there's no time to lose now. They'll be running off somewhere to hide, and he has to run down these fucking stairs and the whole length of the building before he'll have them in sight again! And what's with the girl? Now he'll have to do both of them. Can't have her blabbing to the cops. Two for the price of one. Bad business. He bolts after them like the Running Man, taking the stairs three at a time.

"Follow me," says Marcie, taking the lead.

"Where to?"

"Trust me."

Marcie feels like she's been transported back to her childhood when she spent her time running around the neighborhood playing chase, and tag, and capture-the-flag, and hide-and-seek, and all those other games that suddenly have become the ticket to their immediate survival. Back then she was the best! The fastest runner of her group. The winner at those endless summer games. Running faster than the boys. Outwitting them! Her heart beats wildly, just like it used to when she was zipping along on her carefree teenage feet. She used to do this kinda stuff all the time. Sure, back then it was all make-believe kids' games of course. But so what? She can actually save them! Or maybe. At least she can try ... She dodges left, into what seems to be some narrow utility passage between two apartment buildings. She doubles back, sprints across a small parking lot and dives over a low wall. Max sticks to her like glue.

Back on their feet they're up and running again. Max looks over his shoulder and sees that the hitman is now running behind them, catching up.

"He's gaining on us."

Marcie glances off to the right. Her attention is drawn by some sort of flashing light down there ... down there in the bayou. Of course! The bayou! That's a great idea! Why didn't she think of that before? She leads Max over the embankment.

"You're not planning on going down *there* are you?"

"Sure am."

Still running, "I'm not so sure that's such a great idea. Those are sewers. Let's talk about this first."

"Trust me. Unless he grew up in this neighborhood, I don't care if he's the fucking Terminator, he'll never find us in there."

They run down the grassy sloping hill leading to the concrete banks. She runs along the water's edge, then suddenly yanks Max's arm, drawing him into a side tunnel.

"Are you sure?"

They're now in what appears to be some sort of a concrete tube-like tunnel, about eight feet in diameter. It's pitch black. Their feet splash in the shallow water as they run. Max is having trouble running in the darkness.

"I can't see anything."

"That's the point. He can't either, but I know where we're going. He doesn't. Just follow me. Within five minutes he'll be totally lost, I guarantee it."

"I don't know ..."

But there's no time for discussion. They run, every once and a while branching off down a side tunnel. Max follows blindly, stumbling behind Marcie, winding further and further into the maze.

After what seems like an eternity Marcie stops.

"Ssshhh. Listen," she whispers. Complete silence. They smile. "What'd I tell you? We lost him." She grabs Max in a victory hug. "I knew it. This trick never fails."

"You're amazing, Marcie."

"I know. This is so cool. It's like a real life Tomb Raider!" They stand there in the dark, pressed together, their feet in the dank stagnant water, hearts thumping.

"Wait. What's that?"

"What?"

"Shit."

"Footsteps."

"It's him!"

"He found us."

Marcie starts running. Max in tow again.

"He's really good, this guy," whispers Marcie as they run.

"So what now, Lara Croft?"

"Don't worry. I've got something else in my bag of tricks." She chuckles whisperingly ... "I always wanted to say that."

Then she stops in front of a ladder bolted into the wall.

"What's the plan?" asks Max.

"Wait till you see this. It's awesome! We're going up to this parallel tunnel that will double back and then come to a crossroads. He'll never be able to follow us."

They clamber up the ladder and run in the dark for what seems like ages. Suddenly Marcie stops and Max runs into her, almost knocking her over.

"Sorry."

"Sshhh!"

"Hear him?"

"No."

They wait, ears straining.

"I told you we'd lose him this time," she whispers.

They wait another minute and then they hear it. Damn! Those footsteps again!

"Shit! Who is this guy?" says Marcie starting to run again. As they run, Marcie mumbles over her shoulder, "I'll bet he's an Indian."

"An Indian?"

"Yeah. It's just like what's happening to us here. Didn't you see that film where Paul Newman and Robert Redford had to jump off the cliff to get rid of the Indian tracking them?"

"Yes I did."

Reflective pause. "It didn't work out so good for them, did it?" notes Marcie.

"No, it didn't," agrees Max, still running behind her.

"Do you remember the name of the Indian tracker guy?" she whispers over her shoulder.

"No."

"You know, the one that was so good he could track anyone. Damn! What was his name? It was Count somebody. No ... Lord something or other. Hell, I can't remember."

They keep running. Max notices that the tunnel they were in before seems for some reason to be blocked off, leading them here, where there hasn't been any side tunnels branching off for a very long time. And the tunnel they're in now just seems to keep on going further and further ...

All of a sudden she stops running. He feels her stiffen with fear.

"Why are we stopping?" he asks.

"We're lost."

The tunnel has dead-ended at a large closed metal door that looks like it belongs on a submarine.

"What's this door?"

"I don't know. I've never been here before. We must have taken a wrong turn back there where it was blocked off."

They listen behind them. Straining their ears. Silence. Did they shake him? The seconds tick past.

Then they hear it: the distant echo of his footsteps growing nearer.

"What should we do?" wonders Max out loud.

"I don't know."

Ike's footsteps grow closer by the second.

"I don't think we can go back," says Max. "I have the impression there haven't been any side tunnels for a long time."

"I know. If we go back down the tunnel, we'll run right into him."

"Well, then we don't have a choice." Max steps up to the door. Luckily it opens. He steps inside. Marcie follows. She gropes along the wall, finds a switch, flips it, and a light comes on. It's blinding after the pitch black. When their eyes adjust they see they're in a small concrete room. A complete dead end. No way out other than back through the submarine door they just entered leading straight to the hitman.

Max steps over to the door and heaves. It slams shut with a deafening metal clang, closing and locking them inside the little room.

"You think he won't be able to open the door?" asks Marcie hopefully.

Max shakes his head gloomily. "He'll shoot through the latch with his gun."

"I was afraid you'd say that."

Ike's footsteps come closer. A few seconds later Max and Marcie shudder as Ike throws his weight against the door. It holds, for now.

"Hi guys," says Ike's voice. "What'sa matter? Cat got your tongues?" He bursts into his characteristic gallows laughter. It resonates eerily through the steel door and reverberates into the small concrete room. Marcie grips Max's hand.

"Well, we had some good fun, now it's time to finish up," says Ike cheerfully.

"Are you an Indian?" asks Marcie through the door.

The question puzzles Ike. "No. Why do you ask?"

"You know, like the tracker."

"Oh!" laughs Ike. "That was a great film!"

"You remember his name?"

"Of course I do. Lord Baltimore."

"You're right! It *was* Lord Baltimore!" says Marcie. Max wonders if she's masterfully stalling for time, or simply buffing up on her seventh art trivia.

Meanwhile, Max's mind is racing. Scrambling for some way out of this mess. The far wall of the small room is literally covered with pipes. There's a large cast iron wheel mounted behind a column. "What's that?" he whispers to Marcie. She shrugs her shoulders. He steps over to the wheel for a closer look. Hmm ... looks like the type of thing that would control a valve somewhere. And given the submarine door on this little cement room they've locked themselves into ...

Max's eyes suddenly light up with hope. He tries to turn the wheel, but it doesn't budge. He turns to Marcie, "When you're done chatting, could you give me a hand?"

Marcie joins Max and they both try turning, but it doesn't budge.

"Damn!"

A shot rings out, blasting into their eardrums. Ike's laughter follows in the wake of the bullet. "I figure another shot or two and this door will open. If Butch and you got any last words, you might as well start saying them."

Max and Marcie keep tugging on the wheel, but it's rusted tight.

Ike fires again on the door ... The lock won't hold much longer.

They both realize it's over. In a few moments the tall curly haired non-Indian guy with the long nose will blast through that door and shoot them. Dead.

They put everything they have into one last earthly heave.

And somehow ...

... The wheel starts moving. They smile wildly and keep turning. Faster and faster. As they turn they hear what sounds like a whole lot of water roaring in the distance.

Marcie is grinning like the Cheshire Cat. "He's gonna wish he called in sick today."

Outside the door, Ike is wearing his sardonic cruel smile that suits him so well. He's looking forward to killing them. This has turned out to be an excellent evening. Much more fun than the typical walk in and plug 'em standard routine hit he'd planned on. So far it's been even better than being tucked in bed with a bottle of wine watching Leo and Kate. And after this next bullet the lock will give and he'll step in there and finish them off. A perfect conclusion. A job well done, and another two tattooed notches under his belt. He starts to aim at the lock mechanism, and then he hears something. What is that? He lowers his gun.

... Is that the sound of rushing water? *Yes Ike, it is.* And it's coming from the huge wave of water now flooding the pipe directly next to him. He doesn't even have time to change the sardonics on his smile before he's knocked violently off his feet and swept down the tunnel at a terrifying speed.

Marcie and Max jump into a victory embrace.

"We did it!" she yells, her cheeks flushed with excitement. "Can you believe what we did? It was fantastic!"

"You were great, Marcie!"

They hug and dance wildly. Together, as a team, they stared death in the face once again and they triumphed. In that moment they share a bond so strong it makes protons and neutrons look like attractional dilettantes and superglue look like Play-doh. She reaches out. Bringing him closer. Holding him. They fall back on the concrete floor. They'll both remember this magical moment together for as long as they live.

The question is ... *how long would that be?*

61. When You Want
Something Done Right

IKE WALKS into what appears to be an abandoned warehouse in the middle of nowhere. He's limping, with his arm in a sling, and his face slashed and bruised from last night's high-pressured body surf through those endless concrete tunnels.

"Sit down, Ike," I say.

Ike glances at the two muscle-bound AZ men in suits flanking me. He glances uneasily at the small hacksaw, pliers and bolt cutter displayed suggestively on the stylish coffee table next to the armchair where I'm sitting. Kramer is sitting next to me.

Ike sits, remaining calm. A true professional. He's prepared to face up to the consequences of having blown the hit. Nevertheless, he'd clearly like to leave the meeting with as many of his body parts still attached as when he arrived.

"You failed us, Ike."

"Yes, but I'll make it good. I'll get him this next time, don't worry, mate. I'll do it right off."

I stand up. "There won't be a next time. Do you know why, Ike?"

Ike shakes his head.

"Because you already screwed this up once and we don't have the time to sit back and see if you're going to screw it up a second time."

Ike nods and swallows hard.

"Yes, Ike, I'm afraid I'm going to have kill Max *myself*."

62. Dotting The i

I'M LYING IN THE SAND next to my surfboard with my eyes closed. The waves are breaking heavenly. The sun is radiant, the sea breeze refreshing. I can hear Virgil and Stacy's laughter from down the beach where they're surfing and frolicking together. It's by all objective standards a perfect day.

And I feel perfectly miserable. I've tried to "move on" and put the whole thing behind me, but ever since Dot shut that door on me, I've been feeling like this. I don't know, maybe some things you're just not meant to get over.

My thoughts swirl. I've got a lot to deal with. Max for one. I should be thinking about the Max situation, not Dot. Maybe a quick nap first to calm down. I close my eyes. The sun feels good. Slipping off into that peaceful space between sleep and consciousness.

My thoughts drift back to the Hollywood party a few days ago ... There I am sitting on the piano bench. She's sitting next to me. She just asked me to come over to her house. And now I'm supposed to answer ...

"Wow. Come over? To your house? Uh ... yeah. That'd be great."

"Cool." She smiles.

But suddenly I feel like I'm taking some sort of a turn. A right turn? A left turn? A wrong turn?

She starts getting up.

"Uh wait. I'm sorry. I guess I really can't do this."

She sits back down. Looking at me with her beautiful eyes. Surprised. Embarrassed.

I'm stammering. Feeling like an idiot, or worse. "Look, I'm sorry. I really like you. And I'd really like to go to your house, but you see, I just got dumped by my girlfriend and I ..."

She looks at me. Clearly wondering how on earth my getting dumped is preventing me from wanting to come over to her house for the night—

"Yeah, I guess that doesn't make any sense. Anyway ... she dumped me, but I'm still hoping somehow we can get back together. But of course I know that's *so* ridiculous 'cause there's no way she's ever going to take me back. But if I go home with you now. Oh, God. It's sorta crazy. We've been together since grade school and I've only ever been with her. So, if I ... uh ... I mean, she'd totally know, and I wouldn't be able to look her in the face."

She doesn't say anything. Just nods. Then reaches into her purse for a pen and writes her telephone number and e-mail on a piece of paper and hands it to me.

"You're sweet. Call me if you want. If you feel like talking or something."

I smile at her. And she leaves.

I lie there in the warm sand. Half asleep. Half not. Eyes closed.

Then. Suddenly. Out of nowhere. Certainly with no warning or prior consent, an image flashes on my eyelid screen. It's me and Dot, ages ago. But I can see it clearly. As if it's now. As if I'm actually reliving the moment. Like some B-movie dream sequence.

We're in high school. Our class is on that traditional end-of-school-year overnight fieldtrip to the coast. We're camping in tents spread over those beautiful Oregon dunes. Security is, at least on paper, well thought out by the teachers and volunteer parent chaperones. We're put to bed in our respective segregated tents, with a keen eye out for any hanky-panky. But Dot has it all planned out as meticulously as a prison break, and we manage to sneak away unobserved.

Of course I'd spent countless guy hours talking about it with friends. Had (of course) bragged about already doing it, and had (of course) seen everything you could imagine downloaded from the Internet. But I'd never done it. And to tell you the truth, I guess I wasn't quite ready. But Dot's in charge of everything.

Once far enough away from camp, she chooses a secluded spot between two dunes. We strip shyly and climb into the same sleeping bag. Despite my Internet education, we don't have a clue what to do. I'm petrified. But thank God nature has a way of sorting these things out, and after a few rough starts everything falls perfectly into place.

I remember clear as day. Dot starts trembling all over and moaning softly. For a second I'm really scared. Afraid I hurt her. But then she starts squeezing me tighter with such a look of joy in her eyes that I get it. And almost instantly, like a thunderbolt from the heavens above, the shudder runs through me as well.

We lie there, on our backs, holding hands, looking up at the infinity of stars.

"My God," she whispers. "It was so wonderful. So perfect."

"Wow," I say.

"It felt like time just stopped. Like we were the only ones in the universe. Like our souls had merged together. Like we were in between two ticks of a clock. Just you and me."

She's looking straight into me, in the moonlight, seeing straight inside, to whatever scared insecure screwed up little guy I am, underneath all the layers, at the center of it all. Sand sticking to her hair.

And I look into her eyes and see in that instant that she's completely devoted. Completely in love. That every atom in her body is resonating for me. With me. Despite all my faults and shortcomings. Despite it all. Passionately. Together. She kisses me.

How could I have lost that? That kiss? That magic? *What have I done?*

And then, as abruptly as it began, the images fade. I try to hang on. But it disappears. With an overwhelming feeling of loss and sadness, I open my eyes and look out to sea.

Lying there, staring out at the sea, I get it. Despite the candlelight dinner and the slammed door, everything is *still* pointing in one direction. Diatonically. Canonically. Andantally Contabally. She's my *cadenza*, my *coda*, my true unique *da capo*. Always has been. Always will be. My telos. That one central point in my life.

Virgil, with his board under his arm, is sprinting up from the surf. Stacy is riding out a wave in the distance. Virgil puts down his board and sits next to me in the sand, dripping wet.

"Awesome break."

"I'm through with the break."

"What?"

"Nothing."

"What's with you?"

I don't answer. Virgil's eyes go wide. "Oh no," he groans. "You're not going to flip out and pull a disappearing stunt like Max on us, are you?"

But he sees it. He sees that somehow I've just made this huge decision. *Huge.* I've just decided that I'm going to do anything it takes to get Dot back. I know it sounds stupid. It probably is stupid, or crazy, or both. And I'm probably going to get totally burned. But I'm going to try. I'm going to give it everything I've got. Completely. Only then will I know.

Virgil's looking at me now with some sort of inner smile thing going on. "Oh for Chrissakes, David. This isn't what I think it might be, is it?"

"Yowza," I respond.

And Virgil gets the message. As clear as the UV's sinking into his tan. *"As you wish"* is all he needs to say.

I get up and start running towards my bungalow.

*   *   *

Thirty minutes later I finish dressing and am about to head over to the jet for Portland when Gwen's voice announces that Sal is on the line.

"OK, put him on."

"We found Max," says Sal.

"Where?"

"In a roadside motel in some small town in Texas called Milagro."

"OK, let's do it."

"When?"

"Now."

It's time to finish what I started. This is the last step. Then I'll be free. Free to get back my life. To get back Dot. To start again where I left off.

The jet's waiting. I'm all packed.

There's just one last thing I need to do now. I walk across the room and open the safe.

Max's gun is sitting there, of course. Right where I left it.

I reach in.

*   *   *

"Where are we going, sir?" asks the pilot with his professional no-nonsense British accent.

"Back to Portland."

"Yes, sir."

"But first we need to pick up Kramer in New York, and then make a short stop in a town called Milagro, in Texas."

"Very good, sir."

"Land at some little private airport where they won't bother with any security checks."

"Of course."

And as the jet takes off, my thoughts are all homing in on one central point ... *Dot*.

63. Project H

AFTER THE BAYOU ESCAPADE, Marcie and Max hitchhiked out of town with the idea of crossing the border into Mexico to lay low until the whole hitman situation cools off.

Countless dusty miles later, hot and exhausted, they check into a random roadside motel in a small desert town called Milagro. And that's where they are now, lying together in their motel bed.

"Max?"

"Yeah."

"How many times have we almost died together?"

"That would be two. One with the pills on the hill, and then a second time in the bayous."

"Let's stop there, OK?"

"Definitely."

"Promise?"

"I do."

She snuggles up closer to him. Then she hears something. Far off. Maybe she hears it before any other mortal could hear it. After all, she's been listening for so long. From far away it grows louder until it becomes audible. The rumbling of a Harley Davidson motorcycle makes its way through the thin motel walls where it is distinctly heard by Marcie, and completely ignored by Max.

Normally, her heart would skip a beat at the sound of a Harley. But for the first time since she last heard Lucky's bike zoom away from her forever, her heart remains constant. Completely unmoved by the motorcycle's call. And this makes her very happy. She looks over at Max.

"You're the one, Max," she says.

He lets the words soak in, thinking they are, without question, the finest words he's ever heard.

"So are you, Marcie."

"You wouldn't be pissin' on my leg and telling me it's rainin', would you Max?"

"No."

She folds into his arms ... wild, crazy, sweaty, passionate, cry-out-loud, over-the-moon love.

Afterwards, deep in the night, Max lies there, staring into the darkness. He listens to the soft rhythm of Marcie's breathing. Her head is cradled on his chest. He can feel her heart beating softly through her skin.

"Max?"

"Yes."

"You're not sleeping."

"No. Just thinking."

"Will you tell me something?"

"Sure."

"You said you figured out your telos on the hill when I was telling you about my life."

"That's right."

"Then you said you'd show me, and you took me to meet Bernie and Zoey."

"Right."

"You haven't told me everything. There's something else."

Max suddenly looks bashful. Like a little kid caught in the act. "Oh, I don't know."

"Tell me, Max."

"It's silly, really."

"Tell me."

"It's just a crazy idea."

"Tell me, Max. I saw you outside talking with Bernie."

"Ah, you did, did you?"

Marcie nods.

"It's just the ravings of a sappy old fool."

"Tell me."

"Well ... out on that hill with you I started thinking that there was something terribly wrong with us if lives like yours and so many others across the planet can be destroyed because of something so insignificant as a small sum of money, while at the same time such huge amounts are constantly wasted. I suppose I just never thought about it before. All you needed was a little helping hand and you would have been back on your feet. Because of such a trivial detail, a beautiful life gets destroyed. It happens every day ... families losing their homes for lack of a few dollars rent and ending up on the street ... right here at our doorstep. Not to mention all the children starving across the world and all the other horrible inequities.

"Of course I'm not inventing the wheel, or even coming up with anything remotely original. There have always been a few altruistic souls out there trying to make the planet a better place. And I suppose that's exactly the point. A handful of altruism doesn't do it. It doesn't even *begin* to fix the problem. Doesn't even begin to heal the injustice. After all, it is our world. We're responsible for it. And that's when I realized that maybe the problem lies deeper. That maybe the problem lies with *us*. Do you see what I mean?"

"Not really."

"A young man I know named Virgil used to carry on about evolution all the time, though I never really paid much attention to it. I'd always just taken for granted that human beings aren't very nice creatures. Think about it. Other animals kill for food to survive. We're the only species that kills and inflicts pain for pleasure. Remember the Roman coliseums? The more pain and blood and gore, the more the crowd cheered. Or take the Nazis and other recent genocides. You'd never see such orchestrated atrocities in the animal world. Nothing on the Nature Channel could ever come close to the endless catalog of savagery humans have achieved. When it comes to loathsome collectively coordinated brutality, our species wins, hands down.

"But we are who we are for a reason. It's how we got here. Human beings rule the Earth because we've evolved better than all the other species over the past millions of years. We've used our opposable thumbs and frontal lobes to dominate every other inhabitant of the planet by excelling in every savagery conceivable. We fought our way here, tooth and nail. Burning rainforests, waging wars and genocides, slaughtering untold species into irremediable extinction. Survival of the fittest. Besting all the other species on the way up the DNA ladder to the top."

"OK, so we're the bad boys on the evolutionary block. What does that have to do with your telos?"

Max chuckles. "Well, I'm coming to that. As far as I can see, we're basically still running on the same old program. Sure, we've dressed it up a bit to feel modern and civilized. We're no longer chopping each other's heads off or spending afternoons in the coliseums cheering as gladiators butcher each other, but the fundamental motivational driving force is still the same. Everything about our society is geared towards competition. Societal success is gauged by money. Forbes is nothing other than a list of the best competitors, the champion gladiators. And I should know. I was personifying the program more than anyone on the planet. Taking it to the limit and beyond. And that's how I know the program has run its course. Maybe my failure to feel happiness wasn't the disease. Maybe it was a signpost towards the cure. Competition has brought us to where we are now. But it's not the end of the line. Why should it be? We've been constantly evolving over millions of years. There's no reason to think it stops here. Maybe it's time we call into question the competitive survival strategy that brought us this far. After all, do we really want a world where we walk past homeless people on the street and do nothing about it?"

"But what can we do?"

"That's just it. None of us thinks we can do anything. So we don't. Today everyone talks about everything being global. Global markets, global communication, global economics, global strategy, global warming. It's the buzzword of our time. But we've completely left ourselves out of the equation. Now that the human race has become truly global we have to realize that the *race* part is over. We're here! Together! At a crossroads. Perhaps it's time to balance things out.

"Replacing dog eat dog with dog help dog."

"Exactly. But I see you smiling. I know. We've all heard it a million times. In fact it sounds so corny we dismiss it without thought. Discarding it immediately as cliché. As spurious cerebral spam. We're far too evolved and sophisticated to take stock of something as mundane and pedestrian as a cliché. But life *is* short. Today *is* the first day of the rest of your life. You *can't* buy happiness. It's not what you take out, it *is* what you put in. It's all true. But of course we don't pay any attention. We're too intellectually advanced with our magnificent cerebrums and expensive cars and cell phones and satellites to actually stop and realize that the simple pleasures really *are* the best, and that you really *do* have to seize the moment. We're just too busy, or too selfish, or too shortsighted, or simply too programmed by self-serving competitive genetics to see the obvious."

Marcie smiles.

"OK, you're thinking this sounds like just another sort of new-fangled new-age utopian communism ... But of course communism couldn't work. You can't legislate evolution. The change must come from within. The way it's always happened throughout evolutionary history. Through mutation. But maybe the next mutation isn't genetic. Maybe it's conceptual. Moral. Because we want to."

"So what are you saying? That in order to evolve, people should give their money away? 'Cause I really don't think you're going to get many followers if that's what you're pushing."

"No, I'm thinking of something else. Let me put it another way. What did you feel when you saw Zoey jumping into Bernie's arms?"

"Well ... I felt one of the greatest bursts of happiness that I've ever felt in my entire life. I can still feel it every time I think of them."

"Exactly. Me too."

"In fact, since then I've been wondering about the next one ... already looking forward to creating another miracle."

Max is nodding. "Happiness. It's not just the goal, it's the *means* to the goal. You get it by giving it. By making others happy. Deep inside we feel it. But maybe some evolutionary trick in our brains holds it under wraps to keep us competing tooth and nail. Maybe it's the best-kept secret in the world. But if somehow the word could just get out there, it would cause a revolution without the *r*. It would change the way we're running the planet."

"But how could we get anyone to listen?"

"Exponential distribution ... Math."

"Math?"

"Yes. Exponential logarithmic propagation. It's like the old story of the peasant who gave the king a beautifully handmade chessboard, and when the king asked what he wanted in return, the peasant said simply one grain of rice on the first square, two grains on the second

-458-

square, four on the next, etcetera. Of course the king immediately agreed to what seemed such a good bargain. But the twenty-first square called for over a million grains, and it would take more grains of rice than existed in the whole kingdom to fulfill the bargain."

"I get it."

"Such widespread change requires a catalyst. Like the ape who first transformed that stick into a tool. Of course, who knows how many people tried before us and failed? Perhaps we'll fail as well, but we can try. It will be our project ... *Project H*. We'll wander around creating as many good deeds as we can. Call them miracles if you like. And every time we'll ask the recipient to pass on the miracle: *two times*. And each time that person will feel the incredible joy that you and I felt with Bernie and Zoey. Happiness by helping others will become contagious. The rest is mathematical. Helping one person so that person becomes inspired to help two other people, thereby setting up an exponential chain reaction of planetary magnitude."

Marcie is staring at him, eyes wide with awe. "That's what you were telling Bernie out there on the lawn, isn't it?"

"Yes. He wanted to know how he could ever repay me, and I told him all he had to do was find someone who needs his help and pass on the miracle. *Twice*."

64. Amor Vincit Omnia

DOT WALKS NEXT TO GREG under the rainy grey clouds of Portland. She wonders if she's really doing the right thing. They've decided to have a very small ceremony. Just an exchange of simple vows in the local church tomorrow afternoon with her and Greg's families. As she walks down the damp street in silence she feels a shiver of hesitation run from the top of her head to the points of her toes.

*   *   *

MAX IS DEEP IN THOUGHT while Marcie sleeps peacefully next to him. He's thinking about his predicament. Sooner or later the David/Kramer alliance will succeed in finding him, even after crossing the border down south. Bounty hunters may be expensive, but they eventually deliver. And that's putting Marcie and him in grave danger. He's turned it over in his mind from every angle, and there's only one solution: *kill David and Kramer first.*

*   *   *

KRAMER IS NERVOUS sitting in the jet with me on our way down to Texas. His hands are constantly fidgeting about, as if looking for something to grasp on to. I can tell he has something to say to me. Finally he says it.

"I don't know, I've been thinking, and I'm not sure this is such a great idea," he says.

"What do you mean?"

"I'm just not so sure we should be doing something like this ourselves. We should just leave it to the pros. They'll take care of it, and we can just pay 'em and forget about it."

Kramer can tell by my expression that I really don't like what I just heard him say.

"Well, Larry, that was what you were supposed to do. Remember? You were supposed to take care of Max while he was defenseless as a baby in prison. Right? And the pros screwed that up and Max escaped. And then you hired Ike, which didn't work out too well either, did it?"

Larry looks down at his coffee cup as if the answer were hidden inside. "I know. We had some bad luck. It happens. But I think we should give the pros another try before doing something like this *directly* in person."

"We don't have time for another screw-up. This is our problem, and we need to deal with it now, before it spins completely out of control. Max is smart. If we don't get him, he'll get us."

We spend the rest of the trip in silence. Fine by me. I'm sick of talking with Kramer.

The jet lands and Kramer and I step down to the tarmac. It's a discreet private strip out in the middle of the desert. The night is as black as Texas tea.

*   *   *

AS WE DEPLANE, THE PILOT NOTICES the glint of dark metal in my jacket pocket with that characteristic bulge.

"*Why would David have a gun?*" he wonders to himself. "Well, this *is* Texas. Bloody Yanks."

*   *   *

AN AIRPORT EMPLOYEE IS WAITING on the tarmac for us, holding open the door to the Rolls. Kramer and I climb in and we drive off. We're out in the middle of nowhere. Rolling along this strip of desolate highway through the flat Texas desert stretching forever into the night.

The Rolls slows and pulls over to the shoulder. *Why?* The barrier between us and the driver starts rolling down. Kramer looks questioningly at the driver to see what this is all about, and as the barrier rolls down, Kramer can't believe his eyes—

It's Max!

The driver of the Rolls is Max! Dressed up in a chauffeur's uniform, pointing a gun straight at Kramer.

"Oh no!" says Kramer, eyes wide with fear.

"Oh yes," says Max, "but David first."

He turns the gun on me, point blank at my heart. With a happy smile he says, "Goodbye David," and pulls the trigger.

Kramer screams at the shot, and I slump over.

Then Max aims at Kramer, who's now white as Caspar.

"I should kill you, Larry, because you betrayed me and you deserve to die. But I'm not going to. I'm going to let you live with the guilt of what you did. And I want you to keep everything about what happened completely secret. I'll be watching you. And I want you to disappear. Start over as a good and honest man in some other country where no one knows you. Otherwise I'll come by for a visit."

Kramer can't believe the miracle. Max isn't going to kill him! He's so happy he can hardly breathe. He doesn't dare say anything.

He just glances nervously at the slumped-over body on the seat next to him and nods.

"Now get out," says Max.

Kramer fumbles with the door latch a second then spills out of the car, closing the door behind him.

The Rolls starts driving away, leaving Kramer behind in the dust.

I sit up and watch with a grin as the driver pulls off the Hollywood-perfect Max-mask with its wild mane of Max-hair to reveal Sal's bald head.

"That mask sure was uncomfortable," complains Sal.

"Yeah, but you looked great," I laugh. "And the voice remix was fantastic. Every bit as good as Mission Impossible. Look out Tom Cruise."

Sal smiles as he drives. It was fun to spook that asshole Kramer.

I roll down the window to let the smoke smell from Sal's blank dissipate.

"How much longer to Milagro?" I ask.

"One hour. You ready for Max?"

"Yeah, I'm ready."

*   *   *

MAX IS SLEEPING in Marcie's arms. A knock at the door wakes him. It's a soft, almost imperceptible knock. With a pang of fear, Max first assumes it's another hitman. But would an assassin knock at the door?

Max wakes up Marcie, motioning for her to be quiet. The knock softly knocks again. This time she hears it too.

"Hitman?" she gasps in a frightened whisper.

"I don't know, but I don't think a killer would knock like that."

"Who then? No one knows we're here. Did you order another pizza?"

"I wish I did. Anyway, now you have to go hide. Right away. Go on, go hide."

"Max, this is a *one-room* motel room ... there is no place to hide."

"In the bathroom."

"That's *so* not going to happen. I'm staying with you."

He smiles gently. "Your *are* with me, Marcie. But if there's shooting, the safest place is the bathroom. They want me, not you. Now hurry into the bathroom and stay there till I come get you."

She scowls, but knows he's right. He kisses her and shuts her worried face behind the bathroom door. Then he puts on his pants and carefully moves towards the front door, trying to stay out of some imaginary direct line of fire just in case whoever it is suddenly decides to shoot through the door like they do in the movies.

Marcie (of course) immediately reopens the bathroom door a crack to watch. She's shaking from head to foot. Scared to death.

Max looks cautiously through the peephole. At first he can't believe his eye. But he's quick to react. He throws open the door.

"I'm going to kill you," says Max.

He clenches his fist to swing.

From her hiding place in the bathroom, Marcie watches Max open the front door.

Standing there is a guy. A young guy just standing there. He certainly doesn't look like a hitman. He just looks like some normal young guy in an expensive jacket.

Then she sees the flash of black metal and the bulge of a gun.

And what is Max doing? Oh my God, he's gonna punch him! Max is gonna punch a guy who's got a fucking gun!

Strangely, at that moment, her whole life flashes before her eyes: there she is as a baby with her mom ... Look! Her seventh birthday opening up Mr. Biggles ... and now bombing some test in high school ... and there's Lucky roaring away on his bike. And there she is working the register at Wal-Mart ... It all seems so fast and pointless. But wait! Only dying people have their lives flash before their eyes like this right before they die. Does that mean the hitman at the door with the gun is going to start to shoot at Max, but when he hears the scream he'll change his aim and the bullet will come straight and hit *me* in the head right through the crack in the bathroom door? Please don't let that happen. Don't let him hurt Max *or* me. Make him go away!

And in that split second as she watches her life zip by in fast motion while Max's fist speeds down towards the guy's face, she decides to scream to warn Max. Even if it means taking the bullet right between the eyes. Even if it means dying right then and there, brains splattered all over the cheap sea-green bathroom tiles. To try to save Max it's worth it. Without the slightest doubt.

She opens her mouth to scream.

But Max is already in motion. And as he swings he notices that David is reaching into his jacket pocket for the bulge.

*   *   *

THERE'S MAX standing in front of me.

I reach into my jacket to finally finish off what I began.

In the background, behind me, you can just barely make out Sal's silhouette. He's smiling. He's enjoyed making it all happen according to my plan to destroy the old Max to make way for the new ... The bogus Singh letters, setting up Niki the prosecutor, manipulating Kramer's greed like a marionette, saving Max before Snowman could do his dirty, planting the fake black box I threw out into the ocean to mislead Kramer, sending Bald Bearded Guy in with the little red sleeping pills for Max and Marcie, putting the Miami key in Max's pocket while he was unconscious, making sure Max and Marcie got away without getting themselves or someone else killed during the Miami robbery, modifying the aim on Ike's pistol so he'd screw up his hit, then leading them into the bayous with the flashing light and into the room with the water valve to flush Ike on his way ...

And Marcie? No, of course not. Marcie wasn't part of the act. She was just following her own telos. Things like that can't be rigged. They just happen when the chemistry is right, like when that first cell divided itself in the primordial soup.

And now, for the final twist in the deoxyribonucleic strand:

Max ...

... Who, at this precise instant, just in time to avoid smashing his fist into my face, sees the black box in my hand, and suddenly understands.

Epilogue

If you skipped ahead to this last page, resist the temptation and go back. As the Guru said, sometimes there are no shortcuts ...

... And yes, Dot, this all started off as an e-mail. But since you're not answering my calls or actually reading my e-mails before deleting them, there didn't seem much point in stopping this one till you got the whole story.

So here it is: *the whole story.*

We'll be arriving in Portland in a few minutes, where I'm going to print this out and leave it on your doorstep.

We're all here: me, Max, Marcie, Bernie and Zoey. I've convinced everyone to go out for pizza at Nemo's. My fairytale ending would be for you to call me now. We'd stop by and pick you up on our way back to the Island. I'd really like you to meet everyone. There's so much to do! Project H has begun. Even as you read these words, the miracles are spreading.

I♥UD

PPS: What happens next is ... up to you.

LaVergne, TN USA
09 June 2010
185534LV00003B/3/P